D1827115

ORDINARY PEOPLE

Part XI

PHIL BOAST

Order this book online at www.trafford.com
or email orders@trafford.com

Most Trafford titles are also available at major online book retailers.

Print information available on the last page.

ISBN: 978-1-4907-8836-4 (sc)
ISBN: 978-1-4907-8835-7 (hc)
ISBN: 978-1-4907-8837-1 (e)

Library of Congress Control Number: 2018941295

Because of the dynamic nature of the Internet, any web addresses or links contained in
this book may have changed since publication and may no longer be valid. The views
expressed in this work are solely those of the author and do not necessarily reflect the
views of the publisher, and the publisher hereby disclaims any responsibility for them.

Any people depicted in stock imagery provided by Thinkstock are models,
and such images are being used for illustrative purposes only.
Certain stock imagery © Thinkstock.

Trafford rev. 04/23/2018

www.trafford.com
North America & international
toll-free: 1 888 232 4444 (USA & Canada)
fax: 812 355 4082

Table of Contents

Chapter 1

EMOTIONAL LANDSCAPES

For the short span of time that she had been there, she had been just another face in the by now quite small crowd of onlookers. The policemen had put coloured plastic tape across the entrance gate, forbidding entry to any who were not a part of it; forensic specialists, contractors brought in to dig the pits below the stones, in order to uncover the mortal remains of those who they were now certain would be there, and such police investigators as were still investigating. Occasionally journalists and reporters were allowed entry, but the interest by now was more of the kind which ordinary people show in the face of so extraordinary and significant an event. To have been there, that was the thing, once the news had begun to find its' way across the vast and immediate network of communication which spread across the nation, and across the world. Stories could thence be told over pints of ale or glasses of wine; first – hand accounts of the quite distant views of the still smoking ruin of that which had been a house, which could be glimpsed at places through the still bare trees, and where the mysterious women had lived, who had now died so mysteriously. Such general interest would wane, in time; articles would be written, and read, until something new took the attention of the masses, and by then only specialists and academics would continue to think of it, and wonder at this strange place, and so it would not be entirely forgotten. It had become a part of English history now; a secret place, which had kept its' secrets hidden so well for so long, and its' fascination would endure well beyond the lives of those who had now gathered to see it.

And here for a quite short while had been Megan Thomas, who had come for a different reason. When she had left here to begin her vigil in the village of Middlewapping, she had taken her passport and credit cards, her sewing machine and such clothes as she had needed, so she could continue to live without much inconvenience, and all else which had been the stuff of her life would in any case be gone now; burned to so much ash in the inferno. There would be nothing left which would connect the house to her, or her to the house which had been called Farthing's Well; nothing to come here for, really. But still, she had come, because this is the way of people, and she had to see for herself, so that she could begin to believe something so unbelievable. They were dead now; Fiona, Sharon and Corinne, the three women who had been so much of her life, and the last resting place of Eve would not after all be her last resting place; the most recently dead would be of the most interest, and by now she would lay on a sterilized metal examination table, so that they could try to work out what had happened. But of course, they would never know. They would speculate as to how the three women had died, how the fire had started, and they would look for next of kin, but these had not been ordinary women, and this had been no ordinary fire. They would wonder at the stones, and the bodies which lay buried beneath them, but there was no one left now who could explain. No one except Megan Thomas knew the long, dark history of this place, or its' ancient connection to a Manor House so many miles away. Jane Mary was buried there now, where she had died, and nobody would make the connection, for how could they?

Such wanton sacrilege; the desecration of the graves in the interest of examination; the ritual ended so horribly; they should have been left in peace, to go back to the earth as Mother Nature had intended, and now this.

And so she stayed only for a little while, and nobody would notice her, or remember that she had been there, and after only a little while Megan Thomas walked quietly away, who had just been another face in the crowd, and she would not return. This was not the place, and she had other pressing matters to attend to, such as where she would sleep tonight. She must find somewhere where she could find quietude, and a place to think, for now she had much to think about. But she had been here, at least, and the end of it all was a place from which to start.

On the morning of Rebecca's so unexpected arrival at the Manor House, Victoria awoke at a little after eight o'clock, as was her habit if she was not working in London, and thus had not set her alarm clock. Her first impression of the waking world was that she felt more tired than was usual, and during her first moments of consciousness and before she had opened her eyes or raised her head from the pillow, her mind unconsciously began to register such essential matters as where she was, and what day of the week it might be. And then, as her mind began to quite slowly leave its' sleep state behind, she began to regain knowledge of certain more detailed aspects of her life; little Henry had a slight cold, this was not a working day, it was winter time, and so on. But now came a different feeling, and a sense that this was not an ordinary morning, and only then did she open her eyes and raise her head, and so did the reason for her unusual feeling and her uncommon tiredness become apparent, for the reason was sleeping soundly beside her. The final part of her awakening took somewhat less time; the sense that something was different had scarce done justice to her circumstances, and as the mist of her thoughts finally cleared and the memory of the last few hours of her life returned like a flood, she put her head somewhat heavily back on the pillow and stared at the so familiar ceiling of her bedroom. Christ...A night of passion with her lover, and before that...before that she had been sitting on the steps of the Manor, and she had been crying, and then they had both been crying. And so did Victoria relive in no particular order the time since she had been awoken in the small hours of the morning, and recalled as best she could everything which had happened, and everything which Rebecca had said. Making any sense of that would take a little longer, and would require a conversation with the person who slept beside her; she had gone to bed last evening alone and had awoken this morning with her beloved, and that which had happened in between was something significant. And even as she relived the events of the night, she began to work on understanding their most immediate implication, such as how on earth would she explain this to her parents? She began to mentally run through certain possible invented scenarios; Rebecca had caught a late flight from somewhere, or had just turned up spontaneously, oh and by the way she has a baby, whom she happened to leave somewhere. Had she been expecting her? Well yes, but she had neglected to mention anything to anybody, which was remiss of her, it was true. Whichever way she looked at it, however, nothing was really working by way of sensible or credible explanation; she would have to wing it; see how the conversation developed, so to speak. She was an adult, after all, and her affairs were really none of anyone else's business, but she knew that that did not really work either; she lived under their roof, and some explanation was in any case needed, and would be reasonably expected. Added to this was the complication that on the evidence of last night Rebecca was not currently of sound mind, and lord knew how she would awaken, and how the first meeting between her and her parents would go, however her appearance might be explained. She momentarily considered the idea that she should keep her hidden until the house was otherwise empty, presenting her as having just arrived in the interim prior to her parents' return, but she didn't think they were in fact going out today. Or perhaps she could smuggle her out somehow, and find her alternative accommodation until she was more certain of the situation, and of Rebecca's state of being, and thus her presentability to the world beyond the two of them. But that was all rather impractical, wasn't it, and the tangled web of deceit may well in the end contrive to ensnare her; better not to lie, at least, although a deal of fabrication and dilution of the facts of it, whatever in fact they were, would be needed to at least make it through breakfast.

She pushed the covers back and sat for a moment on the edge of the bed, looking around her bedroom as though she might glean therefrom some kind of inspiration, or at least an easier or simpler way forward, but none was forthcoming. Okay, so concentrate for a moment on the emotional aspect of the whole thing; she was of course glad beyond expression to see her beloved again, despite prior misgivings regarding their reunion, which had in the event proved to be well enough founded. Victoria's emotional focus had shifted of late, and now her primary source of happiness or otherwise lay in little Henry, but that was a different kind of love, and love was not a finite resource, to be distributed accordingly. No, she still loved Rebecca as much as ever, which was a good thing, despite being of little help with her current dilemma, at least in any practical sense. She put on her bathrobe and walked across the corridor to her bathroom, where she did her morning ablutions before returning to dress in jeans and a casual shirt. She opened the window wider, the better to dispel the residual aroma of stale tobacco left from the night; she needed a cigarette now, and coffee, and hoped that she could make it to her step before encountering any of her family. If she saw Michael first then she would debrief him, at least, but that was as may be. She thought momentarily that she might wake Rebecca, so that some kind of coordination of accounts might be achieved, but she quickly thought better of this; better she do it alone and tell Rebecca that which had not really happened retrospectively, and in any case Rebecca was so fast asleep that to wake her would mean further delay, and she wanted to get this done; she had delayed long enough. One more deep breath, and Victoria opened her bedroom door, and tried to prepare herself for whatever might follow. Rebecca had always been trouble, so what the hell was new, anyway.

For Sally Parsons this was a normal working day. That is to say that she was working in the main London office, and was not on any troubleshooting or other tour of the outlying offices or branches of the bank for which she worked. On occasion she would drive to London, if for some reason this was more convenient, or the trains weren't running properly, but for the most part on such days she would park her car at Queenswood railway station and take the commuter train to the city; this way she could use the hour or so of her journey to catch up with her work, or prepare for the day ahead. On this day, however, her computer remained in her bag, and in fact were she to think about it she would realise that she hadn't actually taken it out all week. But she wasn't thinking about it, which was perhaps the point. The passing fields, cuttings and woodland were enough, now, and then suburban London and the small, dirty city where she worked, along with the few million other people who lived here, or who made their daily journey to the heart of the country of England. In another life she would scarce have noticed the so familiar landscape, so intent would she have been on her work, but that was last week, before...Well, before Percival had come back into her life. In truth and in a sense he had never been away, since the first time that they had come together, but since he had left her she had felt his absence in her life, like a hollowness which haunted her days, just as now she once again felt his presence, so no, he had never really gone. But anyway he had come back now, and if she felt inclined to behave like a love – struck teenager then so she would do; she had earned the right to feel like this, and anyway it was a good feeling, and the work, which had once been so important, could wait. Nothing was the same, now. Whereas before, in the other life, she would have welcomed the opportunity to get away from her office and travel the country, now this would mean not going home, and so not seeing Percival, if she was going to see him, and if she was not going to see him then there was always a chance that she would see him anyway, because that was the way that they had always been. And so she made up her mind that the next time something had to be done in Manchester, or Bristol, she would delegate if she could. In any case this day would pass without incident, and it would not be until her journey home that anything of any particular importance would happen. She had been quite late leaving the office, and although the days were getting longer now, dusk was descending on the passing fields, and then her mobile telephone rang.

The morning continued well enough at first for Victoria. As almost always she went first to the nursery, where little Henry had eaten a good breakfast, and he who was by and large a good sleeper had indeed slept well during the night, his cold symptoms having abated. A few moments with Abigail to discuss her sons' wellbeing and the day ahead, and then to the front steps, avoiding the kitchen and thus possible premature meetings with her family, and so foregoing coffee for now. She lit a cigarette; the morning was cold, but not as cold as of late, so perhaps the worst of it was over. For a moment the memories of warm winter holidays in her youth invaded her thoughts; visions of palm – fringed beaches; she was not on the whole much of a one for palm – fringed beaches, and felt the heat as well as the cold, but at that moment a palm – fringed beach felt like quite a good idea, and she wondered momentarily when the next time would be that she would see one. She had sat here only a few hours before, with Rebecca beside her; Rebecca who had killed again, but she must not let her thoughts go there yet; this must be taken in stages, and establishing her presence in the house was the first stage.

Thereafter her morning became more difficult, as she knew that it would, and the first encounter with the rest of her family was with her mother, who stood now at the great front door.

'Victoria, dear, I thought I would find you here.'

'Good morning mother.'

'Yes, good morning; since we are all here, your father thought that it would be a nice idea if we all ate breakfast together.'

Yes, I'm sure he did; bless you father, and curse you also.

'Oh, very well, I'll be in shortly.'

'It's almost ready, so don't be long, and you'll catch your death out here.'

'Yes, I'm just coming...'

So it would be all of them; no chance to spread the word quietly of Rebecca's arrival. Well so be it then; her guest had arrived late at night, so what of it; and what of it if her guest was Rebecca, what business was it of theirs? All she had to do now was to convince them all of this, which might prove difficult in view of the fact that she could scarce convince herself. She put out her cigarette and stood up, hoping that the music that she would shortly face would be gentle music, but she was far from being convinced of that, either.

'Hi Sal, it's Polly.'

Polly Yates, who had been a part of the circuit for years, and so had become a fairly good friend to Sally, thanks to conversations over dinner tables and in various kitchens, but they had not otherwise spent time together. The circle had diminished over the years; people had moved away or started families, but Polly and George had not had kids and had stayed in the town, so this was to be a dinner party.

'Hi Polly...'

Just phoning to say that Fiona and Ray are having a get – together tomorrow night, if you're free?'

'Tomorrow..?'

'I know it's short notice, and Saturday would be more usual, but there it is.'

'Who else..?'

'Not sure yet, Maggie and Mike are away, and Wendy isn't certain as usual, but I daresay some of the other usual suspects will be there.'

'Okay....'

'Is that 'okay' you'll be there?'

'Yes, sure, I'll come.'

'Right; see you there, then; I haven't seen you for ages....So will you be bringing anybody?'

'No, just me...'

'Fine then, well, see you tomorrow then; you're breaking up.'

'I'm on a train.'

The connection was broken, and Sally put her telephone back in her bag. So, Fiona was trawling, and Sally would make up the numbers; somebody or bodies must have pulled out, but she was perhaps being disingenuous; Sally actually liked Fiona, but had never got on with Ray, who thought rather too highly of himself and his opinions. He had also made inappropriate suggestions to her on more than one occasion, and one Christmas he had tried to become too familiar with her under the mistletoe. Wendy was never certain that she would come, but always came anyway; Wendy the actress, who didn't seem to act very often but rarely missed an opportunity to be dramatic, and pretend that her life was busier than it actually was. She had recently embarked on her third marriage, but Sally couldn't recall the name of the latest husband; Paul, or Peter, or something. Sally was less often invited to such events these days; she always came alone, didn't drink alcohol any more, and in truth scarce entered into the spirit of things, and certainly as not far as any single men present were concerned. She occasionally heard news, usually by accident, of events such as these to which she had not been invited, and in any case she didn't always go if she was, but she felt a new and different lightness of spirit, now, and it might be quite amusing to go. She wouldn't ask Percival to go with her; she would offer, but he probably wouldn't go anyway, and certainly he would not wish to. If Sally's popularity had waned amongst her friends then Percival had never had any in the first place, on the rare occasions that he had accompanied her during their first time together. The thing was that the women tended to like him, without saying that they liked him; the animal attraction was very obvious, and she had a sense that their saying that he was no good for her was as much as to say that he would be better for them, and since they couldn't have him....anyway this tended to make the men dislike him. It was also true that on the wrong evening, if somebody expressed opinion with which Percival disagreed, which he often did, then he had a way of winning the argument, being for the most part and by several degrees more intelligent and more eloquent than the general assembly. He had thus quickly gained a reputation for being rather rude, which was unfair, really, but anyway for the good of all concerned and for the sake of the maintenance of her friendships, she had stopped taking him with her. And so she would go alone tomorrow, and she would be happy to do so, because she was happy, now, and although it meant her not being with her beloved, she could always make her excuses and leave early. Would she tell them that she and he were back together again? Hell yes, she would tell them. Queenswood railway station, and Sally walked from the train with a smile on her face and a spring in her step, and she had scarce noticed the journey.

Breakfast in the grand dining room, Susan was working this morning and served eggs Benedict with tomatoes, and her father ate a kipper, he being rather partial to them, whilst being the only one in the family who could abide eating them, or even their rather pungent aroma. Victoria took her place opposite Michael and her mother, and poured herself orange juice.

'Good morning, Victoria.'

'Good morning father.'

'You okay Vics; you look a bit as though you didn't sleep well.'

This was Michael, who Victoria knew well enough could equally well be a help or a hindrance in such situations as this, probably without intending to be either.

'I slept quite well, thank you.'

'Oh, right…so little Henry feeling more himself this morning is he?'

'Yes, he's much better, thank you.'

'Well I do hope Nathaniel doesn't catch whatever it is.' Said Lady Beatrice

'It's a cold, mother, not the Black Death.'

'Yes, well, even so….'

'As coincidence would have it I've been reading a bit about the Black Death,' said Lord Tillington 'which wasn't I believe called the Black Death at the time; 1665 – 66 was the last great plague; the King and Parliament fled London, the King took his court to Salisbury and Parliament went to Oxford. Then came the great fire, of course, which rather saw it off, so to speak; killed all the rats, I daresay.'

'Husband, dear; that is hardly a subject to be raised over breakfast, do you think?'

'I didn't raise it; anyway I had no idea that my family were of such sensitive disposition; hasn't put me off my kipper in the least.'

'So anyway, Victoria; are you going to town today?'

'I don't expect so, in fact there's…'

'It's just that I've a dress to be picked up from Cuthberts; I've had some alterations done.'

'Well, as I say, I have no plans to…'

'If you are going in,' said Michael 'there are a couple of things I need from the stationers; new print cartridges and so on.'

'Look; I'm not going into town, okay?'

'Oh, right…Well, just asking.'

'Well stop bloody asking…There's something I have to tell everyone.'

Which rather stopped the conversation in its' tracks, and took it to a new place; such a perhaps unwarranted outburst from the daughter of the family would have been nothing unusual ten years ago, but here was a manifestation of Victoria which had been rarely seen for a long time. Something was up, and the silence now awaited whatever it might be, until it was broken by her father.

'So pray tell us, dear daughter; we are all ears, I'm sure.'

'Well then, the thing is...Rebecca's here.'

And now a different kind of silence, whilst this piece of intelligence was taken in and a first reaction sought for, and it was Lord Michael, who despite enjoying his kipper put down his knife and fork, and was again the first to break the collective contemplation.

'Ones' faculties may not be as they once were, but I confess that none of them can detect her presence amongst us.'

'She's asleep upstairs; she arrived late last night.'

'From whence does she come...?' This was Lady Beatrice

'I'm not really sure, actually. We were only...Well, we only spoke for a short time; she was tired, you know? Anyway she's here, and, well, I think she may have been through some kind of emotional trauma; she is not quite herself.'

Which was about as good as she could do, and she hoped that she was still on the tightrope; still within the boundaries of telling the truth, but not too much of the truth. She believed that she was, but staying there might prove difficult. Lord Tillington had seen his daughter and her beloved grow from childhood to womanhood through their adolescence, and was no stranger to the emotional landscape of young women, which he knew was rather at variance with his own gender. He was also well enough aware that their more recent coming together had not been without its' difficulties, therefore for Victoria to make such reference gave the matter significance, but she was not quite done yet.

'You also may as well know that she now has a baby daughter; her name is Florence.'

The silence this time did not last so long, and once more it was her father who ended it.

'So, dare one ask whether Florence also currently resides upstairs?'

'No…She…Rebecca has left her somewhere, in good hands and only temporarily.'

'Whilst her mother recovers from her emotional trauma, perhaps?'

'Yes, exactly…'

'Well, well, here is a turn up for the books, as it were, although I confess I have never understood that expression.'

'May we ask who is father to the child?'

This was her mother, whom Victoria expected to be the main inquisitor.

'I don't know; as I say, we only had a brief conversation.'

'It must have been brief indeed for something so fundamental not to have been mentioned. So may we take it from this that she is not in any kind of a relationship?'

'She is in a kind of a relationship with me, mother.'

'You know very well what I mean, Victoria.'

'If you mean is she in any kind of a relationship with a man, then I think not, but that doesn't preclude her having a child if she so wishes, does it?'

Florence's father, whom none of those present knew was Florence's father, had thus far been silent in the matter, and Victoria now exchanged looks with her brother; come on then, help me out, or are you just going to sit there and say nothing? Michael, however, was for now lost for anything constructive to say, and was concentrating rather on his eggs Benedict, so it was left to his father to try to pour oil before the friction became harmful, and removed the delicate skin of moderation which currently covered the discourse. The child was named Florence, after Rebecca's now deceased mother, and they had known Florence, of course, and knew that she had been searching for her daughter for a very long time.

'Well, we are none of us strangers to a woman having a child without the inconvenience of having a man about the place, and I daresay we may glean more when Rebecca is feeling more herself, or at least a less traumatised manifestation of herself, may we not? In the meantime she is of course welcome to stay here, pending her emotional recovery, so to speak, but she will I presume wish to be reunited with her child as soon as may be.'

'Yes, of course, and thank you, Papa; she...well, she only came out of necessity, and I'm sure she never intended to bring Florence here.'

'Which may be just as well, otherwise the house may start to feel rather like a nursery; babies all over the place, productivity seeming to be rampant in this regard at the moment, but does she have anywhere else to live?'

'Not as far as I'm aware, but I'm sure something can be sorted out, and for all I know she may have made plans. I really don't think she'll be here for long, but I have to see to it that she's okay, at least.'

'Yes, well one would not wish to see her turfed out on the street prematurely, as it were; what do you say, Beatrice?'

Lady Beatrice had not missed Rebecca during her extended absence, and whilst she had assumed that she had not gone forever, her return and the manner of it had done nothing to improve her mood, or her feelings toward her daughters' lover. And now she had a child, so what was to be made of that?

'Well, I suppose we have no choice in the matter, do we, but I do wonder how any mother could so abandon a new born child without very good reason.'

'She has hardly abandoned her in the way that you imply, mother, and perhaps she has a very good reason,' (such as saving the lives of your grandchildren) 'and despite what you may think of her, I hope that none of us will be too quick to pass judgement.'

'I will judge as I see fit, Victoria.'

'Yes, of course, but she may stay for a little while, at least?'

'Well I suppose she may, since as I say we have little choice in it, so long as you father agrees.'

'I believe' said his Lordship 'that it was I who first suggested the idea, so on this occasion I do indeed agree with myself, and if that is an end to the matter for now then one would quite like to continue enjoying ones' kipper.'

And it was an end to it for now, and it had not perhaps gone so badly as Victoria had anticipated, due in large part to her dear and in the end blessed father, and from here she could at least move on to the next stage, which could only begin when Rebecca had woken up. Breakfast thereafter was an awkward affair, and Victoria left the table at the first polite opportunity, and only now did Michael, who followed her out, contribute to the matter, catching up with her on the back staircase.

'Listen, Vics; if she needs somewhere to stay she can always move into number seven for a bit, my tenant having disappeared so mysteriously.'

Ah yes; the woman called Megan, who Meadow had warned her about, but who had now gone; the one that got away.

'Thanks Mike, it may not come to that, but its' good to know that the option exists; I'd cover the rent, of course, assuming that Rebecca has no money.'

'Don't be silly, that wouldn't be necessary. I was going to contact the agents today, but I'll put it off until I get the all – clear, as it were. Anyway she paid six months in advance on the rent, which makes her disappearance even stranger.'

It's a lot more strange than you know, Michael, but she would not tell her brother how he had so unwittingly helped the black witch, as had she; not unless and until she told him everything. So instead she smiled for her brother, and continued her progress up the stairs. Breakfast done, but who knew where they would be by lunchtime.

Rebecca was still asleep. Victoria was loath to leave her again, lest she awaken and make her way downstairs alone; Victoria must speak to her before she encountered anyone else. Nevertheless she spent the remainder of the morning with Henry, and therefore also with Nathaniel, checking with some regularity to see if Rebecca had awoken, finally taking a shower, and taking no care to be quiet when she returned to her bedroom.

'What...What the fuck's going on?'

So, finally she had awoken.

'It's okay, you're at the Manor; I'm here.'

Rebecca sat up, and having established her whereabouts and the identity of the speaker beyond reasonable doubt, she placed her head back on the pillow and closed her eyes, but there was still doubt, albeit unreasonable doubt.

'Jesus, Vics....'

'You want coffee?'

'God yes, but...I really am here, aren't I...This isn't a dream, is it?'

'No, it's not a dream...'

'I don't remember coming here.'

'You arrived late last night, or rather early this morning.'

'Yes, but....I have no memory of that...'

'Do you recall what happened after you and I met?'

'I think so; we made love...Yes; that I remember.'

'Well that's something, I suppose...'

'I thought perhaps I was dreaming then, too.'

'No, you weren't dreaming, but you really can't remember anything before that?'

The burning...The old house, the death, and Helena had been there...Of course, that she would never forget, in all of its' terrible detail, but between that and coming here, and how long that had been was a blank.

'What day of the week is it?'

'It's Thursday.'

Which was little help, really, since the recent days had passed without knowledge of ordinary things, such as the day of the week; she had been somewhere where such things are not thought of. The witches were dead, she had made that happen, but then her world had gone dark, and she could recall nothing.

'They're dead, Vics.'

'I know; you told me last night.'

'Yes, I told you; on the steps...'

'Yes, on the steps.'

'Oh god, do your parents know I'm here?'

'Yes, of course I told them; I told them that you had had some kind of traumatic experience; that you weren't feeling quite yourself.'

Despite herself and her present thoughts, Rebecca laughed quietly to herself for a moment.

'You were always the mistress of understatement, my love. And what did they say?'

'They said that you could stay here for while, until you were feeling better, but I also told them about Florence.'

Rebecca sat up now, and this time she stayed there; Victoria sat on the edge of the bed and offered her a glass of water, which Rebecca drank quickly and thirstily.

'Florence...'

'Your daughter, you remember her?'

'I have to get back to her, Vics.'

'Yes, well all in good time, assuming that she's in good hands; right now I don't think you could look after her, do you?'

Rebecca stared ahead of her for a moment; her eyes were bloodshot, and her hands were shaking somewhat, but she was coming to, slowly.

'No, I suppose not...I don't think I can quite look after myself at the moment. I had to do it, Vics; I had no choice, you understand that, don't you? Please say you understand.'

'Right now I don't understand very much, Bex, but yes, I know that you had to do it.'

Rebecca held her hand out, and Victoria took it.

'It was for little Henry, and Nathaniel; they were in grave danger. I never wanted to go back there; to be as I used to be, but there was nobody else.'

'Yes, I know, but it's alright now, and Megan has gone, so everyone is safe.'

'Gone...?

'She left the house a couple of days ago.'

'A couple of days...?'

She had remembered talking to the woman called Megan; when she had been in her heightened state she had been aware of everything; she was so in tune with world around her around her that she could feel rather than see the three women; she knew exactly where they were; she could hear them breathing before she had entered their rooms, and they had been sleeping; in the end it had all been so easy. But one of them had awoken and tried to use her telephone, and that was when Rebecca had spoken to Megan, yes, that was it...And then she had set the fires, but after that... After that there was nothing, so had Helena looked after her and brought her here? Yes, that must have been what had happened;

she must have had a kind of nervous breakdown, or something, which had never happened to her before, but Helena had to have driven her away from that place. She could think of no other explanation as to how she had got here.

'Christ....'

'Bex; when we talked on the steps, can you remember what else we talked about..?'

'What...yes, I think so.'

'You said some things then that I didn't understand; there are some things that you have to explain.'

'Yes...Yes, of course, I'll tell you everything; I want to tell you everything, but not now, and not here.'

'Sure, we have to get you out of here; I mean you can stay here, but...'

'But we need to get out; yes, I agree; we can't do it here.'

'So, can you...I mean are you okay to get up?'

Rebecca smiled, then; the smile was weak, but it was something.

'Yes, I'm okay to do that; I have to believe that this is the worse that it's going to get, Vics; that things will get better from now on.'

'Of course they will; we're together, now.'

'And have you forgiven me for everything that happened before, with little Henry?'

'Yes, I forgave you for that a long time ago, although there was nothing to forgive, was there; that much at least I now understand.'

'So have you seen Meadow?'

'Of course; she and I have spoken at length.'

'She was...She's an amazing person, Vics; I don't know how she did what she did, but...'

'I know... Look, take a shower and I'll find you some clean clothes, then we have to get you past my parents, and we go into town, agreed?'

'Sure...So what did you tell them?'

'Only that you weren't feeling well; we'll have to tell them something, Bex.'

'Of course...'

'Judging by how you were last night you're better than I would have expected this morning.'

Both women smiled now.

'It must be your influence. This has been a terrible ordeal, Vics; please understand that I didn't want to do any of it, but... Well anyway the come – down might be hard; there may be a delayed reaction, I can't know that yet.'

'Well we'll just have to watch you then, won't we? First stage is for you to freshen up; you can stay here for a few days, I daresay, but we need to think of where you and Florence are going to live after that.'

'I know....'

'Don't worry; we'll sort something out.'

Rebecca stood up and put on Victoria's bathrobe; Rebecca had never really carried very much by way of surplus body fat, but she was thinner now than Victoria could remember her being for a long time; in truth Rebecca had scarce eaten in days, not since she had been driven away from Percival's cottage, and the process of ritual and meditation had begun. Victoria made up her bed; sometimes in extraordinary circumstances it helps to do ordinary things. The bedroom was cold, now, so she shut the window, dressed and found some underwear and clothes which Rebecca could wear. So, she had dealt at least initially with her parents, and now Rebecca was awake; all she had to do now was see them through their first meeting.

In the event, their escape was easier than she might have anticipated. By now Michael had left the house, and her father had perhaps decided to make himself scarce; he would have understood, and would probably have gone to his study; he would see Rebecca soon enough. Therefore the only person whom they encountered on their way out of the house was her mother, who would have been waiting for them, and now happened upon them at the foot of the back stairs.

'Rebecca; how delightful to see you, however unexpected has been your arrival...We haven't seen you here for such a long time.'

This was typically her mother; despite earlier conversations she was now charm personified.

'Hello Lady Beatrice.'

'I understand that congratulations are in order.'

'Yes, thank you.'

'I'm sure we all look forward to meeting Florence, when you are quite well enough to bring her here.'

'Of course; I'll bring her soon, I'm sure.'

'We're just going into town, Mama, so I can pick your dress up after all, if you would like?'

'Oh, don't worry dear, I'll pick it up myself one day, but won't you both join me for coffee before you go, and you can't have eaten yet, Rebecca.'

'It's okay Mama; we'll get something in town.'

'Rebecca really shouldn't go out without at least a warm drink inside her; it's still rather cold out.'

'She'll...We'll be fine, really.'

'Oh very well, if you're sure...So will you both be here for supper?'

'I'm not sure what we're doing yet, so don't have anything made for us; I can cook something later if necessary.'

'But, ummm; thank you for letting me stay here, Lady Beatrice.'

'It's a pleasure, my dear; stay as long as you need to.'

'Right, well, we'll be going then; see you later.'

'Indeed...'

Rebecca's need for caffeine was by now quite extreme; she was still finding some difficulty focusing her thoughts and having ordinary conversations, and they had agreed that a quick escape was the higher priority. Victoria noted that her mother's charm offensive stood in stark contrast to their brief conversation over breakfast, and in truth she had often wondered which was the truer manifestation of her mothers' attitude towards those around her; whether her generosity of spirit when she actually encountered people did indeed override her apparent feelings toward them when speaking privately. There was often in these situations an undertow which could take a given conversation in a quite different direction, but her mother was mistress of staying just on the right side of sarcastic, and just on the right side of patronising. But still, perhaps Victoria herself was now being disingenuous; perhaps better give her mother the benefit of the doubt, as she usually did, but in any case the two younger women crossed the entrance hall, took two of Victoria's coats from the coat – stand, and made their way out into the cold, free air; they had made good their escape, and that was for now the important thing.

Both were quiet on the way to town, Victoria concentrating to an unnecessary degree on her driving, and Rebecca staring at nothing in particular out of the passenger side window. Perhaps it was relief at being together and having the world to themselves, where Rebecca could allow her thoughts to wander as they would, but there were heavy things to discuss which could not be discussed whilst waiting in traffic queues. Victoria found a space in an in – town car park, before any further progress was agreed upon, but they needed a venue.

'So, are you hungry?'

'Not really.'

'You should be.'

'Coffee first...'

'Dawson's, then...'

The best coffee in town and the only place which would provide the intimacy and ambience which would suit their discourse, so they walked the short distance to the old town, and found an alcove in the coffee house away from the world. Isaac Dawson recognised the two women; one of them he knew was daughter to the Lord and Lady, who came here only occasionally, the other he knew of less well, but he hadn't seen either for a long time.

'You ladies take a seat; I'll bring the coffee over.'

And so they sat down opposite one another in a quiet corner, that being the easy part. Rebecca was distracted; Victoria sensed that she was finding her way back from a place where she had never been with her, and could never go, which she supposed went with the territory when ones' lover was a witch, but something had to be said; it had to begin somewhere.

'So; where the hell do we start?'

'Why don't you tell me about your year?'

And so did it begin; Victoria talked about Meadow and Keith, and all that had happened since the night when Eve had come to the Manor House. We know much of her life during this time, so the better part of the monologue need not be relayed here, but there was one incident which both knew would need to be talked about.

'We had a party in the garden to celebrate the wedding of Ash Spears and Samantha.'

'Was that late summer?'

'Yes.'

'I wondered why there was a marquee in the garden. I came there, in the early morning.'

'I know.'

'How...?'

'I don't know, Bex; I just knew that you'd been there.'

'I couldn't...I couldn't see you then, and that's something which I don't expect you to understand; it was just the wrong time, for both of us.'

'Sure, whatever; it doesn't matter now, anyway.'

'I was heavy with Florence, then. After that I went west, to the white house, where I stayed until she was born; Charlotte looked after me; Charlotte and the others. She was born on the same day that Rose...The same day that Nathaniel was born; did you know that?'

'Of course not; how could I know that?'

'No, of course; I'm sorry. That was such a tragedy, wasn't it?'

'It was terrible; Mike blames himself, though he's no reason to.'

'It was Rose's decision, I'm sure. Mike must be otherwise pleased though, to have provided the first legitimate son and heir.'

'The next Lord in the line; yes, of course he's...He's delighted. Although it was hard for him, when Nathaniel was in hospital, and he thought that might lose both of them.'

'Well, at least that didn't happen, and Nathaniel's okay now?'

'Yes, he's fine; I'll introduce you later. So what about you, Bex..?'

Which would be the harder part of the conversation, and which started in a hard place.

'What about me?'

'Well for a start, are you going to tell me anything about Florence's father?'

'No...That is, there's nothing I can tell you; you know as much about him as I do.'

'I hardly think that's likely.'

'Well anyway, it doesn't matter, and he doesn't know he's father to my child.'

'That at least you have in common with me. So you'll never see him again then?'

'That I can't tell you...Look...Let's not talk about that, can we?'

There was for a moment a new awkwardness about Rebecca's demeanour, which indicated to Victoria that she was not being told everything, and in fact she had not been told anything, but she let it pass, for now.

'Okay, whatever...So what about Florence; can you tell me about her?'

And so passed the next two hours of their lives, which included two more cups of coffee; they spoke of the Christenings, and of Percival, and how he was now Godfather to little Henry. Victoria relayed such information as she could regarding the people who lived in the village, and they spoke at some length about Charlotte, and the white house, the conversation becoming ever less intense and controversial. That which was not discussed, or indeed mentioned again, were Rebecca's so significant words on the steps in the early morning of this same day. The people in the temple, the man by the stream, and the mother; people who she had apparently killed, but who were they all? Victoria sat opposite a murderess, and she would one day know everything, and Rebecca would tell her, one day, but there are times when the wish to know and to tell are seen off by the difficulty of knowing, or telling, and neither wished the conversation to stray back into darker places. They were together again, by whatever tortuous and difficult route that had come to be, and better that this be enough, for now.

Victoria could see that Rebecca's thoughts drifted sometimes to the place where she could not go, and her distraction led Victoria to believe that she should not pursue her enquiry, lest with it she push her beloved back where she could not follow. And both knew that they had at least negotiated the most difficult part of their conversation; Rebecca had lied about her child's father, and Victoria had been less than entirely truthful regarding Nathaniel's paternal parentage, and both had got away with it, so far at least.

By now it was mid – afternoon, and both of them were hungry. They ate at a local bistro, Rebecca bought clothes, which Victoria paid for, and they did not return to the Manor until early – evening, by which time once again only a passing conversation was had with Victoria's mother; she had seen Rebecca through the first day, and tomorrow she would surely be better, and better able to deal with a meal with her family. By nine o'clock Rebecca was sleeping again, and Victoria said goodnight to her son, and then went to her step for her last cigarette of the day. It had been a particular day in her life, and she was glad that she was not working tomorrow. People had died; people who had wished her son dead, and one of them at least still lived, and of that they would have to speak again. But for now she let her beloved rest; sleep, the great healer and restorer, and now she herself felt the need for restoration; she put out her cigarette, and walked once again through the grand front door of her home. Tomorrow would bring what it would, for today she believed that she had done enough.

Megan Thomas found accommodation at a guest house on the coast; one of the few which had stayed open during the winter months. She would presently look for more permanent lodgings, but here her room had a sea – view, and she could take long walks along the beach, something which she had always liked to do, and she preferred the seashore in wintertime. The three people to whom she had been closest were dead, and would be buried in a way and at a place that she would not know, and she needed time now to see off the sadness of that, and the sadness of her loss, and to come to terms with her new circumstances. She was alone now, and she was the last of them, and she had failed, in the end, if indeed this was to be the end, and that question above all others would occupy the waking thoughts of Megan Thomas during the next days of her life.

Chapter 2

THE EDGE OF THE WORLD

The thaw, when it came to this part of England, and thus to the village of Middlewapping, would come quite quickly. Daytime and then night time temperatures rose and then stayed above zero degrees, something which was welcomed by all of its' inhabitants, but had particular implication for some. With care, and provided that the work is covered at night, foundations may be dug and laid, and stone may be shaped and made ready. Builders know, however, that brick and stonework should not be laid in sub – zero conditions; even with the use of chemical accelerants, and even if the work is covered with tarpaulin overnight, there is a risk that mortar will not cure or set properly, and may quickly degrade. During the deepest winter months, therefore, those whose primary source of work involves outdoor construction must find other gainful employment, where it is available, but such people will watch the weather, and wait for warmer times, and in our tale such a person is Keith.

And so it came to be that within one week of the coming of southerly winds, which bought with them rain and low, insulating cloud cover, Keith returned to a job which had had started and then abandoned when the snow and ice had come. This was a stone wall, which he had begun to build along the two external boundaries of a fairly large house quite near the town centre. He had built a smaller but similar wall during the late autumn, which had been much admired by the local inhabitants, and he had successfully gained three other contracts as a result, thus securing enough employment for several weeks to come. Obtaining work was one thing, however, but the work still had to be done, and Keith knew well enough that his prospective clients would not wait indefinitely, however highly regarded his workmanship may be. Thus it was that on the first day on site, Keith did not arrive alone, but was driven there by a certain William Tucker, who had also picked up Damien Fotheringay, and these three would form the most part of a team, who would work together to see to the walls' construction. Damien was already more than proficient in the craft of stone – walling, as was the fourth and final member of the team, who was uncharacteristically late, it now being five minutes past the agreed meeting time of eight o'clock.

Keith showed the others around the site, and explained the work to be done, which was in fact by now straightforward, Keith having already dug and laid the foundations. Important aspects of the work were ascertained, amongst the most important being where tea could be made and drunk, and lunch and so on could be taken. This was in fact a timber summerhouse, set in the back garden and somewhat away from the main house, which the clients had made available, and which benefitted from electrical sockets and a table and four chairs; relative luxury to those more used to garages and garden sheds representing their only shelter from inclement weather conditions. Keith had bought an electric kettle, tea – bags and sugar, each had bought a cup, and so Will set to making tea whilst Keith and Damien unloaded tools and equipment, which included a cement – mixer.

'So; who are the clients?'

'Couple of gay guys who just got married; they mostly stay in London during the week, but anyway they'll be on honeymoon for a couple of weeks, so we've got the place to ourselves.'

'Perfect...So who's the fourth man?'

'Yeah, you've not met him yet, have you...'

'You've worked with him before though, yes?'

'Oh yes, many times…He's not quite like other people.'

'In what respect..?'

'Better I let you judge for yourself; he's good at what he does and he's got a phenomenal work output; just don't try to borrow his shovel, or any of his tools for that matter.'

'Okay, well thanks for the warning. Local boy, is he?'

'Lives just outside the village; thing is, I've never known him be late before; must have got a puncture or something.'

'What does he drive?'

'He doesn't; he rides…'

At that moment and with some ado a bicycle of the old – fashioned variety entered the front garden of the property, upon which sat Mike, who stopped his contraption next to Will's Land – Rover. Strapped or otherwise attached to the bicycle were a shovel, a sledge – hammer, an iron bar, a tool bag and various other facilities, including the longest spirit – level that Damien had ever seen.

'Morning, Mike.' Said Keith

'Good morning; I apologise for my late arrival; I have had a puncture en route, for which I have had to affect a temporary repair. I will make up the lost time at the end of the day.'

'Maybe you're overloading the bike.' Said Damien

'I have ridden many miles so laden, but cannot take account of nails left on the carriageway, and I do not appreciate such unwarranted remarks.'

'Okay, well; just saying.'

'Anyway,' said Keith, who already felt the need to intervene between his two co – workers, after only their first encounter. 'don't worry about it, we haven't got going yet, and Will's got a brew going.'

'Then we will all be late starting work.'

'It's the first day on site, Mike.'

'Then I daresay some latitude may be allowed.'

'This is Damien, by the way; Damien, Mike...'

'Pleased to meet you, I'm sure.' Said Mike

'Likewise...'

'I discern from your accent that you are from the west of Scotland.'

'Then you discern correctly.'

'A place of great natural beauty, and on my two brief visits there I have found the people most welcoming, though the food was not to my taste.'

'Sorry to hear that...'

Mike dismounted and began untying his equipment.

'Yeah, get unpacked, then I'll show you 'round.'

'I am already familiar with the site; I came yesterday for a brief inspection.'

'Oh; right....'

'Unfortunately my activities were noted by a neighbour, and I was apprehended by the local constabulary on suspicion of trespass and suspicious behaviour.'

'What...You were arrested?'

'They let me off with a caution having ascertained my true intent; I gave them your details for verification.'

'Nobody contacted me; I suppose they must have believed you.'

Having laid out his tools on the driveway, Mike wheeled his now somewhat lighter bicycle away and leaned it against the side of the house; Keith and Damien exchanged looks.

'Christ, where did you find him?'

'He's okay once you get to know him, I think...'

'How long does that take?'

'I'll let you know...'

'So; which is to be my stint?'

This was Mike, who had now rejoined them and was as usual inspecting or perhaps re - inspecting every detail of the site, which included picking up a handful of building sand and running it carefully through his fingers.

'I thought you could do the front pillars and the walls to either side.'

'With corner and end pillars, I see.'

'Follow the foundations.'

'And what is to be the finished height of the wall?'

'About six feet, although we'll see how the courses run out; couple of inches either way won't matter.'

Apparently satisfied, Mike now walked away to examine the foundations of his stint, leaving Keith and Damien alone once more.

'Well, this should be fun...'said Damien

'Never a dull moment with Mike around, oh and by the way never ask his opinion on anything; you'll hear them anyway but don't encourage him.'

'I'll try to bear that in mind, and don't touch his tools, right?'

'Yeah, he's sensitive about that; I once saw him lay a guy out cold for using his brick – trowel without asking; he kind of takes the direct approach to any such transgressions. Not many people can work with him, to be honest; I've known guys walk off site, but he's a true craftsman, you know; never met anyone so focussed once he gets into it. In the evenings he surfs the net voraciously for information on just about anything; he's a mine of information about things that most people have never heard of. Oh, and his other occupation is making teddy – bears.'

'You what...?'

'Don't ask, and don't laugh if the subject comes up.'

'Guy lives alone, right?'

'How did you guess?'

'I mean, whatever gets you though the long winter evenings, you know, but the guy's built like a brick shit – house; I'm having difficulty imagining him with a needle and thread.'

'I think his bears fetch a good price these days; much sought after, it seems. He doesn't use his real name for that; everyone thinks they're made by somebody called Wendy Smith; they're easier to market that way, apparently.'

'Christ...Anything else I should know?'

'I think that about covers it.'

'Tea's ready...'

This was Will, whose primary role aside from making tea would be to supply the three others with stone and mortar. Profits from the job were nevertheless to be shared equally between the four men.

'Okay,' said Keith 'let's to the summer house...'

The work, once started, would be progressed quickly and with aplomb, but in the beginning there must always be tea, and anyway, it had just started to rain.

On this morning, which was the second morning since Rebecca had arrived at the Manor House, Victoria awoke at about the time that Mike had reached his place of work. She showered, and by the time she had returned to her bedroom, Rebecca was also awake and sitting up in bed.

'Good morning, you; how are you feeling..?'

'I'm not sure, yet...'

'Well, we'd better get you out somewhere today.'

'Sure...'

'Let's take the dogs out; go to the coast or whatever.'

'Good idea; yes, that would be nice.'

'I have to go to work tomorrow, Bex.'

'I know...I know I can't stay here; I just need more time, you know? I need to get my head to a place where I can string two thoughts together.'

'You can stay in Michael's house on the Green, if that helps. There's no one living there now...'

'I see...I mean; would that be okay?'

'Mike suggested it, actually.'

'So could I bring Florence there?'

'Of course, why not..?'

'Right...Well that sounds...'

'We can call in there today if you like; see what you need. Mike will have it cleaned and so on, but you'll need bedding and such, and whatever you need for the baby.'

Victoria realised that this was how it would have to be; that she would need to take control of Rebecca's life until she was able to take control herself, and she had to somehow reunite her with Florence as soon as was reasonably possible. Rebecca needed a focus; something to take her mind away from recent events, and bring her back into the real world.

And at least in the village she could keep an eye on her, and she would ask Meadow to do the same.

'You need to make a plan, Bex.'

'I know, and I will, but there're things I need to sort out first...I need to see Helena.'

'Is that a good idea?'

'I wasn't alone down there.'

'I know, but don't you think your focus should be elsewhere at the moment?'

'Helena is the reason for all of this, and I need to know what happened...But you're right, let's get out; I need to see the sea.'

'Okay, well go and take a shower, then, then we'll plan our escape. You'll have to see my parents sometime, you know?'

'Yes, of course...This evening...I'll be fine, Vics, just not yet; let me have today with you; there are things I need to tell you, and things I need to get straight.'

Despite a delayed start and occasional inconvenient showers of rain, the morning in the garden of number twelve, Cedar Drive, was in the end sufficient in its' productivity. Mike had begun constructing pillars which would eventually define the entry to the garden and property, whilst Keith and Damien worked together on the longer side boundary wall. By agreement, no mid – morning break was taken, and at one o'clock, tools were put down, and the four men made for the summerhouse. Few words had been spoken between them since work had begun, beyond those necessary for the continuation of work, but now they sat together to take their repast. Will, who once again made the tea, had brought a round of cheese which had broken when being removed from its' mold, and so could not be sold, and this he cut four ways, for the delectation of himself and his fellow workers.

'This is superb cheese, Will;' said Keith 'Em's really getting the hang of it, isn't she.'

'She's got some really good cheeses coming on line now, and yeah, it's quite successful as it goes, but she still needs to make more, and sell more.'

'Meadow sells all she provides for the deli; it hardly touches the ground, apparently.'

'She needs to get into some bigger retailers though; she's going to Norgate Market next week; see if she can get a foot in the door there. If that takes off she'll really have to get going; buy more goats and so on.'

'And she does the whole thing by herself.'

'I help out when I can, but it's basically all her; she couldn't afford to pay anyone, and anyway she enjoys it, you know?'

'Sure; well, good luck to the lady.'

And so the conversation went, and only a little later was a subject touched upon which would cause any discomfort, and it was Mike, who was reading a newspaper, who raised it, having thus far been uncharacteristically quiet.

'I see that there is still much uncertainty and controversy regarding the house which burned down in Kent. DNA tests have revealed that many but not all of the dead women were related; as many as seventeen generations of women may be represented, and some of the women were probably sisters to one another, or were otherwise related.'

There had thus far been little discussion in the village regarding the burning of Farthing's Well. Aside from Keith and Damien, those who knew anything of the house had not met since the news had broken, and nobody outside the Manor House as yet knew of Rebecca's return. Keith and Meadow had talked of it, though neither had been to the house, and two days after the incident it had been Damien who had brought the matter to the attention of Sophia. They had been relaxing after their evening meal, she was reading on the settee and he had sat at the dining table and was reading a newspaper.

'Christ...Have you read this?'

'Have I read what, sweetheart?'

'It seems that your spooky witches coven has burned down.'

'What...?'

'They don't know what caused the fire, yet, but three women died in the blaze.'

Memories of their visit to the house returned for both of them, and they were memories which neither wished to dwell upon. Sophia had been the first of the white witches to discover the house's location, and the first to go there, but she had not been the last. She joined her beloved at the dining table, and both now read the article together.

'But...I don't understand; I mean how?'

'Seems like it's a mystery, so far anyway... I suppose it could have been an electrical fault, or somebody could have fallen asleep smoking a fag, but skullduggery has not been ruled out, and bearing in mind what you and I know about the place.... Could be somebody has been handy with a petrol can and a box of matches, wouldn't you say?'

'Yes, but...Only the inner circle knew of the house, and... Well, I don't know....This would be murder, wouldn't it?'

'Och ay, bonny lass; in the first degree, I expect...'

'But how would they have got into the place?'

'Well, I doubt if the average Joe on the street could have done it, and why would they anyway, but if it was one of your lot....A witch could have pulled it off, don't you think?'

'I don't know...I suppose so, but who? I mean Rebecca wouldn't have known of it, unless...'

'Unless what?'

'Unless somebody told her, but I mean, who...?'

'That, bonny lass, is the million dollar question...'

'I mean it may not have been her, of course, assuming it was anybody.'

'But from what you've told me she had more reason than most, right?'

'Yes, but...Well yes, I suppose she would...'

'I find it hard to believe that this was an accident, bonny lass. It would also coincide with the disappearance of what's her name...'

'Megan...'

'Ay, Megan; she's gone now, and maybe somebody took it upon themselves to deal with the rest of them, which could be the reason for her swift departure.'

Only a few more minutes of discussion had passed before Sophia had made a telephone call; Charlotte must already know, surely, but she wanted to be certain, and anyway, a meeting of the inner circle would have to be called; she was certain of that, at least.

In the summerhouse there followed a moment of silence; Will knew nothing of anything regarding the house, and both Keith and especially Damien knew that it was something best not talked about.

'Ay, well, it's a mystery, to be sure...'

'For such a pagan sect to exist for so long is probably unique.'

'Oh I don't know,' said Keith 'other pagan religions exist, don't they; Druids and so on?'

'This was or presumably still is a purely female sect, and clearly secretive; I have never read of such a thing before.'

'Probably because it's secret' Said Will

'I suspect that they are witches.' Said Mike

'Witches..? Said Damien 'Surely not in this day and age..?'

'I have heard tell of a witch living in the village of Middlewapping, though I give little credence to such an idea.'

'Ludicrous...' Said Damien

'Ridiculous...' Said Keith 'Anyway I suppose we should get back to it.'

Will now took more of an interest in the conversation; he knew of the witches, of course, and took note of the quickness of the denial by the two others present who knew of them well enough. He would raise the matter with Keith later, but for now the lunch break was over, and the four men left their lunch – boxes on the table, and returned to their respective tasks.

Number seven, The Green was as Megan had left it, and as Meadow and Keith had seen it when they had come in search of her. Commercial cleaners would be employed soon, but for now the house was full of the sense of the witch having been there. They went into each room, Victoria always ahead, and neither spoke until the short tour was complete, and they stood once again in the lounge. It was Rebecca who spoke first.

'There are ghosts here.'

'Don't be silly, it's just a house, and it's perfect for you, for now anyway. It means we'll be able to see one another, at least.'

'Yes, I know.'

'Mike was going to get the house cleared, but we might as well leave the furniture for now, and buy whatever else you need. You have to start being practical, Bex; you need somewhere for you and Florence, and why not here?'

'Okay...Of course I can see that it's ideal, in a way.'

'Well then; we'll have today, and then tomorrow you need to get together everything you need for now; we need to get you sleeping here by tomorrow night, then when you're ready you can go and get Florence.'

'Yes, I need to see her now.'

'So you need to get ready; I can help, Bex, but you need to pull yourself together, you know? I'll speak to Mike about getting the cleaners here tomorrow morning, if we can, then it's up to you. Whatever's happened you need to think of the future now.'

'Of course...'

'So, let's go and have the day together; I'd like that as well, then tomorrow you get practical, okay?'

On the quite short journey home in Will's Land Rover, little conversation took place; all were content with the days' work, and Keith was pleased that Damien and Mike had seen the first day out without serious confrontation. Mike he knew was as meek as a lamb unless provoked, and Damien was diplomatic up to a point, but only up to a point, but there had been no friction between them, and from now on it would be less likely to occur. It was not until near the end of the journey that Will raised a subject which he had been contemplating during his afternoon labours.

'So like, what's the deal with the house that burned down; what do you guys know that I don't?'

Keith and Damien exchanged looks, and Keith nodded; Will was okay.

'It's a coven,' said Damien 'black witches who were intent on the end of the Tillington dynasty; apparently the first Lord killed one of theirs, or something, and they've been after them ever since. Sophia and I went there; place creeped me out, to be honest, but now it seems somebody else has been there, and they seem to have gone with murderous intent.'

'Right...Rebecca being prime suspect, I suppose; she's quite good at setting fire to buildings; I saw her handiwork down west when I took Victoria down there.'

'So what was that all about?'

'Oh you know; it was just another sect who pissed her off, so she took some of them down and gutted their temple; it was before your time in the village. We've been dealing with this kind of crap for a long time, have we not, Keith?'

'Never a dull moment around here...Sects and witches all over the place; can't move for them some days, meaning no disrespect to Sophia.'

'And it looked like such a nice place when I moved here, and now I end up living with a witch; what were the chances...?.'

'But nobody's seen Rebecca, right?' Said Will

'Not for a long time,' said Keith 'but something must have spooked Megan, who it now transpires was one of the black sisterhood; she even got into the Manor House, she was making a suit for his lordship.'

'What...?'

'I know; unbelievable, but Sophia worked out who she was, and now she's gone and this happens. Meadow was all for confronting her, but she'd gone by the time we got there.'

'The women have not been idle, have they?' Said Damien

'It seems not.' said Keith 'You know, in the old days it was easier; guys beating up other guys for some stupid reason; I did some of that myself back in the day, but you kind of know where you are with that. With women it's more complicated.'

'Women are always more complicated.' Said Damien 'And more dangerous, it seems; you don't want to be pissing the women off around here; might find your house burned down or your offspring slaughtered.'

'Yeah, or you might end up dead.'

Will pulled onto the track which ran along three sides of the village Green, and pulled up at its' far end, outside number one. Keith and Damien left the vehicle, and Keith concluded.

'Okay, see you tomorrow; let's make it a seven fifteen departure.'

'Right you are...'

'And, you know; best not repeat our conversation to anyone outside the circle.'

'What conversation?'

Keith slammed the passenger door, which was necessary to ensure its' closure; Will pulled out left onto the main road, and headed homeward and to Emily, something which always gave him a good feeling. Will had had a sense for a long time that things were happening in the village from which he and Emily had been deliberately excluded, and he was okay with that, up to a point, since he was certain that it was done for good reasons. But today he had learned something new, and it was something which he would tell Emily, and about which she would no doubt make further enquiry.

When important things need to be thought about, or talked about, or when changes are happening in the lives of people, they will often go to the sea. Meadow had done so when she learned news of her father, Percival had found refuge here after his abduction and near death, Michael and Elin had come to the coast to try to work out how they felt about one another, and Keith had taken Tara to the ocean, when her second album was finished. Megan had come here, now that her friends had been murdered, and her home destroyed, and now here were Victoria and Rebecca, who had let the dogs loose to run at the sandy waters' edge, whilst they sat on rocks at the foot of the low cliff. Perhaps some primitive instinct draws people to the edge of their world; here would their most ancient ancestors have lived; the first people to come would have come to places such as this, and here they would have stayed, only eventually making their way inland along rivers, through forests or over moorland, into the dangerous unknown. Perhaps when big life is happening people need a big horizon, and a sense that something else lies beyond their vision, over the edge of the world, but anyway whatever the reason, here they will often come.

And Rebecca the murderess had killed again, so that Victoria's child would be safe, and Michael's child, which was not really Michael's child, would be safe. Victoria lit cigarettes for them both, whilst Prince and Bathsheba played in the shallow water, running inshore as the gentle waves broke over them, before running back into the water to make it happen again; they were both water dogs.

'So where do we start then, Bex; I mean is the danger really over now?'

'I can't be sure, Vics, but I think so.'

'How can people hate other people so much?'

'I understand anger, Vics; I understand how it feels to want to kill, but this was very old anger, and not children; never children. Whatever is right or wrong, killing a child is always wrong. I would have waited for them; I would have found another way, but there was Helena.'

'So did she or does she have some kind of power over you?'

'In a way, or at least she did. Her mother was Helen, who was the head of our order, and who was always good to me, but she was turned by the black witch, Eve, and she tried to kill me, or rather tried to make me kill myself, which is the same thing, really, isn't it? And so, well, I had no choice but to kill her, did I? Nobody knew that apart from Sophia, although Rosalind suspects, but then Helena worked it out, somehow, and she would have used that knowledge against me. This was her idea; that we should kill them, and try to end it once and for all; this was her anger, because through me they had killed her mother, and I understand why she was angry; they killed my mother as well, so I know how that anger feels.'

'But are you quite sure you won't be discovered, by the police, I mean?'

'I don't see how; nobody outside the coven will connect me to anything; Charlotte will know, but we can keep our secrets.'

'I hope so, but how will Charlotte know?'

'Helena will tell her, and if not I'll tell her, but she will know, anyway; even if she just reads about it in the newspapers she will know that it was us.'

They were silent for a moment; they had the small cove to themselves, as the two dogs played their innocent games; Bathsheba was braver in water than Prince, and she swam out some way beyond the point where the waves were breaking, before swimming back through the surf.

'So tell me about the people in the temple; how many people did you kill then?'

'What does it matter?'

'It doesn't really, I suppose.'

'You were stupid to go there, Vics.'

'I know, but Will got us out; he was very clever; had he not been there I don't know what would have happened. But the thing is, how do you do it, Bex?'

'How do I do what?'

'How do you live with all the things that you've done; how do you get up in the mornings and do ordinary things, knowing that you've killed all of those people?'

'I don't know...I think you just...It's like you put it all on ice; you hide it as best you can in the coldest and deepest part of your soul, and let it thaw out slowly in the warmth of good things that happen, and good things that you do, and you hope that one day you will wake up and it will all be gone; melted away, you know? And then you tell yourself that, well, there was always a reason; that things were different, then, and that now you are a different person. You look for justification, because that's all you can do, and hope that you are able to convince yourself that somehow you were right; that justice has been done. I thought it was over, Vics. I thought that I could just let things be, and try to make sure that no harm came to anyone; that that would be enough. But then Helena came, and so it started again, and I had to learn it all again; how to be like that, and in the end it was so easy, and you know I think that's the most frightening thing. That I can turn myself back into somebody who can kill people that easily. That the same hands which carry my child, and can work clay into delicate shapes and create beautiful things, and which I use to make love to you, can also destroy; take the life of another person; of all the things that I'm good at, that is the thing which sets me apart from other people; the thing which I do better than anybody. And I have you, you know? And now I have Florence, and I want to give her all of the love I have, so that slowly the love will somehow make up for all of the hatred; that the good things will be enough to counter the bad things; in the end it all has to balance, doesn't it?'

'I don't know, my love; perhaps.'

'You don't hate me for it, do you?'

'No...No, I made that decision; that I would love you and stand by you no matter what you've done, and I know you didn't do this for yourself. I'm a hopeless mother, Bex, but every time I hold little Henry I tell myself that perhaps he's only alive because of you, so how could I ever hate you? You did something which I would never be brave enough to do; what you did was very dangerous, wasn't it?'

'Of course, looking back, but before and at the time you don't think about that; you can't let yourself think about it; you have to become somebody with no fear; it's one of the things I've learned how to do.'

'Well, don't do it again, okay? I lost you once, and I don't want to lose you again. One thing I know now is that my life is empty without you.'

'Looks like you're stuck with me, then, unless I get myself killed.'

'Yes, it looks that way. Anyway, I'm hungry; let's find somewhere to eat, shall we?'

'If you like, but let's stay a bit longer; this is such a beautiful place, and the dogs are having such a good time.'

'Okay.'

'I have to go west; I have to talk to Charlotte, and get Florence, and get the house ready; there's so much I have to do, and I feel as though it all starts when we leave here.'

'Do you think you'll be okay?'

'Of course; what choice to I have? I have to put everything behind me, and hope that…Well anyway, it's all about Florence, now; I'll do it for her, and for us, so sure, I'll be okay. And I'm so lucky that Mike's okay with me taking the house, I know that.'

'Well, the last resident left in rather a hurry, and Michael has no idea why.'

'So how much of any of this does he know?'

'Nothing, and that's how I intend to keep it, for now, anyway.'

They were silent again, the tide was coming in, and dark clouds were building over the sea; both knew that it was soon time to go, but Rebecca had something else to say. Amidst all of her troubles, something in particular was troubling her.

'There's one thing above all else that I don't understand; I mean I've relived everything which happened, and everything which I did, I've been over it in my head so many times, but….I lost some time, and it must have been quite a long time. Try as I may I still have no memory of leaving that place, or how I got to the Manor.'

'You need to speak to Helena.'

'Yes, I know, but something happened; something isn't right, and I just can't make anything of it. That should not have happened; it makes no sense.'

A few minutes later they left; anyone watching from the cliff – head would have seen two women engaged in earnest conversation, an innocent enough scene, just two friends or perhaps lovers out for the day, walking their dogs. No one could have known that one was a witch, and the other daughter to a Lord and Lady, and nobody could know or even imagine the

secret things about which they talked. Only the waves heard
them, and the waves were about their own business, and paid
them no mind.

Sally kissed Percival goodbye in her Mini Cooper outside
number fifteen, Hanover Street, at a little before nine o'clock
in the evening. He had, with little hesitation and as she had
predicted, declined her offer to join her, and instead wished her
a pleasant evening; she would get a cab home. Hanover Street
consisted entirely of large, four – storey terraced houses, an easy
walking distance to the town centre, the properties being much
sought after by those who could afford them, and much desired
by those who could not. This was somewhat later than usual for
her arrival at a dinner party; she had in fact been dressed, made
up and ready to go in good time, but just prior to her scheduled
departure she had come over uncommonly sexually desirous,
and had quite spontaneously seduced her man in the kitchen,
which had lead to their having sexual union on the settee. Sally
had, just prior to Percival's return to her life, upgraded and for
the most part downsized her lingerie, something which she had
convinced herself to be coincidental, but was probably not in fact
coincidental, but had perhaps been more instinctive. In any case
it made the matter of seduction a still easier thing, but now she
had to refresh herself, change her underwear and re – touch her
makeup, all of which further delayed her departure. She changed
into briefs which were no less sexually provocative in nature, but
for the remainder of the evening that which she wore under her
quite modest, sequined dress would be her business only.

Fiona, who was hostess for the evening, welcomed her at
the door, the remainder of the participants being already
seated at the dining table, enjoying sparkling white wine and

pre – dinner canapés and waiting for the main culinary event. Fiona was a dance – instructor, and Ray, her husband, who worked in insurance, was seated at the other head of the table. He was the only other person who stood up to greet the new arrival, something which he did with that which as far as Sally was concerned was inappropriate enthusiasm, and something which was noted by all, especially Fiona. Polly, who had been instigative in Sally's invitation to the evening, rented premises in the old town, from which she had for several years run a florist, and George, her husband, was a Real Estate agent. Wendy the actress, who was currently unemployed, had brought her newest husband, Paul, who directed or otherwise assisted in theatre productions, and the only other people present were Mark and Lucinda, who were both primary school teachers, who taught at the same private school. Both were in the process of divorcing their respective spouses, having recently and quite accidentally fallen in love with each other in the staffroom. This in fact caused some controversy within the group of friends, as Sylvia, Mark's wife, was popular amongst them, but Mark was a particular friend of Ray's, and so had on this occasion won the right to sit at table, and now he brought Lucinda. Fiona and Ray had a large dining table which could comfortably seat ten or sometimes twelve people, and tonight there were nine people, there being other notable absentees, of whom we will hear in a moment.

'High everyone, sorry I'm late.'

'So are we; we're all starving,' said George 'what happened; get a bit carried away on the exercise machine or something?'

'Something like that...'

'I've got some non – alcoholic wine in the fridge.' Said Fiona 'It's okay, Cava will be fine.'

'Good lord,' said Ray 'has she actually started drinking again?'

'Actually she never stopped.' Said Sally 'She was just particular about when she drank, and who she drank with.'

'Ouch...' said George 'I believe one has just been put on ones' place.'

'Anyway, uuum, cheers...' said Fiona 'It's lovely to see you, Sally...I'll get the first course through.'

Sally took a large mouthful of her drink; she felt energized by her love – making, and indeed by her life in general since Percival had come back to her. And yet, at the same time she felt a sense of inner calm which she had not felt for a long time. This was positive, creative energy, which did not have to be worked off on her cross – trainer night after night, but could find a different and better release. She was no stranger to being the only one without a partner at such gatherings; the rogue female, but tonight was different, because her life was different. She knew anyway that everything was not as it appeared; that Fiona and Ray, and Polly and George had their marital difficulties, smoothed over with a veneer of shallow conversation and excellent dinner parties, but the false smiles and barbed comments gave them away. So, let the men want her and the women talk about her; tonight she was happy; tonight she felt like a free woman, because she knew that she was no longer a free woman.

Percival had driven home, and parked Sally's car down the lane beside his side door. Aside from a barely adequate turning place at the far end of the lane, it was too narrow for two vehicles to pass, and Percival had long ago agreed with the farmer that he would keep the lane open to allow access for his tractor, but in fact this only happened occasionally for the transport of livestock or equipment into the field, and Percival was not expecting any tractors tonight. He was feeling tired, and had planned a shower and an early night. He had only been home for a few minutes, however, when his door knocker sounded. Lulu looked alert but not concerned, but Percival wondered who would be calling on him at this hour of the evening, and what this might portend. He opened the door with some trepidation, therefore, but as it was the person standing outside was in fact somebody whom he was glad to see.

'Fancy a beer?'

So here was a different take on his evening; they should talk anyway, and he had not seen Keith alone for some time.

'Sure....'

Lulu also sensed that her quiet evening at home was about to be interrupted; an event was about to occur, so she walked to the kitchen and sat by the hook. The three of them walked the short distance to the Dog and Bottle public house, which had once been stabling for the Manor House, when lanes had only needed to be wide enough for two horses to pass, or for a horse and cart at most. There were a few customers in, but they found a table in the corner, Lulu settling down beneath it to keep a watchful eye on proceedings. There was always an open fire in the inglenook during the autumn and winter months; there was never a fire – guard, however, and the dimly lit room always smelled of smoke. No doubt this was in contravention of various health and safety regulations, but nobody ever complained, except in jest, and Nigel the worthy if somewhat caustic landlord kept a good pint of Old Thumper, which made up for the somewhat smoky atmosphere.

'So; what's new, Keith?'

'Oh, you know; life goes on...I'm back to proper work now that the big freeze is over.'

'And how's Tara doing; she's on tour now, is she not?'

'Yeah, she's away for a few weeks, starting in Japan and the Far East, and then all stations back to London via America and Europe; it's going to be an amazing adventure for her, as long as she can deal with it, you know?'

'She'll be fine, won't she; she's a well grounded person, as far as I can see.'

'She's so well grounded you have to kind of dig her out, sometimes; that's not really the thing; I just hope she can deal with the rock – star lifestyle, and I hope she finds her big - stage confidence.'

'Have you heard from her?'

'She's in touch, sometimes, but we're trying to encourage her independence. Lines of communication between kids and parents are manifold these days; there's no excuse any more, which in some ways is a good thing, and in some ways it isn't. This is her adventure, you know, which seems to be going okay so far, but Tarragon's not an open book, you dig; she keeps a lot inside.'

'Sure...'

'Have you heard the albums?'

'I downloaded the first one; it's good music, and she's got a good voice; I mean it's a voice you recognize; she has a unique style; she should go far with it.'

'Well, we'll see, but even if this is as far as it goes she's gone far enough anyway; I still have to tell myself that it's my daughter singing, you know?'

'Yes, I'm sure; so how about the other two?'

'Rosie's doing well, I mean at school and so on; she's the best of them academically.'

'She still doing the witch thing?'

'Yeah, and that doesn't seem to be anything but a positive; she says it helps her concentrate and whatever, and we trust her with it. She's a person who's really come out of herself these days. It's funny, you know; she's the one I feel most protective about.'

'You mean as far as the attentions of young men are concerned.'

'I suppose....'

'I can see how that could be; she's what one might call drop – dead gorgeous for one thing. So how's Basil doing?'

'Yeah, he's finding his way in the world, and uniquely amongst my offspring he's found love; he and Emma are really tight, you know? I think wherever she goes post – school he'll go with her, but I'm not concerned about Bas; he'll make out okay whatever he ends up doing, which probably won't be university; I don't think the education system will be able to keep him within its' bounds; he's too much of a free spirit. Anyway; my round, I think...'

Conversation around the table was amicable enough during the smoked salmon, with avocado vinaigrette for the two vegetarians, who were Wendy and Lucinda, and it was not until beef Wellington or nut roast that perhaps inevitably the subject of Farthing's Well was raised, and it was George who raised it.

'Bloody weird business in Kent...'

'You mean the house that burned down?' Said Fiona

'It wasn't the house that was weird; it was the people in it, and the women they've been digging up from the garden.'

'I think it's awful just exhuming all of those people;' said Polly 'why couldn't they have just left them in peace?'

'It's a place of archaeological and historical interest.' Said Ray

'But one of them had only just been buried, hadn't she?'

'Yes, but they weren't to know that, and anyway they'll probably get a decent Christian burial now...'

'They clearly didn't want a Christian burial, and there was nothing indecent about the way they were buried.'

'What; no coffins and unmarked graves?'

'Coffins are just a waste of wood, and they weren't unmarked, they were just anonymous, and as far as anyone knows they probably knew very well who was buried there.'

'Who's 'they', that's the point.' Said George

'Witches, so they say...' Said Mark

'Oh come on,' said Polly 'that's just pure speculation.'

'It was probably one of these bloody separatist houses,' said Ray *'the ancient order of feminists'* or what the fuck ever.'

'And what would be wrong with that?'

'Ancient order of lesbians, more like.' Said George

'Ditto my last question.'

'I still reckon they were witches.' Said Mark 'I mean there's supposed to be one living in your village, isn't there Sally?'

'The witch of Middlewapping...' Said George

'Yeah, Sal; what's that all about?' Said Ray

'It's all about nonsense.' Said Sally

'So, you don't know who she is then?'

'Witches exist, I'm certain of it.' Said Wendy

'From whence comes this certainty..?' Said Polly

'I mean come on Sal,' said Ray, who despite or perhaps because of his frustration in regard to Sally seldom wasted an opportunity to make her feel uncomfortable 'for all you know she could be living next door.'

'I assure you that she isn't.'

'How can you be so sure?'

'Because there's a pub on one side of me and a single guy living on the other...'

'Okay, so two doors down then, or whatever; I just don't get how you can be so certain, unless of course...'

'Unless of course what?'

'Well, there you are; a woman living on her own; keeps herself to herself...'

'Ray, for heaven's sake...' Said Fiona

'Are you saying that you think I'm a witch?'

'I'm just saying; you know...'

'If the cap fits, right...?' Said George

'Or in this case the pointed hat...' Said Ray

'Stop it, you two.' Said Fiona

'We're just kidding, right Ray?' Said George

'I don't think you should joke about something about which you know nothing.' Said Wendy

'It's okay,' said Sally 'I'm not offended.'

'I note that you haven't denied it, either.' Said Ray

'You may think what you like, Ray.'

'Watch it Ray,' said George 'she might start using her bewitching charms on you.'

'Well that wouldn't take much, would it?' Said Sally

'Yes, well I think it's time for a change of subject, don't you?' Said Fiona 'Would anyone like more wine; Ray dear, fetch a couple of bottles for the dessert, will you? That's if we've all quite finished?'

'I didn't raise the subject,' said Sally 'and I'm happy to discuss Ray's feelings for me, if he wants to.'

'Okay, enough everyone,' said Polly 'I'm sure it's just the wine talking.'

Polly was by nature a peacemaker, a reconciler of differences, and Sally ever and anon wondered why she had ever married George. George was currently involved in an ongoing affair with Claudia, who was married to Simon, a fact which was a well kept secret which everybody knew about, and Fiona knew better than to have invited them, despite their being a part of the circle of friends.

'So, I suppose we should talk about burning buildings.'

Keith had bought beer to the table, the first having been consumed quickly, and here was something which both men knew that they should talk about, although for their own reasons both did so with some reluctance.

'Yes, I suppose we should.'

'So have you seen her witchiness?'

'Not since the night she came to see me, which was a few days before the fire, but I told you about that.'

'So did she seem like, fired up, if you'll excuse the expression?'

'She was making ready to do something, that's for certain, and now I think we know what it was that she did.'

'Yeah, like killing some more people; stuff like that....'

'That kind of thing...'

'Christ...So where is she now, I wonder?'

'I'm trying not to think too hard about that.'

'Still, you know; ancient curses and infanticide aren't nice either; someone had to try and sort that out. One could say that they had it coming.'

'She'll justify it, the same way as she's justified killing all the other people.'

'And do you agree with her justification?'

'I'm not really sure what I think, which is mostly how I feel about the stuff she gets up to.'

'It's a tough call, but you know, witches seem to live by their own laws, so maybe it's not our place, you know? Those who live by the sword get their houses burned down...'

'Whilst they're still in them.'

'Exactly...So we let her off then, do we?'

'I've given her the benefit of the doubt so many times, I suppose once more won't make much difference, not that there is anything we can do about it now anyway.'

'The trouble is that you can't help liking her, you know?'

'Yeah; there's that...'

'I mean if she could stop killing people, I sure she'd actually be quite a nice person...So; any news of the chicken strangers?'

'No...That's to say, nothing new...'

'Meaning what?'

Rebecca would return soon. She would first be reunited with her child, but it would not be long; Victoria, or perhaps her wish to see Victoria, would see to that, and Keith of all people should know what was happening, or that which could be about to happen. Percival had kept his secrets before, but things were different now, in ways that he couldn't be certain of, but he was certain that he would need Keith on his side if and when the time came. Things were in place now; the pieces were moving, and he could not with any confidence predict the outcome.

'Meaning there're some things that I should tell you.'

Do they require more ale?

'Yeah; I'll get them in.'

Raspberry Roulade, and Sally was by now feeling quite drunk. The conversation had found its' way into safer waters; matters financial and the state of the country in general. Politically speaking, those assembled were for the most part of right - wing persuasion, although Polly had more sympathy for the less fortunate sectors of English society than did her husband. Paul, the newcomer into their midst, would have called himself a socialist, being against that which he saw as a divisive and divided society, and both Mark and Lucinda had sympathy with this viewpoint, despite teaching in a private school and thus being de facto a part of the division. By general and mostly unspoken consensus, politics were not discussed at such gatherings, the only other social transgression being the mentioning of the nowadays ever so sensitive subject of matters of the heart. Ray, however, was also quite drunk, and was still smarting from Sally's former remarks, and was out for revenge, and so he transgressed. Sally was on her own now, but everyone knew that she had once been in love, and that it had not been she who had ended the relationship.

'That guy that you used to be with, Sal; what was his name...'

'Are you referring to Percival?'

'Yeah, that's him.'

'What about him?'

'He still around..?'

Fiona and Polly exchanged looks across the table; what was Ray doing?

'He lives in the village, yes.'

'Seen him lately?'

'Quite lately...'

'He was a pain in the arse, as I recall;' Said George 'not that we saw much of him.'

'Well, he....He wasn't much of a dinner – party person.'

'Guy thought he knew everything.' Said Ray

'Well, he clearly got under your skin then, didn't he?'

'Couldn't abide the guy, that's all...'

'Could that be because he did know everything, do you think?'

'What...? So are you defending him now?'

'I'm just wondering why you disliked him so much.'

'I thought he left you, and now you defend him; as I recall you were a mess after he left.'

'Ray, stop it.' Said Fiona 'I'm sure Sally doesn't want to be reminded of that.'

'I'm touched by your concern for me, Ray, but I'm quite better now, thank you.'

'Better off without him, anyway;' Said George 'used to work in the city, didn't he?'

'As I recall he wasn't working last time we had the pleasure of his company.' Said Ray

'Yes, well, he made quite a lot of money when he was younger, so he doesn't really need to work anymore.'

'Living off his ill – gotten gains, no doubt...'

'His gains were no more ill – gotten than anybody else's; he was just better at it than most people.'

'So you still see him, then?' Said George

'Most days, yes...'

'What; you bump into him in the village, or what; call 'round for a cup of tea, does he; talking about old times..?'

'Actually we're back together again.'

Fiona and Polly exchanged looks again, everybody looked at everybody else, and then everybody looked at Sally.

'Sal, you didn't say anything...' Said Polly

'Well, I wasn't sure how welcome he would have been, but I'm sure now.'

'I'm sure Ray didn't mean anything by it, did you Ray?' Said Fiona

'Look, it's okay, really; I'm glad to know what people really think; it's better than being dishonest, don't you agree? And now I think I should be going; back to the cauldron, you know?'

'Sal, please stay...'

This was Fiona, who had just seen her dinner party descend into disaster, and was wondering who was most to blame for that, and whether anything could be salvaged from the ashes. Wendy, who had been uncharacteristically quiet for most of the evening, but had been rather enjoying the spectacle, made a last – ditch attempt on behalf of her hostess.

'Look, can't we all just kiss and make up?'

But Sally was already on her feet, and making for the coat – stand.

'Let me call you a taxi, at least.' Said Fiona

'It's okay, I'll walk to the rank; it's not far and I could do with some fresh air. Thanks, Fiona, the food was lovely, as always. Bye, everyone...'

There were vague mutterings from around the table, where 'everyone' was trying to work out exactly what was going on, and how to react to it, and to this so sudden departure.

'Oh, and George; next time you see Claudia, be sure to give her my love, won't you; I'm sure we all miss her company.'

Sally left the room, and then the house, and walked out into the free air, and away from the trail of social destruction which she had just left in her wake.

Percival, Keith and Lulu left the pub sometime after closing – time. They walked together to the end of the track, which took them past number three, which prompted a question from Keith.

'Sal not around tonight..?'

'She's out with friends; dinner party.'

'To which you were not invited?'

'I could have gone, you know...'

'Sure.'

'I mean Sal's friends are okay as far as they go, but I'm more of a beer and pasty kind of guy; I don't have much in common with them, as it goes.'

'I feel you...Mind you, you and I aren't exactly cast from the same mold, and we do okay.'

'That's different.'

Keith might fairly have expected expansion upon that statement, but apparently Percival felt it unnecessary, and in any case none was forthcoming. They parted company at the end of the lane.

'Thanks for calling 'round, Keith; we needed to talk.'

'So it seems; it's been a most enlightening evening. So now we wait for developments, yes?'

'Yeah; let's just see how it goes. If it all works out then nobody else need be involved, which is the way I hope it plays out, but stay vigilant, okay?'

'I'm on red – alert, and for what it's worth I think you're doing the right thing.'

'I can but live in hope of that, and there are risks, of course. If it goes wrong then I could have made the situation worse, but I've come to the conclusion that to do nothing is no longer an option.'

'Yeah, I can see that, and there were always going to be risks.'

'Yes, I suppose so.'

Percival reached his cottage, and took his shower, several hours later than he had planned. He was unsure whether he would see Sally tonight; she might wake him up drunk at some hour of the night, it would not be the first time. He fell asleep anyway, and in the event would not awaken until mid – morning, which was the first time he had gone the whole night for a long time, and he woke up alone.

Sally arrived home at sometime after midnight. She was not sure why she had done it; why she had risen so eagerly to the bait, and why she had made so free with the wrecking – ball. She hadn't planned any of it, and she probably wouldn't be invited again, but there had just been so much cut glass around; expensive, crystal glass, the type which shattered easily. And she had been drunk, sure, but it was more than that, and she had never so misbehaved in the usually so polite and uncontroversial company of her friends before. But something was moving deep in the soul of Sally Parsons, which had not yet taken form, but had nothing and everything to do with dinner parties, really. Something was changing the way that she behaved, and the way that she saw the world, but as yet whatever it was had no identity. She considered going to the cottage; Percival had planned a quiet night in, and would probably be asleep, or writing. On further consideration she took a glass of water upstairs, took two painkillers as a first response to the hangover which she knew was coming, took off her clothes and got into bed. Sufficient unto itself had been the evening, and Percival would be there tomorrow, which was all that mattered, really. She fell quickly to sleep, taking that last and happy thought into her dreams.

Chapter 3

SUNDAY

'Em....'

'What ails thee, oh love of my life?'

'Nothing ails me, but I'm not sure about Blossom; she's making really weird noises.'

This was Sunday morning, and life on the smallholding which was Jacob's Field had begun early, as usual, Will and Emily having been fairly abstemious in their alcohol consumption on the Saturday evening, and having retired to bed at a moderate hour. This was now mid – morning, and Emily was in the kitchen making coffee, having already milked the goats and poured the days' product into churns, and removed the days' cheeses from their molds. Will was doing maintenance jobs about the place, as was his wont on Sunday mornings, and thus did he find his beloved. Blossom, the pot – belly pig, now resided in her quite large, purpose – built brick enclosure, which Will had built, and which benefitted from a corrugated tin roof over half its' area; she had settled in well to her new accommodation, and seemed well enough contented with life in general. She was for the most part a quiet creature, only grunting enthusiastically when it was time for her twice daily feed, and otherwise enjoying any waste – products from the kitchen, potato peelings being amongst her favourite delicacies, and now she was making weird noises.

'What sort of weird noises?'

'I don't know; somewhere between grunting and moaning.'

'She's never done that before; what else is she doing?'

'She's lying down in the far corner.'

'Bloody hell, you don't think she's having her babies, do you?'

'Could be...She's been making a kind of nest thing for a couple of days.'

'Yes, I know; maybe she's at the end of her gesticulation period.'

'If you mean gestation, then yeah, could be; all depends when she started gesticulating, which we can't know, of course.'

Emily poured the coffee, and they walked together to the enclosure, where they found Blossom as Will had left her, and she was indeed making uncharacteristic noises.

'Oh Lord...Do you think she's alright?'

'She's being unusual...'

'Yes, she...Look...! Look, look, look; Will, she's just had a piglet!'

'That's a relief; if had been anything else I would have asked for our money back.'

A small, pink form had appeared in the rough nest of straw and twigs, and was making its' first, blind attempts to stand on its' four legs.

'Oh...my...god...Isn't that just the most beautiful thing you've ever seen?'

'Well, I can think of a few things, but it's up there...So old Tom was right then, bless him; I told you he knew his pigs.'

'Do you think we should call a vet or something?'

'What's a vet going to do?'

'I don't know; make sure she's okay, I suppose.'

'She seems to be doing okay on her own. I mean old Tom said she was seven years old, so she's probably done this before a few times.'

'Yes, I suppose so....Look, she's had another one!'

They sat on the wall of the enclosure, drinking their coffee, and watching as Blossom gave birth to the first of her litter. Lady had by now joined them, and was standing with her front paws on the wall, the better to see what was going on.

'Look, Lady,' said Emily 'Blossom's having a happy event.'

'I wonder how many happy events she's going to have.'

Will took Lady's head under his arm, and she licked his face.

'You're going to miss her, aren't you, when Rebecca finally comes to get her.'

'Sure, but I've been thinking about that, and I think we should get a dog; place like this needs a dog, and he or she would be company for you during the day. I mean I know you're not short of animals, but dogs are different, aren't they?'

'Of course, and I think it's a lovely idea; I want a big dog, though; a Labrador or something, or some kind of shepherd dog...Look, that's the third one, isn't it?'

'It's the next one after the second one, so yeah, I guess so, unless she's having them out of sequence. She's really banging them out now.'

'And the first one's already almost started to walk; that's amazing.'

'It's kind of staggering about, anyway; looking for milk, no doubt.'

'So, do you think she will then?'

'Do I think who will what?'

'Do you think Rebecca will want Lady back?'

'No idea; she's got to come back herself, first, and there's no news of that as far as I'm aware, and now she's been up to her old tricks, making free with the box of matches, so who knows what's going on?'

'And killing more people....I mean bloody hell, Will; where does it all end?'

'I suppose when all the bad witches are dead, or have given the curse up as a bad job.'

'It's just all so, I don't know, unbelievable, really....Look, she's just had number four...I mean, Christ, sometimes I wonder, you know, whether we did the right thing?'

'What, you mean going to find Rebecca, and unleashing her particular brand of hell and damnation onto the world....'

'It was my idea to go and find her, you know?'

'Well, who knows, and who knows what would have happened if we hadn't; probably Victoria would be dead, and probably so would Rebecca, once she had outlived her usefulness to the chicken – stranglers. We can't possibly know what would have gone on, any more than we can foresee an end to it. You did everything for the right reasons, Em.'

'And I suppose Rebecca would say the same thing, at least about the witches.'

'You didn't kill anyone, that's the essential difference.'

'I killed the man from London.'

'That had nothing to do with witches or strange cults; anyway it was an accident, sort of.'

'I accidently hit him on the head with a saucepan.'

'You had no homicidal intent, that's the point. Anyway that kind of scum doesn't deserve to live; you did everybody a favour. Five....'

'I just hope it ends up alright for everyone, that's all, even Rebecca.'

'It never really ends though, that's the point. Stuff just keeps on happening...You know, I once had a conversation with Peter Shortbody; he's a nice guy when you get to know him, not that I know him that well. I think he would like everything to stop happening, or that at any given time everything would be different; he kind of thinks of things which aren't there, but could be there; makes no sense to me, really, but it's a different way of seeing the world.'

'It's a bit early in the day for existentialism.'

'Yeah, sorry; went off at a tangent...Anyway right now what's happening is that our pig is giving birth to quintuplets, which is a good thing; make that sextuplets...'

'What comes after that?'

'No idea, if she has any more we'll be in trouble.'

'She's doing really well, isn't she...? This is just sooo exciting...'

'She's doing great; we'd better keep feeding her up; she'll have a lot of mouths to feed; we may have to eat more potatoes.'

'Indeed....Oh my Lord; look who's coming.'

Somebody had just entered through the kissing gate and was walking toward them, and it was somebody whom neither had seen for some time.

Sunday mornings on the bus were a particular time for Keith and Meadow. Neither had to work, and nowadays it was a rare thing for any of their offspring to be demanding of their time or attention. Tarragon in any case had been away at university and thus quite independent for a long time, and now she was gone abroad, Basil was most often with Emma, and Rosie for the most part kept to her quiet self. It was thus a time when father and mother could wake at a later hour, and bring herbal tea to their bed, where they would talk of their lives and their children, and sometimes they would make love. On this particular Sunday morning, however, Basil came on board the bus as Meadow had put the pan to boil for their herbal beverage, and he was holding something in his hand.

'Oh, hi love; everything okay with your world?'

'Well, there's a hurricane in the Caribbean that I could do without, and there's unrest in the Balkans, and generally too many people with not enough to eat, and too many others with too much money, but I'm doing okay on an individual level. I bought you something to read; I got it yesterday afternoon.'

He handed her a popular - music publication, which was opened on the page containing an article about the beginning of a tour by a certain group of musicians.

'Oh, okay, thanks; does she get a mention?'

'She does indeed...'

'So; what are you and Emma doing today?'

'I'm not sure yet; maybe go to town.'

'Do you have enough money for coffee and so on?'

'Yeah, think we're okay; if not I can always sell my body.'

'I know it's tough being so young, Bas, but one day quite soon you'll be earning your own money.'

'Sure...Anyway school days are supposed to be the best years of your life, aren't they?'

'Don't believe everything you hear.'

'That's a relief...'

'So will you eat with us tonight?'

'Yeah; we'll be around, in fact we'll cook if you like.'

'Okay; that would be nice.'

'I would reserve judgement...Anyway, see you later; it's a good article.'

'Well thank you again, young man.'

He left, she smiled to herself and the water in the pan began to boil; she took the drinks and the tabloid publication into the bedroom, where Keith was still in the process of waking up.

'What are you smiling about?'

'Your son; he's growing up fast, in a good way.'

'Of course he is; chip off the old block is our Basil; takes after his father.'

'Apples never falling far from the tree, yes..?'

'Well in that case I don't know which tree Rosie fell out of.'

'The same tree as the others, I assure you.'

'Well she must be the exception, then; what's that?'

'Something for us to read; another one of our apples...'

'Hello, you two.'

'Hello Daphne, how lovely to see you.'

'Yeah, hi Mrs P...'

'Well, I haven't been here for such a long time, which is remiss of me; my word, how this has all changed; you've done so well.'

'Thanks; we've been quite busy, and look, you're just in time to see our pig giving birth.'

'Oh I say, how wonderful...'

'Six so far, and here comes number seven, I think.'

'Seven; my word...'

'So Mrs P; would you like some coffee..?'

'Yes, thank you William; that would be most acceptable.'

'Right; I'll put the kettle on then.'

'Are you sure you don't need to be here to see the births?'

'It's okay; once you've seen one piglet you've seen them all, really; Em'l keep count.'

Will left for the kitchen, leaving Emily and Daphne to oversee the birthing. With one last effort Blossom produced her eighth offspring, after which she seemed more relaxed, and became her usual quiet self, which indicated that the eighth would be the last. By now the others had begun to find her milk, and soon all eight piglets were feeding voraciously.

'I think that's it; said Emily 'eight healthy piglets; that's not bad is it?'

'It's very good, but where did you find such an enormous pig?'

'She's huge, isn't she; Will found her. Anyway, I suppose we should leave them in peace for a bit; let's go and have coffee, shall we?'

'Dead Man's Wealth in Japan.

Yes, dear readers, yours truly Gina French has had her docket signed to follow this rock revival of the moment to Tokyo, at the beginning of their latest and rumour has it their last world tour. The coffers won't cover my staying with them across the rest of Asia and beyond, but Europe beckons, and I'll be in London to see the end. But this two – gig show is the beginning, but I mean, Japan? Hardly the place, one would have thought, to warm up a rock – music performance; the Japanese are a notoriously hard bunch to crack, staying apparently nailed to their seats regardless of the inducement to do otherwise, as if they were watching a performance of Mozart. One might expect polite applause at the end, but one might not expect very much else.

But then I had forgotten a couple of things, the first of them being a certain Ms Aiko, who had them standing up in a state of some excitement virtually before anyone had so much as played a note. The lady has, it seems, captured the imagination of the young Japanese, and has become iconic in Japanese music culture, and we know how cultural the Japanese can be when they get going. And the band marketed their commodity well, putting her centre - front of stage between the two other guitarists, and giving her the chance to show her particular talents with a base solo somewhere near the end of 'Sometimes it Hurts'; I mean a base solo in this day and age; what the hell's going on here?

And then there's Ashley Spears, the man himself, with his quiet and mysterious charisma, who shows up at one gig, and then at another gig, and nobody quite knows what he gets up to in the meantime. The man has always been an enigma; he looks like a rock musician, sings in front of a still adoring world like a rock musician, writes all those songs, but when he's not doing that he keeps it close to his chest; my postman is probably more outgoing, and yet there he stands, talking to fourteen thousand people and better like he was drinking tea with a couple of mates. Somebody should tell him that nobody talks to audiences anymore; that went out with headbands and Spangles, but on stage you can't shut the man up, bless him. No surprise then that his first words to the audience were spoken words; 'Konbanwa Japan', which I am reliably informed means 'Good evening Japan', which got them all going, and after which he kind of rambled on a bit in English about how great it was to be here, thanks on behalf of the band, blah blah blah, and seemed to finish tuning his guitar (I mean, really?) before finally giving a casual nod in the direction of Rick Talbert to count them into 'All Screwed Up'; oh yes, the music, and within four bars the audience were up and dancing like there was no tomorrow; job done, and from then on he had them eating out of his hand, chop – sticks and all, and nobody sat down much during the rest of the evening.

And tonight was a special night in other ways; I have always held a candle for Tara Knightman, who also has her own brand of mystery and quiet modesty nailed off – stage, and who appeared as if from nowhere to make her two solo albums. And here she was on her first big stage, wearing a dress which barely warranted the description; the young lady has legs as well as a voice like nectar, which she weaved around and behind the voice of Ash spears like an enchantress. The well tried and tested sound of DMW has been rent asunder, and will never be the same again; a siren now moves amongst them, and by the end of the show one was left wondering how he ever did it without her. And she sang two of her own songs; 'The Devil in Me' and 'Hell Can Wait' respectively from the first and second albums, and the audience were there for her, and she sang her heart out for them; it was for me a moment of pure musical magic, which has established the young lady once and for all in the small world of big music, where one hopes she remains for a long time to come.

Oh yes, and now there's a flautist in the line – up; another first for this so unusual and ever – evolving band. Who she is and from whence she has come took me some time to find out, but it turns out that her name is Evelyn, and she's Ash's sister, so there's a thing then, just bring your sister along, why don't you (and this incidentally makes it four – three to the girls), and the flute worked; not much solo work but she kind of jammed along with the rest of them, and it sounded good. This is musical evolution in the making; a new sound has come to these old and well worn songs, and the sound is deeper than ever, and better than ever. And okay, I'll stop gushing in a minute, this supposed to be being an objective, detached, journalistic appraisal of a rock concert, but music is supposed to stir the soul, is it not, and when I walked back to my small Japanese hotel room after the show my soul was a mess, and that doesn't happen very often.

So what else can one say? Individually they each played their part; drummers are usually just drummers, but Rick Talbert has turned drumming into an art – form, and Samantha Rodriguez was superb as always; such musicians don't get together very often, but when they do something special happens. And as a whole the band was tight for a first night, given the diversity of their various instruments. At least, that is to say that they started somewhere, and twelve bars later they ended up at the same place, and what happened in the middle was kind of organic, but it always sounded good, and they all, the formerly stage - nervous Tara included, were clearly enjoying themselves enormously.

You can get more details on line as usual, and Google the play – list if you want, but I can't leave without mentioning the grand finale, which was the third encore, and was 'Reason to Believe'. *The song lasted for about ten minutes, included Al Talbut at his*

guitar – playing best, and was also in the realms of the magical.
Ash Spears has never sung better than this, and the band has never
sounded this good; if they really are to hang up their spurs at the end
of this tour then the world of music will have lost something unique
and irreplaceable. But for now this was a beginning, and for now
the world awaits, and if they can win over the Japanese so easily, the
rest should be a stroll in the musical park, shouldn't it?'

They finished reading the article at roughly the same time,
and then took a moment before Meadow broke their mutual
contemplation.

'She's singing her own songs; in front of that many people'

'Yeah...She wasn't sure, was she?'

'No, she wasn't, but that's amazing, isn't it?'

'Takes after her mother...It's the apples and trees thing again.'

'I can't sing, Keith.'

'I was talking about the amazing part.'

'Well I'm not going to argue with that, and I'm not going to
ask for a second opinion, either.'

'Take my word for it.'

'Okay, you old charmer...But I mean, god, Keith; she's really
making it, isn't she.'

'Yep...I told her on the beach that she should have faith in
herself.'

'Well, it looks as though she was listening, then.'

'It was just words; it had to come from her.'

'I know, but she listens to you, although you may not
think so.'

'What do you mean?'

'Well, she's always had to take second place to Rosie in your
affections, hasn't she?'

'I love all of our kids, you know that.'

'Yes, I know...She really enjoyed her time with you the other day; you should try to do more of that kind of thing when she gets home.'

'Sure...I mean you don't think it's an issue with her, do you? Like she resents Rosie or anything?'

'Tara's not a resentful person, but you should try to have time with her, that's all I'm saying.'

'Okay...Okay noted, mind you, after touring the world as a rock musician I don't expect I'll even get a look in, do you?'

'I wouldn't be so sure; Tara's not the kind of person to let fame and fortune go to her head, either; that's why I think she'll be okay.'

'Of course....I mean I do love her, and she knows that, right?'

'Yes, she knows that, Keith. So let's have this moment for Tara, shall we; our clever, brave and beautiful daughter, wherever she is.'

During the course of this morning, two telephone calls were made and received, which were differently significant for those making and receiving them.

At the white house, centre of the coven of white witches, Charlotte had been giving much thought to the matter of the burning of Farthing's Well, and she was certain that it was only a matter of time. She was not surprised, therefore, when the telephone rang, the number of which was known only to the inner circle, and to one other person, and nor was she surprised that the caller was that one other person.

'Hello...?'

'Hello, it's me; Rebecca.'

'Hello Rebecca.'

'I, uuum...I've been trying to 'phone Amanda, but she's not answering.'

'I see...Have you spoken to Sophia?'

'No...'

'But you've tried to 'phone Sylvia and Maria, yes?'

'How do you know....? Are you monitoring my lines of communication; in fact are you cutting my lines of communication?'

'I answered your call, Rebecca.'

'Where is Florence?'

'Florence is with Amanda; Florence is fine, and now you wish to be reunited with her, of course.'

'Yes, of course.'

'Then I'll have her brought to the white house.'

'Are you holding her to ransom?'

'You have to come in, Rebecca; you have to give account of yourself, and everything which has happened.'

'And this is a condition of my seeing my child?'

'I wouldn't put it like that; you may come for Florence whenever you wish, but you will see it as you will. You are a part of the sisterhood, Rebecca, and you must be held to account; what you have done could affect all of us.'

'How do you know what I've done? You've spoken to Helena, of course.'

'When was the last time that you spoke to her?'

'About...About four days ago, why..?'

'I need to speak to you, Rebecca. When shall I expect you?'

'Tomorrow; I'll come tomorrow.'

'Very well then, I will have Amanda bring Florence here.'

'Fine; so Florence is well, then?

'Yes, Florence is well.'

'Until tomorrow, then...'

'Go to the cafe; you will be picked up, as usual.'

The line went dead. Charlotte would now have other telephone calls to make; the others must be informed, and as many of them as possible should come, although she knew that it would not be convenient for all of them. So, Rebecca was well enough, then, although Charlotte could not assess her state of mind, but she was glad to have spoken to her, at least. But then there was Helena, and therein lay a bigger mystery. Nobody had spoken to or had news of Helena since before the burning, which was a strange thing, and something which concerned Charlotte greatly. Helena, it seemed, had simply and completely disappeared.

The recipient of the second telephone call was Sally. Sally had spent Saturday morning recovering from her Friday night, after which she had gone to the cottage, but Percival was not at home, and nor was Lulu, so she assumed that they were out walking in the woods. She made coffee and waited for half an hour before returning home, and she did not see him until the evening, when he called at number three. Neither were particularly in the mood for alcohol, or for going out, so they stayed at Sally's home and watched television, and ate lasagne which Percival prepared, and drank a glass of red wine. They had always been able to do this; alone amongst the women whom Percival had had relations, with Sally there had always been an easiness; a sharing of domesticity, where neither had made any particular demand on the other, other than that they be together. There were things that they could have discussed; Sally could have given account of her Friday evening, and Percival could have relayed the salient parts of his conversation with Keith, but neither felt so inclined, so nothing was talked about other than the most mundane, such as which television programme they should watch, and both were content with this state of being. When less comfortable things are happening in a persons' life, a person will sometimes look for and in any case appreciate comfort where they find it.

And then, late on Sunday morning, when she was preparing lunch and Percival was once again out with Lulu, Sally received the telephone call;

'Hello...'

'Hi Sally, it's Polly.'

Which led to a slight increase in Sally's heart – rate, and a mild feeling of heat rising within her; this may not be an easy conversation, and it certainly was not one that she had been expecting.

'Oh, hi Polly...'

'I hope you don't mind my calling, but I really couldn't leave things as they are, or as we left them on Friday evening.'

'I see...I think perhaps I owe certain people an apology, you especially, probably; I don't really know why I was so badly behaved.'

'Well you certainly hit some raw nerves, but I don't think any apology is needed, unless it goes both ways.'

'I see...Well thanks for the endorsement.'

'I wouldn't go so far as to call it that, but Ray was out of order, frankly, and so was George.'

'If you're talking about the things they said about Percival, then it's really okay; I know full well that Percival was never liked, which is why I didn't bring him.'

'Would he have come anyway?'

'Probably not...'

'And calling you a witch was really beyond anything.'

'I didn't...I mean I really didn't take that seriously.'

'No, I know, but even so...Anyway the evening really fell apart after you left.'

'Oh dear...'

Fiona did her best, but Ray was drunk by then, and the tension between them was palpable, in fact it was bloody obvious, and then Wendy finally kicked in and piped up with her usual high - feminist anti — all — men line; by the time we got to coffee and mint — thins it was quite beyond rescuing.'

'If Wendy hates men so much, why does she keep marrying them?'

'George said exactly that...'

'And what did she say?'

'She didn't really have an argument, except to ramble on a bit and say that Paul was different.'

'She said that about the last one, as I recall.'

'Yes, I know....'

'Christ....'

'And well, things aren't exactly hunky — dory between George and I, either. In fact you might as well know that I'm seriously considering divorcing him.'

'What...? I mean, oh dear, I think....'

'What you said about Claudia, well, it really bought it home to me, you know?'

'Whoa; don't start blaming me...'

'I'm not blaming you, but...The thing is, you're right, of course, I mean everybody knows what's going on, and I'm starting to ask myself why the hell I put up with it.'

'Well, good for you, again, I think...So have you said anything to him?'

'Not yet...I mean it would be complicated, you know?'

'It always is, isn't it?'

'Everything's in his name; I mean the house, really. We've got a joint account, but there isn't much money; it would all be about the house...But look; keep this to yourself, will you, nobody else knows.'

'Not even Fiona?'

'*Not even her...*'

'I see...But I mean...So I'm wondering why you're telling me.'

'*I don't know, really...I suppose because you're detached from it all, in a way.*'

'Well, I seem to be doing my best to detach myself, anyway; I don't suppose I'll get many dinner invites in the future.'

'*What you did wasn't that bad, Sally. I mean all you did was expose the fault lines, and if the fault lines weren't there, you know..? And anyway you don't really care, do you?*'

'No, I suppose not.'

'*Well look, I mean we can't really do this over the 'phone; can we meet for a drink one evening?*'

'Ummm; yes, sure, if you want...'

'*I mean I know you're busy....*'

'I'm not that busy, and I'm working in town at the moment...I'll call you in the week.'

'*That would be great; I'll see you soon then, and you know, I'm glad to have talked to you.*'

'Me too...'

'*Best to clear the air, you know?*'

'Absolutely...'

'*And you know, I'm very glad you're back with Percival, regardless of what certain people may think of him.*'

'Certain people can think what they like.'

'*Of course...*'

'His bark's worse than his bite, Polly.'

'*Yes, I'm sure, and I've honestly never thought anything bad of him, apart from when, you know....*'

'Sure...Well anyway, see you soon.'

'*Okay, bye.*'

During the latter part of this conversation Percival had entered the house; it was now raining outside and man and dog brought some of the wetness in with them; Lulu shook herself dry and Percival removed his coat, and took a clean kitchen towel to his hair.

'Whose bark is worse than their bite?'

'Yours, my love...'

'And who, pray, have I been barking at?'

'Nobody; well not recently, anyway; that was Polly.'

'She's the florist, is she not?'

'Yes....'

'I'll be sure not to bite her next time I see her then; I'd hate to make a liar of you.'

'It was a strange 'phone call, actually.'

'Oh yes; how so..?'

'Well, I haven't told you this, but I was quite badly behaved on Friday evening. I sort of mentioned the fact that her husband is having an affair with Claudia, and now she's thinking of divorcing him.'

'Because of what you said..?'

'Well, no, but it could have been a catalyst.'

'Who's she married to again?'

'George, the estate agent; you only met them once, at Mark and Miranda's house; she's quite skinny with short dyed – blondish hair, and he looks like an estate agent.'

'Yes, I vaguely remember; I've seen her at the florists, anyway; I don't particularly recall him though.'

'He remembers you; you argued for most of the evening about third – world poverty; I think you won the argument, and I don't think he's forgiven you.'

'Oh him; yeah, I kind of remember....so did she not know that George is having an affair with what's her name?'

'Claudia; oh yes, everyone knows.'

'But nobody's mentioned it in polite company before, is that it?'

'I suppose so....Mark and Miranda have split up now, and they're getting divorced as well; he's now with someone called Lucinda, who's divorcing her husband, who's called John, but I've not met him.'

'Christ...Makes you wonder why anybody bothers getting married, doesn't it?'

'Some marriages last.'

'They'd probably last just as well without the marriage; ...Any coffee made?'

'Yes, I suppose so...No, I'll make some.'

'It's the relationship that matters, not the ridiculous and very expensive charade that people go through; nobody believes in God anymore, and the sanctity of marriage seems to have left by the back door. It's okay, I'll do it.'

'You gave Rose away at her wedding, was that a charade?'

'In that instance I can see why they would have wanted to legitimise any future offspring, so that the Lordship might continue, which is ironic, really.'

'Why; you mean because Rose died?'

'What...? Yeah, that's it.'

'But Nathaniel's now legitimate heir anyway, isn't he?'

'Yes; forget I mentioned it; Christ I need coffee...'

This was one thing which Sally knew full well; that if she and Percival made it work this time; if they found a way to mix the oil and the water, and somehow manage to grow old together, they would never be married. She was fine with that; in truth she had never seen herself being married, and this was the only man that she had ever loved, and he was right, of course; it was the love that mattered. Nor had she ever wanted children, and she knew Percival's views on the matter, and perhaps oddly she thought it more of a shame that he would never be a father than that she would never be a mother. He went to the kitchen to set the coffee machine in motion, and she followed him there.

'The odd thing is that she 'phoned me, of all people, and I'm apparently the first to know about the impending divorce, assuming she goes ahead with it.'

'She's alright though, isn't she; Polly?'

'Yes, I've always liked Polly.'

'Apparently she likes you, too.'

'Apparently so...'

'Well, it's good to know who your friends are, and if she's reaching out I guess you should respond...So you're meeting her then?'

'Yes, I'll meet her...I honestly thought I would be a complete social pariah after Friday. And I know what you think about my friends, Percival.'

'They're your friends, Sal; it's none of my business who you call your friends, and friends are important.'

'You don't have many, and you seem to do okay.'

'I just think it's more about quality than quantity.'

'So you think I should rationalize; be more selective, is that it?'

'No, I'm not saying that; you and I are different, and maybe that's just a boy – girl thing, you know? Women do social networks better than men; don't let me influence you.'

He poured two cups of coffee before the machine had completed its' process; he was still damp from the rain and definitely needed caffeine.

'The thing is, I think you're right...'

'I haven't said anything to be right or wrong about; I said it's up to you who you spend your time with.'

'I know, but I think you're just being diplomatic; I made up my mind after Friday that there are certain people that I really don't want to see any more.'

'Well then that's different, and if Polly's about to become a free woman, and she's one of the good guys, then see her and take it from there.'

She laughed.

'Did I say something funny?'

'No, my love; not really; you just have a way of putting things; you make it all sound so easy.'

'I can't see what's difficult about it.'

'It isn't difficult, in theory, but people are connected, you know?'

'It sounds as though your friends are becoming less connected with the passing of time...Anyway how's lunch; I'm hungry'

He lit a cigarette, and having dealt with the nicotine and caffeine cravings, Percival's thoughts turned to food, this for him being the natural order of priority.

'It's in the oven; it'll probably be ready by now.'

Will had made coffee by the time Emily and Daphne reached the kitchen, and he was keen to hear a progress report.

'Well; how many now?'

'Looks like it's going to be eight...' Said Emily

'That's a good litter, or whatever you call it.'

'So what will you do with them all?' Said Daphne

'We haven't really talked about it, have we Will?'

'Not really; I mean she's such a huge pig we weren't absolutely sure she was pregnant, but we might end up keeping the girls and selling the boys; get a breeding programme going, if we can find a stud pig.'

'Well that should bring some money in, then; I wonder how many of each there are; you'll have to sex them and find out.'

'So anyway, Mrs P,' said Emily 'I haven't seen you around the village much lately, not that I'm there so often these days.'

'No, well, I've been away, actually; in hospital, in fact.'

'What...? Nothing too serious, we hope?'

'Well, quite serious, actually; I had to have a growth removed, but I've had the all – clear now, so I hope that will be the end of it.'

'Oh good lord; Meadow didn't say anything.'

'I asked her not to; I didn't want people to worry unnecessarily.'

'You should still have told us; we'd have come to visit you.'

'I know you would, bless you, but that's just the point; I didn't want to be a nuisance; you're clearly busy enough as it is. Anyway I'm on the mend, now; I can't do certain things yet, and I still tire easily, but thank goodness there's not much to do in the garden at this time of year.'

'If you ever need a hand, just let me know.' Said Will

'Bless you again, William, but I'm sure I'll manage; I always long for the spring at this time of year, and it'll do me good to keep active, when I'm able to be active again. Anyway let's change the subject; I suppose you've heard that Rebecca has come back?'

'What...? No,' said Emily 'we didn't know that.'

'She and Victoria went to number seven two days ago, and yesterday Rebecca went there alone, laden down with household goods, so I think we may assume that she will be taking up residence.'

'Really..?'

'Yes, I rather fear so...I have never trusted that woman, and you would do well to steer clear of her. Lord knows where she's been, but I would rather she had stayed there; she seems to bring trouble wherever she goes.'

Daphne stayed for lunch. She was pleased indeed to have time with her young friends, and Emily in particular was glad to see Daphne. It was she, after all, who first researched the history of the land which had always been called Jacob's Field, and had made the link with Emily's ancestors, and so had been a significant influence in Emily's life. And Daphne had supported Emily after the death of Vincent, and a closeness had existed between them ever since. She departed in the early afternoon, she and Emily promising to see more of one another, and Emily would make a point of visiting whenever she was in the village.

'Okay, well, see you then, Daphne, and I hope you get better quickly.'

'I'm sure I shall. Nothing is absolutely certain, yet, and when one has a scare like this it does put ones' life in perspective; it makes one appreciate ones' time, aside from anything else. Of course you are both far too young to even think of such things, but if I may proffer some advice, make the most of everything; when one gets to my age one realises that life is always too short. And you are lucky to have each other, and to be so happy together; never forget that, will you? There is so much hatred and disharmony in the world, and even in our small village, so make the most of each other, as well; to be in love is a wonderful thing; don't lose sight of that.'

They walked her to the kissing – gate, and did not speak until they were almost back at the house, when Will broke the contemplative silence.

'God, that was heavy...'

'I hope she's going to be alright, Will; I can't imagine the big house without Daphne living there.'

'She's a tough old bird; she'll be okay.'

'Well, I'm going to go and see her, anyway.'

'Sure...Meantime I suppose I should get on with sexing the pigs.'

'I don't much like the sound of that; do you want me to give you a hand?'

'It's okay; by the time I've done I'll be an expert pig – sexer.'

'Well don't spread that around; you might get a reputation. She's right though, Will; we are lucky, aren't we?'

'I'm the luckiest guy alive, and it's nothing that I don't appreciate.'

'Good; well then I love you forever.'

Charlotte spent the remainder of the day in quiet contemplation. She cooked and ate her meal, answered her incoming electronic mail, took a walk through the woods which surrounded the white house in all directions, and otherwise went about her usual mundane business, but her thoughts were always preoccupied by one matter, which involved two people. She had let Rebecca go, telling herself that she had not known or at least been certain of her intent, but she had been deluding herself, had she not? Or perhaps better say that she had not thought of it over much, and not as much as she should have done, but had rather let fate take its' course. The coven at Farthing's Well had been burned, likely beyond its' future use, and those who had lived therein had been killed, and she was certain enough now that Rebecca had been responsible for that; that somehow she had discovered the covens' location, but who would have told her? Sophia and Rebecca she knew had a special relationship, so perhaps it had been Sophia, but somehow that did not seem right. Sophia was at her foundation a sensible person, who aside from in an academic sense had no real hatred for the black witches, and would not have put herself at risk to attempt their destruction; her life was moving away from the inner circle, and it was moving in a good way. In any case Charlotte had spoken to her, and she had seemed genuinely surprised at that which had happened, and Charlotte had believed her. But who else but Sophia amongst them knew of the location of Farthing's Well? Sophia had found it, and so she supposed could others, but still, something was not right. And then there had been Helena's absence from the last meeting of the inner circle, and Helena she had not spoken to, and nor had any of the others. The black witches had contrived to corrupt Charlotte's predecessor, and as a result somebody had killed her, Helena's mother, Helen, so Helena had reason enough to hate them, did she not? But if she and Rebecca had formed a quiet alliance, then Helena had hidden the depth of her hatred and her intent well, and Charlotte had not seen it. And Rebecca had a child now, whom she clearly loved, and yet she had put herself in grave and mortal danger by attacking the black coven, so why had she done so now? All of these things were connected, somehow, but Charlotte was at pains to make good the connections. She had long suspected that Rebecca had killed Helen, but she had not until now pursued that line of thought, for where was the point in it? Rebecca had lately been so much improved that she had let the matter lie, and she would never have wished to kill her mentor, of that Charlotte was certain; other and strong influences must have come to bear for that to have happened. But supposing Helena had shared her suspicion? Supposing she had confronted Rebecca, and that they had for this reason agreed to work together, or perhaps Helena had given Rebecca no choice? For Charlotte was now as certain as she could be that Helena had been a part of this, and where was she now?

And it would not have been a spontaneous act. To have so attacked the coven would have taken forethought, planning and preparation; Rebecca would have to have made herself as she had once been; to have turned herself once more into a deadly assassin, and not the gentle mother that she had been when

Charlotte had last seen her. So had they been planning this even when Rebecca had been at the white house, and if so how had she missed it?

So much had happened since Charlotte had begun her tenure as High Priestess. For the most part, she had assumed, her position would entail far more mundane matters; the proffering of advice or resolution of disputes within the sisterhood, but she had inherited from Helen something so profound and disturbing that she had, if she was honest, been ill – equipped and lacking in experience to deal with it. People had died, and people continued to die, and this would likely not be the end of it. And perhaps some of those deaths could have been avoided had she acted sooner, or differently, but it was too late now; what was done was done, and now she would see Rebecca, and that would now be a meeting some significance.

So did Charlotte's thoughts run, and by the end of the day she had changed her mind about something. She would tell nobody except Amanda of her intended and arranged meeting with Rebecca, and even Amanda she would merely instruct to bring Florence to the white house, and would not tell her why until after the fact, and perhaps not at all if it could be avoided. She had better see Rebecca alone, and would tell the others that her appearance had been unexpected. Perhaps that way she could glean more information; perhaps Rebecca would be more open and forthcoming if they were alone, and certain others, Rosalind in particular, who was quick to condemn Rebecca in any case, were not present the first time that she gave her account. If this was against her usual philosophy of openness and of sharing information within the inner circle, and ran counter to the ways of the sisterhood as it now was, then so be it; she knew well enough that hard decisions are sometimes needed, and so did she make up her mind.

In the evening she secured all of the doors and settled to her quite small office in this large house, and wrote her dairies until something after midnight. Eventually she retired to her room, meditated for a short time before finally turning off her light, and drifting into an uneasy sleep. During her meditations she had asked herself a question which she had asked many times before; what was Rebecca, really; she – devil, or protector of the innocent? And what of those who had lived in Farthing's Well, who had kept the anger alive for so long for no benefit to themselves; were they merely would – be child – killers, or did they see themselves as avenging angels, set on revenge for an act of evil done so long ago, which had for so long gone unpunished? Her last thought was a phrase, which came to her head from nowhere; Charlotte had never been a Christian, but she had read the Christian scriptures, just as she had read the Koran, and Buddhist teachings. *'Whosoever shall offend one of these little ones, it were better that a millstone be hung around their neck, and that they be drowned at the bottom of the sea.'* She wasn't certain that she had it verbatim, but it was close enough, and although the offense had not yet occurred, the intent was clear enough.

Good and evil; good and bad intent; the lines between these had been blurred and unclear in so much which had happened since and before she had become High Priestess, but the slaughter of innocents was something which could never be condoned, and with this in mind and in this spirit would she meet with Rebecca, and hear what she had to say for herself.

Chapter 4

VIRTUAL VIRTUES

Upon a former time, when a woman's virtue was seen by others aside from herself as something precious, only to be given away on her wedding night upon pain of disgrace and dishonour, she would often guard such virtue, just as those seeking to take it from her would be at pains not to be seen to be doing so. In such times, a woman and her betrothed would first seek knowledge of each other in other ways, and could be fairly said to know one another quite well by the time they first and at last have sexual union. In the more promiscuous and some might say enlightened age in which our tale is set, a man and woman may fall together within hours of their first meeting, without fear of being outcast or even badly thought of by those around them, and could be said to hardly otherwise know one another at all. And between these two such extremes lies everything else, a place of infinite possibility wherein most people live their lives, and make their choices. Thus may two people grow together, in the physical, spiritual and emotional senses that are the essence of a loving and fulfilling relationship, and these elements may grow at a differing pace, the growing pains often being felt by both, sometimes for years, until a state of harmony is achieved. And if it doesn't work, if the two people find that they cannot be all things to one another, then better they part, and look elsewhere for their lover and soul mate; in the matter of love there can in the end be no compromise, for love, in all of its' bewildering complexity, is in the end the simplest and purest thing.

And for the two people who are to next re – enter our tale, the process of coming together is in a sense still at its' beginning.

They have made love, if such it can yet be called, and so have crossed over one such and so significant a border which separates people who do not yet know each other well. And they have talked together of important things, and felt for each other in a way that people may do in the beginning of their journey of mutual and self discovery, but they have in no sense yet reached the end of that journey, any more than they yet know how far the journey will take them.

For Michael Tillington, heir to a Manor House and an inherited Lordship, the matter is further complicated by the fact of his still seeking a final resting place for the love of his last and now deceased wife, Rose, the first woman who he had truly loved, and he must tread carefully upon the new path which now lay before him; to move too quickly might leave too much of himself behind, which would be good for neither him nor his newly beloved. Nevertheless it was he who had first made that path, or created its' possibility. He and Elin Tomlinson had been acquainted for some years, she being daughter to friends of his father and mother, and she was but a girl and he a boy when they first met, and they grew into manhood and womanhood on quite different ways. And then he had sent her an email, with no agenda whatsoever, the fact of his still being a young man and she by now a beautiful young woman being merely coincidental, and she had read his agenda clearly enough, and had responded in less than tentative manner, the better perhaps to encourage him to write again. And so in due course had she returned to the Manor House for a quite different reason, and so had their journey together at least begun.

As we have heard, Elin Tomlinson was of Nordic extraction, coming as she did from the quite newly reborn and vibrant country which was Norway, whereas Michael was born of the ancient and now decaying grandeur of the English aristocracy. She resided now in England, but her essence remained

Norwegian, and although she knew England well, he knew almost nothing of her country of birth, and this imbalance was something which she knew must be put to rights. Whether she knew this instinctively or consciously is of no consequence, but in any case it was thus that late one morning, Michael received a telephone call at the Manor House.

'Hello Elin.'

'Hello Michael, how are you today?'

'I'm well, thank you.'

'Good, I am well also.'

'Jolly good then; are you at work?'

'Yes; are you free from mid – week?'

'Ummm; yes, I think so; I have no appointments this week which can't be changed or cancelled.'

'Good, I have some leave, and will go to Norway, and I would like very much if we went together.'

'Oh, I see...Well yes, that sounds like a nice idea.'

'Then we will depart on Wednesday morning, and return on Sunday afternoon; I will reserve our seats, but I believe I need your passport details; number, name as it appears on the passport and expiry date.'

'Okay, hang on a sec, I'll get it.'

'I'm quite busy, actually; will you text the information to me?'

'Oh, sure; okay...'

'Good, I will phone you this evening with confirmation of departure time, flight number and which airport we will fly from; it will be Gatwick, I expect. Are you happy to fly standard class?'

'Oh absolutely; it's only a short flight anyway.'

'Okay; we will speak later then.'

Which was the end of the telephone call, and Michael of a sudden was in a good frame of mind, and looked forward to the excursion, and more so to spending the time with Elin. This would be the longest time that they had so far been together, and this would be his first time in Norway. He believed that Victoria had once or perhaps twice been with his parents when they had been quite regular visitors to Elin's parents, but he had always been at school, or university, or then living in Italy, so he had never been. And the journey would be more than literal, for now he would see Elin in her native environment for the first time, and that, Michael realised, was an important thing for both of them.

There are some moments in the lives of people which defy the writing down; some thoughts and emotions the intensity of which cannot in truth be adequately expressed by the written word, or are at least beyond the gift of the author, for which I beg your pardon. In any case one such moment occurred late one morning in the white house, when Rebecca was once again united with Florence, her daughter. She had been driven to the house by Amanda, and on the journey Rebecca was at pains to thank Amanda for so taking care of Florence during her absence. Charlotte was at the door of the white house to greet Rebecca, with whom she must speak, but she knew that any discourse would be impossible before mother and daughter had been reunited, and so her first words were simple, and to the point.

'She's in there.'

Rebecca entered the indicated room, and Charlotte and Amanda went together to Charlotte's study, where they waited and talked of other matters. And if words are sometimes inadequate, then so at times are peoples' ability to deal with the tidal wave of emotion which comes over them, and such was the case at this moment for Rebecca. She lifted Florence and held her in her arms, and she cried freely, for at such times it can sometimes be all that a person can do. Later she would try to rationalise and come to terms with that which she had done; how could she ever have left her child? How could she have put herself in danger, when she now had so much more than her own life to lose? She would in time tell herself that which she had told herself a hundred times; that she had had no choice, and that what had been done had to be done, but these were not thoughts for now; now was just for now, and the sheer joy and relief of the most simple thing as holding her child, and knowing that she would never leave her again. That from now on her life would be devoted to the welfare of the helpless infant whom she had born, and brought into a hard and difficult world. From now on that would be her all, and her reason, and she needed no other.

On the appointed day Michael and Elin met and kissed hello in the concourse of Gatwick Airport, an airport with the capacity to cater for less people than it actually at times had to cater for. They found a table in a less than perfect but adequate eating establishment, and ate a late breakfast together, their flight leaving at just after midday. Michael knew nothing of their intended visit to Elin's homeland, where they were apparently to spend the first two nights in her family's residence in Oslo, before moving to their other, smaller house on the west coast, returning to Oslo for their flight back to London on Sunday. Thus would Michael see Norway's foremost city, as well as the rugged beauty of the Norwegian coastline. The short flight was uneventful, and they arrived on time in the clinically efficient Oslo airport, which had more than adequate capacity and facilities for its' clientele, before catching the underground train which would take them to suburban Oslo, the train in fact being over - ground for most of the journey. The more northerly latitude had seen to a drop in temperature, but the air was clear and the weather would remain sunny for the whole of their stay. A short walk from the railway station took them past a small arcade of shops and cafes, and thence into an area of gentile, high – end, two storey housing, each house being set in its' own grounds, and Elin's parental home being one of the largest properties. The design and layout of the house was unusual, each of the large, well appointed rooms interconnecting around a central, spiral staircase. They dropped their overcoats and overnight – bags in the kitchen, she set the kettle to boil and gave him a brief tour of the ground floor of the house, and more briefly still of the quite large garden. Michael had been speculating during and in truth before the journey as to what would be their sleeping arrangements. They had already slept together at the Manor, of course, but he was as yet uncertain as to the depth of their relationship in the more general sense, and a gentleman does not like to presume; a woman's virtue, even once given, may after all be reclaimed at any time. They drank their coffee quickly, and then;

'Shall we shower before we go out, then I will show you the harbour - front if you would like.'

'Yes, I would like that.'

They ascended the spiral staircase, and went directly into that which he assumed was her bedroom when she was in residence, which had a large double bed and in common with the rest of the house was thoughtfully and stylishly designed and ornamented; nothing anywhere was out of place, and the decor was everywhere simple but tasteful, and certainly not cheap. Any doubts which he had harboured regarding their mutual status were quickly consigned to history when she removed her skirt and blouse, and put her arms around his waist.

'I think now I would like to have sex; would you also like to do so?'

'Ummm...yes, that would be.....'

She removed the rest of her clothing and lay down on the bed. In truth and despite any hopes that he may have held in this regard, he was for a moment taken somewhat aback by such familiarity so soon after their reunion. But it was only for a moment, and given such visual and other stimulus his physical and hormonal self soon took control of the situation. Apparently, for Elin at least, their relationship had in this particular regard moved on more quickly than he had supposed, and she was waiting for him to catch up, and more immediately she was waiting for him to remove his clothing.

'So, Rebecca, I bid you welcome back; I've made tea for us.'

Charlotte had told Amanda that she may leave, and that her duties as regards the child were over, for which she thanked her on her own behalf as well as on behalf of Rebecca. The inner circle of the sisterhood had cared for Florence; Sylvia and Maria had played their part and proffered advice where it was needed, but Amanda had been the prime carer, for which she would be generously compensated, Charlotte would see to that. And so anyway Charlotte and Rebecca were left alone, as Charlotte had wished it, and thought it best, and having at least in part and as far as she could recovered herself, Rebecca had carried her now sleeping infant into the dining room, where she found Charlotte waiting for her.

'Thank you.'

She took her place opposite the High Priestess, Charlotte poured tea, and they exchanged smiles. They had after all lived together during the latter part of Rebecca's pregnancy, and had come to know one another, and had become friends, in a way.

'Rebecca, my dear, first let me say that you are welcome to stay here for as long as you need.'

'Again, thank you.'

'Do you have somewhere to go with Florence?'

'I can live in the village, in the house belonging to Victoria's brother, Michael.'

'I see...Well, whether or not that is wise we can discuss in due course, but before that there are things which you and I must talk about.'

'I know...'

'The point is that whether this be done now, or tomorrow, or whenever you are ready doesn't really matter; these are heavy things, and if you would rather have more time with Florence first...'

'Has Amanda gone?'

'Yes, I told her she could go.'

'I barely had time to thank her.'

'There will be other times for that, I'm sure.'

'And the others...?'

'They don't know you're here; I thought it was better that way.'

Charlotte was watching Rebecca closely, and at those words she relaxed physically, and her expression and countenance changed instantly and for the better.

'It seems I can't stop thanking you, but I have to say I'm bloody relieved; I was expecting the third degree, to be honest.'

'I thought it best that it be just you and I; I will of course have to relay that which you tell me, and your honesty is something which I must insist upon; there will be no more lies or half – truths, Rebecca. I regard you as a friend, but I am head of our order, and as such I have a responsibility to everyone, and you have a responsibility to answer my questions truthfully.'

'I will; it's time that the truth is told, and you already know more than anybody; nobody but you and I know who Florence's father is.'

'And so it shall remain until you think otherwise; that isn't what we will talk about, but whilst on the subject, do you have milk for her?'

'I hope so, yes...'

'Well we've got by so far, so I'm sure that we can manage. So, to other matters; do you want to talk now, or should we wait; the point is that I need you not to be distracted in any way.'

'Well, let's start and see how we get on, shall we?'

'Very well then...'

At this time of the yearly cycle, when the sun at such latitudes rises late and sets early, Norwegian days are short, and by the time they had showered, caught the train and travelled the quite short distance to the coast, Michael and Elin emerged at the portside in darkness. Here were restaurants and bars, and leisure cruisers of all sizes were docked along the harbour awaiting the next day, and warmer weather which would bring the next tourist season. Despite the darkness the view of the fjord was impressive, everywhere distant lights shone along the coastline and from the islands which lay just offshore.

'Tomorrow we can take a boat trip, if you would like?'

'Yes, I would like that very much.'

They ate at one of the restaurants which overlooked the harbour; Michael imagined that they would be crowded during the summer season, but this evening they had no problem finding a table.

'I owe you for the flights.'

'I really don't mind, Michael; the flights were not expensive.'

'Well then, I'll pay for the food while we're here.'

'As you would like...'

Michael would soon learn that in so doing he would quickly reduce and eventually pay off any financial deficit; whatever else Oslo may be, it was not a cheap place to visit; the Norwegian people clearly enjoyed a high standard of living, and dressed and dined accordingly. During the next two hours they caught up with the last few years of their lives; having been at least acquainted during former years they had a vague sense of each other, but Elin in particular was clearly wishing to put substance to the outline. She wanted to know why his first marriage had failed, something which was easy for him to explain, and then how he had married a prostitute, and how that brief marriage had been, which was less easy. She told him of the few men with whom she had had brief romantic attachment, and in her turn why the attachments had been severed, always it seemed by her. They learned of lesser things, such as their respective favourite food, and at some point somehow the subject came around to sport, and she asked him to explain the rules of cricket, an undertaking which was quickly abandoned, lest it take the whole evening.

'Stop...I don't have a clue what you are talking about, and no clue as to why people would even wish to play such a game.'

'Well, I suppose you have to be born to it, really.'

'Yes, I suppose you do; you are such an Englishman, Michael.'

Which of course he was, quintessentially so, just as she was Nordic. Her ancestors had been farmers and builders of fine boats, who had raided the English coast as Viking warriors, come in search of gold and treasure, most of which was hoarded in the Abbeys and churches of Northumbria, where they had first come ashore.

Amongst the next days' activities she would take him to a museum, where they had on display four such boats, which had been diligently reconstructed, and had been buried containing the bodies of noble people, along with some of their worldly possessions. Otherwise almost nothing was left as physical testament to the early Nordic pioneers, or how they had lived; nothing was written down, since they had had no writing, the records at least of their invasions rather coming from places which they had invaded. Michael lived with history; he woke each morning in his ancient ancestral home, and his own country was everywhere steeped in the past, and abounded with historical buildings. Oslo was by comparison a new city, in a country which had relatively recently re - found its' place in the world, and where there was a sense of newly found prosperity and wellbeing for most of its' citizens. There were, it appeared to Michael, far less of the social and economic extremes which so defined the country of Britain, and almost none of the creative energy which it so often spawned. Here it seemed to Michael were a people quite content with their lot, who sent ships now laden with goods to their nearest trading partners, all thought of other invasion being consigned to ancient and largely forgotten history. Michael spoke not a word of Norwegian, but even if had not had Elin to guide him he need not have been concerned; everybody from the people who Elin met by chance who were of her acquaintance to the young girl who served the coffee spoke perfect English; whatever else they had brought back from and since those early invasions, they had most assuredly brought the English language.

During the rest of their stay in the city she showed him some of the capitals' most visited attractions. She took him to a sculpture park, where were displayed the finest works by Gustav Vigeland, who had sculpted his finely wrought naked human figures during the nineteenth and twentieth centuries, and from thence they climbed to the less formal parkland above Oslo, which afforded fine views of the city and harbour, and of the ocean beyond. They ate their meals out, and returned to the house only to sleep and make love, which they did three times during their time together; Michael was counting, Elin was not.

'First of all, Charlotte, I'm going to ask you to break your vow of absolute truthfulness to the others.'

'I see; well that's not a good start, is it? I assume it's to do with what happened at Farthing's Well?'

That took Rebecca a moment; she had been there, and had done the things which she had done, but now the mere mention of the name of that place gave her pause, and sent cold and horrible shivers through her soul. She could no more go back there now than she could fly.

'It's...It's not actually to do with what happened; rather it's to do with why it happened.'

'Go on...'

'First I need your assurance; just on this one thing; everything I tell you hereafter you can do with what you will, but you will understand when I tell you why it must stay between you and me, and it might help if I tell you that Sophia already knows, and has known for some time.'

'I see...Very well then, I make no promises, but rather you must trust my judgement.'

'I killed Helen; it was I who murdered the last High Priestess.'

So here was the first truth revealed to Charlotte, which she had long suspected, but here it was in its' stark and hard reality, and now it was Charlotte who took a moment to absorb the fact of it.

'Tell me...'

'She was turned by the black witch, Eve; I don't know how, or when, but I came to see her, to seek her advice; I found this place, and have long known its' location, even before your tenure. So I went to see her, after my own mother had been murdered, and she...She tried to overpower me; she gave me the knife and told me to kill myself; that there was no hope for me, and it was better that I...but anyway, somehow, and to this day I don't understand how, but I resisted her, and so I cut her throat; it was her or me.'

'So...'

'You'd best let me finish; you can ask the questions later.'

'Very well...'

'I told you that Sophia knows, but Helena also guessed, and that was the power that she had over me; it was her idea to...To do what we did. She had me form an alliance with her, knowing that I had killed her mother, under threat of revelation, and so I agreed to work with her, and for no other reason.'

'Other than saving the lives of the Tillington children..?'

'That could perhaps have been done another way; you may have helped with that; that is to say that the sisterhood may have helped. I'm not saying that I'm not glad that they're dead, and I believe that they deserved death, but I would not have gone against them with only Helena by choice. Helena understood, you see, that I had no choice but to kill her mother, and this was to close the matter between us, so I agreed.'

'And have you spoken to Helena since?'

'No; in common with the rest of the inner circle, I have been unable to contact her, for which I have you to thank, do I not?'

'There is one essential difference, Rebecca.'

'What's that...?

'I can't contact her either; her house stands empty, and nobody has heard from her.'

'I see...Well that's strange, then.'

'Strange and worrying, don't you think?'

'But I mean she must be okay, otherwise how did I arrive at the Manor House?'

'What are you talking about?'

'She brought me there; it must have been her, although... Although I have no memory of the journey; she must be hiding for some reason.'

'Listen, Rebecca; I think we are getting ahead of ourselves; you must tell me everything which happened, beginning from your arrival at Farthing's Well; tell me everything that you can remember.'

By contrast to their city residence, the Tomlinson family home on the west coast was set in rugged, open countryside, within a small hamlet of similar houses, but otherwise having few other buildings within visual range. Another impression with which Michael would return to England was of a country where the anyway quite small population was centred in a relatively few towns and smaller settlements, between which were vast areas of rugged and inhospitable emptiness. It reminded him in this respect of Scotland, which was perhaps not surprising since the two were at similar latitudes, and had a similar geography.

This house was smaller than the city residence, but was equally well appointed, and Elin had driven them to the house in her car, which she kept in Oslo for her occasional visits such as this. This was late on Friday afternoon, which would give them a full day on Saturday by the coast, after which on Sunday morning they would drive back to Oslo for their flight. The free day was spent driving on mostly empty roads in order that she show him some of her favourite places, and favourite views along the rugged, indented coastline. They walked cold, windswept coastal paths, and once descended to the beach, before retiring to the warmth of a local restaurant, where they ate finely cooked fish. Elin it transpired rarely cooked for herself; she disliked the activity, preferring when in Canterbury to pick up a takeaway or other convenience food on her way home from work. Thus in such small ways did they learn more of each other, and the remainder of their time together passed quickly, until early on Sunday evening they found themselves once again in the concourse of Gatwick Airport, where they would say goodbye. One further noteworthy occurrence happened during their journey, which was about half an hour into the flight. She had turned to him and smiled.

'Michael...'

'Yes?'

'Have you ever had sex on an airplane?'

'What...No; mostly I watch movies, and such.'

She said nothing more, but continued to look at him in a certain way, which left little doubt as to what she was thinking.

'I mean...Are you serious?'

'I have never done such a thing either, but we may not see each other for a while, and it would certainly be fun, don't you agree?'

'Well, I suppose...But I mean, how?'

'The stewardesses are about to bring the refreshments; now would be a good time.'

She unbuckled her seatbelt, and then she unbuckled his seatbelt; apparently her mind was quite made up and no further discussion was necessary. She took him by the hand and they made their way to the convenience cubicle at the rear of the cabin.

'I'll go in first; when there's no one looking, follow me in.'

And so he followed her in; she was removing her briefs in the confined space, and having done so she turned from him and placed the palms of her hands against the partition wall.

'You'll have to be behind me; I will try to remain silent throughout.'

He was a Lord in waiting; a respectable member of the English aristocracy, and here he was about to have sex in a toilet; this was not at all proper, was it? His moral and intellectual self were rather against the idea; his physical self, however, appeared to have no such compunction, and he was hardly by now in a position to refuse, was he; here was very much a lady in waiting. And after all, he supposed that it was really only a matter of perception, and if one closed ones' eyes one could be anywhere. So he lifted her skirt and got on with the business in hand, hoping that there would be no turbulence during the next few minutes, which could make things rather awkward, the activity being somewhat awkward in any case, and this would make it four times.

They made their exit without being noticed, although a stewardess gave them something of a knowing look on their way back to their seats, Elin not having quite managed to be silent throughout as had been the plan. The remainder of the flight was somewhat less eventful, although they had missed the refreshments trolley, and we now rejoin them in the airport arrivals lounge, where they were to say farewell.

'Well; thank you, Elin, it was a most enjoyable time.'

'I'm very glad you think so, and I also very much enjoyed myself. So, shall we see each other again soon?'

'Oh yes, of course; I'll 'phone you during the week, shall I?'

'Yes, that would be nice.'

One final kiss and she turned to leave, and was quickly lost in the crowd;

Michael made his way to the long – term car park. On the drive home he relived the events of his time away, preferring not to dwell overlong on the most recent of them; not that he had not enjoyed the experience, but even so, it was definitely best not dwelt upon, and certainly he would tell nobody of it. As he approached the gates of the Manor House in the mid – evening, one final thought occurred to him, which was not for the first time. He had been half – expecting to meet her parents during the trip, or at least some of her friends, for why else would she have been going to Norway? So perhaps after all her sole purpose in going was to be with him, which he supposed was a good thought with which to arrive home.

Rebecca took a deep breath and gathered herself; perhaps she couldn't do this now after all, but she knew that it had to be done, and would there ever be a good time? She had better try, anyway, and she was in a safe place now, where fear and horror could be put aside, for now anyway.

'What I remember well enough is that there were three of them, and that we killed them.'

'How did you get there?'

'In Sophia's car; we left it about a mile away, down a country lane.'

'And how did you enter the house?'

'That was easy; it's...It was an old house; the window latches were not secure.'

'And then....'

'They were sleeping, upstairs; once we had ascertained their numbers...Well, then we killed them; you don't need to know how, but two of them would have known nothing of it.'

'And the third..?'

'She almost escaped, but...Well, from her I learned that there was another of them, living in the village, and that her name was Megan. I made her telephone her, and I spoke to her; she's gone, now, but she remains at liberty.'

'And is she the last of them?'

'Yes; she's the last of them.'

'I see...so then?'

'So then I set fire to everything which I could, everywhere; that was also easy; my last memory was of the house burning, and then, well after that I remember nothing until I was at the Manor House. It was late in the night by then, and Victoria took me in; she took care of me, and we spent two days together; on the second day I began to get the house ready, and now, well, here I am.'

'And what is your last memory of Helena?'

'She...She said that she would kill one of them, so I left her to...To do that; I had to stop the third one escaping, you see?'

'But afterwards; you don't remember seeing her again?'

'No; as I say, I must have blacked out, or whatever.'

'And yet you walked a mile to her car in the darkness, and then she drove you to the Manor House.'

'She must have looked after me.'

'But don't you see how strange that is?'

'Yes, of course I do, but I can offer no other explanation.'

They paused for a moment, whilst Charlotte took in everything which Rebecca had so far said. Florence stirred, but did not awaken in her mothers' arms. Something was wrong; Rebecca had lost control, somehow. Of course she could simply have gone into a state of deep trauma, and her nervous system could have shut down altogether; Charlotte had read about such things happening. But in her then state of mind and being that was unlikely, to say the least; surely if she was to go into such total shock then that would have happened later, and not during the act itself, and she seemed to have recovered remarkably well after such a still short time. But then, how else could she have escaped unharmed, and how else could she have travelled so far, unless Helena had been with her?

'And that's all you can tell me?'

'Yes, that's all there is to say.'

'And of course you left no trace of yourselves there.'

'They will never find us, or connect us to anything; we were careful, and well, the house is gone now.'

'Hi Mike; good trip..?'

Michael had by now showered and changed into casual trousers, slippers and bath robe, and had gone to the kitchen to prepare himself a light supper of beans on toast, the latter of which he was now buttering. Here he encountered his sister, who had just seen Henry to sleep and had come to make her bedtime drink.

'Oh, hi Vics; yes, it was very enjoyable.'

'Good; so any impressions of Norway?'

'How many words do I get?'

'Three...'

'Cold, beautiful and... shallow...'

'How, shallow..?

'Oh I don't know...I mean they're nice people, don't get me wrong; I just think they could do with a dose of adversity; shake things up a bit.'

'Adversity as in the way you and I live, you mean?'

'Guilt at lack of adversity would do it; just something to latch onto, you know?

'Sure....So how's Elin?'

'She's very well.'

'Yes, I'm sure she is, but that's not what I meant, and by the way your beans are boiling rather furiously.'

'Oh, right....Do you want some; I never eat a whole tin and the rest usually go to waste.'

'Sure why not; I'll make more toast.'

'Have one of mine; I'm not that hungry.'

'Are you okay, Mike; you don't look like someone who's just got back from a romantic holiday with their new lover.'

'Sorry; just tired I expect; I mean we got along fine, you know; everything worked out well in terms of sex, and so on.'

'That's not what I meant either.'

'What did you mean, then?'

'I mean how are you two getting along, you know...If it's none of my business then tell me to shut up.'

'No...No, it's fine; ask away, only I don't know what to say, really.'

'Any chance you could expand upon that?'

'I suppose I'm trying to work out how I feel about it all, you know?'

'"It all' being Elin, yes?'

'Yes, of course.'

'Well give it chance, Mike, you've not known her that long yet; that is, you've known her a long time, but not like this.'

'No, I know....'

'Anyway if it turns out that she's not the one then there's no shame in that; you're not committed to anything, are you?'

'Again, no...I mean she's a fine person, you know? She's good company and all, and I like her very much.'

'But you don't love her, is that your point?'

'Not in the way that...'

'Not in the way that you loved Rose...So maybe it's too soon, Mike; maybe you're not ready to love anyone else yet, and that would be absolutely understandable.'

'She's just so completely different from Rose; Rose was passionate, and unpredictable; Elin sort of acts as though she's got everything worked out.'

'Well perhaps she has, even if you haven't.'

'Yes, perhaps that's it, but there doesn't seem much depth to it, if you see what I mean.'

'Cold, beautiful and shallow, yes..? So will you see her again?'

'Oh yes, I haven't given up on it yet; I suppose I should go to Canterbury next; see where she lives and such.'

'Canterbury's nice anyway, but be careful, Mike; take it one step at a time, you know...Don't commit to anything until you're ready; she's your first relationship since Rose, but it doesn't sound as though she'll be your last, and she certainly doesn't have to be. You're still a young and extremely eligible man, don't forget that, and for heaven's sake don't get her pregnant.'

'She's got that sorted; I've seen the pills. I don't think she's gold – digging, Vics.'

'I'm sure she's not, and anyway I don't think she has to be; the family aren't exactly poor, are they?'

'Not in the least; have you seen their houses?'

'Not for a long time, and I'm sure they've moved house since then.'

'Very impressive, anyway, and Norway's not a cheap place to live; two people eating out and you kiss goodbye to a hundred and fifty quid, and the food's nothing special.'

Michael laughed.

'What's funny?'

'Well talking of food, I'm just as happy eating this, to be honest, and here we are discussing the deeper aspects of my love life and eating beans on toast; we should be drinking Chardonnay, or whatever.'

'Champagne, surely...Anyway I'm hardly the best person to advise when it comes to relationships, am I?'

'Nevertheless you're the only person I'd listen to…So anyway, talking of relationships, how's Rebecca, and where is she for that matter?'

'She's away getting Florence; I expect she'll be back in a day or so, then she'll move into number seven.'

'Does she have everything she needs?'

'She'll get by; she's Rebecca…'

'And she's still not told you who Florence's father is?'

'No; she's keeping that to herself for some reason, which is a mystery, actually.'

'Since if you don't know the person, where's the harm in telling you, right?'

'Exactly…I'll get it out of her one day, though; she can only keep her secrets from me for so long. So anyway, I'm to bed via the front steps.'

'Are you working tomorrow?'

'Yes, unfortunately…'

'You don't have to work, Vics; it's not as though you really need the money, is it?'

'I need the sanity, Mike; if it's a choice between that and full – time motherhood I'll put up with it.'

'Yes; it's a pity one can't pick them up when they're sixteen, or whatever.'

'That's exactly what I intend to do. Anyway, if you need to talk, Mike…'

'Sure…Well goodnight then.'

'Goodnight, and thanks for the beans.'

'Least I can do…'

They smiled, she departed, and Michael took the plates to the dish - washer.

She had to let Rebecca go. She had stopped the first interrogation; Florence was waking up and would need Rebecca's attention, and anyway Charlotte had needed to collect her thoughts. Rebecca would stay at the white house for two nights, and during this time they spoke many times of the night that Farthing's Well had been destroyed, and the three witches killed, but in the end no further significant information was forthcoming, so no more progress could be made. Charlotte would summon the others in due course, but for now she made her excuses, and kept them away. There was another scenario; perhaps everything was not as Rebecca had assumed, but if that were the case then how had she survived, let alone escaped to safety? Perhaps Rebecca was right in regard to Helena; that she had gone to ground somewhere, ashamed perhaps at that which she had done, but Charlotte would in that regard not rest easy until Helena had somehow contacted her.

And so for now, what of Rebecca; she seemed well enough, and well enough able to take care of her child, and she was quite determined to return to live in the village, even in the house that Megan had lived in, despite the fact that Megan was still at large. How much Rebecca had indeed been the innocent party in the matter, only there on Helena's instigation, and how much she had herself wished to kill those who threatened the lives of Victoria's child, and her brothers' child, Charlotte was in the end quite unsure. Rebecca had not tried to make a virtue out of necessity; she had not tried to gain the moral high ground, where she could better have defended her actions, and so Charlotte had not judged her. There was nothing really to be done or thought of now in that regard anyway; they had done what they had done; Helena had indeed hidden her intent well, and she would be answerable for her actions, if ever she returned. But she had not returned, and therein still lay the biggest mystery. But Rebecca was keen to leave, and she could not have stayed indefinitely, and Charlotte could not and would not now hold her any longer than she wished to stay.

And so they said goodbye once again, and this time Rebecca left with her child carried on her back, and that had been a happy reunion. The black coven had been destroyed, and perhaps that would be the end of the matter, but there were still too many questions, and after Rebecca's departure Charlotte closed the door of the white house with heavy heart. She would call the others to meeting, but not quite yet; first she would meditate upon the last few days, to see if by doing so she could understand that which so far defied her understanding.

'Hi, my love; what are you doing?'

This was Meadow, who had been working late at the delicatessen organizing the stock, and had come home to find her beloved in front of the word – processor.

'I'm writing another short story; I had an idea at work a couple of days ago and thought I'd run with it and see what fell out. Eventually I'll have enough to go to a publisher; one of these years anyway.'

'So what's it about this time?'

'It's about a wall, kind of.'

'A wall....Sort of like the one you're building?'

'Well no, although it may have given me the idea, but this is like, a really big wall.'

'So you're writing a story about a big wall...'

'Yeah, although the story isn't really about the wall itself, but, well, anyway, you can read it when it's finished.'

'Then to that I look forward. So have you eaten?'

'Yeah; I fed the wee ones...you..?'

'Yes; I ate some of the stock whilst I was counting it.'

'Fair enough...Less to count that way I suppose.'

'And now it's a shower and bed for me.'

'Okay, see you on the way back.'

'Keith; Rebecca's back...'

'What...?'

'Daphne came to the shop today; apparently she's moving into number seven.'

'Christ...We'll have to start calling it the witch house. I wonder if Percival knows.'

'I've no idea, but everyone will know soon enough, I think.'

'Yeah, I think they will; I'll go and see him tomorrow; in fact we'd better have a meeting; Sophia and Damien, and so on.'

'Yes, I think you're right.'

'It's been peaceful around here lately.'

'Well, we can only hope that it stays that way, for all of our sakes...'

'What are the chances, do you think?'

'I don't know Keith, my love; I honestly don't know...'

Chapter 5

GRANT MASTERTON'S DREAM

'Grant Masterson had, for as long as he could recall, been
fascinated by the wall, or more specifically, although all aspects of
the vast structure interested him, he had been especially fascinated
by its' origins, and this was despite the fact that he had never seen it.
He had seen photographs of it as a young boy, but any attempt on
his part to glean any historical or other information were met with
the swift and decisive rebuttal that he was too inquisitive, or that he
asked too many questions about matters which did not concern him;
curiosity could get him into trouble one day, so better just accept
things as they are, for his own good. His father was the only person
who had ever expressed tacit sympathy with his cause, but since he
would not see his father after the age of sixteen, when he reached
his age of independence, he thereafter lost even this support. He had
seen one of the numerous quarries from which the stone had long
ago been hewn, shaped and transported the several kilometres to the
construction site; a vast and deep rent across the landscape, which
had now in part been turned into a small and partly subterranean
leisure park, but he had never been granted permission to get close
enough to see the wall itself, or anywhere near. Even had he been
permitted to enter any of the sectors closest to the wall, he would
still have had to cross the two kilometres of land which separated the
wall from the city, which fell under the control of the Ministry of
Empty Space, and into which few people had ever ventured.
    That which he knew of the wall was that it spanned the width
of the island from north to south, and from coast to coast, a distance
of some one hundred and seventy kilometres, and that it divided
the island into two approximately equally sized provinces, known

simply as the Western Province and the Eastern Province. The crude but clearly structurally sound stonework, which rose to a height of some ten meters at its' lowest point, and more than twenty at its' highest, bore testament to the age of the wall, and the skill of the craftsmen or women who had built it, but as far as he or anybody else that he spoke to knew, no records existed as to when it had been built, or indeed and more importantly, why it had been built; it had simply, it seemed, always been there. As a young man he had attempted to make official enquiry of the Ministry of History, but such enquiry entailed such a complex and bewildering process of form – filling, requiring so much explanation as to why he was seeking such pointless information, that after two years he had abandoned his quest. Apparently the Ministry of History had no sense of its' own meaning; history began as long ago as anyone could remember, beyond which there was, it seemed, no point to it.

The wall had along its' length a total of eight approximately equidistant tunnels, the wall being in the order of ten metres wide at its' base, and mid – way through each tunnel were eight solid and heavy iron doors, which were wide and high enough for one person to walk through, and which were closely and diligently guarded on both sides. As far as anybody that he had ever spoken to knew, however, nobody had ever been through them, from either side. It was, theoretically at least, possible to do so, since no law was enshrined in the constitution preventing the free movement of people between the two provinces. In order to do so, however, moving east to west, it was necessary to obtain form 66795/D from the Ministry of Immigration, which could only be obtained once form 45723/C had been completed, and form 45723/C was only obtainable from the Ministry of Population Movement, once form 66795/D had been completed and submitted to the relevant authority, which was the Ministry of Population Movement. Grant made the assumption that it must be similarly and practically impossible to travel the other way, from west to east, since, as aforesaid, nobody had ever heard of anyone crossing between provinces, either going east or west. Grant had once written a letter of complaint regarding this anomaly to both ministries, but this had been five years ago, and he still awaited a reply. Thus had he abandoned his quest, but he carried his fascination for the wall into his youth and beyond, and he had never given up hope of seeing it, if only from a distance. To get close enough to actually examine it in detail or even to touch the wall was a dream which only the most foolhardy would harbour, but Grant Masterson had always been a dreamer, and some would have it that he was indeed a fool.

At the time in which our tale is set, Grant Masterson was twenty three years old, and was thus now only two years away from his marriage year. He was one of approximately three million souls who lived in the Eastern Province, and had lived all of his life in Zone 33, a typical suburban mid – rise sprawl within the administrative sector, having government buildings at its' centre. At the age of twelve he had been allocated his career in the Ministry of War and Civil Strife, and since then his education had been entirely vocational, leading inevitably to a position in one of the Ministry's sixty three departments. He had begun his full – time working life as a junior and then senior clerk in the Department of Armaments, a posting which he found somewhat tedious and frustrating, since in fact there were no armaments. To have studied so hard for years, only to end up in such a seemingly pointless occupation was anathema to him, although he knew better than to complain, and so kept his head down, and bided his time

It was somewhat to Grant's relief, therefore, that his time in the Department of Armaments was in fact quite brief, before, about a year later, he gained promotion to the position which he now held, which was second in command of the Department of Statistics and Probability. This department employed twenty six people, and was one of the smaller departments within the Ministry. Indeed it was true to say that the Ministry of War and Civil Strife, which had until quite recently been two ministries before the two had been merged, was in its' entirety one of the smallest, since in living memory and far beyond, there had been no war, nor indeed had there been any civil strife. There was no contact with anyone from beyond the island, indeed no other land – mass was known of, the horizon stretching away in all directions and none had ever ventured beyond it, the only boats which existed being the small trawlers used for fishing the inshore waters. Both provinces enjoyed ample fertile land, mineral wealth, and an abundance of fresh water and oil, and both therefore enjoyed a similar and quite adequate standard of living, so there was really nothing to fight about, and thus nobody to go to war with.

Each week, it was the job of Grant's department to submit a report to the head office of the Ministry. In this report was firstly a statistical analysis of the total amount of war and civil strife which had occurred in the province during that week, using information obtained and collated from various other Ministries, and which since Grant had joined the department and long before had always been nil. The second part of the report was a summary of the probability that war or civil strife would occur in the foreseeable future, taking into account all known and predicted factors, and always the probability had been presented as being naught percent. That was, until about four years ago. To this day, nobody knew how it had happened, and since it was before Grant's tenure he could shed no light on the matter. Perhaps it had been a misunderstanding between internal departments, or perhaps more simply the all important form 95711/K had been filled in wrongly, a simple clerical error, perhaps, a slip of the pen or a moment of distraction. But however it had occurred, on a particular and very significant week, the probability of war with the Western Province had risen to one percent.

Now, whilst it was true to say that nobody crossed the border between provinces, telephonic communication was not uncommon, and indeed in certain respects a state of openness at least in this regard had existed between east and west during less suspicious times, cables having been laid and connected to a common junction box at the border. In any case, whether by design or accident, intelligence regarding the increase filtered through into the Ministry of Conflict, which was the equivalent Ministry in the west, and this set early alarm bells ringing within and amongst those who worked there. The next week, word had reached the Department of Statistics and Probability that the Ministry of Conflict had reacted unfavourably to the apparent anomaly, and had itself set the possibility of war between the two provinces at two percent. Though still not a significant percentage, a seed of mistrust and suspicion had for the first time been sown between the provinces; perhaps after all the other province had intent to invade, or were secretly manufacturing weapons in preparation for its' occurrence, and in that case a recalculation of probability was necessary. Three percent became five percent, and a compound process had begun, until, within the space of one year, a greater than fifty percent possibility of war was predicted, and reported. Here it must be said that Grant Masterson suggested to his superior and indeed the heads of other departments on more than one occasion that perhaps this was merely a statistical rather than an actual problem, and that surely lines of direct and official, ministerial communication should be opened, and dialogue begun between the provinces. This suggestion was immediately and forcefully rejected, particularly and most significantly from the Minister of War himself, who by now had seen his importance within the government increase exponentially, and had seen a considerable increase in his budget and workforce. The Minister was most insistent that there would be no dialogue until a significant and sustained reduction in the percentage of probability had been reported from the west; until then, the figures spoke for themselves. And in any case, by this time a new department had been formed within the Ministry of Information, which was rather cumbersomely called the Department of Facts regarding the Western Province, and the propaganda had begun. The Western Province was first accused of provocation, and of warmongering. According to the newly formed Department, it was a fact that it was quite possible that the Western Province already possessed a huge arsenal of weaponry, which was increasing daily, and that its' army now possibly stood at over ten thousand strong. In due course it was reported, via reliable sources, that moral decline in the Western Province had reached such depths that alcoholic beverages were now being manufactured, and being drunk openly in the streets, and even that people were able to choose who they were to marry, and thus have children with, and even when they were to marry. Neo - primitive beliefs in an omnipotent god had possibly begun to resurface, just as in olden times in the east, and it was also a possible fact that people from the East and West were ethnically, culturally and genetically different, the Eastern people being superior in all of these respects. The sanctity of life would mean nothing to such people, and if they did not respect life, were they really any better than animals, bent on the destruction of civilisation as it was understood east of the wall?

And so of course, a practical response was urgently needed. Government funds were initially diverted from the Ministry of Leisure and Recreation and later others, to facilitate the opening of new factories in Zone 45, one of the foremost industrial zones, which was set several kilometres apart from the rest of the city. Taxes were raised overnight from seventy to eighty percent to aid the war effort, human resources were redistributed to work in the factories, the sole purpose of which was to manufacture guns, uniforms, missiles and missile launchers, grenades, bullets, and all such requirements *of ground warfare. In due time, workers from the Ministry of Food and Agriculture were reassigned to build more factories for arms production, and tractors and other farm equipment were decommissioned, the metal from their working components being melted down and reused. Soon thereafter food rationing began, and luxury items such as soap became only rarely available in the shops, each zone having its' own, government controlled supermarket, and each individual or family being allocated a time in which to shop, for whatever there was left to shop for.*

Meanwhile, with each passing week the probability of war continued to increase, until, given the huge investment in the new arms industry, and once the probability had risen to better than seventy five percent, many said that the matter had become a self — fulfilling prophecy. War, for the first time in living memory, and perhaps for the first time ever, was now more or less inevitable.

And so the final stage in the process was begun; missile silos and launchers were moved into position within the two kilometre exclusion zone, final trials were carried out over the ocean, and all was made ready, the Prime Minister himself making declaration over the public address system that the Eastern Province was at last in a state of complete readiness for war. All relevant forms had been completed, signed and countersigned, and all that was now needed for its' inception was his word, and the official stamp to be put to the three hundred and sixty three page document which gave official government sanction for a pre — emptive or responsive strike to be made.'

Keith stopped writing for the evening, which was by now turning into the night, and he had his own wall to build in the morning. Meadow would be sleeping, and he had not seen Basil or Rosie since the early evening, when he had cooked for them and they had eaten together. For a while and before he slept he cleared his head, and thought of matters relating to real — life, lest he take his story to bed with him, and perhaps inevitably his thoughts turned to Rebecca. So, she was back then, and that was something to consider; he would go and see Percival tomorrow. But for tonight he closed down the word – processor, undressed and got into bed as quietly as he could; life on his imaginary island would wait until tomorrow.

During the train - journey home from work during this mid – week evening, Sally made up her mind to 'phone Polly. She did not wish their meeting to encroach upon her weekend; weekends were for Percival as far as was possible, so she would see her the next convenient week – day evening, be it this week or next. She was to eat and pass the evening at the cottage, and almost certainly the night, although the absence of absolute certainty in this regard lent a degree of excitement to her romantic life. The fact of their living so close, and that they could equally well spend evenings and nights at either residence was something which she and Percival were finding their way through, and they did not always sleep together. She still liked to be alone at home sometimes, when she would carry out her exercise routine, catch up with her work and have time to herself; this was how she had lived for months, and she did not wish to entirely abandon her former life. In any case she was conscious of not pushing their newly re – found love for one another beyond the point of tolerance for either of them; she had no wish to break it again, and Percival had his own life, after all, and he was in essence a loner, and she would respect that. There was often a point during their evenings together when the matter of sleeping arrangements was resolved one way or the other. At the cottage she might say something like *'Okay, well I'll go home then, shall I? I've got some work to catch up with for tomorrow.'* And he might say '*I was hoping you would stay, but okay, if you want...I'll probably do some writing anyway.*' And then they would kiss goodnight, and then they might not stop kissing goodnight, and she might stay anyway, and she actually found herself enjoying the uncertainty of it. In a way it was like being constantly at the beginning of a relationship, and later in her fantasies she might sometimes pretend that she was, and they were, if she was of a mind so to do. Percival could be as he really was to her; the man that she had loved for so long, but with a little mental agility on her part he could for the moment become a complete stranger, and either way it worked for her. In her darkest moments she might even imagine that she was an unwilling participant in the matter, and he would not always know which manifestation of himself he had been. Anyway tonight she would shower and 'phone Polly before she went to the cottage, and the way that she was presently feeling she might wear something which would tip the balance in favour of her being invited to stay, and see how it went from there. But then her telephonic plans were thrown out of kilter somewhat when her telephone ringtone sounded just after she had arrived home, and it was about the last person that she would have expected to hear from, who called from a number which she did not recognise.

'*Despite the anti – western propaganda which had been fomented during the build up to war, there were nevertheless still a few dissenting voices within the upper echelons of the government. The statistical likelihood was indeed that the Western Province was as ready for war as was the east, of that there was no doubt, but as yet there had been no actual physical or visual evidence that this was the case. It was also true that, if the west did indeed possess weaponry to the same degree or anything like*

the same degree as the east, then both sides now had the ability to as good as utterly annihilate the other. Missiles in large quantity could now be launched within hours, collectively carrying such a massive pay – load as to be able to wipe out virtually the entire population of those living on the other side of the wall, or at least render the continuation of life, never mind civilised life, a virtual impossibility. A ministerial bunker had been dug and provisioned at the easternmost shore of the island, so the administration of society could continue in any eventuality, but otherwise the woeful inadequacy of the civil defences which had been constructed would likely see to it that, if things went badly, there would be virtually no society left to administer.

Secret meetings were held behind closed doors; those Ministers thought to be most sympathetic to a less aggressive and more conciliatory approach were recruited to the cause, until after several weeks of tentative dialogue, a meeting of ten of the Ministers with the Prime Minister was requested, and granted, and so perhaps after all could another way forward be found.

The meeting lasted for several hours, during which the case for dialogue with the west was put forward, and though this would be too complex and long - winded a matter to write of here, the Prime Minister was not in the end unsympathetic. There were, however, voices in high places arguing equally vociferously for a swift and pre – emptive strike; everything was ready, to strike first would give the Eastern Province a huge advantage, so why delay? On the other hand, argued the peacemakers, they would be shooting blind, since no intelligence existed as to where the enemy's weaponry was centred, and where most of its' population currently resided, and supposing they missed? Supposing only twenty percent of the missiles were effective, then the enemy would be free to fire its' retaliatory strike against a virtually defenceless people, and they may be more fortunate in their aim. The war could be won or lost on a matter of sheer chance, and to lose would be utterly disastrous.

In the end, about one week after the definitive meeting, the Prime Minister had taken council and weighed up all arguments, and had made his decision; the future of the war was to rest on the shoulders of one person, and here is where a young man named Grant Masterson once again enters our story.'

'Hello....'
'Hello Sally; it's Ray'
What...?
'Ray...This is a surprise.'
He had never called her before, and how had he even got her number? Certainly she had never given it to him, and nor she was sure had Fiona; probably he had looked uninvited at his wife's phone contacts.

'Yeah, well, the thing is I 'phoned partly to apologise for Friday; I know I was out of order.'
'It's of no consequence; forget it, I have.'
If he was expecting reciprocal apologies for her behaviour, then he could go on expecting.

'Yeah, well anyway, I was also wondering if we could meet up sometime.'
Are you serious?
'What do you mean?'
'I mean for drinks or coffee after work or whatever; I mean just as friends, you know; no agenda...'
Which was about the most ridiculous thing that Sally had heard for a long time; when it came to Ray and her, there had never been anything but an agenda.

'I don't think that would be a good idea, do you?'
'You don't....'

'No, I don't; I mean for a start what would Fiona think of our meeting?'

'Well to be honest, things are a bit rocky between Fiona and I at the moment.'

Yes, I know they are, which makes the agenda even more rather than less likely, and how would your meeting with me help the situation, do you think?

'Oh dear, I'm sorry to hear that, but I still don't think it's a good idea.'

'Look, Sally...I mean I'm in a bit of a mess about it to be honest; I just need a friend, you know?'

A friend with the body of a Goddess, which you have long since had designs upon; that kind of friend, yes? This was a side of Ray which she had not seen before; Ray, the ever confident and often brash was reaching out, his marriage was on the rocks and she had no intention of being his running – mate through the break up, if it happened. On the other hand he was a friend in apparent need, and she owed Fiona no particular allegiance.

'Just an hour of your time, that's all.'

'I'm not taking sides, Ray.'

'I don't expect you to; I mean maybe Fiona and I can patch it up; I just need to talk it through, that's all.'

'And you think I'm the person to do that with?'

'I don't know, but right now I don't know where else to turn.'

'How about turning to Fiona; your wife, you know?'

'I need someone who's detached from it.'

'And you think I'm detached from it? I mean what about George; man to man, you know?'

'I think George has his own problems right now; it would be a bit like the blind leading the blind.'

'A kind of mutual fucked - up marriage society....Sorry, that was uncalled for, but look, I'm not meeting in secret.'

'I'd rather Fiona didn't know.'

'It wouldn't look good on the CV; I can see that. Look, I'll meet you for coffee or something after work; I'll give you an hour but if anybody asks I'm not denying it, and any talk or even hint of anything happening between you and me and you won't see me for dust, agreed?'

'Agreed..Absolutely...'

'Okay, so when..?'

'How about tomorrow..?'

'Meet me in the White Hart at seven.'

'I'll be there, and you know, thanks Sally.'

She ended the call and took a moment to consider it, and why in fact in the heat of the moment she had agreed to meet him. The last embers of a dying friendship, perhaps; innate feminine curiosity to see what kind of state he was really in, or a way by which she could flaunt herself in front of him one last time; here I am and you can't have me; I'm happy now, and I'm not the wallflower anymore; the final victory. She did not think that this latter was the case, but had to admit that if it were it would not be for the first time; she had done enough flaunting to last the poor guy a lifetime. She would go straight from the train, to the nearest public house from the railway station that she would be seen dead in, drink a Vodka and Tonic and then go home when his hour was up.

In any case she had to smile ironically to herself; any plans she had to quietly and selectively detach herself from this particular small social network had gone by the board, at least for now; it seemed that however much she may wish to leave, they were after all reluctant to let her go. In a moment she would 'phone Polly, party to the other failing marriage, but first she would take a shower; better to at least put some thinking time and neutral activity between the 'phone calls.

'Grant was walking the short distance back to his small apartment on the third floor of block C, after a relatively uneventful day at work, when his progress was impeded by two heavily – armed security guards, two more coming from behind him to prevent his retreat; thus surrounded, a man dressed in a suit and mackintosh stood before him.

'You are number M3567449. Your name is Grant Masterson.'

These were statements, and not questions. Grant felt a cold shiver of fear rise through his body, and for a moment he broke out in a cold sweat. Despite working for the Ministry of War for all of his working life, he had never seen a gun before, and what was this; was he being arrested, and if so, what had he done? There was no time, however, for further speculation.

'Yes...'

'You will come with me; there is somebody who wishes to talk to you.'

A vehicle pulled up beside the group; an armoured and windowless jeep, into which Grant was quite gently pushed; he was ushered to a seat, surrounded by the four guards; the man in the mackintosh was he assumed in the front seat of the vehicle, although the back section in which he sat was totally enclosed. They drove for that which Grant estimated was somewhat over one hour, which meant that by the journeys' end he was forty five minutes beyond the boundary of Zone 3, this for the first time in his life. The vehicle stopped, one of the security guards opened the door and Grant was taken by the arm and led out of the vehicle. They were in some kind of underground sub – way; concrete walls and floor, lit by dim electric light. The man in the mackintosh did not speak, but Grant assumed that he was to follow, and they walked to a lift – shaft. The man opened the doors and indicated that Grant should enter.

'Where are we?'

'You will see.'

The man pressed a number on the control panel, then somewhat to Grant's surprise he left the elevator as the doors were closing; Grant was on his own for three floors, his feeling of anxiety rising to ever greater levels; whatever this was, it could not be good news. At the fourth floor the doors opened, and now a single security guard ushered Grant into the longest corridor that he had ever seen. They walked for perhaps fifty metres, which was nowhere near the corridor's end, before the guard stopped at a grey – painted, unmarked door, which looked no different from the other many doors that they had passed. The guard knocked, and the door was opened; Grant walked in, and the scene before him was one which for a moment stopped the breath in his throat. He was in a large, sparsely furnished room which had white walls, and contained only a huge conference table. To either side of the table sat five men, and five women. He recognised two of the people from photographs in the daily newspaper; one was the Minister of Justice, and the only female that he recognised was Minister of Food and Nutrition. His attention was drawn, however, to the man who sat at the head of the table, whom he recognised well enough, for there sat none other than the Prime Minister himself. Grant was rendered quite speechless, and for a moment his senses ceased to function entirely. Everybody knew the Prime Minister, of course, his photograph was almost daily smiling out from the front page of the newspaper, ever giving encouragement to his now beleaguered and much put – upon public, but few ever saw him in person, much less under circumstances such as this. Furthermore, it was he who now spoke, and he spoke directly to Grant.

'Mr Masterson; please be seated.'

Grant sat at the only available chair, which was at the near end of the table, opposite the Prime Minister. The Prime Minister had several sheets of paper in front of him, as did some of his Ministers, but otherwise the table was bare apart from glasses of water in front of each person, including Grant. Grant was suddenly thirsty, but dare not pick up his glass lest his hand shake too much, and he spill the contents on the shiny wooden surface of the huge table, the like of which he had never before seen.

'You will no doubt be wondering why you have been brought here.'

'Yes...Sir...I...'

'Well then let us enlighten you. You are something of a rebel, are you not, Mr Masterson?'

'I...I don't know, sir...I work hard enough, I believe...'

'Oh yes, of that there is no doubt; your superior speaks highly of you, it seems, but nevertheless there is a rebel in you; you record speaks for itself.'

'My...Record, sir..?'

'As a young man you asked many questions regarding the wall, and you made persistent application to visit it; you have since written letters of complaint to the Ministry of Immigration and to the Ministry of Population Movement, and you have....You have quite recently suggested that the statistics which come from the very department in which you work are questionable. Do you deny any of these things?'

'I...No sir, I cannot deny that these things are true.'

'And do you still believe it; that the statistics are questionable?'

'I don't know, sir. I merely thought...'

'Yes; what did you merely think, and please feel free to drink the water; it is not poisoned.'

Which sent a ripple of gentle laughter around the table; it was apparently obvious that his mouth and throat felt like sandpaper, which was making him rasp rather than speak his words. He took a drink, and took a little encouragement from the lighter moment. Surely if he was to be arrested then it would not be this way, but if not that, then what was this?

'I merely think that some verification is needed; that the statistics in themselves are insufficient to...To warrant the war effort, *far less the actuality of war, and the inevitable and catastrophic loss of life to which it would lead.'*

There; it was said, and whatever his fate may now be, there was no going back from here. For a long moment there was silence around the table, and all eyes were on him, until;

'I see; that is very much as I had thought, and it is well put, and that in fact is why you are here.'

'Sir....?'

'You see, Mr Masterson, there are those in far higher positions than yours who agree with you.'

The Prime Minister nodded to the man who sat to Grant's right, who now passed two sheets of paper across until they were directly in front of him. If the events of the last two hours of his life were unbelievable, then apparently this was to continue.

'Do you know what these are?'

'Yes sir...Of course...'

'Yes, of course you do, for they are something which you have long sought after, are they not?'

In front of Grant were two forms, completed in his name and only requiring his signature. They were forms 45723/C, and 66795/D, the two forms needed to cross into the Western Province. For a moment Grant could only stare at the forms in wonderment, but he was still at a loss as to what they meant, or implied.

'I will come straight to the point, since time is pressing. We need somebody to cross the border. We need someone to verify that which we almost certainly know; that the Western Province is prepared or is preparing for war. This mission will be top – secret, known only to those who sit at this table. You will have less than one day; you will cross the border at dawn tomorrow, and if you have not returned or made contact by midnight of the same day, then we will launch our strike against the Western Province. The mission is dangerous, and you may of course not survive, but you will be doing your province a great service. Do you accept the mission?'

Grant for a moment was at a loss; here was his dream come true; not only to see the wall, but to cross over; to walk through one of its' eight tunnels into the Western Province. He could and probably would be shot or arrested the moment he walked through the door, this he knew well enough, so what was really happening here? The Prime Minister was as war- hungry as any of the worst of his ministers, if the news reports were to be believed, so was this merely an exercise in appeasement; lip service paid to dissenters so that he could claim that he had made every effort to prevent the war? Grant quickly concluded that this was indeed the case, and that he was to be the sacrificial lamb who would see the Prime Minister's ultimate ambition fulfilled, and yet he also knew what his answer must be.

'Supposing....Supposing I refuse?'

'Then you will be imprisoned until the war is over, then I cannot say what will happen to you; after that I cannot say what will happen to any of us.'

'Imprisoned for what?'

'We have the Minister of Justice here and you ask me such a question? You may name your crime, or we will name it for you; you will be imprisoned because you sit here now, and we cannot now let you go free, so what is your choice?'

So it was time then; the decision must be made, but really there was no decision, was there? He had heard reports of the few who had ever been released from the State Prison, and death seemed like a better alternative, and anyway, to see the wall before he died; to actually see the door open before him, and to walk through...He looked once more at the forms before him, the same person who had given him the forms now held a pen for him to take. So; speak the words, then.

'I accept.'

There was a palpable reduction in tension around the table, and the Minister of Food and Nutrition actually smiled at him; she had a nice face. He could have asked the question, of course; of all of the three million people who lived in the Province, why had they chosen him, but what would now be the point? The Prime Minister stood up, and so did the rest of the gathering, but he had one more thing to say;

'*Then we all wish you good fortune. You will stay in the Ministry tonight and will be briefed, as far as we can brief you; you carry a great responsibility, Mr Masterson; I hope for all of our sakes you are up to the challenge.*'

The meeting was over; the security guard entered the room, and now Grant was led back along the corridor to the elevator, and to the place where he would spend perhaps his last night in the Eastern Province, and in all likelihood the last night of his life.'

'Hi Polly...'

Sally had taken her shower and was drying herself in her bedroom; she would be expected for dinner soon, but she had time to make the call; she would check her emails later at the cottage.

'*Oh, hi Sally...*'

'So, how are things with you?'

'*Oh, you know; could be worse.*'

'That bad, huh...So, shall we meet up then?'

'*Sure; I'd love to if that's still okay?*'

'Well I can't do tomorrow, but Friday I can do.'

'*Fine; I'll be closing the florists about seven; should have caught the last of the weekend guilt – flowers by then.*'

'You're becoming cynical.'

'*Well, is it any wonder?*'

'I suppose not.'

'*Right then...*'

'Listen...You may as well know that the reason I can't do tomorrow is that I'm meeting Ray after work.'

'You're what...?'

'He called me earlier; wants to meet for a drink; talk about his matrimonial issues, as you might call them, and rather foolishly I said I would; he didn't sound particularly happy.'

'Christ...'

'Not a word to Fiona, okay? I mean there's nothing in it, believe me, but it's better she doesn't know.'

'And therefore better that you hadn't told me.'

'I know, but I want everyone else to know that this is strictly above board, should it ever come out.'

'Well just watch yourself with him; he's been after you for years.'

'I'm quite well aware of that, and there's no moment of weakness for me where Ray's concerned.'

'Anyway you have Percival now.'

'Exactly, and I intend to tell him, too.'

'And he won't mind?'

Sally laughed.

'No, he won't mind; he'll probably say something like 'what the bloody hell are you meeting him for...?'

'Well, he's got a point....'

'Oh come on; I'm just trying to be the Good Samaritan for once in my life; apparently I'm the only one he can talk to.'

'Is that so...?'

'So it seems...Anyway, see you Friday; I'll tell you all about it then; I'll come to the florists, shall I?'

'Sure...Where would you like to eat?'

'Anywhere you like; we can talk about it on the way to wherever it is.'

'Okay; 'til Friday then.'

So there was the second meeting arranged; Sally dressed quickly and left the house, which she and Percival always called the house, and the cottage was always the cottage, although his was in fact the larger property. She very much wanted to see him now, and anyway, she was hungry.

Of the next few hours of Grant Masterson's life we need not hear, save to say that another of the men who had sat at the huge table spent two hours with him, talking him through his mission, as far as that was possible, and that he was made comfortable in the small, Spartan room which would serve as his sleeping quarters, and given food, water and everything else that he needed. At the end of the evening he lay down on his bed, and considered all that had happened since he had been walking back to his apartment after such an ordinary day, and he would sleep little during this night.

He was awoken sometime before dawn, and taken back to the basement where the same jeep was waiting for him, and this time he was offered the front seat; it would be just himself and the driver; from now on he was on his own. The journey took them through that which Grant assumed was Zone 1, and for the next two hours and more they travelled past barriers and through districts which looked much like his own Zone, until finally they were waved through a heavily armed road - block and the road led away from any buildings or permanent structures. And now that which Grant saw once again stretched his believe to its' limit. Everywhere and as far as he could see in the still semi — darkness were missile launchers, troops about their early morning business, and such other paraphernalia of war as he could scarce have imagined. He knew, of course, that arms manufacture had been going on for years, but to see the results of that manufacture for himself for the first time was something for which he was ill prepared. For this had he and his fellow citizens gone without many of the most basic comforts which they had been used to, before this had all started; before, somehow, the probability of war had risen so significantly to one percent.

And then, as the journey continued, and as the early sun lit up his small world, he saw before him in the distance the wall which he had seen in photographs and in his imagination since he had been a young boy. In its' actuality it was far more impressive that he had imagined it to be; a vast, winding structure which disappeared from view to north and south, and rose here to a height of some fifteen metres. A few minutes later the jeep pulled up a few paces from the wall, near the entrance to one of the shallow, arched tunnels which had been built into the wall during its' construction. And here was that which to Grant was the strangest thing; he had imagined the gates to be heavily guarded, as he had heard that they were, but there was nobody; not a soul could he now see, save the driver. He could see behind him the missile launchers in the middle - distance, but between those and the wall there was nothing. The driver, who had not said a single word to him throughout their journey, now alighted from the vehicle, as did Grant. They walked together the last few paces, and then Grant did something which in even his wildest imaginings he had not believed that he would ever do; he touched the wall, running his fingers over the rough stonework which had been the work of craftspeople back in a long – forgotten time. The driver now ushered him to and then through the tunnel entrance, to the iron gate itself, which was in semi – darkness beneath the dark stonework; the driver undid padlocks and pulled back vast iron bolts to top, bottom and centre, before with some effort opening the gate by a few centimetres on its' huge hinges, which complained at being so disturbed after so long a time. He had left just enough room for Grant to squeeze through, for although he was quite tall, Grant was also quite thin, and now the driver spoke for the first time.

'Well; good luck; say goodbye to your homeland, I don't suppose you'll see it again. You're a braver man than I am, or more foolish, *perhaps, but war this will make fools of us all before the end, I think, and most likely dead fools.'*

'Thank you...'

Grant levered himself through the gap, the gate was closed and secured noisily behind him, and he heard the sound of the Jeep being driven away; the driver clearly had no wish to stay longer than was necessary.

He stood for a moment, waiting. Surely he would be apprehended; surely armed guards would appear at the tunnel entrance in front of him at any moment, and ask his business, or perhaps they would merely shoot him where he stood, but there was nothing. He put his hands in the pockets of his raincoat, and walked the few paces to the tunnel entrance, and looked upon the Western Province for the first time; the first time indeed that anyone from the east had looked upon it.

What Grant saw was not that which he had been expecting. Since the evening before, when had been told that he would soon be standing here, he had speculated as what he would find, but it had not been this. In the first place, there was nobody in sight. The wall stretched away to the horizon in both directions, just as it had on its' eastern side, and it looked no different. But all else was empty space; roads and rough tracks crossing a flat, open, dusty, treeless plain, the nearest sign of human habitation being a line of buildings, perhaps a kilometre away, which he assumed was the outer limit of the town, or city. No weapons, no missiles, no army encampments; nothing. Well then, there was only one thing to be done. With one final glance around, he began walking toward the buildings, his black, patent - leather shoes picking up dust as he walked; he would approach the town in full view, but what of it; secrecy and stealth, at least on this side of the border, had never been a consideration.

He walked for perhaps half an hour, taking no account of roads or tracks, but heading straight to one building which for no reason he had made his target. He was close, now. Surely soon a welcoming committee would be sent out to meet him; certainly he would be watched, so perhaps sniper – fire from one of the windows in the upper storey of the low – rise buildings; he would be an easy target for any marksman; a single shot would see to it. But still, nothing happened. He had reached the buildings by now, and walked past the first line, whereupon he found himself at the end of a long, straight street, lined on both sides with apartments, shops and office buildings. Vehicles were parked on the verges; whatever else the west possessed, it clearly had its' own car industry, the model, for there was only one, being not dissimilar to the cars which were produced in the Eastern Province. Rats roamed openly in the streets and amongst the waste paper and general refuse which lay about, hunted by packs of dogs, which, he was pleased to observe, ran from him as he got closer; he had never been comfortable around dogs. But still, there were no people. The closed shops were full of the kind of products which had been available during better times in the east; the current fashion here was clearly for mid – length skirts, and brighter colours for both men and women than he was used to, and a far greater range of styles. He found a vending machine which dispensed free drinking water, at which he slaked his thirst, and he urinated in a side alley before moving on. He walked for two or three hours through empty streets; here was a whole, self contained town, part of the urban sprawl which seemed to go on without end, as it did in his own province, and it was completely deserted.

He sat down for a moment on a bench by the street - side, and wondered what to do now. How far should he walk before he gave up, and made the telephone call from the nearest public telephone; he had tested one along the way, and it was active, so that was at least something. He was mid – way through his deliberation when he heard in the distance through the otherwise silent streets the unmistakable sound of a car engine approaching. The vehicle was in sight now, and soon it was upon him, and stopped where he sat; there really was no point in hiding; he had to understand what was happening. The vehicle was in fact an open – topped jeep with the roof off, and inside in the front and front passenger seats sat a young man and a young woman; the woman was driving, and the man was first to speak.

'What the hell are you doing, brother?'

Which was a good question, so honestly was probably the best policy.

'I was...taking a rest.'

'Are you lost, or what?'

'Yes...'

The man and woman exchanged looks; what do we have here?

'Well, look; you'd better come with us; this is the final sweep, and we were just about to give up, you know? You very nearly got left behind.'

'I see...'

'So, are you coming or what?'

Grant stood up, and climbed into the back seat of the vehicle.

'I'm brother Peter; this is sister Fiona; what's yours, man?'

'I'm...I'm brother Grant.'

'So what's the deal; how come you missed the convoys?'

'I...I've been sick.'

'Right...Well, now you've been lucky; you could be the last of us.'

Sister Fiona found a gear, and they began a journey which Grant estimated to be of about two hours duration, during which time the scenery did not change very much; just more deserted towns, interspersed with tracts of agricultural land, in which were growing crops which were for the most part familiar to him. The houses and buildings were of slightly different design and colour, and aside from the emptiness there was a slightly different feeling, but that which struck Grant was the familiarity; there were more similarities between the Western and Eastern provinces than there were differences. Brother Peter and Sister Fiona talked to one another on occasion during the journey, which was generally in a southerly direction, but they spoke little to Grant, who was clearly a little strange, and was observing everything around him with uncommon interest. For Grant, the most noteworthy thing was a huge oil refinery, which dominated the landscape towards the end of their journey; a journey which ended at the coast. Grant had never seen the ocean, except in pictures in newspapers, and for a moment the sight of it once again sent his senses into free – fall. But even that emotional overload was quickly eclipsed by the sight which now lay before him. For they had entered a deep – water port, and here, tied along the wharf, were boats the size of which quite literally took his breath away; huge liners, capable of carrying hundreds if not thousands of people. And then it struck him almost as a physical blow, and it was as much as he could do to prevent himself from exclaiming, for now, at last, everything became clear to him. The total lack of weaponry, the deserted streets; the oil refinery, the attitude of his driver and her partner; everything, and he could not now help but laugh out loud. For years, probably, and who knew how many years, whilst the Eastern Province had been building weapons of death, the Western Province had been building ships.'

A quiet evening at the cottage, and Percival had cooked lentil bake; the first time he had made such a thing.

'I've come to the conclusion that it's a bit weird eating the flesh of other animals, not to say barbaric; I think Keith and Meadow have got that one right.'

'So are you going vegetarian then?'

'Thought I'd give it a go...I mean I know we evolved into flesh – eaters, but that was before we had brains, you know?'

'Fine by me; I hardly ever eat meat anyway.'

'Anyway I made lentil bake; I looked it up on line, it's got lentils and such in.'

'As the name would suggest...'

'Indeed.'

Both decided that the lentil bake was delicious, and otherwise the evening went without event. When it came to time to go, or stay, it was Percival who asked the question;

'So have you got work to do?'

'Always...'

'Okay; I'll get down to some writing then.'

'It could wait 'til tomorrow, I suppose.'

'So are you staying then?'

'Am I invited?'

They made love, gently; it was mid – week love making, and no work or writing got done. They were drifting into sleep, she with her head on his shoulder, when she first mentioned her newly made social arrangements.

'Are we doing anything tomorrow evening?'

'Nothing planned, why?'

'I'll be a bit late home; I'm meeting Ray after work.'

'He's the insurance man, isn't he?'

'That's him.'

'And he's married to Polly, right?'

'No, sweetheart, he's married to Fiona.'

'Right...What the hell are you meeting him for?'

Sally smile to herself.

'He wants to talk to someone about his marital problems; I said I'd give him an hour; we're going to the White Hart.'

'Well if he tries anything on, let me know; I'll set Keith on him.'

'Don't worry, I've got that covered. Then on Friday I'm going out with Polly.'

'And which one's she divorcing?'

'She's the one who's married to George.'

'Right...So why doesn't Polly marry Ray; Fiona could marry George; problem solved, wouldn't you say?'

'Sort of permanent husband – swapping; I'll suggest it, shall I?'

'Tell them it was my idea.'

'Okay...'

Sally was all but asleep, but Percival had something else to say.

'I've been thinking....You and I should go away somewhere for a few days.'

'Where..?'

'Wherever you like; you're owed some leave, aren't you?'

'Lots of it...'

'So where would you like to go?'

'I'll tell you where I've never been.'

'Where..?'

'Paris.'

'What...? Christ we'd better put that right. Let me know when you've booked time off and I'll get the tickets.'

'Okay...'

'I love you, Percival.'

But Percival was already asleep; no matter, she would tell him again tomorrow. She fell asleep in the warmth of their afterglow, and they both slept soundly until morning.

"...ell, here we are.'

Grant became aware that Brother Peter was speaking to him from the front of the vehicle.

'I'm sorry...?'

'I said; here we are.'

'Yes; thank you.'

'We assume you've missed your allocation.'

'Allocation...?'

'Your place on a ship; your sector was cleared weeks ago.'

'I don't think he's from that sector,' said Sister Fiona 'are you, Brother Grant?'

This was the first time that she had spoken directly to him, and she had not spoken unkindly.

'No....I'm not from that sector.'

'Then what the hell were you doing there..?' Said Brother Peter 'Look, if you've been sick, or whatever, just show your I.D. to the port authorities; mostly these are cargo ships now, but they'll reallocate you, I'm sure.'

'I.D.....'

'Yeah; your I.D...I assume you have your I.D. card with you, or is that too much to ask?'

'Hush, Peter,' said Sister Fiona 'I'm sure Brother Grant has his I.D, don't you, Brother Grant?'

'Actually, no...'

'By the stars...' said Brother Peter 'Do you have any money?'

'Well, not really. That is, I've got a few Credits with me, but I don't suppose they work here, do they...'

Fiona and Peter exchanged looks again, and it was Peter who spoke.

'Where did you say you were from?'

'He didn't say, did you, Brother Grant...'

There really was no point in lying.

'I'm from the Eastern Province; I came across this morning.'

A moment of disbelief, and to be sure that Grant was not joking with them, but when his expression remained serious, the matter required serious dialogue.

'But that's impossible; I mean nobody's ever done that before... How did you make it across, the gates are guarded.'

'Actually they're not,' said Sister Fiona 'the last guards were decommissioned yesterday; the wall's been cleared now; it could just possibly be true.'

'So, you mean you just walked across?'

'Yes, I just walked across.'

'How many of you..?'

'It was only me; nobody else came, and nobody else will come.'

'So....So what are you then; some kind of a refugee, or spy, or what?'

'I'm not sure what you'd call me...A spy, I suppose. You have to leave; you have to get these ships gone by midnight.'

'What are you talking about?'

'At midnight they are going to rain death and destruction on the province; there'll be nothing left.'

Brother Peter and Sister Fiona were clearly now at a loss; of course they were, for they could not have known that they had just given a ride to the only person in living memory to have crossed over, and now it was Grant who spoke.

'Look, it's okay; I know that you have to arrest me, and that you'll probably kill me after what I've seen, but you must believe me; it seems that most of the people have gone, am I right? So everyone must leave by midnight; that's when they're launching the missiles; I saw them this morning, and there are hundreds of them. I'm here to report what I see, but I won't do that; I won't go back even if you release me, so do whatever you want with me, but please, just get everyone away.'

'These are the last ships,' said Sister Fiona 'the final ship to leave is due to weigh anchor at ten o'clock.'

'Then be on it; don't leave anyone behind...Look, can I get a coffee?'

'What...?'

'Before you have me arrested,' I'd just like one cup of coffee; you have coffee here, I've seen it, and all of the glasshouses were decommissioned years ago; we don't have coffee anymore.'

Even when coffee had been available, it had cost about half a days' credit earnings for a cup, but even so Grant had sometimes indulged himself, but there had been no coffee for a long time. Brother Peter laughed.

'Man, are you for real?'

'I'm telling you the truth; look, if you don't believe me...'

Grant pulled out the few notes from his trouser pocket; everything else; all forms of identification had been taken from him yesterday in preparation for his mission, but they had left his money. It was enough credits to buy a meal, or perhaps two, but it was no good to him now, so he gave it to Brother Peter, who examined it closely. It was Sister Fiona, however, who spoke first.

'I think coffee sounds like a good idea, don't you?'

'We can't....'

'Sure we can; we have to wait somewhere for the port police, so why not in the cafe? Are you hungry, Brother Grant?'

'Actually yes, I'm very hungry.'

She got out of the vehicle, and somewhat more reluctantly so did Brother Peter, and Grant did likewise. In common with the rest of the province, almost all of the shops and restaurants along the quayside were already closed down, but one cafe had remained open to serve the few hundred people who remained to load the remainder of the cargo. They found a table, and Brother Peter bought coffee, soup and bread; Grant had not eaten since last evening, and realised for the first time that he was indeed very hungry. The two people who carried his fate in their hands left him for a few moments, and stood in earnest conversation before returning to the table, and Sister Fiona, who had been the quieter of them hitherto but who now seemed to have taken control of the situation, was acting spokesperson.

'We don't quite know what to do with you, Brother Grant from the Eastern Province, but since we believe that you are being honest with us, or at least that we have to believe you, we will be honest with you...This is the last day, you see; there really is nobody left who we can take you to; things are chaotic enough as it is; everything is about leaving, now, and we...Well, we are at a loss.'

'I see...'

'We are a part of the Coordination Committee, and such we have things to organize, and we will leave you for a while; don't try to run; your only hope now is to stay with us. We will be back as soon as we can, and we will see what can be done.'

'I'll be here.'

And so Grant finished his soup and coffee, and waited. During that which remained of the afternoon he walked the quayside; trucks were being unloaded; timber crates and sacks, the contents of which he could only guess, were being transported to the huge hold of the nearest ship. There were three ships in dock, and during the time that he waited, one of them weighed anchor, and to much fanfare made its' slow way out of port. He watched the huge vessel as it made open water on its' last voyage, and wondered at such an exodus; how many ships had these people built, and how many times had each ship returned here to pick up so many people, and where were they all going? He had not asked; he made the assumption that the less he knew, the greater chance there was that he would survive, and he knew that the danger was far from over. Peter and Fiona had shown him only kindness, but he was still the enemy; the only one here of an enemy which was now set on the annihilation of everyone that he met, and saw. And he understood their dilemma; they had not become friends; that was too strong a word, but they had connected, as people will, and that would make it harder for them to turn him over to the authorities. He could be useful, of course, invaluable, even; he had first hand and intimate knowledge of the Eastern Province, and there was something else for them to consider, although soon it would be too late to make a difference. So perhaps after all they would just leave him here, the last person standing on the dockside as the last ship departed, waiting to be blown to pieces by his own people; there would be some kind of strange and befitting justice in that. He could perhaps have stolen a vehicle, made a telephone call and made it back to the wall in time; he had never driven a car but it didn't look very difficult. But he knew that he would not do that, not having seen this; he would rather die now than go back to that place, and that life, even if he were allowed to live; he would sooner have his last hours as a free man, even if it was only a few hours. No; he would take his chances with Sister Fiona and Brother Peter.

Darkness had come before he saw either of them again, and now Fiona came on her own. He was leaning on an iron railing, looking out to sea, when she came up behind him and took him by the arm.

'Come with me, and don't say anything.'

Together they walked along the wharf; everywhere were people making their final preparations to leave, and they passed by unnoticed, until finally they reached the gang – plank which led into one of the two remaining ships.

'This may not work, and if it doesn't then I'll have to turn you in, I'll have no choice; just stay close to me.'

They walked up the narrow timber ramp together, she in front; the guard at the entrance to the boat checked her identification, although he clearly knew her and they exchanged smiles. The guard looked at Grant suspiciously.

'He's with me; he's lost his I.D. and papers; I'm dealing with it.'

And that was that; the guard was about to speak, but did not get the chance; Fiona walked quickly away and Grant followed her, and he could only guess how close it had been. Without speaking further she led him through the vast ship, up two flights of iron steps and finally through a door and into a long, narrow corridor, which Grant assumed was accommodation. She stopped at door number *fifty three, unlocked the door and led him into a cramped cabin which contained a single bed and not very much else.*

'This is my cabin. I've made the trip several times and have certain privileges. You can stay in here until we leave. There's bottled water, and if you need to pee or whatever, use the bucket. You are very lucky; on any other night but this, this would not have been possible.'

She turned to leave, but Grant had one question.

'Why are you helping me?'

'It hasn't been just me, but if we hadn't helped you then the revolution would have been pointless.'

And with that she was gone, locking the door behind her. Grant sat down on the bed, then removed his raincoat and shoes and lay down; suddenly he felt extremely tired. So there had been a revolution, and Grant wondered what manner of repressive regime had been overthrown in order that the ships be built, and war avoided, but that would have to remain a question for another day, if there was to be another day.

He must have fallen asleep. In any case the next thing of which he was conscious was a gentle rocking motion, which for a moment made him feel quite sick, and for a moment he was disorientated, until he remembered where he was. He stood on the bed and looked through the small port – hole; the quayside was moving, and the huge engines increased their volume as the ship was gently steered away from the dock - side, and out into the open ocean. So, he had made it then, at least this far.

Within a few moments he heard the key turn in the lock, and Fiona returned, looking a little less tense, but not entirely relaxed.

'Okay; we're on our way. The voyage will take five days; you'll have to sleep where you can; nobody will care now. Water and meals are provided but here's some money if you need anything; it's not much but it will suffice. For the rest of the trip, forget I exist; we'll meet up again at the other end.'

'And what will happen at the other end?'

'I don't know yet; I need to think, and to talk to some people.'

'I don't know how to thank you.'

'Well don't; I didn't do this for you; I did it because I believe in what we're doing.'

'Sure...What time is it?'

'It's just gone eleven o'clock; we were late departing; don't you have a pocket - clock?'

'I could never afford one.'

He smiled, and she returned the smile. He walked along the corridor and out into the chill night air, and leaned against the iron rail, watching the dock and the lights along the shoreline gradually recede as they made open water. Everything today was a new experience, and he had never been on any kind of boat before. He was still there when the night sky lit up, red and yellow. The light came first, followed shortly afterwards by the sickening sound of explosions as the first missiles landed. It must be midnight, and for the first time the probability of war between the provinces had reached one hundred percent. He could have telephoned them; he could have stopped all of this, but where would have been the point? There was nobody there to kill anymore, and there would be no retaliatory strike; they would assume that they had won a great victory, so let them assume; they would know soon enough when the army poured like so many ants through the eight gates, which would probably be tomorrow morning at first light. All they would find would be so much fire and rubble, and the bombed – out remains of that which had been a society and culture much like their own. There were no differences between them, genetic or otherwise; these were not animals, as they had been told, bent on their destruction, but rather people who had chosen peace, and new horizons.

The bombardment went on, hour after hour, until there was nothing to see but a red dot in the otherwise jet – black ocean; one final great shaft of white light lit the sky as the oil refinery exploded, and then, eventually, there was nothing more to be seen, as the place which had once and always been his home disappeared below the horizon. Grant Masterson still had no idea where he was going, but wherever it was, he kept the faith that it would be a better place than the place from which he had come. If this was his dream come true, then he would dream, for as long as the dream would last.'

Chapter 6

MEN IN SUITS

For Sharon Tate, the days since the fire had been difficult, not to say traumatic. To lose ones' home and ones' closest friends and support in one terrible night was something which she was finding it hard indeed to come to terms with, as was the acceptance of how lucky she had been, if anything about this utter catastrophe could be said to be lucky. In the first place she was a light sleeper, and had heard and been otherwise aware of her would – be assassin at the last moment, and so at that which would otherwise have been the last moment of her life she had instinctively reacted with her lithe, dancers' body, and rolled away just as the blade had struck the mattress. Thereafter she had just enough time to register that her assailant was female before launching her counter – attack, which caught her would – be killer completely off – balance, and she had struck her head against a hard object; perhaps it had been the wall, or her bedside cupboard, it was impossible to tell in the darkness, but in any case it had been enough to render the young woman unconscious, whoever she had been. All of that had been more or less instinctive, but thereafter rational thought had entered the arena, and she had known better than to turn on her bedroom light. The house was under attack; she heard sounds from below her, and now in the darkness she had made her slow and deliberate way towards the door, stopping to quickly dress in jeans, pullover and shoes, and to take her wallet, car key and passport from the drawer; if she were to escape this, then she would need these things at least, and her thoughts were now only of escape. She made her way into the corridor, where she waited, trying to assess her current situation; she was wide awake now, and her witches' awareness took over, and this was far worse than she had thought. By the time she made the head of the stairs, smoke was already rising between bare floorboards and up the stairway; whoever they were, they were burning the house. Where were Corrine and Fiona; how many of them were there, and where would she encounter them? Holding her breath as best she could, she more quickly now descended the wooden stairs, and once on the ground floor she was at a loss; should she make straight for the front door, her nearest and now only point of exit, or should she first try to find the others, or apprehend the arsonist, before the smoke overcame her? In the event the decision was made for her, as she encountered a second woman in the hallway, and this woman she recognised, even in the dim, smoky haze; this was the witch Rebecca. For a brief moment they faced one another through the smoke; Sharon had just enough time to register the hatred in Rebecca's eyes, which was tempered only by the surprise at seeing her; she was supposed to be dead by now. Rebecca made her move, but Sharon was quicker, and stronger, and she pushed her attacker back into the lounge, where she must have lost her footing, but whatever had happened Sharon had time to close and lock the dividing door. She now opened the front door, thus ensuring her own safety; her eyes were hurting, and she had taken in some smoke, but now at least she could breathe again, and she must think quickly. Flames were already coming through the downstairs windows, the heat she assumed having broken or melted the glass, and the furthermost parts of the house were already aflame. Of the others there was no sign, and her next action was done without much thought, other than that to let Rebecca die was not the way. She once again held her breath and lifted her pullover up to her mouth; she re – entered the house, unlocked the dividing door and dragged Rebecca's now limp and apparently lifeless body through the hallway and out to the front of the house. Perhaps in any case she had been too late; the heat and smoke in that which had been the lounge had been all but unbearable, but then, the body moved. Rebecca coughed as she regained consciousness, her first breaths of good air going in deep and quickly as the organism overrode all else and fought to survive, and now in the light from the inferno their eyes met again. The hatred which Sharon had seen before was gone; all thought was now on survival, and in Rebecca's weakened state it was an easy thing for Sharon to beguile her; she spoke the words which she had learned many years before, and Rebecca was hers.

'Well; here I am as promised, and mine's a Vodka and Tonic.'

Ray was already at the White Hart when Sally arrived, sitting at the bar with a pint of ale, and now she stood beside him having come directly from her train. Having bought her drink they found a table in a quieter part of the quite busy Public House, which was at this time of the day a commuters' pub, the commuters being at the home end of their daily journey to and from the capital city and its' environs, and the early evening was usually its' busiest time. The clientele, which was for the most part male, were here for after work alcoholic refreshment, some having more sociable meetings with colleagues away from the office, others on their own. Men in suits and overcoats taking the hard edges off a stressful working day before returning to hearth and home, where for some such as Ray a different kind of stress awaited them. They worked hard, these men, in jobs which for the greater part they did not enjoy, to support a lifestyle which they often wished could be different, but they were caught in a vicious entrapment where one part of their lives depended upon the other, and they could give up neither. And so almost every day at this time they drank alcohol with others who understood, although nobody talked about it; what was the point, because what other choice did they have?

'So; what do you want to talk about?'

'Oh come on, Sally; don't make this harder than it is...'

'Sorry; seemed like a reasonable question, or shall we pretend that we're not here to talk about your marriage and see if it sort of turns up in conversation?'

'Okay...It's just difficult to know where to start, that's all.'

'Well, take your time; we've only got an hour and if we're lucky we might be able to avoid the subject altogether.'

'I thought you might be able to help, that's all.'

'Well I'll help if I can, but I really don't know what I can do; have you thought about getting professional help, you know; go to a marriage guidance councillor?'

'We haven't talked about it, and I wouldn't know how to suggest it, even if I thought it was a good idea.'

'Well you're clearly both discontented, so let's start with how this discontent manifests itself; what's going on between you?'

'It's easier to say what's not going on between us, and it hasn't for a long time; not really.'

'And who's to blame for that, do you think; I mean Fiona's an attractive woman, so without wishing to go too deeply into it, does she not want you or is it the other way around?'

'Both, I suppose....Lately it's just so hard to get close to her in that way, or any way for that matter, and so you kind of give up trying, I think. I mean you know she takes dance classes in the evenings sometimes?'

'Yes, I think I knew that.'

'She's got one tonight, for example, and I find myself looking forward to the evenings that she's not around, you know?'

'Well that's not good...'

'Yeah, right, and the thing is, it's not even that I don't want to be with her.'

'So what is it, then?'

'I don't know; it's just easier, I suppose; life is more peaceful, you might say. And I've only got her word for it, you know; that she's doing a dance class, and she's home later than she used to be.'

'So do you think she's being unfaithful to you?'

'I don't know; probably not, but I'm not certain...'

'Well you can never be certain, but I think you should give her the benefit of the doubt in that respect; innocent until proven guilty, you know; statistically, the woman in a marriage is far less likely to be unfaithful than the man. She's probably just taking dance classes, and is probably not in such a tearing rush to get home these days, things being as they are; maybe she enjoys the time away as well. I mean if she knew that you and I were meeting she might be forgiven for thinking that something was going on, which it isn't, but it might look somewhat suspicious, don't you think?'

'Yeah, I suppose...'

'And by the way I told Polly that we're meeting for a drink, just so that you know.'

'You did...?'

'I told you this isn't going to be a secret meeting, Ray; I'm not going to be a part of whatever's going on between you, but you've really got to do something about all of this, assuming that you both want to, of course. So you haven't actually talked about divorce?'

'No, not as such.'

'Well something has to happen....When was the last time that you went away together; that sometimes helps, I'm told; make or break kind of thing.'

'We had two weeks in Bali last year; it was a disaster; I mean I tried, you know, but it just wasn't working between us, I mean sexually, you know?'

'It isn't all about sex, Ray.'

'Yeah, I know, it's different for girls, right?'

'Of course; I mean everybody wants sex, but it has to be in the right circumstances.'

'Yes but Christ, I mean white – sand beaches, candle – lit dinners outside every night; how much more right do the circumstances have to get?'

'Well, it's emotional as well as environmental circumstances, but I take your point...So how about you?'

'What about me?'

'Are you being faithful to her?'

'Chance of being otherwise would be a fine thing.'

'Which is hardly the attitude, is it? Not if you ever want things to work out between you.'

'Well, you know...'

'Stop right there; I told you that whatever you feel for me isn't on the play – list; it isn't going to happen, Ray, and I'm not even going to talk about it.'

'Still, I can have my fantasies, right, and I do, believe me.'

'I really don't want to know about your fantasies; I'm not the problem, Ray; maybe I'm a symptom of what's going on, but I'm not the cause.'

'How do you know?'

'Oh come on; you don't love me, Ray, in the same way that you must have loved Fiona once, and maybe you will again. I mean if you don't mind my saying so you're displaying the classic signs of a mid – life crisis, but your relationship with Fiona's the most important relationship of your life; you married her, you know? Men of your age often go through this, but it passes, I'm told; can't you just go screw the secretary or something; get it out of your system?'

'You haven't seen my secretary.'

'So screw somebody else's secretary; then you'll get the guilt, then you'll begin to realise how lucky you are to be married to Fiona. The grass really isn't always greener on the other side; it just looks that way.'

'If you'll excuse the cliché, right..?'

'Sorry, Ray, but this is just one big cliché; next you'll be telling me that your wife doesn't understand you, at which point I might just walk out, by the way, but I mean just look around you; how many of these men are rushing home to their loving wives; the malcontent is palpable. But you know, people work things out, Ray, but you have to put some effort in; tell her that you love her and treat her with a bit more respect; in fact a lot more respect.'

'By screwing somebody else..?

'That's just sex, and so long as it's between consenting adults and you use a condom there won't be any long – term damage done, if it's part of a process. I'm not advocating unfaithfulness in a general way, but you're obviously wired up about proving your own sexuality, so go prove something to yourself if you have to, then go back to the woman who loves you.'

'How do you know she loves me?'

'Because I can see how much you're hurting her, even if you can't.'

'Have you spoken to her?'

'No, I haven't; I don't have to.'

'So what's this then, feminine intuition?'

'You could call it that, but I prefer to call it the bloody obvious.'

'Christ, I'm feeling guilty already, and I haven't even done anything...'

'Why do you think I'm talking this crap?'

'So is this psychology, then? Putting me through some kind of virtual affair just so I can feel guilty about it without actually doing it?'

'The punishment without the sin; is it working...?'

'Yeah; it's working....'

'I mean I could take you home now and fuck your brains out, but I'm not going to do that, because it really wouldn't help the situation.'

'If you say so...And anyway then you'd be unfaithful to Percival, and women are never unfaithful, right?'

'I didn't say never, but it's not going to happen; I'm not taking responsibility for your problems, one way or the other.... Just go home and say you're sorry.'

'What; for not having an affair..?'

'No, not for that...You have to make her feel important again, because she is important; she's the woman you love, otherwise we wouldn't be having this conversation.'

There was silence for a moment while the man considered; the way she had put it, it was all so obvious, but sometimes when a person is this deep in the woods they are unable to see the trees, and the theory of it was far more easy than the practice.

'So what about you, then..?'

'What about me?'

'I mean things are working out for you this time around?'

'Things are working out fine, thank you, but we're not here to talk about that, either. Look, I should be going, you know?'

'I haven't had my hour yet.'

'It's okay, I charge by the minute, and I really don't know what else I can say. Just get a grip on yourself; go home, open a bottle of wine and put some candles on the table for when she gets home, and for Christ's sake don't tell her you've seen me.'

'I thought it wasn't supposed to be a secret.'

'There's such a thing as being too honest.'

'Anyway you've told Polly.'

'She won't say anything; I'm seeing her tomorrow evening; I'll tell her to keep her mouth shut.'

'Okay...Okay, but supposing I do all that; say sorry and so on, and it doesn't work, you know?'

'Then say it again; she may not believe you the first time, but she will want to believe you, and that's the important thing; saving your marriage may be work in progress for a while, and right now she probably hates you, which is a good thing, by the way.'

'Christ; women...'

'I know; can't live with us, can't live without us; must be tough, and I know that's another cliché, but clichés are clichés for a reason. I'm not going to say "try seeing things from her perspective" because men can't do that, but pay attention to her; try to imagine you're meeting her for the first time; love needs constant rebirth or it dies, and if that works then everything else will follow.'

'And what if in the end and after all of that it doesn't work?'

'Well then divorce her; there's no magic formula if it really is over, but at least you'll have tried, and you'll walk away with a clear conscience, and that'll be important, if it happens.'

Sally stood up to leave; he finished the last of his beer.

'Well, thanks, Sally, I think; I don't know what else to say.'

'I hope it helped...'

'Yeah, it helped, I think, and I really am sorry about last Friday.'

'Forget it...Look, you're a good man, Ray, otherwise Fiona wouldn't have married you; you just have to let the good man out, that's all, and it will work, if you really mean it.'

'I know I've not always been good to her, and especially lately; that at least I can see...'

'Well then start from there and go and be good to her; if you're good to her for long enough then eventually she'll forget the bad times; she'll want to do that as well. How're things at work, by the way?'

'What...? Oh, you know, I'm making it up the ladder; head of department now for my sins, and I should make it into the big room eventually; it puts iron in the soul but it pays the mortgage.'

'Yes, well Insurance isn't the kind of career which lends itself to too much excitement...You ever think about changing jobs; you know, go for a complete re – invention?'

'I've thought about it often enough, but the mortgage doesn't seem to go away.'

'You could buy a smaller house; there're only two of you, after all; do you really need all the bedrooms, and there are cheaper areas to live in.'

'Well maybe I'll try to sort my marriage out first, then do the rest of my life later.'

'It might be part of the same deal, you know?'

'Are you saying I'm boring?'

'No, but if your job's boring then it isn't helping you, is it; I mean as a whole person, if you'll excuse another cliché.'

'Okay but I mean, you work for a bank, right, and I'm guessing that you've got a mortgage, so isn't this the pot calling the kettle black?'

'Well I'm not married for a start, and I doubt if I ever will be, and as it happens I'm paying the last mortgage instalment this month; I went for a quick pay – off; it's hurt sometimes, especially at the beginning, but it will have been worth it, and houses weren't so expensive when I was buying.'

'Well good for you, so you'll be giving up the job soon then, is that it?'

'Nothing's ruled out...'

'Really...? But I mean you're a shining example to everyone of a successful career woman.'

'There're plenty of those around these days, and lately I've started asking myself, you know; is that how I really want to be remembered? Anyway we're not talking about me, remember, and I really should be going.'

'So am I allowed a kiss goodbye; just as friends?'

She walked around the table; he stood up and she offered him her cheek, and he kissed her; friendship officially reinstated, which Sally caught herself being pleased about, actually.

'So, are you going straight home?'

'I think I'll have another beer first; she won't be home for a couple of hours anyway, and I need some thinking time, and probably some Dutch courage.'

'Well don't get pissed; that won't help either.'

'Just one for the road, you know?'

'Well, see you then, and good luck.'

'I'll let you know how it goes...'

'Don't make that a priority. We may not see each other for a long time anyway; I imagine that I've been struck off certain people's dinner party guest lists.'

'Does that worry you, if it's true?'

'Not really; not at the moment, anyway...'

They smiled goodbye and Sally walked through the suits, attracting some attention as she did so. She commuted with about as many women as men, so she assumed that the women must go home; perhaps to cook the evening meal, or perhaps just to go home. At the beginning of the brief meeting with Ray she had no idea how it would go, or even how she would react to their encounter, but she thought that she had given fairly good account of herself, or at least she hoped she had. In the end she had felt sorry for him in all of his male stupidity, but then she knew in some deep place that it worked both ways; that she would never know how it really felt to be a man; she could only ever have a woman's perspective.

She thought that she might shower and change at the cottage this evening, assuming that Percival was home; she kept clothes there for such an eventuality, even though they were not living together; not really, anyway. But if she was going for the whole package; if she really was going to change her life, then who knew what might change in that regard; right now, as far as Sally Parsons was concerned, nothing was certain apart from her love for Percival. Everything else was subject to further and deep consideration, and she had been thinking for some time now, and especially since a certain man had come back into her life. Did she really want to be a woman in a suit all of her working life, or should there be more to it than that? With this question making its' way once more through her mind she walked back to the station car park, for the last part of her own journey home.

Sharon centred herself, as she had long ago learned to do; even and perhaps especially in extremis one must always begin from the centre; she knew that she did not have long, and in the time she had she must think clearly. Leaving Rebecca where she was lying, she made one circuit of the house, which was by now everywhere in flames. She opened the back door, which for some reason was not yet so affected, and through the smoke she saw the body of Fiona lying inside. She dare not go to her, the smoke was by now too intense, and the flames too close, and in any case her body was limp and unmoving; she was dead for certain. This was fact now, to which she would allow her emotions to react in time, but not now; Fiona was dead, and there was nobody else; Corinne was nowhere to be found, and nor was there sign of any more attackers; there had only been two of them. By the time she returned to Rebecca, she was certain that there was nothing more to be done. Corinne she assumed must also have died, as must the woman who had tried to murder her in her sleep; there was no possibility that anyone would survive now who had not already made their escape. Rebecca was trying to speak, but the words would not come; she was in thrall now, but she was breathing more normally; Sharon had gone back for her in time, before she had been completely overcome, but she had only just been in time. So think, Sharon; the heat from the inferno was now all but unbearable even where she stood, and the fire – services would surely be here soon; somebody must have seen the blaze, which must be visible now from a long distance. Her instinct to stay at the place where she had lived for so long, and not to leave the people whom she loved, fought for a moment with her common sense, and the knowledge that she must leave this place as far behind her and as quickly as she could. But then there was Rebecca, who was now quite at her mercy. She could make her walk back into the flames if so she wished, to burn in the fire which she had made, but whatever it was which had made her go back for her now made her think again. There had been two assassins; only two, and why only two? There were deeper things beyond this which perhaps would not be revealed if Rebecca were dead; the white coven must be involved, but why had there been only two; that made no sense. She had no way into the white coven; Eve had known its' location, but Eve was gone now, and they would be vigilant; Rebecca was their only weakness. But if she was not to kill her, then what; her own safety must now be paramount, and with Rebecca with her she could not be assured of that; even in her present condition, Rebecca should not be trusted, or underestimated. She could walk her to the road and leave her there, but time was pressing, and anyway then too much might be revealed when they found her. So, to the car then; the coven had shared a car, and here Sharon had also been fortunate; she had been the last to use it, and so had the car key in her bedroom when the attack had come; had the key been elsewhere in the house she would not have found it, and would have had no means of quick escape. She lifted Rebecca by the arm and guided her to the vehicle, and onto the back seat, where she lay down without protest. Whether it was her near – death in the fire or Sharon's witchcraft which now made her so compliant was something which Sharon had no time to consider. She started the engine and drove up the lane to the gate, which she left the vehicle to open. She looked back briefly at that which had been her home; even from this distance and with her eyes still stinging and wet from the smoke, she could see that the upper storey was now on fire; flames had engulfed the entire building; it would be utter destruction. She got back in the car and turned out onto the road; at this point the direction was unimportant; just to escape, and she had escaped just in time. Fire tenders and police cars passed her, sirens wailing; they would be there in minutes, but they would be too late.

So, she was free; somehow and by some stroke of good fortune she had made it out of and away from the burning house, and alone had survived the assassination. She had her credit cards and some cash, and the clothes which she now wore, which included no underwear, and she had the witch Rebecca semi – conscious on the back seat. The short term strategy had worked; she had done okay so far, and now she could begin thinking further ahead, and the next consideration must be where the hell she was going.

Sally's story now moves forward a day, to Friday evening, where as arranged she arrived at the florist at just before seven o'clock, as Polly was clearing up for the day.

'Hi; I won't be a minute.'

'It's okay, take your time.'

'So where would you like to eat?'

'I don't really mind; Fredo's?'

'Sure, I could do Italian...'

Less than one hour later they were seated in the restaurant, and had ordered pasta and a bottle of red wine as recommended by the house.

'So,' said Sally 'I suppose we may as well get the Ray thing over with.'

'I didn't like to ask...'

'What, in case it turned into a night of unbridled passion with your best friends' husband?'

'Well, you never know...'

'Then let me put your mind at rest; we had a drink, talked about his marital issues, and it all took less than an hour.'

'Okay well then I'll ask; how was he...I mean...'

'I know what you mean, and he's fairly pissed off with life at the moment; classic male in his forties stuff, you know?'

'So did he talk about Fiona?'

'Sure; most of the time actually, or rather his relationship with her; I told him she still loved him and that he should man – up and get his life and marriage back on track.'

'And how did he take that?'

'He was drinking on it, but I think it'll be okay, although you never know; it takes two to want to put things back together, doesn't it....'

'Indeed; it must have been odd for you, though; I mean you're part of the reason for it all going tits – up in the first place.'

'No I'm not Polly; not really. I'm just the unattainable woman; the person who would magically put everything right in his life, and I could be anybody. It's not me, it's what I represent; the greener grass, you know?'

'Do you really think so?'

'Yes, I really think so.'

'And did you tell him that?'

'In so many words, yes, and by the way I told him that you knew I was meeting him, but please don't say anything to Fiona. If he manages to pull off the great re – meeting of minds and bodies then it's best if it's seen to come entirely from him.'

'Rather than you...Sure, I can see that...Okay, I won't say a word, and if questioned I will deny all knowledge of such a meeting.'

'Good...That's done then.'

'And she's not really my best friend; I mean I love her to bits but she can bitch as well as the rest of them if the need seems to her to arise. She hasn't always treated Ray as well as she might; it sort of works both ways.'

'Well, it's down to them now to sort it out, one way or the other; I've done all I'm going to do.'

'Sounds like you've done enough, and I mean that in a good way, which is something I never thought I'd hear myself say.'

The pasta arrived; both had foreknowledge of the generosity of the dishes served at the establishment, and both had forgone a first course.

'So what about you then; since I seem to be getting down to brass tacks with people at the moment; how are you and George?'

'No better, frankly...'

'So you haven't had the confrontation yet?'

'No, not yet; it's been more a matter of minor skirmishes than a full on battle, if you see what I mean. And the whole bloody ridiculous situation with Claudia seems to be going on, at least he's not denying it, so I make the assumption....'

'Oh dear, I'm sorry...'

'Ms Green Grass herself...I mean what the hell's he doing; there's no way that she's going to leave Simon; he's got far too much money for one thing, and she likes her creature comforts does our Claudia. I'm sure that for her George is just a distraction, you know?'

'Well, maybe it'll burn itself out.'

'And maybe I won't be around to witness that happening. Perhaps I'd better send him to you; you seem to be able to talk sense into people, men in particular. Christ, what is it with men; I mean Fiona's fit; she's a dance instructor for heaven's sake.'

'That's what I told Ray; maybe the problem is she's not a twenty five year old dance instructor anymore.'

'She wasn't instructing then, but I know what you mean. Anyway let's change the subject for a minute; I'm getting quite depressed; I'm not a twenty five year old florist, either...So, what about you; you're back with Percival again, so what's that all about?'

'He sent me an email from Japan, then Indonesia; then he called me from Denmark.'

'So it was a cautious and staged approach, then.'

'I suppose you could say so.'

'And then you met up?'

'Yes, of course we met up.'

Of a sudden Sally felt angry, which surprised her somewhat, and for a brief moment she tried to analyse the reason for her anger. It was quite alright if people wanted to talk about their dying relationships, but she and Percival were nothing to do with that, and nothing to do with them, for that matter, and she had no wish to talk about her feelings for him, nor his for her, nor even how they were reunited. It was as though talking about their love in this so negative a context might contaminate it somehow, which was stupid, really, but they had never accepted him, so they didn't get to talk about him; keep him out of it. She had tried to keep the anger from her voice, but the anger had been unexpected, and Polly had caught the nuance.

'Sorry, did I touch a nerve?'

'What...No, sorry, it's nothing; do you want dessert?'

'Sure; I'll ask for the menu.'

They stayed for another hour, ate Italian trifle and drank espresso coffee; at some point the conversation drifted back to Polly's impending confrontation with George, but no conclusions were drawn, and Sally found herself increasingly keen to be leaving. There was nothing after all that she could do from the female perspective which would help; giving advice to a woman was different from giving advice to a man, and she did not presume to do such a thing. All she could really do was offer a sympathetic ear, and her sympathy bank was by now feeling somewhat depleted. The two women parted friends, and with a promise to meet up again soon. She had met two of the four wounded parties to the two failing marriages, and her sympathies in the end were all with Polly, who was lovely, after all, and she understood her frustration. She supposed that it would require the transition between frustration and anger for Polly's extremely long fuse to be finally exhausted, and that, she also supposed, was not now long away. And as for Ray, well, he would do as he would, and perhaps all would be well, and perhaps not; on the battlefield of love between men and women, there would always be casualties.

In the first instance, that was to say having given the matter initial thought, Sharon had nowhere to go. She had broken ties with her family; her parents lived abroad in any case, and with her two brothers and one sister she had had no contact for years, they lived several counties away in any case, and in truth she had no one outside the coven whom she could really call a friend. Since coming to live permanently at Farthing's Well at the age of seventeen, she had led a particular life, which nobody would ever have understood. Sharon was a professional dancer, who at the age of twenty eight was approaching the end of her dancing career, but she looked and danced young enough to prolong her stage time for a few more years, and aside from the dancing she kept herself fit. It was the kind of work which saw her travelling the country and sometimes abroad, and in either case being away from home for prolonged periods of time, until a particular show had run its' course, at which point she would return home and rest, and look for the next contract. She was currently out of work, which was a common enough occurrence, and she was not concerned, but now she had no home, and she cursed herself for leaving her telephone on her bedside table; now she would have to make the telephone calls, and she would have lost some important telephone numbers. There were people with whom she danced, but with most of them she enjoyed only a professional relationship, and none of them could help her with this particular dilemma. Her only true friends, Corrine and Fiona, were both almost certainly dead, and there would be a time to grieve for them, but this was not the time. She was heading west, in the dead of night, and at some juncture she must have made up her mind where she was going; she must speak to Megan, who she knew lived somewhere by the village Green in Middlewapping. And now she made her second decision, which in fact was not unrelated; she would take Rebecca to the Manor House. She would leave her there, having erased all memory of the journey from her mind. That would be an easy thing to do, and would sow a seed of uncertainty within her; she would not understand how she had got there, and would probably conclude that the other witch, whoever she was, had taken her there, but she would not be certain, and she would never see the other witch again. Rebecca must be taken back to the place where Sharon had last seen her, on the night that Eve had died at the hands of the woman Meadow. There, Sharon supposed, would she return to her life, and to Victoria Tillington, her lover. And that in turn would allow Sharon time to think beyond this terrible night, and to take council with Megan. Being thus resolved she continued her journey, and would arrive at her destination in good time do all that she had to do, before the morning came.

Sally went straight to the cottage; having been embroiled in the cold negativity of other peoples' problems for two consecutive days, she wanted very much to feel the warm glow of her love for Percival, before the chill went in too deep. Her friends had drawn her back in, but she was determined to control how far in she would go; after all, she had her own life and love to deal with, which had nothing to do with them, and tonight she had inadvertently learned to what extent that was true. And she walked in to good news;

'I've booked the flights; we go next Wednesday.'

'Oh that's great; I'll confirm the leave on Monday. When do we come back?'

'Sunday...'

'Perfect.'

'I also booked a hotel; it's some kind of cheap place, but that's how I've always stayed in Paris, it's that kind of city; you okay with that?'

'Of course; however you want to do it, my love.'

'I hope the weather breaks by then; it's all about sitting outside in Parisian cafes, so we'll need overcoats.'

'I can do overcoats...'

She showered and within an hour they were in bed. Tonight she decided would be girls on top; she made love to him, wearing a black and extremely transparent negligee, which lived up to its' name, and which by her own volition she was scarcely wearing anyway during their lovemaking, and was not wearing at all by the time it was over; she loved him, after all, and he was taking her to Paris, after all. And Paris, she decided, was a very good place to discuss the things which she now very much wanted to discuss with him, and she could wait until Wednesday.

Sharon went first to the Manor House. She parked the car outside the driveway, opened the huge metal gate, and half supported the still semi – conscious Rebecca up the long gravel driveway. Having reached the front steps, she left her there, having told her to forget her journey, and to forget who had saved her, and who had brought her here. She must have no memory of Sharon; Sharon would remain a complete stranger to her if ever they were to meet again.

She then returned to the car and drove the short distance to the village Green, parking the vehicle on the main road, out of sight. She walked to and then across the Green, which was bathed in cold, pale moonlight, and no lights showed at any windows; everyone was sleeping, as she had hoped and expected that they would be. She identified the house; number seven, where Megan had held her vigil, and had gained the trust of the Tillington household, which had been her master – stroke. And now she had a problem; how to awaken Megan without drawing unwanted attention to herself. She stood by the door for a moment, but then noticed that the door was not in fact entirely closed, which was odd, but at least she could now enter the house silently. The house was empty. She moved in the darkness from room to room, her eyes now being quite acclimatised, and seeing well enough with only the moonlight to guide her, but there was no one. Megan had gone, and as far as she could see she had left hurriedly and taken certain of her possessions with her; drawers had been opened, and emptied. She sat for a moment on the stairs, and considered this new twist to events. Had Megan known, somehow, that Farthing's Well had been attacked, and destroyed, and so had she fled, fearing for her own safety, and if so, how could she have known? Was it possible that she had also been assailed during the night, and had been taken somewhere, or even assassinated? Upon these things she could only speculate, but there was nothing to be done now. She cursed this new and serious dilemma, for without her telephone she could not contact Megan, nor Megan her; leaving her telephone had been an even bigger mistake than she had imagined.

She walked back across the Green and sat for a moment in the car, which she supposed from now on would be her car, but came to no conclusion, other than that she must leave this place. She had nowhere to sleep, and of a sudden she felt tired. She thought for a moment of her bed, where only a few hours ago she had been sleeping soundly, and she had thought safely. But that was before her life had been turned upside – down, and before she had barely escaped with that life, however it would now be. She wiped her sleeve across her eyes, as she had been doing regularly since the fire, but perhaps it was no longer entirely the effects of the smoke which made her eyes water. She started the engine, pulled out into the still empty road, and left the village and Manor House behind her, cursing once again as she went. They had all been too complacent. They had assumed that their location had been a deeply – guarded secret, as it had been for hundreds of years, and yet somehow the white coven had found them, or perhaps the witch Rebecca and the other woman had been alone in their knowledge and intent. These were questions which must be asked, and for which she must somehow find the answers, and perhaps now she would have to find them alone. But first she needed sleep, and before that water to slake her thirst; she had drunk nothing since inhaling the smoke from the fire, and could not recall ever being so thirsty. Tonight she would sleep in the car, and wake up later this morning in some country lane somewhere, and thereafter she must deal with the next immediate practicalities; she would need to buy clothes, and find some kind of accommodation for the next night, and from there on, Sharon Tate was currently at a loss.

Chapter 7

CONCERNING VARIOUS
VISITATIONS

Assuming that he survived his parents, Michael Tillington would one day, in all legal and official senses at least, be sole owner of Middlewapping Manor, at which point he would be expected to move into the master bedroom which his parents currently occupy. To live thus is an unusual thing; to be born and raised in the sure and certain knowledge that one will die in the house in which one is born is not the lot of most people, but then most people are not set to inherit a Manor House, or a Lordship granted centuries ago by King Henry VIII to Michael's ancient forbear, whose portrait hangs to this day in the grand dining room; the first of an illustrious if for the most part illegitimate line.

Furthermore, Michael now and against all once apparent odds has an heir to his title, and thus to the house and estate; Nathaniel, born to his now deceased and still beloved wife, Rose, and Nathaniel, who assuming that he in turn survives his own father, is set to carry the mantle after Michael has passed away. One day he too will make the short but significant journey from the nursery to the master bedroom, just as his father will have done before him.

Such an inherited honour does not bestow upon its' recipient the power or influence that it once did. In former times, to be a Lord was to be close to the reigning monarch of the Islands of Britain and beyond, which was in turn more or less a guarantee of riches and status, or death, perhaps, if one were to in some way offend said monarch. In the somewhat more meritocratic society into which Michael has been born, however, this is no longer the case. He no longer has the automatic right to sit in the King's chamber, or the Queen's chamber, or to be a part of any privy - council. The House of Lords is predominantly nowadays made up of men and women who were not born to such circumstance, but have for the most part earned the right to be there during their lifetime; they are best or highest in their chosen field or profession, or have otherwise achieved something which is regarded as exceptional.

Michael had no intellectual or philosophical objection to this state of affairs. He was in any case a person born of quite modest disposition, who in truth had no inherent or acquired wish or desire to stand above the common herd, and was for the most part content with his lot, and for the most part considered himself fortunate indeed to have been born into such elevated and quite unmerited circumstance. Nevertheless such was indeed his lot, and he had been raised with a sense of high history all about him; it was in his soul, and the way that he saw the world around him, as well as being quite literally in the blood which flowed in his veins.

In truth Michael had never been close in the emotional sense to either of his parents. In part he supposed this was due to his and their status in society, and therefore propriety, which tended to mitigate against close parental ties. He had been cared for during his early years by his nanny, who was now deceased, and sent to private boarding school at a young age, and so their influence upon him could in a way be said to be somewhat peripheral. He loved them, of course, as children will love their parents, and they in their turn loved him, in their way, but they were in a sense the backdrop to his life rather than the foreground, emotionally and otherwise. Michael's years in Italy had seen off any realistic thoughts he may have had of eventually taking over his father's well established commercial ventures, which had in any case been in decline over recent years, so there was no connection between them in that sense, either, as might otherwise have been the case.

In any event Michael was content enough with his life in the more general sense, and with his modest property business, which may one day grow into something larger, should he ever wish it to do so, but he had at least now gained financial independence from his family. He had ever been at odds with his younger brother, Alexander, there being hardly anything aside from their blood ties to unite them, so different had they been in character and temperament, and though he felt the death of his brother, he quickly recovered from his only moderate grief. It was his sister, Victoria, to whom of his immediate family he had always felt the closest affinity, and here is where his eventual sole ownership of the Manor became more academic than actual, since as far as he was concerned, his dear sister had as much right to the place as did he, and she and her ascendants would live here for as long as it was their wish so to do.

Victoria had not herself had an easy or peaceful childhood or youth, Michael blaming this in part on the influence upon her of their brother, but Victoria had had problems enough of her own. She was happier now, or so it seemed, her still quite recent attempt to take her own life seeming to have in so extreme a fashion laid her particular demons to rest, at least for the present. And now she had a child of her own; little Henry, who had in common with his own child come into the world against the odds. Victoria clearly had particular and occasional feelings toward men, but for the most part her love and desires were directed toward her own gender, and one woman in particular. Rebecca and she had been lovers since they were quite young, and now apparently Rebecca had a daughter of her own, who like Henry had uncertain or unspecified parentage on her fathers' side. At least, the fact of it was that Victoria did not know who was father to Florence, or else she was not telling him, and why should she not tell him if she knew? In any event mother and daughter would soon be living in his house on the village Green, which had been Rose's house, and he was pleased to so help, as long as Rebecca's influence on his sister was in future of a positive nature, or benign at the very least.

It was also the case that if the affairs of his sister's heart were somewhat mercurial in nature, Michael had, since the death of Rose and particularly of late, been giving more than usual consideration to his own future in this regard. If one day he would certainly sleep in the master bedroom, there now remained the question as to whom, if anyone, would sleep there with him.

There was Elin, of course, his beautiful Nordic girlfriend, with whom he had shared pleasant and sometimes passionate times, but there was something about the matter which prevented his seeing their relationship as being permanent, though he could not be certain why he should feel this way, and thus could be no more specific than that. 'Lady Elin' had a certain ring about it, but the lady herself, though good company, had yet to find a path to his soul in the same way that Rose had done, so the question remained as to what was to be done about this. Victoria would have him enjoy the relationship whilst it lasted, and for that which it was, but surely biding time and waiting for something to end was no way to carry on regarding something as important as this. He had a duty, after all, and in a way he was not now only looking for someone to share his own life, but someone who would be as a mother to Nathaniel, who must henceforth in a way be the most important person in his life. And yet to cast himself adrift once more into the tempestuous and lonely waters of emotional solitude was not something to which he looked forward, and on the other hand he could not be anything but honest with Elin; if she was not to be his last love, then better the love end now, for both of their sakes.

Such were the thoughts of Michael Tillington as we now find him, as he is engaged in the business of moving his clothing, official documents relating to his business and a few other personal effects from the new extension, which might one day yield the income for which it was built, but for now somebody else was to move in. This was a certain Pandora Winterton, who had telephoned two days ago. She was to paint his father's portrait, and had become available sooner than she had expected, and much to her surprise and pleasure had been offered accommodation at the Manor House for the duration of the work. And so, for now, Michael would move back into his old bedroom, where he had always slept when in residence at the Manor House; the master bedroom would one day be his, but not he hoped for many years to come. And for now, wherever he slept, would sleep there alone.

Rebecca had been born into the upper - middle class of English society. In the material sense she had wanted for nothing as a young girl, and with some financial diligence her parents had been able to send her to a good private school, indeed some might call it the best of all private schools, and then in due course and for reasons that we have already learned, she was sent to a fee – paying Convent School, from which she had run away, and so in any case against this backdrop had she lived her young years. She had then lived for years in a stone shack, under conditions which were little better than squalid, and which certainly would have been quite intolerable for most people, regardless of whichever strata of society they had been born into. The winters had been cold there, and her only running water had come from a small waterfall which was part of a stream, which fed into a brook which ran beside the track beside which she lived. She had cooked her meals on a single – ring gas burner, when she had cooked at all, and her bed had been hard, and damp during the cold months, her only income coming from the few ceramic works which she could sell in the town of Headwater, and by means of her sometimes prostituting herself to those who attended the temple. And so as she walked across the threshold of number seven, The Green, carrying a bag of food, a rucksack and her infant child on her back, she carried an acquired hardness of constitution which was nothing to do with the way that she had been born, or raised, and everything to do with the way that she had lived thereafter. Here there would be warmth and good shelter, hot running water on demand and a warm place to sleep, so she cared not at all that the house would be sparsely furnished. She had bed – sheets, a refrigerator, a table and chairs, and sufficient crockery, cutlery and utensils with which to cook and eat, and with all of this she was more than content. She would need to buy clothes, most of her former attire being cast away during the feral months of her early pregnancy, but even this was not an urgent requirement. She would carry her child when abroad, and she pulled a drawer from the chest of drawers which she lined with soft blankets, and here Florence would sleep. She had some money which her mother had bequeathed to her, and her studio in the town was still hers to use, so soon she would return to her former craft of making ceramic pots, by which means she could, she hoped, pay her modest way, and feed and clothe her child. She knew that her tenure in the house must be of limited duration; she could not call upon the charity of Michael for long, but that was a thought for later; she could stay here for a few weeks, at least. It was kind of him to offer a place to stay for her and her child, and she could not help but wonder how he would feel if he knew that Florence was also his child, and whether then he would be more or less inclined to help her, but for now at least she could only speculate upon this.

She was also uncertain how her return to the village would be received by others who lived there, chief amongst these being Percival, Sophia, Meadow and Keith, and she would call on them soon; these people had all been a significant part of her recent history, and were as near to friends as anyone she had known since her early school years, and those had been many years ago. That which she had been had made it difficult for anyone to be close to her, she understood this well enough, but perhaps that was over now; here was comfort, at least, and in this place would she make her life, and make her stand, if they came for her. And of course she would go to the Manor, perhaps in a day or two, unless Victoria came to her first. She had lived with Victoria in the village once before, in the house which still belonged to her, and here, in Michael's house, was somewhere where they could be together again, and perhaps together and in time they could once and for all lay to rest the ghosts of all that had happened.

In the meantime she closed the door behind her, and felt for a moment an intense sense of gladness that at last and for the first time she could be alone with her child. It was a strange thing that she and particularly Charlotte had no news of Helena, but no doubt she would be in touch when the time was right. All of that; the terrible night at Farthing's Well, and other things which she had done in her life, she must put behind her, now. She would never again go back there; she would never again turn herself into the killer that she knew she could be; she was a mother, now, and so long as nobody threatened the life or wellbeing of her child, she would live in peace; a peace for which she had yearned for so long, and one day, perhaps, she might even find peace with herself.

From behind the counter of the delicatessen, Meadow had watched as Rebecca had walked across the Green from the bus stop to her new home, carrying her child and her few possessions. There had been talk of a meeting between a few of them to discuss her coming, which had in the end turned into nothing more than a series of conversations between individuals, which had reached no conclusion; what conclusion could be reached, after all? Keith had, as she would have expected, been of the opinion that all would be well, and if it was not then they could deal with any eventuality as and when it occurred; she was just another witch, after all, and Meadow smiled to herself at her man, and at that particular notion.

She was in any case at that moment somewhat distracted by a package which had just been delivered; it was addressed to her, and was from the on – line mail – order book and music club to which she subscribed. She usually kept a book by her, the better to sometimes while away the quieter times of the day when there were no customers, although in truth she would more often lean on her serving counter, observe the world through the glass frontage of her shop, and meditate upon life. But now there was the package, and she had not ordered any books of late, and anyway the package was not really book – shaped. Perhaps Rosie or Basil had ordered something in her name, if so it would not be the first time, and she would leave the package unopened until the evening, when she could make enquiry of them. She put the parcel under the counter, upon which she once again rested her arms. It had been a quiet day; Daphne had called in, as she did most days, and today she had brought with her scones and tea – cakes. Meadow had found herself missing the almost daily conversations with her unlikely friend during the time that Daphne had been in hospital, and her clientele had certainly voiced disappointment that the supply of scones, tea – cakes and other delicacies had ceased temporarily. Daphne looked well enough now, and was it seemed almost fully recovered from her ordeal, and the scones and tea – cakes had been sold in their entirety during the course of the day.

In any case the working day was nearly over now, and Meadow was looking forward to getting home. She had awoken to electronic mail from Tara, which would have been sent from somewhere overnight from a different time - zone, but she had not had time to read it in the sometimes chaotic environment of the early morning, when man and children were eating breakfast and otherwise preparing to depart for the day. In any case, however much she may enjoy running the delicatessen, she always looked forward to getting home, all be it ever so humble a home.

Pandora had called upon the favours of a friend with a car on the afternoon that she arrived at Middlewapping Manor. To have travelled by train with her easel, paints and brushes would have been tiresome enough, but this time she had the additional burden of a suitcase, into which she had hurriedly placed clothes and toiletries, and she had on this occasion already stretched canvas over frame, and so had that to carry as well. One of her subjects had been unavailable to be painted, and so she had 'phoned the Manor House and spoken to his lordship, who had no objection to an earlier start to the work, and it was during the conversation that he had offered her a place to sleep, an offer which she had readily accepted. In any case she knocked on the front door of the Manor, and as per her last and only visit here, the housekeeper had answered, as David, the friend with the car, was carrying her belongings up the steps.

'Hello; I'm Pandora...'

'Indeed; we met briefly once before, did we not; please come in.'

She was shown through the grand hallway to the door which led into the new extension, David following behind with the luggage.

'His Lordship and her Ladyship are out, I'm afraid, and will not return until late this evening, so his Lordship will see you tomorrow morning. I have been instructed to make sure you are comfortable and to ask if there is anything else that you need. The kitchen has tea, coffee and a few basic provisions, but if you need anything further just come and find me; my name's Molly.'

'Right...No...No I'm sure everything's fine, thank you Molly.'

The agreement had been that she would take care of her own catering needs, so she was expecting the use of a kitchen, but she had not expected to have her own kitchen. Nor had she expected her own lounge, bathroom, office and two bedrooms from which to choose. She thanked Molly again, saw David on his way, and did a brief tour of the rooms. Well, here was something then; her own self – contained apartment, and one of the bedrooms would do quite well as a temporary studio, provided her subject was okay with being painted there. The few provisions in the kitchen included milk, eggs, bread, cheese and even some vegetables and fruit; quite enough for her needs today, and probably for a few days, actually, so she would not need to shop, having brought no food with her. She put the electric kettle to boil for coffee and walked back into the lounge; prominently displayed on the main wall was her portrait of Rose, and for a moment tears threatened the back of her eyes; what a terrible tragedy her death had been, and Pandora was gratified that she had at least been able to portray the young woman in all of her beauty, before her beauty had been lost forever. She rarely got to see her paintings once they had been paid for and given over, and this painting in particular she was glad to see again. She collected herself and her emotions; she was here to paint somebody quite else, and must focus now on that. During her career she had been commissioned to paint everything from infants to the very elderly, but this would be her first Peer of the Realm, which would make no material difference to the way she would paint her latest subject, but there was something particular about the matter. She walked outside to a small paved area with wooden seats, which led onto the gravel driveway leading in turn to the side gates, sat down and rolled a cigarette. This would be her smoking place; it was cold, but she was used to that, and the view was nice; fields and woodland, and middle -distant views of the village in places. She had enjoyed her stay in the village when she had been painting her secret portrait of Rose, and was happy to be back here again. She would go into the village as soon as may be, to see Meadow at the delicatessen, and she might even call on, what was his name; Percival, that was it. Rose's lover; she was sure that he had been her lover, although he had denied it, and so had she; still, she had liked Percival. She made coffee and unpacked her few things; later she would set up her easel and canvass, and get herself ready; if his Lordship wished to be painted somewhere else then she would move everything, but she did not think that he would object. Many artists, she knew, would make preliminary sketches of their subjects, but Pandora did not; she worked straight onto the main canvass, and almost always had done. By early evening she had cooked and eaten an omelette, taken a shower and all was set fair for work to begin, whenever his Lordship was ready. She went outside for a cigarette, which this time she embellished with some quite mild marijuana, and recalled all that she could about his Lordship's family. The son, who had been Rose's husband, was called Michael, after his father, and the daughter of the household was Victoria, whom she had spoken to on the telephone. Victoria she thought had a son, and so of course did Michael, although she did not know or had forgotten their names. She knew very little of her Ladyship, but had liked Lord Michael on the one occasion that she had met him, which was when they had agreed that she would paint his portrait, and she looked forward to meeting him again. It was not he, however, who she would first encounter in the big house, and in the mid – evening, somebody else knocked on the door of the extension.

During the mid – evening there came a knock on her door; Rebecca had fed Florence, who was sleeping now, and she had taken a bath and eaten her simple evening meal. She expected that this would be Victoria, and she looked forward to seeing and to talking with her beloved. The person was not Victoria, however, but still, she was not in the least disappointed to see who was standing on her doorstep; love can take many forms, after all.

'Hello Rebecca.'

'Hi...This is a nice surprise.'

'Is it...?'

She walked back into the room and Percival followed.

'I can offer you coffee, but that's about all; I haven't got myself organized yet.'

'Coffee's fine.'

She went to the kitchen, and Percival made for the dining room. That which the house lacked were any easy chairs, or anywhere comfortable to sit, and anyway, Percival had always preferred to sit at a table. She returned with coffee, and water for herself, and sat down opposite him.

'Are you off coffee these days?'

'For Florence, you know; I'm trying to completely clean up; only fresh food; nothing processed, that kind of thing.'

'And yet you bought coffee.'

'Unexpected guests, you know? I don't think you'd come here if there was no coffee.'

'Fair enough....And I suppose this is a no – smoking house now?'

'Open the window.'

Percival did so whilst she fetched a saucer, which would suffice as an ashtray.

'So where is she?'

'She's asleep upstairs; I'll introduce you sometime; now if she wakes up, but she'll probably be out 'til early morning. She's a good sleeper; takes after her mother in that respect.'

'To that I look forward...Anybody else been to see you yet?'

'You're my first visitor.'

'Well then; on behalf of everyone, welcome back to the village.'

'Thanks...Am I really?'

'I'd be lying if I said there was no apprehension going about at your return, as I'm sure you will appreciate, but you're back, at least, which was not a given at our last meeting. So how have things gone since then?'

She smiled, and he smiled in return.

'If you mean was I successful in my...In my endeavours, then yes, I was.'

'Could you be more specific?'

'The black witches are dead; all except the one who lived here.'

'Yeah; I read that there had been a fire; three people dead.'

'Three people dead...'

'And the one who lived here?'

'She's gone, for now anyway.'

'Right...So you think it's over, then?'

'I don't know, Percival; she got close, did she not?'

'Apparently so...'

'I mean Christ; she was making a suit for his Lordship.'

'Yeah, she had some nerve for sure.'

'And nobody even suspected anything.'

'Witches are very good at concealing themselves and their intent; so I'm told, anyway, and it only takes one bad witch, you know?'

'I think Victoria will be more vigilant from now on.'

'Yes, I'm sure, but what about you?'

'What about me?'

'You're kind of exposed here, don't you think? Everyone's somewhat surprised that you're living here, to be honest; that is everyone who knows anything about what's gone on.'

'I'm not going to hide anymore, Percival, and I can look after myself.'

'Well, keep your door locked, and don't talk to any strangers...Keep some witch repellent by the front door; just common sense, really.'

'I'll be careful, and I at least am glad to be back. Anyway, where else should I go? Everyone I love is here; I have better protection here than anywhere, don't I?'

'Do you?'

'Well, there's you, for a start.'

'I don't do witches; that's Meadow and Keith's speciality.'

'No, you just deal with devil – worshipers, which are far worse, in a way.'

'That may be overstating things.'

'Is it...? Look, I know full well as do you that the only reason I'm alive is because of you.'

'Me, rather than anything I've done, perhaps.'

'Really...? I think you've done more than you're telling me; I don't think I'm the only one who keeps secrets.'

'I don't know what you mean.'

'I mean that I don't believe you.'

'What do you not believe?'

'That you went all the way to the west - country just to talk to Tony Blackman; that you just had a conversation with him, and that you left things inconclusively.'

'That's all true; guy wouldn't commit himself.'

'Well that much I believe, so maybe you're not lying, but I don't think you're telling me the whole truth; not by a very long way. You're up to something, aren't you?'

'Am I?'

'Yes, I think you are, but it's okay, you don't have to tell me.'

'Any more than you have to tell me who your daughters' father is.'

'Any more than that...'

'Well, let's just leave it there then, shall we, but the fact remains that you could still be in danger, so look out for yourself, that's all I'm saying, and if anything looks off, or seems off, you tell me, or Keith and Meadow.'

'Still my knight in shining armour, then...I'm lucky, aren't I; not many people have one of those.'

'Yes, well don't push your luck is all I'm saying.'

'I will be careful, Percival; of course I will, I've got Florence to think about now, haven't I? So anyway, what about you; what's new in your life?'

'Sally and I are back together again; that would be new to you, I think.'

'Really...? Well, well, isn't life full of surprises?'

'Why are you surprised?'

'I don't know...I mean the attraction is obvious, both ways, and I don't know Sally well, of course, but well, from what I know of her you're very different, aren't you?'

'Everyone's different; in this case she's a woman, I'm a man, so that's already quite a big difference, but people get by.'

'Yes, but there are degrees of difference, even between men and women...So it's over between you and Louise, then...'

'Yeah, I did that; we were just too different, you know?'

Which made her laugh, which made her realise that she had not laughed very much recently, and also made her realise how much she had missed the man who sat opposite her. Victoria was the main reason that she was here, but she was not the only reason.

'So how did you and Sally get back together?'

'I contacted her; I was seeking her friendship, I think, and somewhat to my surprise I ended up getting the rest of her, as one might say.'

'Friendship not being enough for her, I imagine.'

'I thought I'd be lucky to get that, but yeah, it was all or nothing, once I'd got past the fact that she was pissed with me.'

'And how did that manifest itself?'

'She told me, in no uncertain terms; couple of times, actually.'

'Which I know is about as close as you're going to get to discussing your love life, in fact for you this is positively gushing, but I won't pursue the subject further...'

'That would be best...'

'I confess I am surprised, but I suppose you know what you're doing.'

'That's a hell of a supposition; I wouldn't put your shirt on it. When it comes to affairs of the heart I'm about the last person I'd trust to give myself advice.'

'I mean I know she's an attractive woman, but with you there's always more to it than that, isn't there?'

'She bought me a dog, for a start, so there's that, you know?'

'Okay, I get it; subject closed...'

'So talking of dogs, are you going to have Lady here; she'd give you another line of defence against invading witches.'

'I intend to go and see Emily and Will over the next couple of days; see if it's okay if I take her back.'

'She's your dog.'

'Yes, I know, and I miss her, but they've looked after her for so long now, she must be part of the family.'

'They'll be fine, I'm sure.'

'Well, I'll talk to them...'

'I suppose you could always get them another one.'

'Yes, I could, couldn't I...That's actually a very good idea.'

'Yeah, well I'm full of those.'

'So anyway returning to the subject of women that we love, have you seen Victoria lately?'

'Not very much; did she tell you that I'm Godfather to Henry?'

'Yes, she told me, and I'm pleased about that; in fact I'm more than pleased about it; I think it's wonderful.'

'I was surprised, to be honest.'

'Of course you were.'

'Were you surprised, when you heard, you know?'

'Not in the least, why should I have been?'

'I was unsure of her motivation, that's all.'

Which made her laugh gently again.

'What's funny?'

'You; you're what's funny; you are a very clever and intelligent man, Percival my love, but in certain very significant ways you go through life with your eyes closed.'

'I find it helps, in certain very significant ways...Anyway we went to the big church, which was a first for me, but even so it's an unofficial arrangement, I think; not officially sanctioned by the almighty, at least, but I'm good with that.'

'Well, he'll never have a father, as far as anyone but Victoria knows, so you'll have to take your responsibilities seriously.'

'I intent to...So she never told you, then; who the father is..?'

'No, she's never told me, but then I haven't told her who Florence's father is either, so we're about even in that respect. And I do forgive you, by the way, for telling her about Florence.'

'Yeah; sorry about that; we were sharing confidences.'

'And her confidence was more important to you than mine, is that it?'

'You weren't there at the time, and she would never have forgiven me for not telling her; at least that's what she said, but you're right, I shouldn't have done it.'

'I think Victoria would forgive you quite a lot, actually, but fortunately so will I, and you are forgiven.'

'I'll sleep better tonight for that, and now I guess I should be going.'

'Back to Sally, then...'

'Actually we're not seeing each other tonight; she needs time off sometimes. I just thought I'd see if you were okay; make sure you're eating right, that kind of thing.'

'I appreciate your concern, but I'm eating fine, thank you.'

'So there's nothing else you need to tell me then, about your trip to the eastern counties?'

'No...Well, not about that, but something did happen which I can't explain; something strange which happened afterwards.'

'You mean strange as compared to killing people...'

'The thing is, I have no memory of the journey back; I remember the fire, and...Well, at some point I must have become unconscious, and the next thing I remember was being back at the Manor House.'

'Any idea how that would have been possible..?'

'I had an accomplice; she was the reason that I was there at all, but that's another story, so she must have driven me back, but it's still odd. I mean I've thought about it a lot, you know, but I can't do any better.'

'Maybe you were overcome by the smoke, or whatever; that can happen.'

'Yes, I suppose so.'

'Still, I wouldn't give up on it; there could be a more sinister explanation.'

'Like what?'

'Like somebody wanted you to be unconscious; witches can do that kind of thing, I'm told.'

'Yes, but...Anyway, it doesn't matter; not now, and I'm trying really hard to get past it, you know?'

'Sure; let it be then.'

He stood up, and so did she.

'Thanks for coming, Percival; I'm glad you were my first caller.'

'Thanks for the coffee.'

They walked together to the front door; she put her arms around his waist and put her head on his chest, and breathed out deeply.

'I've just realised how much I've wanted to do this.'

'You should have said something...'

She smiled and released him.

'I won't make you stay, although I could, you know, or have you got your witch repellent with you?'

'Never leave home without it these days.'

'Well, it doesn't seem to be working....I'll see you soon, I hope.'

'I live in the cottage down the lane; any time you're passing...'

He opened the door and left the house. She locked herself in and leaned against the door for a moment, and continued smiling to herself; she was glad to be back. She went upstairs; Florence was sleeping soundly in her makeshift crib, and Rebecca lay down on the bed beside her, and was asleep within moments.

Pandora opened the internal door to her temporary accommodation; she had not expected anyone to visit her this evening, and was not really dressed to receive guests. She was also feeling somewhat unusual due to the marijuana cigarette, but she thought she could hold it together okay.

'Hi; I'm sorry to disturb you; I'm Victoria; we spoke a couple of times on the telephone.'

So here was Victoria; daughter to his Lordship; skinny with an interesting face, not what one would call pretty, or beautiful in the way that Rose had been, but she had the kind of bones that Pandora would like to get her brushes around; it was not the sort of face that one would easily forget.

'Oh, yes, of course, I'm very pleased to meet you. Come in...I mean of course you can come in; it's your home, after all...'

'Well we hope to respect your privacy whilst you are with us, but I just thought I'd see if you had everything you needed; anyway to be honest I was keen that we should meet one another.'

'Me too, actually, and thanks, but I'm absolutely fine; this is all so much more than I had expected.'

'Well, I'm glad you're comfortable. Mother and Father asked me to apologise that none of us were here to welcome you;

they had a prior engagement and I've not long been back from London; I don't quite know where my brother Michael is, but he appears to be out, anyway.'

'It really is no problem; Molly made sure I was okay...Look, I mean this may sound stupid under the circumstances, but can I offer you coffee?'

'Sure; why not. Well tea, actually.'

They smiled, Victoria sat in one of the easy chairs and Pandora went to the kitchen, returning a few moments later with two cups, just as Victoria was lighting a cigarette.

'Is that okay...?'

'Well, not really, at least I don't smoke in the main house, but I saw your rolling – tobacco, so I assume you don't mind?'

'Good lord no, not in the least; I've been smoking outside.'

'Well you might leave a window open tonight, and best not smoke if either of my parents are present, and if anything's said I'll blame you; as a guest you are afforded a certain latitude. Both of my parents used to smoke in their youth anyway, so they can't be so *'holier than thou'* about it.'

Pandora smiled again, and began to relax in the company of this young woman, whom on first meeting and first impression she liked very much. Victoria had had a less than exciting day at the gallery, little Henry was well and in good hands, as ever, and she welcomed the distraction of meeting the woman who would paint her father's portrait, and had painted a certain other picture, of course.

'So, you intend to start work on my father tomorrow, then.'

'As soon as his Lordship is ready....'

'Mother has been on at him to have this done for years, so it was fortuitous that we found you, or rather that Rose found you.'

Their gazes turned automatically to the canvass that hung on the wall.

'I don't suppose it's often that you get commissions of that nature.'

'No, it isn't...'

'She took us all by surprise with that one; caused quite a rumpus, as you might say, but it's a beautiful painting. The dying rose was a nice touch.'

'Thank you, although I had no idea, of course...Anyway I very much enjoyed painting her. Forgive me, but you have a son, do you not?'

'Little Henry; why, would you like to paint him?'

'I paint people of all ages, and I would very much like to paint your portrait, actually.'

'I doubt whether my face would add very much to the aesthetic of the place.'

'I think you're wrong there, if you will forgive me for saying so.'

'Well, get Papa out of the way first; you never know, you might end up doing the whole family. There'd be a certain significance to painting my brother's son as an infant, I suppose; the next little Lord in waiting....He could hang next to his mother, although that might be somewhat macabre, thinking about it.'

'It's a strange thing that I've not met your brother; Rose was quite insistent that nobody should see the painting during its' making.'

'Yes, I'm sure, and one can see why; Michael was as surprised as any of us; we were together when the painting was delivered.'

'I see...Well, perhaps I'll meet him soon.'

'I'm certain that you will; I know he wants to meet you, anyway.'

So here was an opportunity for Pandora to learn more about Rose's family, and the family of the man that she would next paint, and Victoria stayed for over two hours and a second cup of tea whilst she answered questions regarding herself and her immediate relatives, and imparted such information as she could of the history of the Tillington dynasty. It was just before midnight when she made her departure, and Pandora took a second shower before retiring for the night. Portraiture was a particular type of painting; Pandora would lose herself in her work, and could paint for two or three hours at a sitting, but so much depended on the availability and patience of her subject. Tomorrow she would take photographs of his Lordship, so that she could continue work in his absence, and there was always the background to work on, but she would require his presence for quite long periods of time, and how long she would have him for she would learn tomorrow. She fell asleep thinking not of him but of his daughter; Victoria had a sad face, in a way, despite their spending a pleasant and sometimes jocular evening together. She had lived a privileged life, of course, but that was equally of course no guarantee of happiness, and Victoria carried with her the essence of a still young life which had not always been easy. In truth she had learned little of the family when she had been painting Rose's portrait, but she knew that Victoria had once tried to take her own life, and had very nearly succeeded, and having met her Pandora could see how that could have been. She also knew that the love of Victoria's life was a woman, and that there was nobody but her who had met the father of her child, whoever he was. So yes, she would like to paint her, and found herself hoping that she would in any case see more of her during the coming days.

Meadow arrived home to a full and busy bus. Rosie was preparing vegetable curry, which had become her speciality within the close culinary circle of the family, Keith was drinking tea and reading a newspaper, and Basil and Emma were playing a computer game together on Emma's lap – top. She had been fairly certain that any hope of reading Tara's email lay later in the evening, and her assumption was now confirmed.

'Hi everyone...'

Which received varied responses; Meadow poured herself herbal tea, having placed the unidentified package on the dining table.

'Anyone care to take responsibility for this?'

And it was Basil who answered.

'Oh, cool; that would be me, in fact...'

He got up from the floor of the lounge area, took the package and began to remove its' outer cover. Inside were several compact discs; Meadow had come to the conclusion that it was probably compact discs, that which had cast any doubt on the matter being the size of the package, which was bigger than it ought to have been. Basil took out one CD and gave it his mother.

'What do you think, oh maternal one; seriously cool cover, wouldn't you say?'

In quite small lettering to the top of the cover was written 'Tara', and somewhere near the bottom in similar lettering was written 'All That I Will Ever Be.' The background image was of a crowded street, most of the people, who were walking in both directions, were in quite soft focus, the sharpest image being that of her daughter, who was roughly central to the picture, walking with her hands in her coat pockets, and glancing slightly to one side; just a young woman walking down a street, but this was a particular young woman. By now Basil had distributed copies to everyone present, and it was Meadow who spoke first.

'Oh my...When was this released?'

'Three days ago; I've been waiting for it.'

'How many copies did you buy?'

'I forget now...'

'Basil....'

'Okay, I think it was about ten.'

'About ten...'

'Yeah, In fact now I come to think about it, it was exactly ten. I mean I thought you might want to, you know, give some to your friends, or whatever; I'll pay you back, when I've, you know left school and got a job, and such; a couple of years should do it. So how's the anger rating?'

'It's yet to be established.'

'I mean it's not every day your sister brings out an album, so I might have got a bit carried away, what with the emotional overload, but you should hear it; it's even better than the first album.'

'You've heard it?'

'I downloaded it; thought I'd better get some hard copies for those less technically proficient; anyway, CDs are better.'

Meadow took a moment to centre herself; of course this was not the first time that she had seen her eldest daughter on an album cover, but her own sudden emotional overload took her unawares, and for a moment she was quite lost for words. Basil, however, was not.

'Father; place the record upon the gramophone, and give it some decibels.'

Keith, who was also for a moment lost for anything to say, complied, and the bus was immediately filled with the musical introduction to 'A Song to Nobody', which was followed shortly afterwards by Tara's beautiful voice.

Keith and Meadow hugged one another, and then they both hugged Rosie; it was a moment of familial togetherness, and Meadow could no longer quite keep the tears from her eyes. Emma was studying the lyrics on the inside booklet, and it was left to Basil to continue his monologue.

'This is one of the quiet tracks; it gets quite heavy later, but I mean it's absolutely amazing, you know? Ash is definitely writing for her now, you can tell by the lyrics; this is pure Tara, and they're some of the best song lyrics I've ever heard; it's going to go large, you know; this is going to launch my sister in the big – league as a solo artist, only don't tell her I said so or we'll never hear the last of it.'

They played the album whilst they ate their curry, and then they played it through again, the entire early evening being dominated by the voice of the only absent family member. Eventually the children left for their respective rooms in the trailer, leaving Keith and Meadow to prepare the bus and themselves for the night. Meadow brought the lap – top to bed, and she and Keith read Tara's email together.

'Hi Mum, Dad, everyone, sorry I haven't been in touch lately but we've been sort of busy; if we're not performing or getting ready to perform then we're travelling or just doing band stuff, and I've done a couple of interviews for magazines and so on. I mean it's mostly about Ash and the band, but I'm drawing some attention as well, which is nice! I told you Tokyo was amazing, well everything since then has been fairly amazing as well. We're in Hong Kong now, so we're kind of dodging around this part of the far - east, so I'm getting to see something of the cities and so on between gigs; I can't tell you how much I love it out here, and am kind of keeping a mental list of places that I'd like to come back to and spend more time in, which is actually just about everywhere I've been so far. Anyway the really amazing thing is that I'm singing some of 'my' songs, usually two or three every gig, it all seems a bit random really but I think Ash knows what he's doing, and we're sort of trying the songs out, and trying me out, of course, and so far I think I'm doing okay. I can't describe the feeling of standing front of stage and singing to thousands of people; it's absolutely terrifying and

completely thrilling at the same time, but I think it's getting a bit less terrifying every time! When I think of how the songs started; just me and Ash in the church with a guitar, and now there's this; the sound that the band makes in these huge auditoriums is just incredible. Anyway the band are great, and even Ash and Al are managing not to argue most of the time, and everyone, especially Samantha and Aiko are being totally supportive. With Ash's sister, Evie, there are four of us girls here, and we've got together a couple of times for a bit of female solidarity, or just to chat, really, which has been great. Otherwise practically everyone else is male, like the road crew and so on. Ash is keeping his eye on everybody, including me, and I really like Rick, the drummer, who's a real rough diamond but he's been a total gentleman to me. It's just such a thrill to be around these people; they're all such fantastic musicians, of course, but they're great people too, and I love them all. Anyway, I'm sorry, I know I'm gushing a bit but you know this is just such a totally new experience for me; I'm not sleeping much; late nights mostly so I'm becoming a bit of a night – owl and sleeping in a bit; living on nervous energy, mostly. Nobody's drinking much; there's a bit of weed about, somehow, but otherwise everyone's staying sober; it's all about the music these days, which isn't how it used to be I think. Anyway that's me; there's so much to say but I'll tell you all about it sometime. Oh and by the way I think the new album's being released about now, so tell Bas to look out for that, and tell him I haven't forgotten about the O2 tickets. London seems like a long way away right now, and every day's a new adventure, but anyway love to you all, and I'll be in touch again from Cloud – Nine sometime soon. Tara xxx'

Meadow, who had just wiped another tear from her eye, was the first to speak.

'Oh Keith; this is just so fantastic, isn't it?'

'Yeah; who'd have thought it...Our Tara a famous rock musician; what can you say?'

'I don't know, but I'm so proud of her.'

'Me too, as it happens...'

'And the new album, you know...'

'Sure; I don't think it will be the last one either, do you? I mean even if this is the final farewell tour for DMW, Tara won't stop now.'

'Ash'll see to that, apart from anything else.'

'So the band might stay together for Tara. I mean the music world's a strange and unpredictable beast, so you never know, but Ash seems to go on forever, and as long as Ash is around Tara will be fine. Ash is something else, really; I mean you meet the guy and he doesn't look like he could boil an egg, but he's all there when it comes down to it.'

'Funny, I know someone else like that.'

'Actually I'm rubbish at boiling eggs.'

'Me too; I can never get them right.'

'Yeah; tricky things, boiled eggs...How did we get onto boiled eggs, anyway?'

'I think it was you who first raised the matter.'

'Was it...? I must have missed that part of the conversation.'

'I rest my case.'

'What case?'

'Never mind, my love...Anyway I'm sleepy now.'

'I think I'll just read through the song lyrics; pass the CD will you?'

'You'll be word – perfect by the morning, won't you?'

'Probably...Good song titles anyway...'Hell Can Wait'...'Dreams of Winter'...Not sure about 'Turn Me Over', though; what's that all about?'

'Weren't you listening?'

'Yes...I'm just not sure it's the sort of thing my daughter should be singing about, that's all; not when there're other people around.'

Which made Meadow laugh.

'Don't read that one then; she's a big girl now, you know. Anyway enough; stop making me laugh, I need sleep; try not to fall asleep with the light on.'

'Okay...Good night.'

'Good night Keith.'

'Listen, I was just wondering...'

'What...?

'I don't suppose a demonstration would be in order.'

'What sort of demonstration?'

'The song lyrics, you know, just so there's no misunderstanding on my part...'

'No...Not now anyway; I told you, I'm sleepy.'

'Some other time then..?'

'I'll think about it, okay?'

'Fair enough...Good night then'

'I love you Keith, you idiot.'

'I love you too, which means I can't be that much of an idiot.'

'Got me there, big man...'

Chapter 8

A DAY FOR THE ANGELS

Time was the great healer, or so she had heard it said, and now for the first time in her young life Isabella Baxter hoped that it was true. The days passed; she went to school, or sometimes to the library in the town, but spent more of her weekend days and evenings at home now, shut in her bedroom listening to music through headphones whilst reading, or playing her anonymous games of chess with anonymous people via an international on – line chess club. 'Coquette' her on – line name attracted certain attention from the mostly male players, and some tried to engage her in written and sometimes suggestive conversation during the games, but she did not respond, not anymore; she was there to play chess, that was all, and to further hone her already considerable skills at this most ancient and complex of games. Isabella was a particular type of person, who was on the whole and at least academically far more intelligent than her peers, and in truth she did not make friends easily, often finding the company of other girls of her age rather silly and boorish. She saw them become overly excited or upset at the beginning or end of relationships with mostly slightly older men, which she saw little point in, and little reason for that which she considered such emotional excesses; sex was necessary to fulfil her young desires, but beyond that she did not see what all the fuss was about, and so she had little or none of the peer – group support that others might have had in her particular situation.

Even she no longer went to her chess club; there were too many associations, not with the club itself but with playing chess over the board. In any case she would have to go there alone;

her father seldom went during the winter months, suffering rather as did with his health in colder temperatures, and she was less inclined now to venture out alone after dark. Her ambition, to be the highest ranking player at the club, which she had almost achieved, seemed to her now like a pointless and empty ambition. Richard Templeton had been the only player to outrank her, and in truth she had no wish for victory over him, who had been nothing but a friend to her. She had beaten Barnabas Overton, when she had been Agnes Appleby, and that had been perhaps her greatest victory of all, though the game itself had in truth been drawn, but even that seemed now like a hollow victory. Once she had used her young sexuality to seduce and then do harm to men whom she met, who had done her no harm; Malcolm Freeman, when she had been Ingrid with half German parentage, and Larry Chapman, whose name had been written on the mirror, and that had all been about Jed, who had left her without saying goodbye, but she was different, now. When she had first made incognito contact with Barnabas Overton she had been Mirabelle, and had been fourteen years old, and for Paul Stewart she had been Alexa; she had been many different people, but now once again and forever she would be Isabella Baxter, and she had been made different by one night in Dusseldorf, of which she had no memory; she had been unconscious when her life had been changed.

Her intellectual self could rationalise; they had been men, and men will take women against their will, as they always had done, and in the end it was nothing personal; they had not abused her for any reason other than that she was a woman. They had turned her into so much flesh; blind, unthinking and unconscious flesh, and with that flesh, her flesh, they had done what they wished. Barnabas Overton, Neil Finley, Ed Fullerton and Paul Stewart; they must have known Larry Chapman; *Larry says hello'* had been written in her lipstick where she was bound to see it when she woke up, so perhaps it had also been about revenge, and she had not been nice to Larry. So at some moments and on some days her intellect would be in the ascendancy, and on such days she felt better, but on other days her emotions would win the internal and seemingly endless battle which raged within her, and she would become lost again, and it would become personal again, and these were still bad days.

So perhaps then it was just a matter of time; perhaps one day these two parts of her would meet in final confrontation, and there would be resolution between them. Perhaps time would indeed heal, if time was indeed such a great healer, as she had been told. In the event, however, and in a way, help would come from somewhere and from someone from whom she would least have expected it.

'T'was on the bridge at midnight, his knees were all a – quiver; he gave a cough, his leg fell off, and floated down the river.'

The scene is the mess – room of the local Borough Council Parks Department, which is located within the small Municipal Park closest to the town centre, which for reasons that nobody anymore knew is called 'St Agnes Park' or mostly *'St Ag's'* by its' local residents. Other such rooms existed in other parks within the councils' jurisdiction, and at the Municipal glasshouses and outdoor plant nursery, but this was the place where Barrington Thomas most often took his packed luncheon, and this was the park which of all of them was his favorite in which to work. His co – workers would vary from day to day, or week to week, depending upon the work required to upkeep the parks and recreation facilities around the town, and today on this Friday lunchtime and aside from Barrington there were six people present. There was Jake, who was near retirement age and had worked for the Borough Council all of his working life, and here also was Mat, whom Barrington supposed was in his fourth decade, and who drove the tractor – mounted grass – cutter during the spring and summer months; Phil the lorry driver was here, who drove the only lorry owned and operated by the Council, and which was most often used to transport garden refuse and cuttings to the Municipal refuse tip and so on. Here also was Mario, whose father had been an Italian prisoner of war during the second world - war and had not returned to Italy after the war was over, Farah, who was undertaking a compulsory years' work experience within the industry before attending Horticultural College, and Roy, who was currently speaking. Roy was a particular sub – species of human being, who carried within himself a seemingly endless tirade of strange sayings, jokes, anecdotes and so on, which he delighted in daily sharing with his fellow workers. Roy had names for everyone, which tended to come into common parlance within the workforce. Mario, for example, was 'El Gringo' which had in fact nothing to do with Italians, but a certain license was apparently permitted, and nobody seemed to mind or notice, and Farah was affectionately known as 'the nymph', on account of her pretty face and slightness of stature. Barrington in this context was 'the Bishop', having once let it be known that he had a degree in Theology. Such names were most often used when referring to the individual in the third – person, and to his face Barrington was most often 'Barry', Barrington apparently being rather long – winded for the purposes of general conversation.

'So, Barry, what are you up to this weekend; teaching the Epistles to the apostles, are we?'

'Actually my youngest sister May's coming to stay.'

'The boy stood on the burning deck, his feet were covered in blisters; he had no trousers to put on, and so he wore his sisters'. So what does your sister do then, when she's not being the fifth month of the year?'

'She works in the film industry.'

'Nice one; rub shoulders with the rich and famous, does she?'

'I think she meets some quite famous people sometimes, yes, although she's not really in the big league; it's a small independent company; most of what they do isn't mainstream.'

'She a good Christian, like you..?'

'I'm not a good Christian; in fact I'm not a Christian at all.'

'What...? I thought you were a qualified God – botherer.'

'That may be so, but I haven't bothered God for long time now.'

'So what's with the degree, then?'

'That was then, this is now; the degree was a mistake, except in the academic sense; I was set to be a priest, once, so career – wise I'm starting again, you might say.'

This caught the general attention of all present. Barrington had always hitherto been reticent with his co – workers regarding the subject of his former vocation, and the last years of his life. There had been some collective speculation regarding the matter, but the most recent newcomer amongst them had not been questioned directly before, and was fairly sure that he could not keep his life a mystery indefinitely, and anyway, why should he not tell them? A short silence had followed his last statement, and the next person to speak was Phil, the lorry driver.

'You were going to be a priest...Jesus Christ, if you'll excuse the expression. So you were going to be *'Father Barrington'* then.'

'Eventually...'

'So that would be a Catholic priest, would it?

'It would, or would have been...'

'Man that was a lucky escape...They aren't allowed to have sex, are they, except with the altar - boy; that seems to be generally accepted. So what happened; you lose your faith or whatever?'

'Yes, I suppose you could say that.'

'Or maybe you just didn't fancy the altar – boy, right?'

'Phil, for fuck's sake.' said Mat, the tractor driver.

'Sorry man, that was out of order; so is that what you've been doing 'til now then, being a priest and shit?'

'Actually, no, I never made the priesthood, in fact I never started it; before this I was in a monastery for three years.'

Another brief moment of silence followed whilst this intelligence was absorbed by the assembly, and it was Mat who continued the enquiry.

'So you were like; *'Brother Barrington'* then?

'Yes; that was me; semi – closed order, the whole thing.'

'So, I mean what the fuck happened?'

'I had to test my faith to the limit, and I failed the test, you might say.'

'Jesus...So you had to wear a habit; the whole works?'

'The whole works...'

'The abstinence from sex deal would put me off being a priest...'

'You wouldn't last a week.' Said Phil

'I mean it's not natural, is it?'

'No, it isn't.' said Barrington

'There's like, no sex in a monastery either though, right; at least not officially.'

'That's correct, officially or otherwise, actually.'

'So now you're making up for lost time, as it were; is there a lady in your life?'

'Phil; leave the man alone,' said Mat 'and don't forget there's already a lady present, or a nymph anyway. Anyway it's time we were back to work.'

Grass cutting season was not now far away, and Mat would thus soon be back on his tractor, something to which he looked forward; Mat loved his tractor above almost all else, and would at times wax lyrical about the warm wind in his hair and the smell of the new – mown grass. For now, however, he would walk to his place of work with the others. Everyone stood up, Jake, who was a man of few words, rinsed out the tea cups in the sink, and all returned to the final session of their paid employment before the weekend, for which they had just been paid, it being Friday. Barrington returned to the preparation for the spring season of an herbaceous border, feeling pleased that the others now knew something at least of his recent past. He had not so far mentioned anything of his short time in Thailand which had seen him become a heroin addict, and thought better to keep that part of his recent history to himself, at least for now. Doubtless this would in any case not be the end of the matter of his once having been a monk; he would he was sure be the butt of occasional jocular banter, and word would spread quickly throughout the workforce, which was during the working day a close – knit community, of which Barrington was in fact glad to be a part. And so he was pleased, and glad also that he would be seeing May this evening; he had not seen his sister for several weeks, and indeed had hardly spoken to her during that time.

The young woman sat on a bench by the main road, which overlooked the village Green. She had driven past the village often enough, but had never stopped here before, and she took a few moments on this cool mid – afternoon to admire its' historical charm. She was feeling rather nervous and apprehensive, and in truth somewhat stupid, but she must allow these feelings to be overcome by her determination to see this through, if she could; she had given the matter much consideration over the past few days and weeks, and had talked the matter over with Shirley, and they could think of no better way, and better she come alone. And she knew well enough that it may not work; there were so many variables and uncertainties, and if she was unsuccessful then she would simply walk away, and try to think of another way in which she could save her marriage. She had been here a little over half an hour when she saw the bus approaching; so, this was the moment then, and she must gather herself for possible confrontation, or more likely disappointment.

May arrived in the mid – evening. She had flown in from Vienna during the afternoon, having been involved in some shooting for a low – budget but tastefully written and produced film about an English couple who met in a Viennese café, the remainder of the film being set in London. She had called in briefly at her rented apartment in town, to shower and pick up some clothes before catching the train to Queenswood Station, and a weekend with her brother in that which she regarded as her country retreat from the city, and from her busy working life. Barrington had prepared an evening meal of pasta, salad and bread, which he had baked himself, and had just opened a bottle of red wine when his door knocker sounded, after which the door opened; May had her own key, but had knocked anyway out of politeness.

'Hi Batty; how goes dinner, I'm starving.'

The whirlwind had returned, and Barrington was glad to be caught in her unpredictable turbulence.

'Ready, actually...'

'Good, let's eat; I'm glad we're eating in; I'm bushed.'

'I thought we could eat out tomorrow.'

'I'm good with that.'

'Still busy, then..?

'You might say...Tomorrow will be my first day off for about three weeks; I need to sleep, and de - tox, actually; too much coke, you know; need to clean up my act a bit; that wine looks good though.'

Barrington made final preparations for the evening repast, and both sat at the dining table, and glasses were raised.

'Well; here's to your restful weekend; it's good to see you, Maisy.'

'You too; so, how's your life been since we last spoke?'

The school bus pulled to a stop, and students of all ages alighted. Most went to the front of the bus and crossed the road, walking toward the housing estate; only four of them walked in a different direction. There were a group of two very attractive girls and one quite tall and handsome young man, who she guessed would be upper or lower sixth – formers; Basil, Emma and Rosemary would often travel home together, but she was sure that the girl for whom she waited was not amongst them. So perhaps she was not on the bus, then, but as this thought and a feeling of something like relief passed through the woman's mind, another older, very slim girl stepped onto the pavement, and she walked in the right direction across the Green. So perhaps this was her, after all; she had little to go on other than a name, an address and a vague physical description, but it as likely her. So, what to do; she could still walk away, and almost she said nothing, but then she steeled herself and stood up, as the girl was walking quickly away from her. The girl was on her own, at least, and for that she was grateful.

'Excuse me…Is your name Isabella?'

The girl turned around and looked at the woman. She said nothing, but she had no need to; the look on her face told the woman that she had found her.

'Look, I'm sorry to trouble you; you don't know me but my name is Rachel; Rachel Overton.'

Rachel Overton; for a moment the name meant nothing to Isabella, but then she realized; her Christian name was not important, but the surname was the thing.

Still the girl said nothing, but she had stopped walking away, and in fact had taken a few slow steps back toward her, until only a few paces separated them. The girl was looking at her as though she were some strange and exotic beast, and one which might be dangerous.

'I suppose the first thing I should say is that I come in peace…Since I, that is we, received your letter, well, quite a lot has happened, actually, but the thing is, I was wondering whether you would be prepared to meet sometime, to talk about it, you know…That is to talk about the terrible thing that happened to you.'

Still no words; she was clearly searching for something to say; the beast had lost none of its' strangeness, but was perhaps not so dangerous after all.

'So, I mean I know this must be terribly difficult, and I understand that we can't talk now, and that you might need some time to consider, so…Well, let's say that I'll be in Dawson's Coffee Shop tomorrow, at say twelve noon, if that would be a convenient time for you. You know Dawson's I suppose?'

The girl nodded, once, which was her first significant communication.

'Well then, I'll be there, just me, at twelve, and if you would like we can just talk about it, you know? We just want to help, if we can, that's all.'

Rachel had read somewhere a long time ago that ninety percent of communication between people was non – verbal; human beings had a learned and innate ability to read the slightest and most subtle change in the expression and demeanor of others of their species, even those whom they had never met before, and if this were true, and if she was reading this young woman right, then she had said enough. In any case she wished this confrontation to end as soon as may be.

'So; until tomorrow then; I hope you come.'

She turned and walked away; it was done, and there was nothing more to be said. In truth she had not known what to expect; a hail of abuse, perhaps, or unjustified condemnation that she could be married to such a man, or tears of self – pity, but she had seen none of these things; just a look of enquiry, and understandable uncertainty at what would have been a most unexpected encounter. She would go to town tomorrow, which was Saturday, and she would go to the Coffee Shop, with no real sense of whether Isabella Baxter would be there to meet her.

Isabella walked the remainder of the short distance home, bad thoughts racing quickly through her mind; how dare this woman disturb the ashes of her hatred and disgust, just as she had begun to put out their fire. What did she want, anyway, and how could she possibly help? Why the hell would she want to meet the wife of one of them; they who above all of her hatred she hated the most?

But still, by the time she had reached her front door, something else had begun to stir deep within her; perhaps, just perhaps, if she could walk one more time through the fire, she could reach a place where she so longed to be; a place where lay resolution and a peaceful spirit, and just perhaps this meeting and this woman could be a first step on that difficult journey. So, would she go or would she not go; that question was something which would plague her throughout the evening which followed, and which she took with her to bed, and which haunted her half waking state during the night. It was something about which Isabella would change her mind several times before the sun had set and risen again on her troubled young world.

Brother and sister spoke of their working lives whilst eating their spaghetti, and in this matter as with so much about them, Barrington could not help but mark the contrast between them. Her life in this regard was concerned with meeting urgent deadlines and tightly controlled budgets, and dealing with the vagaries of actors, directors, film locations and so on; in the final analysis hers was all about people; his was about trimming hedges or planting out winter or spring bedding plants, and apart from lunch and tea – breaks he would often speak to nobody during the course of his working day. Depending upon the month of the year, Barrington was three or four years his sisters' senior, but at times it felt to him as though they could as well be separated by three or four decades. He had dedicated his early and youthful years to God; she had devoted hers to decadent self – indulgence and living life to the limit, although her innate intellect and intelligence had always seen to it that she pulled out just in time to avoid disaster, and academically she had always fared better than their sister, Erica, which in truth did nothing to endear her to her elder sibling. During the conversation she told him about her work colleagues, and he described some of his to her;

'They're an eclectic bunch, on the whole; horticulture seems to attract its' fair share of eccentrics.'

'Yes, I'm sure. So you're still enjoying the work then?'

'I love it, actually. I mean the wages aren't exactly high and career opportunities are kind of limited, but I'm doing a couple of day – release courses in propagation, plant nomenclature and so on, which is a start, I suppose.'

'Of course it is, and enjoying your work is really important, you know. Remember what you were like after Thailand, and even when you first moved here; compared to that this is good, and so are you. I don't think I've ever seen you this contented.'

'I told some of them today that I'd been a monk, and that once upon a time I was going to be a priest.'

'How did that go down?'

'Well they were surprised, to say the least, and I haven't heard the last of it, but I'm glad I told them.'

'Did you tell them about Thailand?'

'No, not yet, and maybe I won't.'

'It's all a part of it, Batty; how you came to be as you are. So do they know about Miranda?'

'No, not that, either...The reason that it all went wrong...'

'She wasn't the reason, Bats; she was the catalyst, and it didn't go wrong; she was probably the person who rescued your life, in the end, and you know it. So how's it going these days in the Miranda Spool department, anyway?'

'We still see each other, you know?'

'Yes well of course you do, I'd taken that as read, but have there been any recent developments in your relationship?'

'In what sense..?'

'Well I mean, what goes on between you at the moment; how often do you see her?'

'About every week, sometimes twice a week, but mostly it's weekends, and it's not every weekend. I'm not seeing her this weekend for example.'

'And are you happy with that arrangement; I mean generally speaking?'

'As far as it goes, yes...'

'And is she happy with it?'

'I suppose so.'

'Haven't you asked her?'

'Not really; not directly, as you might say...The thing is, I've decided that, well, I have to get my life in better shape before I; well before I take things any further with her.'

'You've decided that, have you, so does she get any say in the matter?'

'What do you mean?'

'I would have thought it was bloody obvious what I mean; so you're sort of parking her to one side, is that it, until you feel ready to take on the commitment?'

'I have to feel sure of myself. I mean I have to feel deserving of her.'

'Oh that's complete crap, Batty.'

'Again; what do you mean?'

'Do you love her?'

'Well yes, of course.'

'How do you know...I mean do you miss her between your occasional meetings?'

'Yes, absolutely...'

'And does she love you, too?'

'Yes, I think so...'

'Have you asked her; I mean do you tell each other that you love each other?'

'Sometimes, I suppose.'

'It's not something that you can suppose; do you or don't you?'

'This is sort of personal, Maisy...'

'Fuck off, I'm your sister; answer the question.'

'She's...Well, we're not that demonstrative, really; I mean sometimes, in the heat of the moment, as it were.'

'So you have heated moments; well that's something, I suppose, but I mean she walked out in front of you, naked, before she even knew you, so how much more demonstrative does a woman have to get?'

'That might have been an accident.'

'Oh that's such bullshit; it wasn't an accident, Batty.'

'Okay, so maybe she just, you know, wanted sex or whatever.'

'Or whatever...Look, okay, so maybe you're both happy with the way things are, but if she really loves you she'll take you as you are, you know?'

'So you don't think she loves me, then?'

'Oh for Christ's sake that's not what I'm saying.'

'So what are you saying, then?'

'It's you that's holding back, Batty; she's probably thinking that that's all she is to you; that you don't really care whether you see her or not; little sister comes for the weekend so, sorry, you know, see you next time.'

'I thought we should have some time together; you're important to me, Maisy.'

'Sure, and I expect she knows that, and she's therefore probably wondering why you don't want us to meet.'

'That isn't it; I mean I'd like you to meet, of course.'

'So 'phone her then; let's all go out together tomorrow night. She sleeps here sometimes, yes?'

'Yes, we sleep together, of course.'

'Well then invite her for the weekend, or tomorrow night or whatever.'

'She might have other plans.'

'Yes she might, but you don't know, which is my point, really; you should know this kind of thing about each other. I mean I understand that you were deeply traumatized by all that happened before, and weren't ready for commitment, or whatever, but that's over now; you're here and you're settled, living in this beautiful house, and now you have a job, so you can even just about afford it, so it's time to take things on to the next stage of your life, don't you think? I'm not saying that you should propose marriage or anything, but you know, relax into it and stop analyzing it, and trying to work out how much of her you are prepared to give, or how much you think she deserves. If she loves you then you being you will be enough, and there's nothing wrong with you anyway; you've got your degree, so she knows you're not stupid, and you've led an interesting life so far; more interesting than most people, so stop looking at the whole monk thing in such a negative light; stop being ashamed of it. How many women can say that their man – friend used to be a monk? It must have broken the ice during a few conversations. Have you met any of her friends?'

'No, not…No…'

'Well there's somewhere to start then; tell her you'd like to meet them sometime; invite her over mid – week, that kind of thing; just be a bit more spontaneous about things; call 'round when she's not expecting you on a Tuesday evening or something. I mean you've known each other quite a long time now so you can't do it all at once, she'll think you've had a brain transplant, but try to change things slowly. Or better, sit her down with a bottle of wine one night and just tell her how you feel, and why you feel it; tell her everything that happened to you, and why she was a part of all of that even before you were together. Keep your secrets from your work colleagues if you want, but you can't keep secrets from her, not forever; lay your soul out before her; don't be afraid to do that.'

He poured them more wine; in truth he never knew what to expect from May, but he hadn't really been expecting this.

'Well, I can't argue with any of that, I suppose.'

'Of course you can't; you know your silly little sister always knows best; go to it, brother; the worst that can happen is that she runs a mile, in which case she didn't love you or deserve you anyway, but she won't. You're better than you think you are, and always have been. You lived with guilt all of your young life, but that's over, now; now you're just like the rest of us, so engage with it all; life is shit, sometimes; we all get burned, but we all have to get through it and get on, you know, so be yourself, and learn to love yourself, and stop trying to protect yourself from harm, otherwise you'll never be able to love anybody else.'

They had eaten quickly and hungrily during this conversation, and now May took the plates to the kitchen, leaving her brother to his muse for a few moments whilst she organized a cheese plate and put the kettle on for coffee. When she returned with plates and cheese, her brother had a question for her.

'So what about you then, Maisy; when you talk about being burned do you talk from personal experience?'

'Well, you know me, Bats; never one to let the grass grow, you know?'

'Yes but seriously; has anybody ever really hurt you?'

'Hell no; not really, I mean I do okay, but when do I get time to have a serious relationship?'

'And does that bother you?'

'Not yet; maybe one day Mr Irresistible will walk into my life and change everything, but that hasn't happened so far; I am the mistress of the one – night stand, but that's all anyone ever gets.'

'Are you sure you're not just protecting yourself?'

'Touche, brother, but no; I've had some offers, you know, but I've never met my Miranda. It'll happen when it happens, you know, but so far I'm enjoying the party too much. You on the other hand have never enjoyed parties; we're different, but don't worry about me; worry about yourself, or rather stop worrying about yourself and do your own life to the full in your own way. No more guilt, okay?'

'Okay; no more guilt.'

'That's my boy.'

She yawned, and spoke through her yawn.

'Oh Christ… I'm sorry…, but I really am tired; I'm going to crash; make some coffee and take it to bed.'

'Of course; we'll eat the cheese for breakfast.'

'Good idea; well, goodnight Batty; we will continue this conversation tomorrow. Oh by the way, have you met Tara what's – her - name yet?'

'Not yet. I think she's on tour with DMW at the moment anyway.'

'So you haven't met Ashley Spears yet either?'

'Ditto; he's hardly ever here anyway, as far as I understand it.'

'This some village, isn't it; I mean not only do you have about the most famous meteorite on the planet, the place is awash with rock stars, and somehow word has got about that there's a witch living here as well.'

'Where the hell did you hear that?'

'I don't know; I can't remember. It's not true, is it?'

'Well I don't expect so, but you're right; one never knows with this place. By the way, Tara Knightman's second album has been released.'

'Have you got it?'

'Not yet.'

'Then we will buy it in town tomorrow; I need to get a few things anyway, and I need to check your wardrobe; make sure you don't need more shirts and such. If you're about to embark on your brave new life, you'll need the shirts...'

'Fine; whatever you say.'

'Right; and sorry about the lecture, by the way, but someone has to sort your life out.'

'I'll let you off; just don't ever stop lecturing me, okay.'

'T'was ever thus, was it not?'

'For as far back as I can remember; the difference is that I listen these days.'

'Well, god and our beloved parents aren't there any more, are they? Or our beloved sister for that matter; you heard much from Erica?'

'Just occasional 'phone calls, one way or the other; you..?'

'Nope...I think I'm permanently black – listed for leading our brother from the straight and narrow paths of righteousness.'

'One day I'll tell her, I expect...'

'Steady on; one can take this honesty thing too far, you know...'

She smiled, and Barrington returned her smile; she left for the kitchen, and thence to the narrow stairs to that which both regarded as her bedroom. Barrington stayed at the dining table and finished his wine; he had much to think about, and she had only been here for a couple of hours. She had as ever and in so short a time blown like a fresh breeze through his life, and she always brought with her the wind of change.

The scene now is Dawson's coffee emporium, and the time is twelve noon. Rachel sat at a table from which she could watch the door of the establishment, and as the first minutes of the afternoon ticked away, she began to think that after all she was not coming; that her hopes of some kind of resolution for all concerned were false hopes. By ten minutes past the hour she had all but given up; she would wait until twelve thirty, and then she would leave. It was then that Isabella entered the premises. She saw the woman, ordered her coffee from the counter, and came and sat at the table, facing her. She was dressed casually in jeans, sweater and jacket, and although there was still a certain nervousness about her demeanor and her movements, she looked Rachel in the eye as she sat down, her expression neutral; waiting, and Rachel had still not heard her speak. Rachel smiled, trying to convey friendship and a sense that she was pleased to see her, but the smile was not returned.

'I'm so glad you came.'

'I almost didn't. So, what do you want to say to me?'

She had a nice voice; it was a steady voice, and there was no anger there, at least. Any nervousness that she was feeling did not find its' way to her vocal expression; Rachel sensed, however, that the anger lay not very far below the surface.

'Well, first of all we are all sorry, of course, for what happened to you, although anything I say in that respect will be inadequate, I know that.'

'We....?'

'The four recipients of your letters; let's start there. None of us knew each other before, but we do now.'

'How did you find me?'

'Through the hotel register in Germany for your name, then the chess club for your address. We've known where you live for some time.'

'So why have you waited until now?'

'We all had our own problems to address, to be honest, and well, as you can probably imagine I haven't exactly been looking forward to our meeting; but anyway, you should know that your letters hit the mark, as one might say.'

'What do you mean...?'

'Two of the relationships have ended, as a matter of fact.'

'Which two..?'

So far it was only questions, as Rachel had expected, as much as she had been expecting anything; short, urgent enquiries, the last being the most urgent of all; her attention now was absolute, as if she were studying a difficult chess position. Whatever else she might be, here was an intelligent young woman, who Rachel was certain would make a formidable opponent over the chess board, not that she had ever played chess. And of course she would want to know the damage that her letters had caused, and Rachel supposed that there was no harm in telling her.

'Ed...Ed Fullerton and Margaret, and Paul Stewart and Patricia; all going through messy divorces, now, thanks to what happened. Ed and Margaret have no children, and Paul and Patricia are fighting over custody of Dawn and David.'

'So did they all admit what they'd done?'

'Yes, some more easily than others, and it took us all a while to make contact with one another, the women, that is, and since then certain of us have met several times, to you know, to discuss the situation, and what to do.'

'So which one of them raped me..?'

Rachel tried once again to put herself in the position of this young woman. Even now details of the night were not complete; it had always been a difficult thing for the four women to talk about, but eventually Barnabas had admitted that it had been he and Neil who had raped her; the others had abused her in other ways, and of course she would want to know who; the question would have burned inside her for a long time, ever since the night in Dusseldorf.

'Listen, before I say any more, I want to be clear that whatever happens from now on, this is not to become a police matter; that much at least we have all agreed upon. Whatever I tell you I tell you in confidence, and with the understanding that nobody will admit to anything in a court of law; everyone will deny everything, and you won't in any case be able to prove that anything at all happened. I'm not here to seek justice for you in the conventional sense; is that quite clear, and will you accept that?'

Silence now for a moment while Isabella considered this. Rachel noted that she had become more nervous now, and her hand shook as she raised her cup, but eventually;

'Okay…Okay, I won't go to the police.'

'You understand that we at least have to protect them from prosecution; enough damage has been done, and we had to give them that assurance in order to get to the truth, so there can be no discussion on this.'

'Fine; I don't want to go to the police anyway; I didn't at the time, because I knew how hard that would be.'

This was the first time that she had given any indication of how she felt; so much had been spoken about Isabella Baxter, and until now none of the four women had any idea of her. For any woman to have been so abused was never acceptable, but it would be easier for Rachel if she liked this girl, and she found that despite everything, she did begin to like her, on first impressions at least. So much harm had been done; the lives of everyone involved had been torn apart, and it would be an easy thing to try to somehow blame Isabella for that; Isabella, the writer of the letters from whence this had all begun for the four women involved, and Rachel had to keep in mind at all times that here sat the victim and not the perpetrator, and this would be easier if she could like her.

'None of us understand how this came to happen; nothing like it has ever happened with any of the men so far as we know, and well, we thought that we knew them, you know?'

No tears, Rachel; there had been enough tears, and this was not the time. She was here to make contact, that was all, and to establish relations with this girl, if she could, before anything further could be done. So; focus, then; this was not the time for introspection, or for wishing for the ten thousandth time that none of this had ever happened.

'So, I mean how have you been, anyway, since the attack?'

'Fucked up; what do you think?'

'I know; stupid question, but I had to ask, and there's no other way of asking, is there...'

'Yes, well I kind of lost it for a while afterwards...'

'You must have been thinking rationally at some point; you were rational enough to find out all of our addresses, and to write the letters; that was clever.'

'Well I got over being a gibbering idiot quite quickly, and I wasn't...I wasn't going to let them win completely, you know? Just walk away and pretend it didn't happen.'

'No, of course...So have you sought any professional help?'

'No...'

'Have you thought about doing so?'

'What, like rape counseling, that kind of thing?'

'Yes.'

'I can do this on my own, you know?'

'Yes, I'm sure; forgive me.'

'You've done nothing to be forgiven for, but if you've come here seeking my forgiveness for your husband, or whatever, forget it. He tried to...He followed me to my room, you know, before it all happened; said he wanted to play chess, but...Well anyway, he must have been thinking about it even then; this was well planned.'

'I know that; this hasn't been easy for any of us, you know, and this isn't easy for me.'

'Sure, I get that, but you came to find me, and now I want to know who raped me.'

'Very well; it was my husband, Barnabas, and Neil Finley.'

That was still a hard thing for Rachel to say, and it had never been harder than this to say it, and she must allow Isabella another moment to absorb this intelligence. Rachel had known so much for so long, and she must allow for the fact that this so significant information was being learned and taken in for the first time by Isabella, who must have been wondering and probably speculating ever since the night of the attack. That it had happened at all was bad enough, but not to know who would have made it all the harder; how could anyone come to terms with that?

'It's odd, then, that it was the other two who...Who you know, split up.'

'We all reacted in different ways, and to different degrees; even to have been party to such an attack is bad enough; it would find the cracks in any relationship.'

'Yeah, I suppose...So what about Neil Finley?'

'He...Well, Shirley, his wife, has been the most supportive of us, to me, that is, in coming to see you.'

'So what about her relationship..?'

'She is also...Well, she is also the most forgiving of her husband, it seems; they will stay together, I think, whatever happens from now on.'

'I see...So how did you react?'

'No better than anybody, but despite everything I still love my husband, which is partly the reason that I'm here. Mostly I, or rather we, at least to a greater or lesser extent, want to see how you are coping, but that isn't the only reason that I came.'

'So what are the other reasons?'

'I think we must all try to find resolution, somehow. I can tell you that there has been so much remorse. None of them came back from the trip to Germany the same, and none of us knew why until we found out what had happened. It was a moment or an evening of collective testosterone – driven madness, and I'm not prepared to give up my marriage until I've at least done my best to try to get things back to where they were before, not for the sake of one evening, but we're some way from that yet, and it may never happen.'

'You mean you might get divorced too, is that it?'

'Nothing is certain yet for any of us; I mean I could more easily have forgiven an affair, I think, or a single act carried out alone, but this was....Well, you know well enough what it was.'

'So what are you going to do then?'

'I'm not certain, yet, and so much depended on our meeting, but now I've met you I'm going to ask you to help me, of all things, which I understand is asking a lot, but well, it may be something which will help you as well, otherwise I wouldn't ask.'

'Help you how?'

It had come to this much sooner than Rachel had expected. All that she had hoped for from this second meeting was to open dialogue which may eventually lead to her main intent, but here was a direct young woman who was talking far more openly than she had perhaps anticipated, so she saw no reason to prevaricate either. She drew a deep breath; so here it was then, the moment which she had been working towards for these past several weeks, and she had not the least idea what the reaction would be to her proposition; anything from instant and absolute rejection to, well, to anything, really.

'I'm going to ask you whether you would be prepared to meet with my husband; with Barnabas, with me there, of course.'

That also took a moment, before;

'I see...So what's this then, some kind of psycho – babble, where victim meets perpetrator, everyone shakes hands and makes up and gets on with their lives as though nothing happened? So that he can salve his disgusting conscience and pretend that he's such a good guy, really, he just made a mistake; it was the other guys who put him up to it, and boys will be boys and all, and now he can put the whole nasty business behind him, and eventually he'll be able to convince himself that I was begging for it anyway; that kind of thing?'

So here was the anger then, and the insults, and this was hard for Rachel to hear, made so much harder by the fact that both were so absolutely understandable.

'I don't see it quite like that.'

'Well how do you *see it* then?'

'He's....I mean I really do understand how you feel...'

'Do you? Anything like this ever happen to you then...?'

'No, of course not...'

'And now you're going to tell me how sorry he is, and how much he wants to apologize to me, is that it?'

'Something like that, yes.'

'Well excuse me for saying so but fuck that; if you've never had this happen to you then you can't possibly understand how I'm feeling. I wonder how much he would want to see me and apologize if he hadn't been found out; if I'd just quietly disappeared and he'd never heard from me again; what do you think?'

'I...I don't know...'

'Of course you know...I met him again, did you know that; we played a game of chess.'

'Yes, I know....Apparently you disguised yourself very cleverly.'

'Well he wasn't in such a tearing rush to apologize then, in fact he couldn't get away from me quickly enough.'

'He was…That was the shock of seeing you, that's all; he didn't know how to react.'

'Well he did react; he ran away like the coward that he is, and now he hides behind you, hoping that you'll be able to make it alright again; that you and I will be able to bond and understand each other in such a female way, and that we'll find it in our female hearts to forgive him; well, that isn't going to happen; you can forgive him if you want and put your marriage back together. Do whatever you want, I don't care, but leave me out of it; I don't ever want to see him or think about him again.'

She was clever, and eloquent, and had maturity of thought and perception which Rachel thought was far beyond her young years; Rachel was twenty nine years old, and was no fool herself, but she was struggling against this so much younger woman, in no small part because from an objective perspective she absolutely agreed with everything that she was saying. But not everything here was objective; this was her husband who was being so eloquently torn apart; the man that she had fallen in love with and married, and with whom she had shared the last seven years of her life. There was no mitigation, but she knew well enough that the young woman who sat opposite her was no angel herself, and if there are straws to be clutched at, then she should try, at least.

'Do you remember Larry Chapman?'

'What's he got to do with anything?'

'He's a friend of my husbands', as it happens, and I know now what you did to him.'

'Yeah, I guessed that they knew each other; someone wrote *Larry says hello* on the bathroom mirror of the room that they attacked me in; did you know that?'

'No…No, I didn't know that.'

'No, well he must have forgotten to mention that small detail, and if you're trying to say that the two things are similar....'

'I'm not saying that.'

'Larry Chapman fucked me in his car, and I told his wife, which is a little different to drugging someone unconscious and raping them, don't you agree? He had choices which I wasn't given.'

'Yes, of course, forgive me.'

'Stop asking for my forgiveness...Look, I don't want any bad shit to happen to you, you know, but what you're asking me to do...To forgive him or any of them or even pretend to forgive them for what they put me through, well, it isn't going to happen. I'm not sure why you're here, really, for me or for you, but of it's for me then thanks, but no thanks, I've dealt with it so far, and it hasn't been easy; I don't trust anybody anymore, and I don't go out alone after dark, and all because of your husband and his friends, so, you know, that's my perspective, so don't ask me again.'

'Fine...I do understand; I was just hoping that for your sake, if you were to meet him and see that he's not the monster that you must think he is, then that might help you as well, in some way.'

'He's a rapist, and the worst possible kind of rapist, and sure, I expect he weeds the garden on Sundays or whatever, and brings you tea in bed in the mornings, but that doesn't change what he is, or what he did.'

'Well then; I suppose there's no point in discussing it any more, is there, but look, please at least think about it. I'll leave you my 'phone number, and please keep it; I'm not a rape apologist and I don't for a moment in any way condone what he and the others did, but if you think you could ever find it in your heart to allow him to tell you how sorry he really is, then, well, that's all I can say, really.'

She handed her a piece of paper on which she had written her contact details; her email address and telephone number. Isabella took it, and put it in her jacket pocket. She had not torn it to pieces, or screwed it up and thrown it back in her face, so that was something at least.

'So what about in the meantime; are you going to leave him or what?'

'I don't know yet; I'll have to think about everything again now, won't I?

'Yes, I suppose you will.'

'I have to hope that perhaps you will change your mind.'

'Jesus...I mean look, you're a nice woman, and I know this can't have been easy, and if he'd like stolen the stereo or punched me in the face or whatever then sure, big deal, I'd forgive and forget, but not this; I was violated in the worst possible ways, and I'm still hurting, so it's more than I can do. I'm not the guilty party, here, and I won't succumb to any kind of fucked – up emotional blackmail.'

'That was never my intention.'

'Sure, well anyway, I'll see you then.'

Isabella stood up to leave.

'I hope so, I really do, and not just for my sake, or for the sake of my marriage; I think...I think you are a very brave and intelligent young woman, for what it's worth.'

'Thank you, and you're okay yourself, so maybe in another life...'

'I haven't given up hope in this one yet, Isabella.'

A final parting smile, and this time it was returned, if somewhat wanly and reluctantly. Rachel watched her leave, and wondered whether her marriage was indeed leaving with her, or whether even now there was some other way.

Isaac Dawson also watched the young sister leave; there had been some heavy vibe laid down between the two sisters, but Isaac had kept a discreet distance, and could only wonder at the subject of their discussion. Isabella Baxter walked down the narrow, cobbled streets of the old town with wings on her heels. If the demons had followed her since her return from Germany, then this day had been a day for the angels.

Chapter 9

A BRAND NEW PHILOSOPHY

Paris, a place of iconic landmarks, churches and monuments, situated throughout a city which is in itself iconic. In common with other cities, the road system of the French capital is barely adequate to accommodate the volume of traffic which moves through and across its' bounds at the beginning and the end of each working day, and at such times the metro system also merely suffices. For those who live within her limits or commute here for their employment, therefore, the romantic repute of the city is perhaps less obvious, but for those with no need to be anywhere at any particular time, the city may still maintain its' aura of beauty and sophistication. Percival had been here before, more than once, and the first time had been with his mother when he had been ten years old. The early years of her sons' life had been hard years for Percival's mother, but she saved what little money she could, and once a year she would take him to the west - country, or to Scotland, so that she and especially he could at least once a year leave the confines of their small flat in Vauxhall, and once a year leave London behind, and breathe freer and better air. Then, when he was in his eleventh, year, she had once again cashed in her hard – earned savings and taken him to Paris, which had been his first trip abroad. Since then he had been back here twice, but he would never forget the first time, and the city had always since then held a special place in his affections. By now he had his favourite areas, and his favourite cafes, and it seemed to him fitting that he should come here now with Sally; that she should become a part of this place, as the place was a part of him.

By contrast, everything about the city was new to Sally, and their days were spent in a tireless quest for her to see, experience and photograph everything, as people are wont to do when in a new and hitherto unexplored place, and Percival was happy to be carried along the wake of her enthusiasm. The Louvre gallery, the Arc de Triomphe, the Eiffel Tower, the church of the Sacred Heart; The Sacre Coeur, which is where we now join them, on their third day in the city. They were staying in an inexpensive Parisian guesthouse quite near to the Seine, which served a basic but quite adequate breakfast, and they would take their lunch wherever they found themselves, and whenever they became hungry, which today was in Mont Martre, and today as usual it was she who became hungry first.

'This looks like a nice place; let's stop here.'

It was a café in which Percival had drunk coffee before; the last time he had been on his own, and this was better.

'Sure...'

The weather was overcast but mild, the worst of the winter having left the city to warmer times, until next year, so they took a table outside and ordered Croque Madame, a glass of wine and coffee, the latter arriving first at the table as requested. They were quiet for a moment; she looked at him and smiled.

'It's everything it's cracked up to be, isn't it?'

'I've always thought that the French had sophistication nailed, and this is still a great city.'

'Still...?'

'It was a city of philosophers once; now everyone's just trying to get by or get ahead like everywhere else, but the spirit's still here, don't you think?'

'Yes I do, and it's unlike you, my love, to wax so poetic.'

'They would have sat in places like this, drinking cheap wine and smoking French cigarettes, discussing the meaning of life, or perhaps the lack thereof; the golden age of existentialism. We live in more cynical and less thoughtful times.'

She smiled again.

'What are you smiling at?'

'Nothing, it's just that you're right, and what better place than this?'

'For what…?'

'For telling you something which I've been thinking for some time now…'

'Oh yes, what's that?'

'I'm thirty years old today; you won't have remembered, of course.'

'Damn; sorry…'

'It's okay, and that's not what I was going to tell you.'

'So what were you going to tell me?'

'That I'm going to change my life.'

It was akin to a kind of deep meditation. When Pandora was painting, the world outside her canvass and all external influences were forgotten, and if on occasion they could not be forgotten, then she knew well enough that she could not or should not paint. She tried always to be the consummate professional, and not to appear too 'precious' as she herself saw it, and she tried always to put herself in the right frame of mind before each sitting with a live and paying subject, but there had been occasions in the past when she had had to apologize, and send her subject or model away until the next time; if her head was not right, then the painting would not be right either. She had, particularly in the early days, torn up completed or nearly completed canvasses, which would have been quite acceptable to her client, because they were not acceptable to her; she had missed them, or got them wrong, and it had to start again. She saw herself as the conduit between her subject and the paint which she applied to her canvasses, each brush – stroke capturing a small part of their essence, until, countless thousands of brush – strokes later, the subject appeared before her in the most complete and accurate image that she was able to create. Moreover some people were easier to paint than others; some would change their state of being and therefore their expression of themselves from one session to the next, and so in a sense became moving targets, whilst others did so in the more obvious way by simply not keeping still during a sitting, and these things would have influence upon how she worked. The craft of her work was the accuracy of her paintwork and the mixing of colours, which she saw as most of that which she did; she was in a sense and in essence a copier, as were all of those who had come before her, and had created the images of the previous Lords whose images adorned the grand dining room of her current place of work. Her art, as she perceived it, was in that which happened beyond this; in the portraying of the image not just of the physical manifestation of her subject, but of their spirit, so that this might live on beyond the bounds of their mortal life.

It was also true that during the painting of a portrait, it was not merely the time spent painting which was important to the work, but the surrounding time spent away from the canvass; the background noise of her immediate life must be calm and relaxed, or a dysfunction would occur which was hard to overcome. During the period when she was working on a painting she avoided excess in any form, and kept her behavior within tightly controlled limits, the balancing factor here being that between commissions she would often seek out excess, perhaps of a sexual or social nature; she would become and remain drunk for perhaps a week, before becoming sober again prior to the next time she needed a steady hand, a clear head and a quiet spirit in order to pick up her brushes again.

In any case in most regards her current commission was an easy one. His Lordship had agreed without hesitation that the painting could be done in the second bedroom of the extension, and so here he would sit, and here she worked. He was an easy and patient subject, and learned quickly enough that there was little or no point in attempting to engage his painter in conversation whilst she was working; she either did not hear him or having heard him she did not respond, which amounted to the same thing. The room and the apartment in general were an ambient and easy environment in which to work, and at the end of a sitting it was an easy thing for her to put down her brushes, wash her hands or take a shower, and then step outside and roll a cigarette; there was no journey home to consider. She regarded herself as a fairly relaxed painter, however the emotional investment which she always put into her work saw to it that she came away from each sitting feeling tired, and sometimes exhausted, but she always recovered quickly. The sessions with Lord Michael would last anything between one and two hours, depending on his commitments or state of mind, and she might paint during his absence, working on the background, or making small adjustments to her days' work. Otherwise she might take a stroll around the Manor House grounds, having been granted permission to do so as she wished, or she might walk to the village for provision at the delicatessen. That which she did not do was to enter the rest of the great house, and if on occasion she spoke with Victoria or Michael, it was because they had come to see her. Since their first meeting, Victoria in particular would seek her out some evenings, once she had seen to little Henry and her own needs, and the two women would sit and smoke their final cigarette or cigarettes of the night together, and Pandora would show her subjects' daughter how the painting was developing. It was also now, however, that she met Michael Tillington, Victoria's brother, for the first time. Here had been Rose's husband, the man set to inherit a Lordship who had married a prostitute, and it seemed to Pandora to be in almost all regards an unlikely match. Her physical attractiveness was beyond question, and had she not come to know Rose she might have assumed that she had been looking to improve her lot and status in life, but there had been none of that about Rose, and their coming together continued to seem to Pandora to be an odd thing. Michael was a man of gentle and unassuming spirit, and he would be a hard person not to like, and Pandora had taken a liking to him immediately, but she could perhaps understand why Rose had taken her young self elsewhere in search of a certain fulfillment, and how therefore Percival had entered the arena of her romantic and sexual life. Nothing had ever been admitted to, of course, so it was only speculation on her part, but the way that she and Percival had been and had reacted with each other on the odd occasion that she had seen them together made her quite confident in her speculation. And then, on one particular morning when she had been walking in the grounds she had met with Abigail, nanny to the two children, and had met Nathaniel for the first time, the next little Lord in waiting, and there was something about the look of him which made her look at him twice. His skin tone was a shade darker than Caucasian, and even at such a young age she caught something in his look or expression which brought Percival to mind rather than Michael, which took her speculation off in a quite new but not unrelated direction. Victoria had not spoken of any father to her child, Henry, so she assumed that he was absent from her life, and in her wanderings about the Manor House grounds and their environs, Pandora wondered as to the certainty of the paternal parentage of either child to the children of Lord Michael. Lady Tillington she would see less often during her tenure at the Manor; aside from a polite but somewhat terse introduction she only saw her from a distance on occasion. Perhaps her attitude to such as Pandora was more typical of people of her status in society; Pandora was after all merely the person who had been engaged to paint her husbands' portrait, but things which had been said or implied by his Lordship made Pandora think that perhaps of all of them, her Ladyship was least able to accept the way that Rose had wished to be portrayed, and perhaps she in part blamed Pandora for the portrayal. It had been a secret painting, after all, and Pandora it was who had captured Rose in all of her radiant sexuality, and she had been for the duration of the painting the only other party to the secret. In any case, Pandora considered that here was an interesting not to say fascinating family, and she found herself increasingly enjoying her first intimate meeting with members of the English aristocracy.

Will and Emily were together in their kitchen when Lady made them aware that something unusual was happening. There were almost always noises from the smallholding, since goats were not always the quietest of creatures, but Lady's anyway acute sense of hearing was particularly well attuned to the sound of the kissing gate, which squeaked on its' hinges when opened; somebody was coming. This was in fact quite late on Wednesday morning; Will had worked with Keith, Mike and Damien over the weekend in order to progress the building of the stone wall, which was progressing well toward its' completion, and so all had agreed to take a days' rest from their collective labours, and Will was at home for the day. Emily had milked early and set her cheese for the day, and was now washing dishes from breakfast and from the evening before, and Will, who was sitting at the kitchen table, was the first to get to his feet to see what or rather who had caused Lady to growl quietly to herself whilst standing by the back door.

'Who's coming?'

'Christ; it's Rebecca.'

'Bloody hell, I wonder what she wants.'

Emily dried her hands and joined her beau by the door.

'I wonder…What do you call that thing that she's got on her back?'

'I think it's called a baby, William.'

'Yeah…No, not that; the thing she's carrying it in.'

'I think it's a *'she'* baby.'

'Okay, so what's she carrying she in?'

'I think it's called a papoose or something; why?'

'I couldn't think what they were called.'

'And that thing on the end of a rope that's walking beside her is called a puppy; a German Shepherd puppy to be precise.'

'What the fuck's she got a puppy for; she hasn't looked after Lady for months.'

'I don't know…Maybe she's forgotten that she already has a dog. She's called Florence by the way, just so you know.'

'Who; the puppy..?'

'No, dear heart; the thing in the papoose…'

'Got it…Well I suppose we should open the door, then.'

'I suppose so…I'd better go and change, don't you think; put a clean T shirt on.'

'You look fine.'

'I haven't even put a bra on yet; I feel indecent.'

'That's what I mean; you look fine; not that I would have noticed if you hadn't said anything.'

'You lie very badly; I've told you that before.'

'Fair enough, and just say that again, will you?'

'What?'

'What you just said.'

'What, about you lying very badly?'

'No, what you said before that about not h...'

'William shut up; hold the fort for a minute.'

'Okay; I suppose it's not every day a homicidal witch comes to the door; better look one's best.'

Emily went to the bedroom; Will opened the door just as Rebecca was approaching. Lady was the first to greet the new arrival with customary enthusiasm, and she and the puppy, which looked to be only a few weeks old, also greeted one another as dogs will do. The puppy rolled onto its' back to indicate submission, and Lady indicated her acceptance of its' acknowledgment of her dominance, and all was well.

'Hi, Will.'

'Hello Rebecca; this is a pleasant surprise.'

'Yes, well Meadow told me that you might be home today, so since you are both here, and I haven't seen either of you for such a long time, I thought I'd seize the opportunity...'

'Sure; well, come in; coffee?'

'Actually I'm off coffee; water will do fine.'

'We have juice...'

'Juice it is then; trying to stay off stimulants for the baby, you know?'

'Sure...'

Rebecca released the puppy, took the sling from her back and placed her child on the kitchen table; the dogs went about their canine business, for the moment ignoring all human influence or presence.

'And this must be Florence, I presume?'

'Indeed.'

Will brought a glass of cranberry juice and two half – drunk cups of coffee to the table. Emily re – entered the room wearing a clean T shirt, Will noticing that she had still neglected to wear any undergarments; a fact which for a moment caused his thoughts to become inappropriate to the occasion, particularly in view of the fact that if anything this T shirt fitted more tightly than the one she had taken off. The briefest moment passed between them; he looked at her, she studiously avoided his gaze; enough said.

'Hi Rebecca; it's great to see you; welcome to the farmstead...'

'Hello and thank you, Emily; it all looks fantastic; you two have done so well; I want a guided tour of everything.'

'Of course...'

Will and Rebecca sat down, Emily went to the table and put her face close to the infant, who was lying quietly on her back and surveying that which she could of the world around her.

'And you, my beautiful one, must be Florence; she really is gorgeous, isn't she?'

'Yes, well she has her moments.'

'Meadow told me what a pretty baby she is; she wasn't kidding, was she? Anyway, it's good to see you Rebecca.'

'You too, Emily; both of you, in fact...'

'So; how are you settling back into the village?'

'Perfectly, thank you; it's so good to be back, I can't tell you...'

'It's a great house; we were really happy there, weren't we, Will; most of the time anyway.'

'It's a lovely house; I'm very lucky.'

'Bit of recent history since we were there as well,' said Will 'I mean after us Rose had her portrait painted, and then we hear there was a witch living there for a while; you must feel right at home.'

'Will, for heaven's sake...'

'What..? There's no secret about people being witches around here these days is there?'

'No; absolutely none...' said Rebecca, smiling as she spoke.

'I mean we three know each other well enough, don't we?'

'Yes, of course we do.' Said Rebecca 'I for one will never forget the first time we met in my workshop; I had no clue as to who you were then of course, and I was a different person then anyway.'

'Yeah; you were kind of spooky and dangerous looking.' Said Emily

'Yes, I suppose I was, wasn't I...I was very unhappy then; I'm much happier now.'

'And alive, which was never a given.' Said Will

'That's true, and I have a lot of people to thank for that, you two included, of course.'

'Yes, well this conversation's got off to a lively start,' said Emily 'most people talk about the weather and what not.'

Which made them all laugh; this was in a strange and perhaps unexpected way a happy reunion.

'So how's Lady?'

'She's been fine as always; I suppose you've come to take her away?'

'Yes, I have, if that's okay; I've missed her terribly, and well, things may still not be safe for me, so I'd like to have her around, you know?'

'Of course...' Said Emily

'I see you've already got another one,' said Will 'although I wouldn't think he'd be much good in terms of security yet.'

'Yes, I picked him up this morning, actually; the breeder gave me twenty four hours to bring him back if he's not wanted.'

'Why would he not be wanted?' Said Emily

'He's not for me; the thing is, you two have been so great about looking after Lady for me, so I thought, well, he's for you, if you want him, as a token of my gratitude.'

'Really...?' Said Emily

'Of course you may not want a dog permanently, and if so then it's fine, I'll just return him.'

'Hell no,' said Emily 'he's absolutely gorgeous; we'd love to have him, wouldn't we, Will?'

'Yeah…Yes, absolutely, if you're sure…'

'Quite sure; life hasn't been easy for me lately, and it wouldn't have been possible to take Lady until now, but anyway, I'd very much like you to have him. This is the kind of place which needs a dog.'

'I was saying that very thing to Will only recently, so, you know, thank you, Rebecca. What's his name anyway?'

'His pedigree name is *'Moonlight Sonata'*, otherwise it's up to you, of course; he's had his puppy injections by the way; I've got the certificate somewhere.'

'Okay, well, we'll give that some thought then; the name, that is.'

She picked the puppy up and held it against her chest; he licked her face, and Florence for the first time voiced her disapproval at having been laid down and thus far largely ignored. Rebecca picked her up and calmed her infant spirit, and Emily smiled.

'What…?'

'Oh nothing; I suppose I never really saw you as a mother, that's all.'

'Do you think it suits me?'

'Absolutely…'

'So how about we show you around then…I mean it's only loads of goats, a few chickens and one huge pig, complete with piglets, but it's home, you know, and it keeps me busy every day.'

'I'd love to look around.'

'Fine then, and you'll stay for lunch, will you?'

'If it's no bother..?'

'None at all…'

'And by the way I tried your cheese for the first time yesterday; it's superb.'

'Oh, thanks, I'm glad you think so; I'm sort of getting the hang of it, I think, at least it seems to go wrong less often than it used to. Lead on, William, and yes, little dog, you can come too.'

Percival said nothing; when somebody makes such a statement there is nothing to be said, really, so he lit a cigarette and waited.

'I'm thinking seriously about giving up my job, for a start.'

Which as and of itself would be a change of some significance.

'I see, and now I think I should ask you why you're doing that, or even thinking of doing it. I thought your career was set fair; that you were everyone's golden girl. You'll be on the board of directors one day quite soon, won't you?'

'Yes, well probably, at least I probably would have been.'

'So, why...?'

'It's complicated, in a way, and in a way it's very simple, but anyway I'll start with the easy part. The thing is, ever since I can remember I've wanted to own a house by the village Green; ever since we used to drive past when I was a kid.'

'Yes I know; you told me.'

'And well, now I've done that; I've paid off the mortgage and the house is mine.'

'Yeah, you said.'

'And so recently I've been asking myself what next, you know? I've denied myself a lot in order to achieve that, and I'm glad I did now, and I love my house, but now I have to think about the rest of my life. I mean what will be my epitaph, Percival; *'She had a good job in a bank.'*?'

'People have done worse, and achieved less.'

'And people have done better, but that's not really the point; I don't compare myself to other people in that way. The thing is, I don't want to deny myself anymore; I mean I made my decision before now; before coming here, but being here just reinforces everything I've been thinking. I've lived a couple of hours away from this beautiful city all of my life, and I've never been here.'

'You're here now.'

'Yes, but what else is there, you know? I mean that's a rhetorical and rather stupid question, but what else have I missed?'

'You can't think like that; that way lies madness. Anyway you've hardly been wasting your time, have you, and thirty isn't old, you know?'

'I know, and that's why I want to do it now, before...I don't know, before I get my directorship and before it becomes too late; before I start telling myself that I can't do without it; the high salary, the pension fund, the share dividends, whatever; I want to let go of the rope, if you understand what I mean, before I get so tangled up that I can't get out.'

'Of course I understand what you mean, but this is all new; give me a minute...'

'Sure, I'm sorry...'

'It's not about being sorry; it's doing whatever you think is best...Christ, that was corny; you see, I'm not quite ready for this.'

'Not ready for me to be different, is that it?'

'You have to be whatever you want to be; it's up to me to adapt; it's your life.'

'Yes, it's my life....But I mean it's not any more though really, is it?'

'What are you talking about?'

'Well, there's you now, isn't there...'

'What do you mean?'

'I mean there's our life together, and I want that so much, and well, let's be honest; how long do you think we have unless things change?'

'Now you've lost me...'

'You're a free spirit, Percival; that's what I'm saying, I think.'

'Am I...? Well thanks for letting me know, I might have missed that.'

'Oh come on; you can go wherever you want whenever you want to; you send me emails and 'phone me from God knows where, you go somewhere and learn to scuba – dive, you get mixed up in dangerous situations and just shrug it off as though nothing in particular's happened; you leave Louise, a woman who you clearly love, or loved, the same way that you left me for her, so where does that leave me now?'

'With me, as it goes.'

'Yes, but you know what I mean, but that's not really it either; I mean sure, take me or leave me as I am, and if you leave I'd survive, but...Well, we're together now, and I don't know why you came back to me, but you did.'

'Why do you think I came back to you?'

'Maybe because I talked you into it, or seduced you, or whatever; you bend with the wind, Percival, in love as in all other things, anyway shut up and let me finish...I mean it's all mixed up with you, and me, and what I ultimately want from my own life, and I'm not sure what that is yet, but what it comes down to is that right now I want to escape from myself, and my well controlled and channeled life, and my fucking career prospects. I mean let's say I made the directorship, what would I be doing? Counting the banks' profits and my annual bonus, and making financial decisions about people's lives, and I really don't want that responsibility, and since you came back, well, I've begun to realize a lot of things, and one of those things is that I don't want that life, either, not really. I'm away from home a lot these days, which is okay, but that can only get worse from now on, and I don't want to spend my weeks in hotel rooms anymore; I'm starting to resent it, you know? And I know it's the price you pay for being successful, but success isn't success, or doesn't feel like success unless…Well unless you can share it with person you love, and I don't want to be alone any more, and I don't just mean week days, I mean ever. From now on I want it to be about me and you, and what's best for us, and how we can get better together. You say that you have to adapt to me, but that works both ways, doesn't it?'

The conversation was interrupted as the wine and food were delivered to the table. For now the food was ignored, but both felt a need for the wine, and Percival lit another cigarette. Sally took it from him and Percival lit another one, noting that women did that sometimes.

'Look, I mean I had intended to do this differently; you know, wait until we were having a candle – lit supper or whatever, and I'm not doing it very eloquently, am I?'

'You're doing fine.'

'No I'm not; I had it so clear in my head, sometimes anyway, and what I was going to say, but it's not coming out right.'

'It's okay Sal, really; I know you well enough to know what you're saying, and sometimes you just have to keep talking until the right words come out; this is me, you know, and we're in a Parisian café, so you know, anything goes, and you can't always plan these things.'

'It would be typical of me to try to though, wouldn't it, and that's the point; I don't want to be like that anymore, so maybe this is the beginning, you know? Perhaps this is the moment when my life changes.'

'Well whatever you have to do and however you are is fine with me; better this be about you, and your life, than about what it is you think I want, but given that all's well however you see things going. To be honest I thought something like this was coming.'

'You did..? How..?'

'I don't know; the way you've been with your friends lately, things like that; I mean I didn't identify the source of your discontent, and I thought maybe it was me, you know, but you've had a restless spirit lately, and now I'm glad I know why.'

'It isn't you, my love, although it is you of course, in a way, but only in a good way. So you're okay with everything then; I mean if I do hand in my notice?'

'Christ, Sal, do whatever you need to; we're not together because you're a successful banker, any more than we wouldn't be if you weren't, or won't be if you're not, if that makes any sense.'

'Yes, it makes sense, I think and I love you for saying it anyway, but the other thing is that I don't really have a contingency plan. I mean what I'm good at and what I understand is the way money works; private and business finance and so on, and of course I have to go on bringing in the bacon, as it were, so I was thinking about some kind of personal financial advisory service, and I understand quite a lot about keeping fit, so maybe I could become a personal trainer, or something; things which will give me more time, at least.'

'Sure, whatever...'

'And I could learn new skills, you know?'

'Of course...'

'And there wouldn't be so much money coming in, in fact there may not be any money coming in for a while, which kind of runs counter to the fact that I want to see more of the world.'

'Money isn't the issue; I've got money, and you know I'll support you in whatever you do.'

'Will you..?

'Of course I will; if this really is what you want then run with it and see what happens.'

'I mean I've got some savings in various forms and in various places; it isn't much but I can live off that, for a while anyway, but any new business or whatever is going to take some time and cash to set up.'

'Look, forget about money, okay? So when are you going to tell them?'

'I don't know yet, but soon, I think; there's no point in delaying, is there?'

'None at all...'

'I mean I suppose I could carry on for a while, and keep saving; that would be the sensible thing to do, wouldn't it?'

'Yes, that would be the sensible thing to do, but this isn't about being sensible is it; sensible's a slippery slope, anyway; there's never going to be a perfect time, except now, if it's really what you want.'

'I just...I just need to know that you're behind me on this; just tell me that I'm not being stupid, or if I am being stupid then tell me that as well.'

'You're not being stupid, Sal.'

'So is it a good idea, do you think?'

'That's not a fair question; this is your decision, so if you've made your decision then don't look back.'

'Okay...Okay, thanks, Percival....God this is exciting; I mean Christ what the hell am I doing?'

'I don't know, Sal, but it seems to suit you.'

'I mean I don't want to or intend to be dependent on you.'

'I would never see it like that.'

'No, I know you wouldn't.'

'I suppose being entirely practical about it, you could always rent out the house for a while; just as a temporary thing, you know, if you needed some regular income.'

'Where would I live?'

'Well there's always the cottage, but I know you don't want that.'

'You mean move in with you?'

'Yeah, I know; bad idea.'

'You said I don't want that; what did you mean?'

'I understand that you want your independence, Sal, so, you know…'

'It isn't what you want either, is it?'

'I don't know what makes you think that.'

'Because…You've never said it's what you want.'

'I assumed it was pointless for me to even suggest it.'

'Okay, well now it's your turn to forget what you think I want for a moment; is it what you want, Percival? I mean do you think we could live together?'

'We almost do anyway, and yeah, I think we could live together; you're the one who's stopping that.'

'I thought it was you.'

'Well then we seem to be suffering from some kind of joint and several misapprehension, do we not?'

'Yes, we do, don't we…'

'Well anyway that's something we can discuss down the line somewhere; keep it as an option, you know?'

'Yes, keep it as an option…Good idea. And in the meantime live together anyway, except in two houses.'

'That should cover it.'

'Brilliant…So….So that's two life – changing decisions over one glass of wine then.'

'Lucky we didn't order a bottle. Look Sal, whatever you do and whatever we do is fine by me; just run with it, you know? Louise was nothing like you, so don't make comparisons; she was kind of wild, you know, and she would never have been anything else, not with me around anyway.'

'And I'm Ms Conventional, yes?'

'Not any more, it seems.'

'Well maybe not, but anyway something else I want to say is that from now on I'll support you too, Percival, in whatever you're still mixed up in with these cult people or whatever. I'll do whatever I can to help, and I know I've always said I won't but, it's what people do when they're in love, isn't it?'

'Yeah, I suppose it is, although my love isn't conditional upon that, either, in fact it isn't conditional upon anything, but thanks, it's good to know.'

'So what's happening there, anyway?'

'I'm not quite certain, but things are moving, I hope, but I'd rather not talk about that now; now is about you, and by the way I'm sorry I forgot your birthday.'

'It's okay…'

'Fortunately, however, I do have something with me which might make up for it.'

'What…?'

Percival put his hand into his coat pocket and pulled out a small, deep red imitation leather box, which he gave to her.

'What is it?'

'I think you're supposed to open it.'

She did so, and inside was a heavy, solid - silver bracelet.

'My God, it's beautiful…'

She put it on; with some effort it just about fit over her quite small hand, and once on it fitted her wrist very well.

'You hadn't forgotten at all, had you, you bastard…'

'Well, I was going to wait for the candle – lit supper too, but since we seem to be skipping that part…'

'I wouldn't mind the candle – lit supper anyway, if it's still an option.'

'Nothing's ruled out; I don't think we're going to run out of things to talk about, do you?'

'Thank you, Percival, it really is a beautiful bracelet, and I'll never take it off, ever. Let this be symbolic of the new beginning of my life, and since we're in Paris, let's call it my brand – new philosophy, shall we?'

'Sounds reasonable to me...'

Rebecca stayed until the mid - afternoon. These three had indeed not spoken for so long that there was much to talk about. Will and Emily had had little to do with the witches, or the intended and attempted killing of the Tillington children, and knew nothing of Rebecca's setting fire to Farthing's Well and the killing of the witches there. Their involvement in Rebecca's affairs had always been much more in relation to the cult, and inevitably the conversation found its' way to the subject, although Emily in particular was loathe to relive old and best forgotten memories, and it was Will who first raised the matter. By now Rebecca had been shown around Jacob's Field, they had eaten lunch of potato bread, eggs and tomatoes, Rebecca had fed Florence and the infant was sleeping contentedly on the settee.

'So, any news about our friends from the west – country..?'

'All's quiet there Will; that part of my life at least is sleeping at present.'

'So that's not where you see your present danger coming from then?'

'I don't know; I hope that I'm in no danger at all, of course, but the witch that you talked about, she who lived in the house before me; she and I may yet have to have confrontation, or she may have gone forever, I don't know.'

'So aren't you taking a bit of a risk then, living on your own somewhere where they can find you?'

Rebecca smiled.

'You aren't alone in thinking that, but I'm not going to hide anymore Will; if she or they come for me I'll be ready for that, and I'm better protected in the village than anywhere else. I know what you're thinking; that I could take Florence away and keep her safe, but I've made my decision. This is where my life is, and where her life will be, for now at least, and I won't let any harm come to her.'

'Right...'

'And it isn't just me, is it; others are deeply involved in what has happened; Victoria and Percival especially, and Keith and Meadow, and Sophia; I won't desert them all the time there may be any danger to any of them. If I'm not here and someone comes looking for them in my stead; well, in any case I've decided it's best for me to be here. What I want more than anything else, and what I've wanted for a long time is peace, and safety for everyone, and I could never rest entirely until I knew that it was all over. Anyway let's not spoil our reunion by talking of bad things which may never happen, all of our lives are moving in positive ways now, and I'm so glad to have seen you both, and to have seen what you're doing here, which I really do think is wonderful.'

When it was time to go, Rebecca picked up her child, placed her in the carrier on her back, and said her goodbyes to her hosts. She walked to the kissing gate, Lady walking willingly beside her on a loose leash, and she left the puppy behind. Will and Emily watched her go for a moment, and Emily was the first to speak.

'Well, that was unexpected, wasn't it?'

'Yep...'

'No mention of the child's father, you notice.'

'Nope...'

'Who's your daddy then, little one?'

'It's probably best not to ask. Did you notice anything strange about her; Rebecca I mean.'

'Not really, why..?'

'That's what I mean; she's not strange any more, which is strange…She's behaving almost like a normal human being.'

'Maybe that's what motherhood does for you.'

'I suppose…Anyway, we've got a dog out of it.'

'Which is brilliant, isn't it, and it was sweet of her; pedigree dogs are really expensive. We'll have to think of a name for him; how about Monty?'

'I could live with that.'

After all the excitement Monty had by now fallen into a sudden and deep sleep under the kitchen table, as puppies will do.

'He looks at home already.'

'Yeah…Em, something's been bothering me…'

'What's that then, dear heart?'

'When you changed your T shirt; why you didn't, you know…'

'How do you know I didn't?'

'Well one can't be certain, of course, but anyway I think we should confirm the matter, you know, one way or the other…'

'I don't need to confirm anything.'

'Yes, well that's all very well, but as the other interested party I think some verification is necessary.'

He turned to face her, and lifted her T shirt a little way above her waistline.

'William, I advise you not to do this.'

Which as it turned out was no deterrent, and he lifted the garment the rest of the way up.

'You're not listening, are you?'

'Sorry; what did you say; I wasn't listening.'

She pushed him away, but made no attempt to readjust her clothing, and thus emboldened the young man took his young lady by the waist and pulled her to him, removing her T shirt entirely as he did so, something which he knew full well would not have been possible without her complete cooperation. They kissed, and for a moment no further discussion was possible, until the kiss was over.

'Have you no shame, sir?'

'Not much…'

'So it seems, and I suppose I should know that by now, and now I suppose you 're going to suggest we retire to the bedroom, are you?'

'Unless you advise against it…'

'You see, you were listening; I knew you were.'

'So what do you think then?'

'What I think is that I give up with you; there really is no hope, is there?'

'Probably not…'

'Anyway I can hardly stand here like this, can I; somebody might see.'

'We live in the middle of a field, Em.'

'Yes, but even so a girl must retain her modesty, even in the face of such unwarranted and unasked for advances.'

'Well, if you put it like that…'

They held hands and walked to the bedroom door, and had anyone indeed been watching it would have been all but impossible to tell who was leading who.

On their final morning in Paris, Percival and Sally took a stroll through the Jardin des Tuileries to kill time before they took a cab to the airport. It was another fine, quite sunny morning, and both had the feeling that spring was not now far away in this city of cities. Sally had by now saturated herself in Paris, and Percival had had at least a little time to consider

Sally's plans for her future, if such they could yet be called, and considered that a final conversation was needed. They stopped for coffee, as was their wont, and as usual they took an outside table, and now, having lit cigarettes for them both, he broached the subject.

'So, what kind of a reaction do you think you'd get if you hand in your notice in?'

'Yes; I've been trying to imagine their reactions.'

'Mild shock, I expect; they won't see it coming, will they?'

'No, and if this is a to be an *are you sure you're doing the right thing*

discussion, then yes, I'm quite sure, my love; as sure as I can be, anyway. I look at my friends; at Fiona and Ray, and Polly and George, and Claudia and Simon, and I'm determined that I'm not going to end up like them; that you and I aren't going to end up like them. I mean you're different, I know that, but even so...'

'Just don't do it for me Sal, that's all I'm saying.'

'I'm not doing it for you; I'm doing it for me, and for us, which is the same thing really, isn't it?'

'It's blurred edges, you know?'

'Of course it is, but that's what relationships are all about, isn't it? Both people in any relationship worth the name have to be strong and independent, and to be doing what they want to do, but where one life ends and another begins is always uncertain, isn't it? You're the love of my life, Percival; if we split then there's nobody else, and there never could be, not like this, and I trust our love absolutely, because what other choice do I have? If you're worried about it then look upon yourself as my saviour, saving me from a life of balance sheets, overdrafts and profit and loss calculations. Without you I would never consider doing this, so of course it's because of you, but it isn't *for* you, and it's the right thing for me to do, and hell, it's only a job, anyway.'

'If you set up a consultancy that's what you'd be doing in any case; balance sheets and so on…'

'I know, but then it will be for me, and anyway that's not my only option; who knows what I'll be doing a year from now.'

'Okay, well go to it then.'

'With your blessing…?'

'With my blessing…'

And so it was done, and enough had been said, about that, at least, but Sally now had something else to say.

'You have to tell me one day, Percival; everything that's happened to you; all about what happened in the west – country.'

For a moment the image of the dell entered Percival's thoughts, as it was wont to do sometimes; Howard's Bench, his incarceration and then being drugged and tied to the stake; the chanting, and the man with a sword who was ready to kill him, and who was now dead himself. It was only a moment, but Percival closed his eyes until the image returned back to the part of him where hell still lived, and from whence the fear had never really gone away; perhaps it would soon, but for now the ghost of that night still haunted him. But for now the moment passed, and he was in Paris again with the woman that he loved, and who loved him, and it was a sunny day.

'I will; one day, when it's the right time.'

They smiled, and finished their last coffee in their last Parisian café, for now, anyway.

'I suppose we should be heading home, don't you think?'

'Which home; your place or mine..?'

'It doesn't really matter, does it?'

'I thought you loved your house.'

'I do, but the cottage has one thing in its' favour; you're there.'

'Well then, let's start at mine, and see how it goes from there, shall we?'

'Sounds like a plan, and you know, thanks, Percival, it's been a fantastic and important few days.'

'Yes it has.'

They stood up, she took his arm, and they walked away into a brave and now less certain future. Sally knew well enough that when it came to love nothing was ever really certain, her friends bore testament to that, but by creating her own uncertainty, by letting go of the rope which bound her to a part of her life, she was sure, or at least she hoped, that her future in other ways would be made more secure, and that was a different kind of balance sheet altogether.

Chapter 10

THE MAKING OF COMMITMENTS

Rosemary Knightman, younger sister to Tarragon and elder sister to Basil, was in her last academic year at school. Late next summer, provided that during the early summer she obtained the necessary grades in her four chosen scholarly subjects, she would be set fair to go on to attend university, and thus begin her further and higher education. In truth there was little doubt in the minds of her teachers or her parents that she would attain the required grades; Rosie was the most academically gifted and certainly the most academically focused of her siblings, and everyone expected her to pass all subjects, probably with distinction. If all was well academically, however, there was one thing which went rather against her in the always competitive matter of securing a place at one of her chosen universities, which was that she would likely have little to offer aside from her anticipated academic qualifications. Competition was such for places at the better universities that they oft times required not only examinations passed with good grades, but other evidence that applicants had interests and abilities aside from their school work; perhaps they might have an extra - curricular qualification, or belong to a particular club or association, or could show evidence of some other achievement or relevant interest within or beyond the school gates. Rosemary did indeed possess other and considerable abilities; she could with little effort have influence upon or sometimes even control the minds and actions of others, she was well versed in one particular aspect of human history, in herbal remedies for illness and injury, and in the ancient traditions of witchcraft, none of which in regard to her university application would be of any advantage or use to her whatsoever. One could scarce, after all, write *'witchcraft'* in any part of an application document asking for other interests, and to be a witch was not a recognized skill or qualification. Once indeed, in darker and more superstitious ages, even to be suspected of being a witch was a virtual guarantee of being burned at the stake, or more usually drowned, or hung by the neck until dead, and whilst this is no longer the case, echoes of such times resonate into our modern and more enlightened world. Most people indeed are not aware that witches actually exist outside the realms of fiction or folklore, and to be a witch is still to lead a secret life. Nevertheless, Rosemary could be a charming and engaging young person if she had a mind; her father indeed would have it that she could charm the very birds from the trees, and her mother was also rather of this opinion, particularly where her father was concerned. She lacked the tall, willowy stature and physical elegance which her mother and sister possessed, but there was no doubt that she was exceptionally pretty, which should confer no advantage upon her at interview, but neither would it work against her, particularly if the interview panel were masculine, and in all regards she would in any case interview well if she reached that stage. She could argue or discuss any point on any subject of which she had knowledge with calm intelligence and clarity, and if she knew nothing of something she could say so with equal calmness and intelligence, and had learned control and mask her emotions, and thus would she hide any nervousness which she would undoubtedly be feeling. People who knew and were concerned for her therefore remained confident that she would indeed succeed in furthering her academic ambition in whichever way she chose, even if she was perhaps naturally less certain or confident herself. Whilst we are with the subject of interview technique, and before we move on to other aspects of Rosemary's life, there was another element to her learned abilities which might be born in mind, which is that it would be a quite easy thing for her to use her craft to influence a panel of interviewers to think in her favour, be they men or women; she may not be able to use her knowledge and manipulative abilities in any official way, but they may have a more practical application if she chose to use them, but she would surely not do so, would she, for to do so would be morally reprehensible, would it not?

In any case she intended to apply provisionally to four universities, all in the south of England, and might in the end be persuaded by her tutor at school to include Oxford and Cambridge in her application, but in all cases her chosen subject was Psychology. Rosie had during the course of her learning become deeply interested in the conscious and particularly the unconscious workings of the human mind; the manifestation of a person which was shown to the world, and which enabled them to live from day to day was, she knew well enough, but a small part of that persons' psyche, and she wished to make that which lay beneath it her realm of study and understanding, so the subject became a quite natural choice for her, and no other subject held anywhere near the same interest.

Despite, previously at least, having something of a reputation for being a somewhat detached and introverted person, Rosemary had always possessed a quiet charisma and something of an aura of mystery about her, which tended to catch peoples' imagination and sometimes fascination, and would draw people to her. She had always therefore made friends quite easily if she so chose, and had in any case during latter times become more open and outgoing of countenance, something which was welcomed by her mother and father, and responded to favourably by her peers. She thus enjoyed an extended network of friends, whilst not having any one friend in particular. She was of a time of life where most of her day was spent with other girls of her age, the boys of her age having by now come to see her and others of her gender as a potential mate, whilst not in general having the maturity which the girls possessed to do very much about it, all of which tended to lend a certain awkwardness to their dealings with the fairer sex. In any case sexual differences certainly played their part, even in the environment of a school; hormonal aspects of being a young person could be overcome to an extent in such an essentially academic environment, but not entirely, and Rosie and her peers were no exception to this general and fundamental rule.

Nevertheless, older men would from time to time enter the realm of such young women, and Rosie had lost or perhaps better say quite deliberately and consciously given away her virginity at the age of sixteen, to a man several years her senior, this occurring whilst at a social gathering which was held at the house of a mutual friend. She had been taught and had come to see her mind and the minds of others as being things of delicacy and subtlety, and thus had always hitherto avoided alcohol or other depressants or stimulants, which would artificially alter the state of her own mind; she had never even so much as smoked a cigarette, and nor did she intend to. However having heard accounts of the experiences of her feminine peers, she decided that she should at least experience certain of these particular aspects of young life for herself. She therefore on this occasion consumed sufficient wine and then tequila to become rather drunk, and the resultant reduction in inhibition saw to it that the ice maiden, for such she was still then regarded, became rather less icy, and thereafter she was no longer a maiden. She awoke the next morning feeling hung – over, and once the effects of the alcohol had worn off she decided that she did not much wish to repeat the experience. That was to say she had not particularly enjoyed the feeling of intoxication, and certainly had not enjoyed its' after effects. The sexual aspects of the experience however were a different matter, and she concluded that henceforward she would for the most part forgo the former, but would remain open to the possibility of the latter. The gentleman who had been fortunate enough to share in her first sexual intimacy was himself at pains to repeat the experience, and perhaps to form a more lasting emotional bond with the young woman, of whom he knew little other than that her name was Rosie, and that she was beyond doubt the most beautiful young woman that it had ever been his pleasure to meet. The young woman, however, made it quite and immediately clear to her peers that she wanted no further contact with the gentleman, polite and gracious though he had been; the ranks were closed, and all enquiry in this regard fell on deaf ears; nobody would assist Luke, for thus was his name, in making further contact with her, and he never saw her again, his function having been fulfilled in quite adequate fashion. He would go on to find romantic and emotional fulfilment elsewhere, but Luke would never quite forget his one night of passion with the girl who had been called Rosie, who had gone from his life as quickly and mysteriously as she had appeared, and he would never have the least idea that he had slept with a witch.

Aside from her above average academic ability and her attractiveness, there was another aspect of Rosemary, or perhaps better say her life, which tended to set her apart from her peers; in the middle and upper – middle class social sphere in which she moved, her contemporaries lived for the most part in quite well appointed detached or semi – detached houses, whereas Rosemary had lived for all of her life on a bus, and since she had been old enough to be left on her own at night had slept in a partitioned – off part of a trailer. Her parents had always instilled in her and her siblings a sense of the unimportance of material goods or possessions beyond the essential, and so she had during her life had little of either, and neither in truth had she ever desired them. It was always possible, of course for children to rebel against such a taught philosophy, but in fact none of the offspring to Keith and Meadow had done so, Rosie being no exception. In part this was a matter of practicality, given the small, private space in which she and her siblings lived, and Rosemary's wardrobe of clothes was sparse compared to her contemporaries, a high percentage of them having been made by Meadow, who was skilled and self – taught seamstress to the family. In this regard as with many things, quality rather than quantity was the watchword within the household. It was also the case that the three children had been raised from birth and through childhood as strict vegetarians, and in this Rosie had never wavered. Tarragon nowadays ate meat from time to time, but Rosemary and Basil had never done so, and it was true to say that Rosie had never in her life consciously eaten the flesh of another animal, and nor had she ever worn leather clothing or shoes.

This in essence then was the backdrop against which Rosemary had lived her young years, and hers was for the most part a happy household, despite its' modesty. Her father and mother loved one another deeply and constantly, and this sense of love and emotional harmony had they imbued and instilled in their children. Rosie saw around her the damage done to her peers by broken or dysfunctional marriages, and the deep and lasting embitterment which resulted, but she at least had never had to thus suffer, and the emotional foundation upon which her life was set was as strong as it was constant, and in her quiet and undemonstrative way, Rosie loved her parents as well as they loved her. Her friends had things which she did not have; they were sent away on exotic holidays, wore the latest imitation designer fashions, and enjoyed lavish banquets and events to mark their birthdays, but oft times their parents were not both present, or perhaps neither of them were, and as she grew older and wiser, Rosemary increasingly understood that her parents had given her something upon which no measurable value could be placed.

Thus have we learned in a general sense something more of Rosie Knightman, and from here on in this chapter we will hear of something far more specific which happened to her one day during these winter months, for her teacher of witchcraft and mentor, Angela, had news for her one evening which Rosie would deem of considerable importance, as indeed she might.

On the Monday morning following their weekend in Paris, Percival and Sally kissed goodbye at the door of the cottage. He had not on this final morning or in the final moments before her departure tried to influence her decision either way, her mind apparently being quite made up. She had left in her sharp, city clothes as always, and wheeling a small suitcase, as she would be travelling the north and midlands of England during the next five days, returning home on Friday. One of her primary arguments, if such they could be called, since Percival was not arguing, was that she wanted this to end; that she wanted to come home every evening, and here was a case in point. In any event Percival would be alone for the week, and she would begin her journey north from the London office, where she would, he assumed, tender her resignation, and begin her months' notice of departure which was written into her contract of employment.

Percival had in truth been taken quite by surprise by her decision; the bank that she worked for was a small, independent bank, which would likely be overtaken during the next few years by one of the larger banks, so her time in its' directorship if she were indeed to be offered it may in any case have been limited, but still, she was about to throw in a promising career, for which she had given him her reasons, but that which Percival was left to wonder was which of her reasons was in her mind the most important. She was, it seemed, about to reinvent herself and her life in a most fundamental way, and though she would have it that she was not doing this for or because of him, he wondered how true this was, or how much a fear of losing him had influenced her decision, and therefore whether her fear of losing him was justified. Percival had led a particular life; he had fought for years with a cocaine addiction during his own very different and lucrative time in banking, which had left its' mark on his psyche, and his way of seeing the world, and he had come to live in the cottage in a last attempt to clean up his life, which fortunately had thus far been successful. How close he had come to total burn – out or complete and lasting emotional or psychological collapse he would never know, but he had survived himself and his former life, thereafter regarding himself as somewhat damaged if still functioning goods. So was she right to doubt his love for her; was he really so unreliable? His love life over recent years had in itself been a somewhat tempestuous thing; he had sailed close enough to Rebecca to feel her anger at the world, and had ended his first relationship with Sally in order to follow Louise into her own and sometimes extreme disillusionment with the business of love, and Rose, of course, had found her way into his soul in a quite different way. He had contacted Sally again at the point at which he had decided that he and Louise would probably in the end destroy one another, and that which remained of their ability to have normal relations with anybody, and he had not known what to expect when he had done so. He would have settled for her friendship, but had instead encountered the anger which Emily had warned him was coming, and with that had also come a clear desire that they should get back together; in the end she had wanted him back more than she had hated him, and in the meantime had become her own kind of sex Goddess, which had also taken him somewhat by surprise, and why had she done that? Had it been done consciously, or was it purely instinctive? Was it perhaps further manifestation of her anger, or to make him see how stupid he had been to leave her, and was it for her benefit or for his, and did it really matter since both so clearly benefitted from the metamorphosis? And now she was apparently about to throw away a safe and financially rewarding career; she would create uncertainty where before there was security; Sally was becoming something which she had never been before, and for now Percival was at pains to know why this was, or how he actually felt about it.

And so on this particular morning, and having kissed her goodbye at the door, Percival finished his coffee and answered emails, eventually walking to the kitchen, where Lulu joined him; whatever was currently occurring in his life, and whatever thoughts currently preoccupied him, this was definitely a going for a walk situation.

'Rosemary, before you go, I have something to tell you.'

This was a certain weekday evening, and Rosie was about to say goodbye to Angela and walk the short distance back to her home.

'Oh yes; what's that?'

'The head of our order has contacted me and requested an interview with you.'

'I see…'

'This is I believe an unusual thing; if you wish to accept, and to meet her, then you would travel to the west – country and go to the coven, which as you know is referred to among us as the white house. I have never been there, and there are indeed few of us who have, so this may be regarded as a particular honour, and a rare opportunity. It is possible of course for all of us to ask advice and so on of our High Priestess, and I have done so myself, but this is done via one of the inner circle, and few of us have ever met her.'

'Right...Right, well I suppose I should go then. Do you know why she wants to meet me?'

'No, not really, other than perhaps your connection to your mother, and to events which have happened in your village, but that is only my speculation, and she has given me no specific indication as to why she wishes to see you. She has also made it clear that this can only take place with the blessing of your parents, which you must seek before any arrangements are made.'

'Why...? I mean surely I can decide whether or not to go, can't I?'

'You are still young, Rosemary, and still in the care of your parents. I will ask them myself if you wish, but otherwise you must obtain their consent; this matter is without question.'

'Okay, well I'll ask them, then.'

'Good, then I will trust you in this; let me know when you have their approval, and I will make the necessary arrangements. The sisterhood will pay the cost of your fare and so on. You would travel by a morning train and return the same afternoon, and since you are presently at school this would of course be at a weekend.'

'Right, I see...'

Rosie walked home through the dark, chilly evening, wondering why she had been so summoned, and why Angela had waited until the end of their meeting to tell her such significant news. Her mother had met with the High Priestess, whose name she knew was Charlotte, but otherwise she knew little of her. Indeed her mother had herself been invited to the white house, but she had never been, but this was different; Rosie was a part of the sisterhood, and as such she could hardly refuse the summons, or request, as Angela had called it, and in any case she had no wish to refuse. She would very much like to meet Charlotte, and perhaps some others from the inner circle, and to go to the infamous white house itself was something which she had never expected to do.

In the end it was to be a long walk. It was a fine, clear morning, and Lulu, who had resided with Keith and Meadow during Percival's time in Paris, was clearly enjoying herself and her freedom. Across the field, through the wood and beyond into open heath – land, where on still, cold days a mist would hang all day in the hollows, but today the wind had blown the air clear, and from high ground a person could see for miles. Percival for the most part enjoyed and preferred the still, comforting enclosure of the woodland paths, but sometimes a wider vista is needed, as if from here a clearer view might be had of one's life, and the wind might blow clarity through and into one's thoughts. The heath for the most part rolled away from the town, having only isolated dwellings and farm houses, but from here one could also glimpse the distant outer limits of the suburban sprawl, as the town spread ever outwards from its' ancient centre. Percival stayed with the higher ground, intending to circle 'round to the lake, and thence home.

By now Sally would be in London, and could perhaps even by now have given her notice; perhaps by now she had officially at least crossed over into her new working life, for which she had no coherent plan, and a month was not a long time in which to make one. Percival had made the assumption that she would take a sabbatical once her contract had ended, perhaps for several weeks, and that she and therefore they would travel somewhere, perhaps to the Far – East where she had never been, but he would leave the decision to her. She had indeed travelled to few places in her life, after all, and her enthusiasm for Paris made him sure that wherever they went she would fully embrace the experience. Hitherto her life had been one of carefully controlled expenditure and debt reduction, but from now on she would be a freer if not a richer spirit, and Percival would have to get used to that. If she had been a safe harbour for his emotional self, then he assumed that she would remain so, but everything else about her would change, and he would of course help her in whichever way he could, whatever had been her motivation. And in the end, what did it matter? Percival had ever been a pragmatist, and had in truth planned nothing of his own life, so he could scare judge others in this regard, and would be ready for whatever would happen from now on in the life of this once and now again significant woman in his life.

Lulu fetched a fox from a small, isolated birch copse some one hundred metres ahead of him, and he watched as the animal fled from safety across open ground; Lulu half – heartedly chased her distant relative for a moment before giving up the chase and running to him, clearly pleased with herself at having disturbed the fox's slumbers. Percival worked to avoid any analogy of Sally being the fox, the bank being the wooded copse, and his being the German shepherd dog, but the thought had flashed briefly through his thoughts. In any case within another hour Percival had circled back into more wooded country, and soon found himself at the far end of the lake. As he walked the path at the lakes' edge, he saw that somebody was sitting in contemplative mode on a bench near the duck – house. He recognized the person immediately, and was pleased to have so come across them; he had not seen them for quite a long time, and the figure looked up as he approached.

'I suppose there's no reason why she shouldn't go, is there?'

This was Meadow, speaking to Keith. They had retired to their bedroom and to bed at the end of the day, Rosie having told them her news, and they saying that they would let her know in the morning whether they would grant her permission to go. (*'Oh come on; what reason could there possibly be for me not to go?' 'Your father and I just have to discuss it first, that's all.'*)

'No, I suppose not; seems to be a big honour, meeting the big witch.'

'I mean it might be different if I hadn't met her, but she seems okay, you know? I never told Rosie the reason for our meeting; not the real reason ...'

'No, I know.'

'There's a lot that Rosie still doesn't know, about what went on.'

'So maybe you should 'phone her; what's her name again?'

'Charlotte...'

'Charlotte; right...Call her and tell her the situation; tell her how much Rosie knows and tell her to keep it that way.'

'It's a pity she has to go on her own...'

'Well she can hardly take a friend, can she; anyway it's just a train journey.'

'It's not that...It just seems like a big thing for her to do alone, that's all. Well, anyway, you're right; I think I have her number somewhere, if not I'll get it from Rosie; I'll call her tomorrow morning, and as long as that happens and I make everything clear to her, and she agrees, then we let her go, yes?'

'Seems reasonable...I mean this being a witch business still seems to be nothing but a positive in our daughters' life, so I can't otherwise see any harm in it, or any valid reason to stop her going.'

'She'd probably go anyway, so better she goes with our consent, provided all goes well with my talk with Charlotte.'

And so it was decided, and the next morning there was a quite long conversation by telephone, and the following Saturday Rosemary found herself on a train heading west. The journey itself was uneventful, the train being quite empty, and Rosie sat opposite a young man with quite long, curly hair and round – rimmed glasses, who wore a well - worn Tweed jacket over a light brown, collarless shirt, and gave off a pleasant and intelligent aura. He spent the journey doing a crossword puzzle from one of the broadsheet newspapers, whilst Rosie read a book, or just passed the time looking out of the window.

At the other end of the train journey there was a short bus ride, and by late morning Rosie was sitting in a certain café by the sea, and here she waited at an outside table, as she had been told to do. She ordered a glass of fresh orange juice, and sat for a while watching the waves break on the shingle beach; this would be a busier place during the tourist season, but now she had the terrace to herself. Despite the time of year, however, it was a quite pleasant morning, with a light wind coming from the ocean, and Rosie was in truth in no hurry to move on. She did not however have to wait for very long; she was expected, after all.

'Hello Reginald; haven't seen you for a while.'

'Hello Percival.'

Percival sat down beside his friend on the rustic bench, and Lulu sat down in front of them, breathing hard and clearly tired but contented after her exertions.

'You look thoughtful…'

'Yes, although I wasn't thinking about anything in particular.'

'Fair enough…'

'I've just been 'round to see you.'

'Oh yes; how was I?'

'I don't know; you weren't in.'

'Yeah, stupid of me…Are you sure you're okay?'

'I think I should carry out some maintenance to the duck house before the spring comes; wood preservative and so on.'

'Good idea; the ducks are doing well, aren't they?'

'Yes, they are. I didn't call to see you for any reason in particular.'

'You don't need a reason, dear chap; call 'round anytime, you know that…So I hear you got your crib back in order again then.'

'Yes; I engaged a commercial cleaner; she came for three days.'

'Big job then…'

'Yes, and then she came back the next day, and she didn't do any cleaning on that day.'

'Oh dear; so what did she do?'

One of the ducks had paddled over to them, doubtless with the expectation of bread or other sustenance, but was keeping a safe distance from the shore, and from the large dog which also there sat.

'Her name is Gwendolyn.'

'What, the duck?'

'No, the commercial cleaner…'

'Right…So did you complain to the cleaning company?'

'I don't mind the name Gwendolyn.'

'I mean about her not cleaning the next day.'

'No, she wasn't supposed to clean the next day.'

'So what was she supposed to do?'

'I'm not sure, but anyway we went for an unplanned walk; we came here, actually; she'd not been here before.'

'Right…No, sorry, you've lost me, so were you paying for her for this day?'

'No, it was not a working day for her; later we ate crumpets; it was a very enjoyable day.'

'I see, I think, so have you seen her since?'

'No...'

Percival thought that perhaps he was beginning to understand; getting to the point of that which Reginald was trying to say would often feel like getting blood from a stone, and he would at times state the opposite of the truth. On this occasion, for example, since he had said that he had had no particular reason for coming to see Percival, Percival now took this to mean that he had had a very specific reason for so doing, and the reason appeared to be a woman called Gwendolyn. He chastised himself momentarily for not being quicker to realize his misinterpretation, but he had got there in the end, which he supposed was the important thing.

'So, would you like to see her again?'

'Yes.'

'So what's preventing you from doing so; do you have her private telephone number?'

'Yes.'

'Because she gave it to you..?'

'Yes.'

'So, what's the problem?'

'The problem is that I don't know what she is.'

'You mean apart from being a commercial cleaner...'

'Yes; that much has already been established.'

'Right...So this is a problem with definition, is that it?'

'Yes.'

'In terms of her relationship to you..?'

'Yes.'

'And that's the reason why you're not 'phoning her?'

'Yes.'

'Okay I think I'm getting there, and my first question has to be; what does it matter, and why does she have to be anything, apart from, what's her name?'

'Gwendolyn.'

'Gwendolyn…Right…Why does she have to be anything other than herself?'

'I fail to see how she could be anything other than herself.'

'My point is, if you had an enjoyable day together, and assuming that she enjoyed herself as well, then why not have another enjoyable day together?'

'I would like to do that.'

'As I'm sure would she; ask her, Reginald; she can only say no, after all. How old is she?'

'I don't know; one does not like to ask a lady's age.'

'Well give me a clue; older or younger than you?'

'Younger, but probably by less than a decade…'

'Well that's fine then; I presume she's not married or anything?'

'No; she lives on her own in the town, and has never been married, and she has no children.'

'So there is no impediment to her becoming your particular friend, then.'

'My particular friend..?'

'If that's how you want to see her. Look, I'm not really sure how qualified I am to advise other people about these things.'

'You have experience; with relationships and so on.'

'It's not all been good or wise experience though, but the point is…Okay, here's the thing; you wouldn't think twice about calling me, or Meadow, or whoever, would you?'

'That's different.'

'Which leads me to think that this particular person means something special to you, emotionally speaking; am I right?'

'Yes, I believe she does.'

'So I daresay that if you had such a good day together then she probably feels the same way about you, and is probably wondering why you don't call her. In this kind of situation the man should make the 'phone call, and it doesn't have to be heavy, you know; just suggest that you meet up again. I don't know what she's interested in, obviously; take her to an art gallery, have a day in London together, something like that.'

Reginald was quiet for a moment, and was clearly thinking. Percival considered a change of subject, but couldn't think of one, and anyway this seemed to be subject to be discussed. It occurred to him that in all of Reginald's life and despite his advanced years, this was quite possibly the first time that he had experienced such feelings for another person, and Percival was aware that he should tread carefully, so he let Reginald be the next to speak. Reginald, however, now stood up and walked that which Percival considered to be an inappropriate distance along the footpath before turning around and rejoining man and dog, the dog by now also wondering what was going on.

'I will 'phone her this very evening.'

'That's the spirit…'

'Yes, thank you Percival, for your good advice.'

'Well it was hardly rocket science; anyone would have told you the same, but I'm glad to have helped; just relax and be yourself. Anyway, I should get back; I'll leave you to your non – specific thoughts, and you know; good luck, I'm sure she's a lovely lady.'

Percival stood, and began walking the now short distance home. Meeting Reginald had been an unexpected and quite welcome distraction from his own considerations, but then nothing regarding Reginald was ever usual, so why should he have expected otherwise? If his cleaning lady had or was to become his lady – friend, then Percival was glad for him, and his walk home was the lighter for the encounter.

'Hello, are you Rosemary?'

The woman had approached Rosemary's table and now stood before her, wearing a pleasant and open expression. Rosemary knew of Maria, who had been her point of contact with the higher witches, but this was not she.

'Yes, that's right.'

'My names is Amanda; when you 're ready we can go.'

Rosie quickly drank the rest of her juice, and was suddenly overcome with a sense of nervousness, which she knew was as stupid and irrational as it was unexpected, but there it was; she was about to meet the High Priestess, the highest witch of her order, after all, of whom she knew nothing.

'Okay, I'm ready.'

They walked together to a car which was parked in the landward side of the café, and Rosie was offered the back seat.

'Sorry, I have to blindfold you.'

'Oh; okay.'

'Weren't you told? It is only a short journey, but we take this precaution with everyone outside the inner circle.'

Rosie complied, for what choice did she have, and allowed Amanda to place a blindfold loosely over her eyes; the vehicle's ignition was started, and after a journey which Rosie assumed was about half an hour the car pulled to a stop and the engine was turned off. The front door of the vehicle was opened and then closed, and Amanda reached in and removed the blindfold, and led Rosie out of the car. They stood before a quite large house, painted white in its' entirety, and with a single front door at the head of a flight of entrance steps which were constructed of brick and stone.

'Well, here we are; I'll see you later.'

'Okay...'

Amanda took her place once again in the drivers' seat and turned the car around; Rosie watched as the vehicle quickly disappeared from view around a bend in the single – track lane, and now she was quite alone with the big house, which stood in isolation within the dense, winter woodland. She walked to the steps and ascended to the front door, which in common with the rest of the house had clearly not been painted in a long time. She stood for a moment at the place where Rebecca had sat after she had killed the mother, Helen, the last High Priestess, and was about to knock when the door was opened. Before her stood a woman in her forties or fifties, who had a pleasant face and countenance, and who now smiled at her.

'Hello Rosemary; my name is Charlotte; thank you for coming.'

Rosie was led into a quite large lounge, where an open, log fire was burning. She removed her coat, which Charlotte took from her. In truth Rosie had not quite known how to dress for such an occasion and such a meeting, so in the end had opted for jeans and practical shoes, and a quite smart red sweater, which her mother had knitted, and she was pleased to see that Charlotte was similarly casually dressed.

'Please take a seat; would you like tea or coffee?'

'Just water would be fine, thanks.'

'Very well...'

Charlotte left the room, which allowed Rosie a few moments of contemplation; so this was to be a one to one encounter, and Rosie was unaware whether there was anybody else in the house, but thought not; such a large and isolated house, and she tried to imagine living here alone. She also tried to assess her first impressions of this woman, who was clearly no ordinary woman, but it was too quick to gain any meaningful insight, other than that she seemed friendly enough, and to be of quite open countenance. She also knew, however, that here must be a very powerful witch, and she did not yet know the nature of her, so she must remain on her guard. In any case the subject of her thoughts now returned, bearing a jug of water and a pot of tea on a tray, which she placed on a coffee table; she then took the seat opposite Rosie, and poured drinks for them both. An old – fashioned tea service on a presumably antique coffee table, which went well with the appointment of rest of the room, where none of even the newest furnishings looked to be less than twenty or thirty years old. Apparently Charlotte read her thoughts.

'Yes, I inherited the furniture from my predecessor, and some of it goes back well beyond her, I'm sure. Most of it is not to my taste, to be honest, but there it is, I confess I am rather lazy about such things.'

Rosie took a drink from her water and said nothing, and Charlotte, who would also be assessing as well as being assessed, made further attempt to put her guest at her ease.

'I daresay that you didn't know what to expect from this meeting, or from me; you were perhaps expecting some wizened old crone, am I right; someone who would be somewhat more in keeping with the furniture?'

The first direct and significant question; the engagement, however it was to be, had begun.

'No...No, not at all...'

Charlotte smiled; she had a nice smile.

'I confess I am young to have inherited my position, which in some ways I daresay is a good thing, but it has disadvantages also. A great deal has happened since the beginning of my tenure; much has been achieved by the sisterhood, many positive things have occurred which I believe would not otherwise have done so, but too much of my thoughts and energy have been directed at events which have happened in your small village, but that is not the reason that I invited you here. I understand from

Angela that you are making good progress with your life as well as with your learning; would you say that this was the case?'

'Well, I suppose so; I mean school's going okay, if that's what you mean, and Angela is a good teacher.'

'Yes, she tells me that everyone is confident as regards your academic success.'

'More confident than me, I dare say.'

'Of course; it is often easier to believe in others than to believe in ourselves; we can but see the world from our own perspective, and only we can truly understand our own insecurities and uncertainties, but it is from these that we draw the energy to continue, and to try to better ourselves, is it not?'

'I suppose so, yes.'

'Well anyway, I wish you well with your school work, and I hope that that which you learn with Angela may help in this regard; learning what is generally known as 'witchcraft' is in my view at least not only an end in itself, but a way by which we can positively influence the rest of our lives; would you agree with that?'

'Yes...I mean I've learned much better how to concentrate, and focus my thoughts and so on.'

'I'm glad to hear it, and that and the fact that you are clearly in any case a very intelligent young woman will, I'm sure, see to it that you succeed in whatever you wish to achieve in your life, and you have learned well certain aspects of our craft, but with this, of course, also comes a certain responsibility.'

'What do you mean?'

'I mean that for example you apparently show a particular aptitude for influencing the thoughts and therefore the actions of others, which like other skills is present in all of us, but some of us are more gifted than others, and few of us learn how to do it.'

'If you're talking about the night that I made Ash Spears play his guitar rather loudly, which I suppose you must have heard about, then that was quite a long time ago, and I haven't done anything like that since.'

'No, I'm sure, and I'm equally sure that you have been forgiven for that particular piece of mischief, and in any case I'm also sure that some people actually rather enjoyed it, but it demonstrates well enough that you do possess a particular skill in this regard, and it is a skill which must be used carefully.'

'Well, I'll try to be careful, then.'

'Of course you will, and please forgive the lecture, but I have seen since and before my time as head of the sisterhood how destructive such powers can be if they become perverted, and used to do harm to others.'

'I presume you are referring to Rebecca?'

'Rebecca is a particular case. My predecessor had great faith that Rebecca could and would redeem herself, and for her sake I have kept that faith. Rebecca lived here, at the white house, during the last weeks of her pregnancy, and during that time I came to know her quite well, and yet she remains an enigma.'

'Well she's moved back to the village now.'

'Yes, I know, and I understand her reasons for so doing, and I am glad that she is making such a life for herself and Florence, but there are still uncertainties surrounding her.'

'What kind of uncertainties?'

'It concerns what we were just talking about; how our powers may be used to do harm to others, and go against our so ancient traditions. You will know, I think, of the black coven which exists in the east, and the curse which was placed on the Tillington household.'

'I know something about it, but not very much.'

'Well then, suffice to say that two of our number, and I include Rebecca in this, went against the coven, and Rebecca would have it that the coven was destroyed, and that all but one of the witches were killed.'

'I see...'

'The one witch is of concern to us, of course, but I remain otherwise concerned; Helena, daughter to our former High Priestess, has disappeared; there is no other way of putting it, and she was in secret league with Rebecca, and now I am most worried for her, and I begin to doubt Rebecca's account of the confrontation.'

'So you think she's lying?'

'No, I don't think that, but I think she may be mistaken; that other powers greater than hers have somehow led her to believe that things are not as they really are.'

'So you think Helena may be dead?'

'Perhaps, although of course I hope I am mistaken in this, but I think we must be prepared for anything to happen from now on. This need be no concern of yours, of course, but be careful, Rosemary. It is always important that you keep your art a secret, but now it is more important than ever; nobody aside from those closest to you must know that you belong to the sisterhood.'

'I'll be careful...I mean my family know, of course, but nobody else, as far as I'm aware, anyway.'

'Well that is as well, and let us hope that nothing bad will happen, but because of my concerns I wish to tell you something else of which you may not be aware; Sophia, who lives in the village, is also a member of the inner circle of our coven.'

'Sophia...?'

'Indeed, and I tell you this so that you will know that there is somebody aside from Angela close at hand, should you ever need them.'

'I see...Well, thank you for telling me.'

'I will of course tell her that you know, but nothing need be said between you, unless you ever feel that it is appropriate or necessary. Sophia was in the first place sent to watch over the village, and to report events to me, but now as you will know she has become romantically involved, and has decided to stay in the village anyway, so that was a happy outcome. And now that our conversation has hit upon lighter matters let it stay there; I did not invite you here to scare you, for indeed there is nothing of which you need be afraid, so long as you keep the secrets of our sisterhood, which I'm sure you will.'

'So what about my mother; and my father for that matter..?'

'What about them, my dear?'

'Well, I mean they, and especially I suppose she has been involved in things, so is she in danger?'

'No, I think not, and I am not concerned for Meadow, and nor do I wish to leave you with the impression that there is any present danger to anybody; as I say, it is quite possible that nothing untoward will happen.'

'Yes, but…How much has she been involved, anyway; I think there're things that she's never told me about; things that she's done, you know?'

'Well that may or may not be the case, but it is not my place to act or speak between mother and daughter; your mother is a wise and gifted woman, and if, and I say if, there are things that she deems best not spoken of then I'm sure she has her reasons, and I do not imply anything by my words; as far as I am aware she has no secrets from you. And now let us talk about you, for my main reason for inviting you here is to learn more about such a young and clever member of our sisterhood.'

'What would you like to know?'

'Anything and as much as you wish to tell me; let's start with your studies; which subjects are you taking, and which universities do you intend to apply to?'

The morning turned to the afternoon. At some juncture they ate a light meal of salad and bread together, and Rosie was shown around the rest of the ground floor of the coven, which she assumed was open to the others of the inner circle, the upstairs she assumed being the private domain of the High Priestess. The only variation from this happened in the mid afternoon, by which time Rosie had began to think that it would soon be time for her to leave to catch a train home, and once again Charlotte had anticipated her, and seemed to have perceived her thoughts.

'Well, my dear, you will wish to leave soon, I'm sure, but before you go I would like to show you something, or rather somewhere.'

She opened an inner door, and led Rosie down a flight of stone steps into a quite small underground room, which Rosie assumed had once been a cellar. Now, however, and once Charlotte had lit candles, she saw that the room contained a rectangular table and seven chairs, and appeared to have no other form of lighting. She assumed that the chair at the head of the table was for Charlotte's use, but she now at one of the side chairs, and invited Rosie to sit opposite her.

'This, my dear Rosemary, may be said to be the very centre of our sisterhood, both physically and spiritually; I have never invited anybody here before who is not a part of the inner circle, but I wished you to see it. I come here alone sometimes to meditate, but its' primary function is for meeting and ritual when the inner circle comes together.'

She placed her hands palm upwards across the table.

'Take my hands for a moment, if you will, and close your eyes.'

Rosie did so, and she heard words that she did not understand, and for a moment she lost consciousness, and thus all sense of the passing of time. When she next became aware, Charlotte was speaking to her in her soft, lilting voice.

'....time for you to be leaving.'

'What..? I'm sorry; I must have drifted off...'

'That's quite alright; I was just saying that you should leave soon.'

'Yes, of course…But how long was I asleep for, if that's what I was?'

'Not long, my dear.'

Rosie was unsure of what time they had entered the room, but a glance at her watch told her that it was later than she had expected. Charlotte now opened the door and extinguished the candles, and they walked back up into the daylight together. She did not have the least idea what had just happened, other than that she was sure that Charlotte had been speaking to her in her calm, beautiful voice, but as to what she had said Rosemary had no idea, other than that she felt better and lighter of spirit than when she had descended the stairs. If she could enter the minds of others and control their thoughts, then here was somebody who was clearly more adept than she, and Rosie would later conclude that she had indeed been hypnotized, or bewitched, or whatever one might call it, and had lost that part of her life and memory completely, for however long it had been. For now, though, her visit to the white house was over, and Charlotte fetched her coat at the front door, which she now opened onto a chilly but clear afternoon.

'Well then, Rosemary, I bid you farewell for now, and thank you again for coming.'

'It was a pleasure, and a real honour, actually.'

'Then it was a shared honour, my dear, and you leave with my blessing. I wish you well with your studies and with your life, and I'm sure I will hear good reports of you from Angela. We have spoken briefly of some dark things, but never forget that the sisterhood should always also be a celebration of everything which has been achieved over the centuries; our lives and my tenure as High Priestess are but a small part of something which goes back into uncertain time, and will continue long into the future. Learn the ritual well, for it is that which binds us with our sisters since the beginning, and until the end. Work hard, my dear, and be happy, and celebrate your life, for it is a wonderful and blessed thing.'

To which Rosie did not really have an answer, and in any case the same car which had brought her here now appeared and was stopped at the foot of the steps, although how that had been arranged with such precision Rosie had no clue, since no telephone call had been made that she was aware of. But now she remembered something, and so had something at least to say.

'Oh god, I nearly forgot; it's not much but I've brought you a small gift; it's my sister's latest album.'

She took a compact disc from her coat pocket, and gave it to her host, who looked at front and back covers.

'This is no small thing, my dear, and I thank you for it; I will very much enjoy listening to it, I'm sure.'

'Well, Tara's got a great voice, although some of the songs are a bit; well, you'll hear…'

'Of a sexually explicit nature, perhaps..? It's okay, I'm quite broad minded; our sisterhood embraces the widest possible manifestation of womanhood; you may be interested and perhaps surprised to hear that we include prostitutes as well as the pious in our number. Some of us are professors and some are home - makers; the sisterhood makes no distinction.'

'So, I mean; how many of us are there?'

'I don't know; I have never counted, and nor do I intend to, but we are many, and of all ages and from all walks of life.'

A parting smile between them, and Rosie descended the stairs and once again took the back seat of the car. She just had time to see the white – painted front door being closed before the blindfold was placed over her eyes.

Percival would have to wait until mid – evening for the telephone call that he was expecting. When it came he was eating his evening repast of vegetables in fried –rice, of which he had made enough to last for probably three days, since he would be eating alone. Any shortfall in his weeks' nutrition would be seen to by Nigel and Susan at the Dog and Bottle, but he had cooked one meal, at least, and felt thus vindicated. When the 'phone rang he left his half – eaten meal on the dining table and took his glass of wine to the desk; he was fairly certain who would be calling.

'Hello…'

'Hi, it's me; sorry, I've been tied up all day in meetings.'

'So where are you now?'

'In the hotel room, finally; just been to the gym and had a shower, and I'm getting room service. I wanted to wait until I was settled before I called you.'

'So….Did you tell them?'

'Not yet, actually; nobody was around, and it was Monday morning, you know, so there was no opportunity, really, and I had a train to catch.'

'Oh well, there'll be other opportunities.'

'I'll have to wait 'til I get back to London now.'

'Sure…'

'Oh shit, here comes supper; that was quick. I'll call you back in an hour.'

'Okay, speak later…'

'I'd better put a dressing gown on; wouldn't do answering the door naked, would it; unless it was to you, of course.'

'Go and get your supper…'

'I love you, Percival.'

'I love you too.'

'Gotta go; bye…'

Percival delayed the continuation of his meal in favour of a cigarette.

There was a new and different dynamic about Sally now, which had been there since their reunion, but Paris had been the beginning of something which he had not seen in her before. She had not after all handed in her notice, or even told anyone that she was leaving, but he supposed that this was only for the reasons that she had given. In truth and to say the least of it he still had his reservations as to what she was doing, or intended to do, and her reasons for doing it, but it had to be her choice. If he was honest, Sally's return to being the most important person in his life had taken Percival by surprise, but there could be no looking back now, could there? If she was prepared to commit to the sacrifice of her career, even if only a small part of that had been done out of fear of losing him again, then he would do what he could to see to it that their relationship made it through whatever was to follow. And something else that he now decided was that he would not feel guilty, whatever happened; this had been her decision, and it was her life. He drained his glass, and said a silent toast to the future. He could not know that the future in this regard would be nothing like that which he currently imagined, for there was somebody else who had quite different ideas, and of this person we will hear in due time.

At a non – specific juncture during the car journey to the railway station, Amanda told Rosemary that she could remove the blindfold; they were safely away from the back – roads now, and had entered the outskirts of the small town. In her blindness since they had left the white house, Rosie had begun to speculate as to the primary reason that she had been invited here. Was it because of her mother, or had it merely been so that Charlotte could meet her, a courtesy which was apparently extended only to the favoured few, or was it perhaps to warn her of possible impending trouble in the village, in which case surely she could have spoken through Angela. Or perhaps again her prime motivation had been to do whatever she had done when Rosie had been under her spell; she had implanted something which Rosie had no access to through her normal thought or memory processes, so she could have no idea as to its' significance. Perhaps that had just been a test, to see whether Rosie could resist her hypnosis, and thus how strong she actually was, or had it been something less sinister; just a blessing or positive words to take away with her; a subliminal gift, imparted from the very heart of the sisterhood, where nobody but the inner circle went, and now Rosie had been there, and why had Charlotte done that?

In any case such speculation was interrupted as soon as she entered the railway station; the train was already standing at the platform, and a swift check of her watch told her that it was about to depart. She ran up the steps and across the pedestrian overpass between platforms, and was just in time; the train began to move even before she had taken her seat. She sat down heavily, and was recovering her breath as she looked across at the person who sat in the opposite seat, her surprise registering at the same time as theirs; it was somebody whom she had seen before.

'Hello, is Gwendolyn there please?'
'Of course Gwendolyn's here; I live alone, Reginald.'
'Yes; this is Reginald.'
'I know this is Reginald.'
'Yes, well the thing is, I was wondering if on the off – chance you might happen to be free of work commitments one day

soon, and if so whether you would like to go to the Science Museum in London; that is, if you would like to.'

'*I see…*'

'I would also be there; that is, we would be going together.'

'*Well I'd rather made that assumption, and I would love to, although I prefer the Natural History Museum.*'

'Of course; the Science Museum was only an example, the point being…'

'*That we would go together…I can be free on Friday, if you would like.*'

'Then Friday it is; thank you.'

'*You're welcome. So where shall we meet?*'

'Where would be convenient for you?'

'*You could meet me here if you like; Flat 6, The Chandlers, May Street.*'

'Yes, that would be very fine.'

'*Shall we say about nine o'clock?*'

'Yes, I will be there at nine o'clock.'

'*Very good then, and thank you for calling, Reginald; I shall look forward very much to seeing you again.*'

'So will I; that is to say that I will look forward to seeing you, too. I had intended to 'phone you sooner, but…'

'*I understand, but you've 'phoned me now, which is the important thing.*'

'Indeed; until Friday, then…'

'*Until Friday…*'

Reginald replaced the receiver of his telephone, noting that his hand was shaking rather violently after so brief a conversation. This was the first time in his life that he had 'phoned a lady to ask her out on a date, which he supposed was what it was, and he had been preparing himself for any reaction, including rejection, but that had not happened. So, Friday then, and he was sixty four years old, but supposed that when it came to such things, whatever such things were, it was far better late than never. He went and sat by his fish tank; he always found that watching his fishes had a calming influence upon him.

A smile, which Rosie returned quite spontaneously, and without further thought; such a thing would have been inappropriate at a first such meeting, but this was not the first time that these two had so met. The first time they had studiously avoided eye – contact, but in the complex matter of human relations this was a different circumstance, and absolute politeness was no longer necessary, and significantly he had been there first; he could thus even speak to her without fear of being misunderstood.

'Well, this is a coincidence, isn't it?'

The young man with the curly hair and wearing the brown shirt and tweed jacket now had a different broadsheet newspaper over his knee and a pen in his hand, and was clearly doing another crossword.

'Yes, it is, isn't it…'

'You any good at crosswords…?'

He had a pleasant voice, and an accent which placed him somewhere near London, and from an upper – middle or upper – class background; it was an intellectual voice, which perfectly fitted his style of dress and general demeanor.

'No; at least I never do them, so I don't know, but probably not.'

'Well here's one across; *'Two ponies, despite two ducks, question mark..?'* Two words, four - dash – seven…'

'It's cryptic then, is it?'

'Very…It's usually the toughest crossword around; I can't always finish it.'

'I probably couldn't even start it.'

'Well anyway, I suppose since fate has brought us together again, we should at least introduce ourselves; my name's Quentin.'

('Quentin; of course; what else would your name be?')

'I'm Rosie.'

'Pleased to make yours, I'm sure; so what brings you to this god – forsaken backwater of our island nation?'

('I'm a witch, and I've just met with my High Priestess.'; no, better not.)

'I've been visiting a friend; you?'

'Visiting an aging grandmother; just in time, actually; she died this morning.'

'Oh dear, I'm sorry...'

'Well, she was ninety four, so life didn't owe her much; she smoked right up to the end bless her; her last fag was still burning when she croaked...Which is ironic, really since both of my parents died of cancer, and neither of them smoked past the age of about twenty. Anyway there now has to be a post – mortem, would you believe; fucking incredible, if you'll excuse my French, I could tell them that she died of being ninety four, but that isn't enough anymore, apparently; there has to be cause of death for the death certificate. You have to get a certificate if you die, which says that you died of heart failure or some such crap; Christ, a light cold would have finished her off. Anyway since both of my brothers work abroad its' left to yours truly to organize the funeral and so on; we'll probably put her in the ground next week, and then there's the will to sort out...Jesus, how do you split a huge house in Clandon where none of us want to live three ways, with sitting tenants?'

'I really don't know.'

'No, of course you don't, and forgive me, I'm thinking aloud and you're the first person I've met....'

'It's okay, really; I've got nothing better to do. So will your brothers come over for the funeral?'

'Yeah, I expect so; at least Tristan will, and Freddy, that's Tarquin, might even make it if there's money involved; which means we'll have more arguments, and Tris will probably end up hitting Freddy, which will end up in another huge family feud which will go on for years. Christ, I'm getting bored just thinking about it, and I know what you're thinking; dodgy nomenclature, right? Our dear departed parents had a way with pretentious names, and Tarquin gets hot under the collar if you call him by his real name, so Freddy kind of stuck, since he was about eight, I think.'

'I think they're nice names; at least Quentin and Tristan; I'm not sure about Tarquin either, to be honest.'

'There you go then…Anyway, your turn; what do you do when you're not visiting friends in far – flung places?'

'I'm still at school, actually; doing 'A' levels; I finish in the summer.'

'What subjects?'

'History, chemistry, maths and English'

'So you're an all – rounder, then; well done. And what university will you end up at, and studying what?'

'Psychology; wherever I can get in, assuming I get in anywhere. What about you; what do you do?'

'I'm between jobs, as one might say; I did three years Geology and Paleontology at Bristol, then mastered in Human Evolution at Oxford; that was last year, and I haven't really worked since; well, nothing relevant anyway, there's not a lot of funding around these days for discovering our evolutionary past, but I remain optimistic.'

'I was thinking of applying to Oxford; would you recommend it?'

'Sure, I mean there're as many wankers at Oxford as anywhere else, and it's not a passport to instant fame and fortune any more, but yeah, it's still a good college.'

'Right, well thanks for the advice.'

'You're welcome; did you notice what the last station was called?'

'Norminster, I think.'

'Then I'm next up; I'm not going all the way home yet; got to stop off and see a man about a funeral.'

'Where's home..?'

'A stones' – throw from Queenswood Station; I awaken to the sound of trains every day; you?'

'Middlewapping...'

'Nice; the quintessential southern English village...'

'Yes, the houses are nice, although I live on a bus, actually.'

'With your mum and dad, I assume?'

'With my mum and dad...'

'Admirable eccentricity...You're not a witch by any chance, are you?'

'What...?'

'The witch of Middlewapping; present – day folklore; people say there's a witch living there.'

'No; nothing like that.'

'That's a pity; I've always wanted to meet a witch...Tell you what...'

Quentin wrote something on the edge of his newspaper and tore a piece from it, which he handed to her.

'No business cards I'm afraid, but if you ever need a paleontologist...'

'Thanks, I'll bear it in mind....'

'In fact give me a ring anyway, any time; I'll tell you more about Oxford; bore you with tales of derring – do amongst the dreaming spires; we were clearly meant to meet up, so let's find out why sometime.'

'Okay…'

He stood up to leave, and placed a small, well - used canvass bag over his shoulder.

'Oh Jesus Christ; you know what? *'Half – century…'*'

'I'm sorry?'

'The crossword clue; a pony's twenty five quid, yes..?'

'Yes, I think so…'

'So two ponies equals fifty, and the two ducks contextualize it; it's a cricketing analogy, a duck being no score, and fifty runs is a half – century; Christ, that's just too obscure, don't you think?'

'It's too obscure for me, anyway.'

The train pulled to a stop.

'I meant it, you know; call me, if you want.'

'Sure…'

'Until the next time then…'

He smiled as he parted, and her last view of her new – found acquaintance was him walking casually along the platform, and he waved his newspaper as the train departed.

So now that which had in any case been a significant day in the life of Rosie Knightman had taken on a new and quite different significance, and even thoughts of her meeting with the High Priestess had for now been eclipsed by a brief conversation with the young man in the tweed jacket. All she had by means of continuing their connection was a scrap of newspaper with a number scrawled upon it, and this she folded carefully and placed in her inside coat pocket, lest she should decide to 'phone him again. She may or she may not, and one thing she had learned first from her mother and then from Angela was not to act in haste where this could be avoided, so she would wait until she had made her deliberations, and then after due process she would 'phone him. In the meantime she couldn't settle to her book, so having bought a bottle of water from the service trolley which passed through the train, she leant her head back on her seat and settled to watching the world go by, and at this moment the world looked to Rosemary like a good place.

Chapter 11

THE NATURE OF LOVE

If there was one aspect of Rebecca's return to a life more normal which to her symbolised this perhaps above all others, it was her return to her small studio in the town, and to her potting wheel. As we have learned, the studio was one of several which formed a small, enclosed courtyard which benefitted from being close to the town centre, but away from its' noisy distractions. The courtyard and its' buildings had once been stabling for horses, before the mass production of the internal combustion engine had rendered such fine beasts all but obsolete. Now the courtyard rang to the sound of small industry; to the labours of Tony the iron – worker, Sam the cabinet maker and others; a small, refined group of craftspeople who had come to know one another during their working lives. They could scarce be called friends, as they had no contact with one another away from their working environment, but they would help one another if need be, and had respect for each other and their need for absolute concentration on their craft whilst they were about it.

On the first morning, Rebecca had placed Florence on her back and a bag over her shoulder, and had caught the bus from the village Green to the town, from whence to the door of her studio, which she unlocked with the key which she had kept with her always, despite and throughout her recent life. Those other artisans who plied their various trades were to a man and woman surprised and clearly glad to see her back. Even Sam the cabinet maker, who by repute amongst them was a stoic, and who seldom spoke unnecessarily to anybody, nodded his acknowledgment of her arrival, whilst others were more vocal, amongst these being Robin, the silversmith, who made jewellery of unusual and individual design.

'Christ, we all thought you were dead, but I see the opposite is in fact the case; you've been otherwise busy, it seems.'

'Hello Robin; this is Florence.'

'Pleased to meet her, I'm sure.'

And so on. Aside from Rebecca, there were two other women who rented workshops; Kim, who made small ceramic brooches and table ornamentation, and Wendy, who worked in batik. Both of these greeted the new arrival with enthusiasm, and welcomed her mother back into their small community, and in truth Rebecca was surprised to say the least by the general warmth of the welcome which she received.

The studio itself smelt musty and of old clay, and was as might have been expected in a state of neglect. Here it had been that she had created her last demon, and left it there for whoever next entered the room, and Victoria it was who had encountered it. Here also one evening had she met Eve, when she had come for Rebecca with all of her murderous intent, but she must now consign all of that to history; that was her past life, and a place to which she never wished to go back, indeed to which she must never go back.

During the morning she begged some off – cuts of wood from Sam, the cabinet – maker, for purposes of making a crib for Florence, which with customary apparent reluctance he provided, after which he quickly constructed the crib for her, asking no payment and seeming to ignore all attempt at thanks. It was a simple, shallow box, built in the finest Mahogany, and would serve its' purpose admirably. Rebecca placed her coat in the crib and enwrapped her daughter in it, promising her soft blankets and linen tomorrow, but having drunk her fill of her mothers' milk Florence quickly fell into contented slumber; the new sleeping arrangements and temporary bedding apparently suited her quite well for now, thank you.

Michael Tillington's small – scale property development business was going along well enough. He missed Rose's sensible and perceptive input into his decision – making, but he had sold two properties recently which gave his enterprise some liquidity, and would allow his further investment without assistance from the bank. He had therefore to all intents and purposes and for the first time in his life reached a position of financial independence; from now on he would be investing his own money in his future, instead of somebody else's, and for Michael this was a good feeling. It was at this time and quite by coincidence that something happened in this regard which promised to move his business to a different and higher level, and it was something which he had not expected. He had begun to look quite tentatively for his next financial venture, and aside from working on – line he had visited certain Estate Agents and auction houses, where he had put in speculative bids where he thought appropriate, with little hope of success. He was more than a little surprised, therefore, when one morning he received notification that one of his bids had been successful, and of all of them it was the one which he would perhaps least have expected. It was also the one in which he had been the most interested; a large, detached property in need of complete renovation, which he assumed would have gone to a larger and more cash – rich developer than himself, but on this occasion everything had worked in his favour, and once all financial and legal matters had been attended to, the property would be his. During the day that he had received the news he began to consider how he might best go about the huge renovation job which he was about to take on. He had developed working relationships with certain builders during the life of his business, and had been variously and moderately satisfied with their performance, but this was to be a different kind of project. Normally he would put the work out to tender, but he knew full well that in this instance cost could not be the overriding factor. In the first place the building was listed, so no external alterations could be made, and whoever undertook such a project must be sympathetic to a building which had stood since the mid seventeenth century. The property had sold quite cheaply, and the housing market was much more buoyant during these times, and a substantial profit was there for the making provided that the work was carefully undertaken; in good condition the house would sell for a very large sum of money. By the afternoon of the day, he had made up his mind, and in the mid - evening he kissed his son goodnight, put on his coat and left the Manor House, walking down the long, gravel driveway; he would not be needing his car on this occasion.

On her first day at the studio Rebecca produced nothing. She took delivery of a consignment of clay, and otherwise set about cleaning her working environment. She swept the walls and ceiling of cobwebs, washed down working surfaces and cleaned the cobbled floor of broken shards and cleaned it as best she could. Finally in this regard she thoroughly cleaned her tools, her kiln and her potting – wheel, and ensured their function for future use. She walked the short distance to the town centre and bought an electric kettle and dried herbal tea, and sandwiches for her luncheon. She went to the craft – shop and bought glazes of various colours, and by the days' end she was ready; tomorrow she would make her first pot, and her working life could at last begin again. She still had money on deposit which her mother had bequeathed to her, but she would need to pay her way as soon as possible, and one day quite soon would have to begin paying for her accommodation, wherever that might be. She could not prevail upon Michael for very long, but neither could she afford the market – rate for renting the house on the Green. She would have to find more a more modest abode for her and her daughter, but however that may be she must turn her thoughts to matters financial, and begin earning cash for her artistic endeavours. One thing which she had in her favour was the fact that the ceramic works which she had produced when she had last worked had become quite sought after, particularly in view of their individuality and scarcity, and she would it seemed have no difficulty in finding a market for her produce. The two craft shops which she had visited had both agreed to buy whatever she made which was to a quality, and advertise the fact that she was a local artist, who would make items to order.

And so it was that for the next weeks of her life, Rebecca would work long hours at the studio; beginning in the mid to late morning, her working day would often not end until late in the evening. At all times Florence was in close attendance, and was closely attended to, and the infant would fall asleep to the gentle hum of the potting wheel, and the other sounds which emanated from those others in the ancient courtyard who worked with diligence upon their respective crafts.

Given their now close domestic proximity, Rebecca and Victoria saw little of each other during these late winter weeks, which would see off the last of the seasons' chill. In part this was due to the business of their respective parenting; Victoria was more often than not working at the gallery during this time, and whilst at home she devoted as much of her time and energy as she could to Little Henry. Rebecca, as we have learned, worked during most evenings, and arrived home tired at the end of the long working day, and having attended to Florence's needs she would most often take a bath and retire immediately thereafter. Aside from needing to earn money as quickly as possible, Rebecca had an obsessive aspect to her nature which saw to it that if she was working then she would give herself over to her endeavours, body, spirit and soul, which aside from the care of her daughter left little room in her life for anything else. It was also true that Victoria knew that her parents would not approve of her spending nights away with her lover, which she knew at the age of twenty nine was ridiculous, but there it was, and it seemed to her a little sordid to sleep with another woman in her brothers' house, when he was being so accommodating about the matter. It was also the case that Victoria felt differently in a deep way towards Rebecca after the killing of the witches, and learning the whole truth about Rebecca's past, whatever had been the reason or justification for her murderous actions. She still loved her, and still would not condemn her, but something had come between them which was not to be easily overcome; a coldness was there, which was not entirely specific in nature, but both felt its' chill. Rebecca did not in any case come to the Manor House during this time, and so Victoria would on occasion go to the village in the late evening, but mostly they talked now of practical matters, and their respective children, and she would always walk home to her own bed. It was also the case that Victoria became increasingly impatient with Rebecca for refusing to tell her who was father to her child, which she plainly knew, so why would she not tell her? No harm would come of it, after all, and Victoria would not be judgmental, since she would not know the father. And there was something else which for now kept Victoria at the Manor during the evenings, and of this we will learn shortly, but in any case their previously often passionate relationship now went through a quiet and contemplative time; Rebecca was remaking her life, and Victoria was pleased indeed to see this, and asked nothing more of Rebecca than that, any more than she was being asked to give of herself.

Upon this particular evening, Meadow was about her needlework, accompanied by Keith who was gently playing his guitar, when a quiet knock came on the door of the bus. Meadow was at the time thinking about her children; wondering where Tara might be at that moment, and how Rosie had been a more contented and confident soul since she had been to the white house to see her High Priestess. There had it seemed been nothing of any controversy discussed, and clearly Charlotte had been true to her word, and had left certain matters unspoken of. Of Basil she need think less these days; Emma and he were clearly as besotted with one another as ever, and the young lady would she expected take her life and the life of their son in her gentle but firm and capable hands as she matured into womanhood; Emma was sweetness personified, but she had, Meadow believed, an underlying determination to get that which she wanted, and she wanted Basil, and in this much at least she had been successful. So taken as a whole, she considered that in all regards life currently went well for her offspring, and their happiness was her happiness. Keith was looking forward to the spring, and warmer weather, when he would be able to take his beloved for longer rides on his motorcycle, and now came the knock on the door, which bought an end to their various contemplations. Keith put down his guitar, and stood up to see who was calling, and it was a person that he would never have been expecting.

'Michael...'

'Hello Keith, please forgive the intrusion; I hope I'm not disturbing you?'

'Not at all; welcome to our humble abode.'

Michael Tillington stepped onto the bus, and he had never been here before. Keith knew Michael passably well from the time that he had built the extension to the Manor, and from their playing together in the cricket team during the summer, but it was true to say that Meadow had hardly so much as met the next Lord Tillington, and had spoken to him only once when Keith had introduced them at the Manor House, on the occasion of Nathaniel's Christening.

'Good evening, Meadow.'

'Good evening, Michael; can I offer you some herbal tea?'

'Yes; thank you.'

'So, to what do we owe the pleasure of this visit?'

Keith and Michael took seats at the dining table, whilst Meadow fetched tea, and Michael took in this confined but cosy environment in which he now found himself. Here had Keith and Meadow raised their three children, and Michael allowed himself a moment of admiration for their having done so, and to compare their home to his.

'Well actually it was Keith that I came to see, upon a specific matter relating to possible future work.'

'Oh yes;' said Keith 'not planning to extend the Manor again, are you?'

'No; nothing like that; it actually relates to my property developing business.'

'Right...'

'Yes...The thing is, I'm about to take possession of a large and mostly derelict period house, which stands in its' own grounds, and which I intend to renovate and sell on, and well, without beating about the bush, so to speak, and having seen the excellent job you did at the Manor, I was wondering whether you would be interested in doing the job for me, if we could agree terms and so on.'

'I see...Which period, how big, and how derelict?'

'Mid seventeenth century, the property has or rather had four bedrooms and two reception rooms, a kitchen and one bathroom, if such it can be called. It's basically just walls and a roof.'

'What are the elevations; brick, stone or plaster?'

'Brick, mostly, with stone quoins; mostly not plastered, at least on the outside.'

'And you've seen the structural report?'

'Yes; it isn't a full structural survey, but it indicates that the walls are structurally sound, although there's no damp – proofing, of course.'

'So we'd have to inject...How about the roof..?'

'That's rather subject to further inspection, but the roof beams seem to be in reasonable condition, as far as I can see, and as far as the report goes. I would hope to re – tile using the existing clay tiles, but I've only visited the property once, so everything is, as I say, subject to further inspection before I or we know what is possible or viable to do.'

'Where is it; it sounds like several months' work, and I'm not into big commutes.'

'It's on the Broadwater road, just across the county border, just outside a small village called Midford; I reckon about forty five minutes.'

'Yeah, I know Midford; it's just a few houses and a pub...I think it's called *'The Greyhound'* or something.'

'Actually it's the *'Horse and Hounds.'*

'That's the one; I've never drunk there, but anyway forty five minutes I can do...So it's a complete re – wire and re – plumb, yes?'

'Yes; I think we could use one of the bedrooms as a second bathroom without knocking any walls down; I want to leave the structure as it is, and end up with three bedrooms; one en - suite.'

'How about the grounds..?'

'They're about a hectare, all told; there was once an ornamental garden surrounding the house, which is called 'Orchard House' by the way, although any orchards there may have been aren't there anymore, and of course the grounds are completely overgrown now, so it would need complete re - landscaping.'

'I know a man who could do that...So do you need to apply for planning consent?'

'I don't think so; it's only grade – two listed, so as long as we leave the outside unchanged we can work inside, subject to building regs of course.'

'Sure... Well, I'm definitely interested....So I'd be a working contracts – manager, then.'

'Yes; I'd leave the running of the job entirely in your hands.'

'Right...Well let's take a look at it; I can take a day out anytime you like.'

'Tomorrow would suit me. The thing is, Keith, this is a very exciting project, and the most ambitious that I've taken on so far, and I want somebody that I know and that can trust on site.'

'Well thanks for the vote of confidence, and sure, tomorrow would be fine. It sounds like it would be as good as impossible to quote for, so it would need to be day – work, if that's okay?'

'That's why I need someone I can trust.'

'Sure...Well I'm into the idea as well, so we go tomorrow.'

'I'll pick you up in the morning; would nine o'clock suit?'

'I'll be here...'

'Good; well that's settled then, and I do hope we can work together on this; it must have been a beautiful house once, and could be again, I'm sure.'

The business of the evening and the reason for the visit thus concluded, Michael stayed only for long enough to drink his tea. Meadow had seldom heard Keith discuss his work before, and was struck as she often was by how focussed and succinct he could be when the need arose. She was struck by another side of his character, however, when he saw fit to change the subject;

'So how's life in general, Mike; any romance on the horizon yet?'

'Keith, that question is indiscreet.'

'It's okay, we play cricket together; gives me the right of indiscretion.'

'Michael; don't feel that you have to answer.'

'No, it's okay, really...Well actually there is someone, although I'm not certain if we have any long – term future together.'

'Local girl is she?'

'She's half Norwegian, actually, but she lives in Kent; her name's Elin.'

'Well good luck with that, or her, or whoever the future brings.'

'Thanks...Well I suppose I should be going; thanks for the tea and see you tomorrow morning.'

After Michael's departure Meadow joined Keith at the dining table.

'He's a nice man, isn't he?'

'Yeah; Mikes alright; no airs and graces, you know, but his Lordship's like that as well, and Victoria's the same...It's only her Ladyship who's a bit up herself.'

'Yes, you said...I've not really met her; that is we weren't formerly introduced. It must be hard for him though; Michael I mean. Whoever he marries will be the next Lady Tillington.'

'He didn't take much account of that when he married Rose, I mean given her former profession and all...'

'He was clearly in love with Rose; she'll be a hard act to follow, I would think. Anyway the job sounds good, doesn't it?'

'Yeah, it does; it would keep the three of us in work for a long time, if Damien and Will are up for it, and there'll be a lot of sub - contracting.'

'What about Mike?'

'I'll see about Mike; he's okay outside, but I'm not sure about the others working with him in confined spaces, especially Damien...Anyway I have to get the job first.'

'Of course...'

'Talking of Damien, I'd better 'phone him; tell him I won't be in tomorrow.'

'Right, well anyway I think I'll turn in; my eyes are getting tired.'

'Sure, I'll be there in a minute.'

Michael walked home feeling pleased with his meeting with Keith; if he had indeed found his contractor then work could he hoped start fairly soon, and he looked forward to seeing the house again now that it was his. On his arrival home, Lady Beatrice informed him that Elin had 'phoned again. He had not returned her last call, and she must be wondering why, but it was not a call that he was looking forward to making; anyway it was getting late now; he would 'phone her tomorrow.

'Victoria, do you have a moment?'

'Yes, of course Papa.'

This was early evening; Victoria had eaten her main meal of the day in London, as she sometimes did, and would not be joining her parents and brother for supper. Father and daughter retired to his Lordship's study, he sat down, she shut the door and took her accustomed seat on the opposite side of his huge, leather inlayed desk.

'So, how do you think the portrait is coming along?'

Lord Michael did not wish to see his portrait during its' making, but would wait until the work was complete; Victoria by contrast saw it most days.

'Very well I think; of course she still has some work to do on your face, but I think she will get you perfectly well in the end, in essence.'

'Yes, well, one hopes that one's essence is worth the getting, but the artist is somewhat reticent in her opinion.'

'Well she would hardly sing her own praises, would she?'

'No, I suppose not...I also suppose that if anyone is qualified to assess the quality or otherwise of a painting it is you, my dear. I understand that she would also like to paint you, as it were.'

'Yes, it seems so.'

'And would you be in favour?'

'I don't know...'

'Well, it's up to you, of course, but I think it would be good idea; we could hang together, so to speak; I would be quite willing to pay for the commission.'

'Thank you, Papa; I mean for the thought, but should mother not be done before me?'

'You're mother would not I think sanction the idea, nor I think would she have the patience to sit still and unspeaking for the long periods of time required.'

Victoria laughed at this.

'And do you think I would have the patience, Papa?'

'I think you can be whatever you have a mind to be, Victoria.'

'Well thank you again, dear Papa, for such a vote of confidence, but what about Michael; eldest child and only son?'

'Michael will wait, I believe; we men are best captured in our elder years, although I don't quite know why that should be the case; perhaps we have better found our essence by that time.'

'Whereas we women are best captured in our younger years, is that it?'

'It's just an idea, Victoria; strictly clothes on, mind you, I don't think we want a repeat of Rose's performance.'

'I hardly think I can compete in that regard anyway.'

'Yes, well without going to deeply into that, I believe you do yourself an injustice, beauty in my view being very much in the eye of the beholder.'

'I believe your opinion may be biased, Papa.'

'That may be so, but facially you have a refinement about you which dear Rose did not possess, beautiful though she no doubt was, and since we are talking in terms of essence, yours is essentially different from hers, and would broker no comparison in any case.'

'And from the neck down all things become equal, yes?'

Which perhaps she should not have said to her dear father, but Victoria was rather enjoying herself, and her fathers' rare and now evident discomfort.

'We stray into subject matter perhaps best not discussed between father and daughter, but staying strictly above the neck, Pandora is of the opinion that you would paint well, and I happen to agree with her, and in any case who am I to argue? Anyway, give it some thought; our artist seems to be happily ensconced in her temporary abode, and would not I think object to extending her tenure.'

'We'll have to start earning money from the apartment sometime.'

'Indeed, but nothing will happen there until the spring at earliest, and anyway certain things must rise above mere financial consideration, must they not, otherwise we're all of us wasting our time.'

'Well then, I promise to think about it.'

'Good...So anyway, speaking of free accommodation, how is Rebecca settling into Michael's house?'

'Well enough, I think, and she's working hard these days at the studio. I'm sure she'll be able to pay her way soon.'

'Well perhaps, and as long as Michael is content with the arrangement...This was his decision, of course, and I daresay he should be applauded for it, but one would not like to see the situation go on for too long, lest resentment set in, in certain quarters, if you understand me.'

'I'll keep an eye on things, Papa.'

'That would be all to the good. We know well enough your feelings for Rebecca, Victoria, but her returning into your life has not been universally seen as a positive thing.'

'I'm aware of that, and I will do what I can to see that the matter does not get beyond us.'

'Very well...And I daresay her daughter is well and healthy?'

'She is bonny in all regards.'

'Good....And dare I ask whether you have gleaned any intelligence as to the child's paternal parentage?'

'None, I'm afraid; she won't tell me.'

'I see, so is she even in contact with him?'

'That I can't tell you either.'

'Yes, well it seems to me that we men are increasingly surplus to requirements once the seed is sown, so to speak; one has a certain sense of redundancy.'

'Not everyone is as Rebecca and I, Papa.'

'Well one can but agree with that, I suppose. I still do not know what manner of trauma Rebecca had suffered prior to her most recent arrival here, and I daresay that you will not see fit to tell me, just as I am aware that other events have happened in your and her lives about which I know nothing, and can therefore have no influence upon, but take heed to my warning, Victoria; be careful in your dealings with Rebecca.'

'I will, Papa; I hardly see her now anyway.'

'We none of us see her; does she feel uncomfortable coming to the Manor?'

'No...No, I don't think so; she's working long hours these days, that's all, and goes nowhere and sees nobody apart from me, and then only when I go to see her.'

'Yes, well anyway, I daresay supper is imminent, so we had best leave it there for now, but don't forget that I'm always here if you need me, not that I daresay I can be of much use to anyone these days.'

'Oh Papa, I always need you, and always will.'

She smiled for her father, who returned her smile.

'It's not that...It's not that I don't want to tell you, Papa, but some things are just best not talked about; not yet, anyway.'

'Well if you ever consider that the time is right...'

'Of course...'

'You have your life to lead, Victoria, and I am aware of the unusual circumstances of our living under one roof, as it were, so I will not press my enquiry, but I see your doubt and uncertainty, which are ever vexatious things for me.'

To which Victoria had no answer, but instead she felt a lump grow in her throat, and tears threatened to reach her eyes, so she stood up, walked around the desk and kissed her fathers' forehead.

'Bless you, Papa.'

'Bless you too, Victoria, and don't forget to think about your having you portrait painted.'

'I won't, if you would really like me to.'

'Well, as in all things pertaining to your life, it's your decision.'

They smiled again, she left the room. Victoria knew her father well, and it may indeed be her decision, but her father had made it clear enough how much he wanted it to happen; to have mentioned the matter once would be mere indication, or mere suggestion, but to have done so twice was tantamount to a plea. Victoria in truth had no wish to have her portrait painted, but for her father's sake if for nothing else she would think about it. Lord Tillington sat for a moment in contemplation before standing; his presence would shortly be required at the dining table.

Orchard House would once indeed have been a beautiful house. Michael made the assumption that it had been built and initially owned by a member of seventeenth century nobility; perhaps somebody who had attended the court of the first King Charles, although it would have been built around the time of the English civil war, which made its' beginnings less certain, particularly since its' actual year of construction was nowadays unknown. Keith and Michael walked the two storeys of the house, carefully examining walls floor – boards and staircases. They checked window and door frames, to see which of these if any could be preserved, and in any case the leaded – light windows would have to be re – framed and reused, so as to maintain outward appearances. Michael showed Keith where he thought that a second bathroom could be added, and Keith suggested the possibility of opening up the loft space and adding another bedroom; certainly there would be enough space for it, and if it were to be added then now would be the time to do so, and there would be room enough for a narrow, quite steep staircase from the landing of the first floor. Having been around the house twice, they emerged once more into the bright sunlight of a calm, clear day. Inside had been years of dust and neglect in the warren of rooms which had once been someone's home, and it felt good to breathe the free, clean air. They walked the boundaries of the property and inspected the quite dilapidated walls, which even so Keith said he would do his best to renovate to an at least serviceable state, and walked as best they could through the overgrown gardens, where only the semblance of that which would once have been paths remained. Finally they returned to the house and sat on a low wall. Both looked again at the facade of the building, and this was a moment of significance for both parties, but particularly for Michael. For the moment and not for the first time he wondered if he had taken on too much, and whether there was a reason that he had won the auction with that which seemed to him to be such a low bid, and he sought reassurance.

'Well Keith; what do you think? I know it's too early to go into detail; just an overall impression...'

'It's doable, of course; basically you can build or renovate anything, but it's a big job. The walls seem okay, which is the main thing, but we won't really know about the roof until we start taking tiles off, or at least get a better look inside the loft; I'll need to bring a powerful torch next time.'

'Of course, but would you still be interested in taking the job on..?'

'Sure; I can do it for you, but like I say I can't really price for it; any attempt at a quotation would be bound to be wildly wrong.'

'Well, as I say, I'd be happy to pay you a day – rate, and you'd be free to take on whoever else you thought appropriate.'

'Well then, all things being equal I think we have ourselves an agreement, or at least somewhere to start.'

'Excellent; that's something of a load off my mind, I confess. I sincerely hope that this will be a mutually beneficial project.'

'Sure...You invest a few quid in this place and it'll be worth a fortune. I wonder when and why it was abandoned in the first place; I mean who owned it before you?'

'I've no idea on either count; everything was done through the Land Agent, of course.'

'Oh well, it's yours now; well done.'

There was something else which Keith wanted to say; something which Meadow had said regarding Michael last evening had struck a chord with him, and now at such a mutually satisfactory moment, he felt emboldened to ask. Meadow would doubtless have called this inappropriate, but she also knew Keith to be a person of some perception when it came to the people around him, and he was nearly always right.

'Nothing else on your mind, is there?'

'I'm sorry?'

'Forgive me, and I mean I know this place is a lot to think about, but you seem otherwise distracted.'

'Well actually I was just thinking; Rose would have loved the house.'

And so the chord was struck again; here was a man who would one day inherit an ancient title, and he had fallen in love with a beautiful prostitute who had died providing the son and heir; the pathos was there for all to see, and Keith had a moment of sympathy for the man who sat beside him. He knew well enough how it felt to love a woman, after all, and to lose Meadow was something which Keith could scarce even imagine.

'It would be a hard place not to love...Anyway I don't know about you but I'm thirsty, and I think the moment calls for a pint of ale; how about we retire to the *'Horse and Hounds'*; I wouldn't mind checking the place out anyway, for future reference.'

'That sounds like a very good idea; you've seen enough here for now?'

'Yep; I hope that Orchard House and I will get to know each other intimately before either of us are very much older; I'll know every brick of her soon; this could be the beginning of a not always beautiful love affair. She'll fight back for sure but we'll get her in the end, so let's leave her in peace for a while longer.'

Aside from any disinclination to leave the Manor House these dark, still cold evenings to see Rebecca, there was something else which kept Victoria at home during this time. There were sometimes exhibitions of contemporary art at the gallery, and she would on rare occasion meet living artists, but most of the artists whose work hung in the great rooms were as long dead as were the subjects of their paintings. It was also the case that she never saw any painting in anything but its' completed form, and the process of witnessing the portrait of her father unfold at the end of each day became a thing of fascination for her, particularly as the painter worked in the classical style. Abstract or impressionist art had its' place, she was sure, but she reserved her greatest admiration for the classicists, and her favourite paintings at the gallery had always been those painted in this style. And so, at the end of most days, once she had showered and eaten, and seen to the needs of little Henry, she would make her way to the new wing of the Manor, where Pandora had come to expect her visits. The two women would smoke cigarettes together, and Pandora would briefly talk Victoria through the days' work, and how the painting was progressing. Their conversations became ever more easy and natural as they grew to know one another better; Victoria would tell Pandora something of her family's history, and something of the lives of those still living; her mother, father and brother, and Pandora would speak of her own life and ambitions. For the most part their meetings were not for long, perhaps no longer than half an hour, although at times they were for considerably longer, and usually on such occasions they took tea together. It happened that upon a certain evening, however, neither would be working the next day; Victoria had the day off from the gallery, and his Lordship was not to be in residence, since he and Lady Beatrice were away visiting friends in Hampshire. On this occasion, therefore, at Victoria's suggestion, both allowed themselves the latitude of drinking a glass of wine together, which became the whole bottle, and then quite quickly became two bottles. The way of any relationship might change under such circumstances; Pandora knew well enough by now the nature of Victoria's sexuality, as had Victoria guessed hers, and it seemed to both of them a quite natural thing to take their friendship to a new level of intimacy. It was a simple enough thing, Victoria saying that which she would usually say.

'Well, I suppose I should be going.'

To which Pandora would usually reply;

'*Sure; see you tomorrow then.*'

On this occasion, however, she gave a different response;

'You don't have to go, if you don't want to...'

And so she stayed, and the artist and the daughter to her subject spent a night of gentle and considerate passion together, and both awoke with the feeling that it had been a good thing, and a thing well done.

The *'Horse and Hounds'* public house turned out to be a deeply rural establishment; a place where the local farmers and trades – people would come for an early evening pint of well – kept ale before going home for their evening meal, or ramblers might stop for refreshment on their way. This was early lunchtime, however, and aside from two such ramblers who were ensconced before their pints of ale and appeared not to be rambling anywhere for a while, Keith and Michael had the only bar room to themselves. The low, beamed ceilings placed the building at about the same age as Orchard House, the ambience being not dissimilar to the Dog and Bottle. Michael bought drinks and they found a table by a window, and raised their glasses to their new enterprise.

'Well; cheers Keith, and here's to our venture.'

'Your health and happiness, sir...'

'Yes, well the health at least I have.'

'And you're working on the happiness, yes?'

'It comes and goes, you know?'

'Such is the human condition, but in your case recent events are still having an influence, I think.'

'Well you know, some days are better than others, and the overall trend is towards improvement, I think, and Elin has helped in that regard.'

'Yeah, Elin...But you're not sure how you feel about her, is that it, or is it her feelings toward you that you're not certain of, if you don't mind my asking?'

'I don't think there's any doubt in her mind, as it happens...'

'So where's the doubt in yours; I mean what's she like, apart from being part Norwegian?'

'She's smart, independent and successful, and damnably attractive for that matter.'

'Man, you're painting a negative picture here...So where's the problem?'

'I don't know…Maybe it's just too soon, you know?'

'And she's not Rose, right?'

'I suppose so.'

'And she never will be, and nor will anybody; you've got to let go sometime, Mike.'

'I know…And I'm going to 'phone her this evening, and I have to make a decision, hence the distraction, even from such an important day as this. I won't keep her hanging on, you know; she deserves better than that.'

'Everyone deserves better than that, but the fact that it matters to you prompts me to advise caution before you throw the babe out with the bathwater, as it were; I mean you aren't going to live the rest of your life alone, so what are you going to do; start looking for love when the time feels right?'

'Yes, it doesn't work like that, does it?'

'Nope; don't think so. I mean this is none of my business, but if she's pulling you out of the doldrums then why not run with it, even if it isn't forever?'

'I suppose I'm just old – fashioned; once I'm committed to somebody, if you understand me… I'm sort of all or nothing. I stayed in Italy far too long, when I should have given up on that disaster a lot sooner.'

'So you want rid of her, is that it?'

'No…No, that isn't it either. I'd miss her if she wasn't a part of my life anymore.'

'Well Jesus man, so the problem's just in your head; let it be, you know; give it some air and see what happens; take it one day at a time, you never know, you might surprise yourself.'

'Yes, I suppose I might…'

'Anyway, look, sorry; like I say it's none of my business… We're here to talk about houses, right?'

'No, I appreciate being able to talk about it; thank you Keith, but I think I've made my mind up.'

During the remainder of their time together, the conversation returned to more practical matters pertaining to Orchard House. By the time Michael dropped Keith at the village, they had agreed a day – rate for Keith, which was more than Michael had been expecting, but he was not about to argue; he wanted Keith for the job, and so should be prepared to pay for him. The overall investment would almost certainly in fact be more than he could currently afford himself, so he would have to continue with lesser and quicker contracts to provide the finance, otherwise he would have to defer to the bank once more, something which he wished to avoid if at all possible. But still, it was in Orchard House that he would invest the most, emotionally as well as financially, and the day had been a good one, in the emotional sense. Michael had not made friends in the village in the same way as had his sister, but here perhaps was taking place the cementation of a friendship which had its' beginnings on summer playing fields, and would continue amidst the mess and chaos of a building site in winter, and he was glad of that. He lived in a Manor House, and Keith lived on a converted bus, so there was something to consider, and Keith had Meadow, and a loving family, and upon that no value could be placed. And good advice was also something without value, from wherever it should come, for in such small ways may lives sometimes be changed.

Rebecca still could not remember. She worked hard during this time, and even by her most exacting standards she knew that this was the best work that she had done; her time away from the studio had it seemed given her a new creative energy, which she embraced with enthusiasm. Her demons; her beautiful demons which had given her a quite different kind of expression during her dark years bore no comparison with anything else; they stood alone in their horror and in her need for them, but now she worked with the clay once more to make pots; objects which could be used as well as admired, and she was working well. She tried new shapes and new glazes; deep and contrasting colour combinations which she had not used before. The turning of the pots on her wheel to create simple, elegant contours was her craft; the same hands which had been used to destroy and to kill now touched the raw clay with the delicacy and tenderness of gossamer, but her glazes became her art, and that which she became known for. She sold to the craft shops, and with the aid of someone known to Robin the Silversmith she created her website, to which almost daily she added new photographs of her new creations. Soon she was taking commissions; she made plates and tea or coffee sets to order, if that was what people wanted, but her pots, some of which stood two or three feet tall, were her finest works, and she employed the services of specialist couriers to deliver them to far – flung parts of Britain, and then to mainland Europe and beyond. There were other practical matters to attend to; she opened a bank account and registered her small business, and from now on if one day she made sufficient profit she would pay taxes to the government for the first time in her life.

But still, she could not remember. How she had arrived at the Manor House after Farthing's Well was something of which she had no clue. She had thought to find out when next she had met Helena, but Helena had gone, and there was no news of her, so what had happened? Was Helena dead, killed by the black witches, but if so who had looked after her, and taken her away from the inferno? Who had in all probability saved her life? On occasion she would meditate upon this, and try to bring back the lost hours, but always that part of her life was closed to her. So perhaps after all there was no memory to be had; perhaps

she had indeed been rendered unconscious, but over time a
different thought began to grow within her; perhaps witchcraft
had been used, but that made no sense, for who would have
done that? Not Helena, surely, for where would have been the
point, and anyway Helena was not strong enough to overcome
her. Finally she would give up, for where was the point in further
speculation; it was still possible that Helena would come out of
her apparent hiding and make herself known to the sisterhood,
but until then there was nothing more to be done, so she let the
matter be.

She rarely saw Victoria during this time. Victoria would
on occasion visit her, but she never stayed, and for now they
had drifted apart as they had sometimes done before, and
Rebecca knew well enough the reason for this. Victoria knew
everything now, and these were hard things for her to know.
She had pressed to know who was father to Florence, but she
would not tell her, not yet. One day she would know, as would
Michael, but for now even love such as theirs would suffer from
such a revelation. They were bound together; Victoria knew well
enough that Rebecca had saved her, and brought her back to
the living world after she had killed herself, and that it was for
her and for her son Henry that she had killed the witches at
Farthing's Well, but these things were known at a deeper level,
where lived their love, and neither of them it seemed could go
there now. So for now Rebecca would work, and tend to her
infant child, and meditate upon all that had happened. Twice
during this time she went to the cottage down the lane, but
neither time was Percival at home, so her love for him she
would also let take its' course. She had her blessed and beautiful
daughter now, and she had her work, and for now this would be
enough. She was not yet out of danger, she knew this, and there
was still much uncertainty, but so long as a life more ordinary
was hers to live she would live it, and be thankful that she had

made it this far, and to this place, and that the demons of her former life had not yet found her.

After the night that she and Pandora had slept together, Victoria would still most evenings go to the new part of the Manor. She still wished to see the painting, but now she wondered whether it was for this that she went, or whether to see the artist was now the greater incentive. There was no initial or residual awkwardness between them; they could not go back to where they were, but they could drink tea and smoke cigarettes and talk together as they had before, and nothing need be said. What was done was done, and perhaps it would happen again or perhaps it would not, and this was understood. Only in one sense did their relationship change during this time, and it happened one night as Victoria was leaving. She was still unsure, and had convinced herself that it was more for her father than for herself, but once the words were spoken it was done.

'You can paint my portrait, if you would still like to.'

'Yes, of course I would...'

'Well then, whenever you have time; goodnight Pandora...'

'Goodnight...'

And so their gentle love affair would continue, but in a quite different way, for such sometimes can be the nature of love.

Michael Tillington arrived home at the Manor with a sense that his life had moved on during this day, although he could not at first identify the nature of the moving. There was Orchard House, of course, but that was after all just a house; a series of financial transactions which would in time he hoped yield good profit, and yet it was more than this. For the first time it was more than a place where people could and would eventually live. This time he would be resurrecting a part of English history; awakening something of beauty and substance from its' long slumber, and Michael had lived and breathed history all of his life. And yet it was more even than this. The ancient timbers and soundly constructed walls would one day all fall to ruin if nothing was done; emptiness must be filled, and it was not enough to look back at that which had been, when there was so much future to be had, and to be made.

So perhaps after all he had been fortunate, to have come across such treasure, and he must stop now looking for negative things where there was so much that was positive; the symbolism was there for him to see, and he saw it well enough; it just took him a while to realise how stupid he was being, and how close he had come to losing something so precious, and it had taken Keith to make him see it.

He ate a light meal alone, showered and let the early evening pass before he made the 'phone call which he had known that he must make, and Elin answered on the second ring.

'Hello, it is Elin here.'

'Hello Elin, it's Michael.'

'Oh, hello Michael, it is good of you to call me.'

Polite words, as Michael had expected, but her tone of voice was somewhat less friendly.

'Yes, look, I'm sorry I haven't returned your calls.'

'Well, I believe I know the reason for that, but perhaps you will tell me?'

'Yes, of course...The thing is....Oh dear, this is rather difficult over the telephone.'

'If there is something that you wish to say to me then best that you say it.'

'I would rather see you; could I drive over tomorrow?'

'I will be working.'

'What time will you get home?'

'I think around eight o'clock, or perhaps later; we are working long hours, presently.'

'So could I come then?'

'I suppose so, if you do so want to.'

'I do so want to...I mean I do want to. The point is, I want to talk about our future.'

'Our future...So do we have a future, then?'

'Yes, but...the thing being that I don't any longer want us to carry on as we are.'

'I see...So what is wrong with us as we are, and what is it that you want?'

'That's the reason, you see, that I haven't 'phoned you; I had to get things straight in my head, and well, now I believe I have.'

'Which things..?'

'You and me, I suppose, although I don't think I'd quite realised it, and well, where we go from here, as it were; what we both expect from one another, that kind of thing. I mean I know that sounds very contrived, and I don't mean it to, because that isn't it, really, but anyway....'

There was silence for a moment; this was not that which she had been expecting, and for a moment she had nothing to say; aside from anything else she was trying her hardest to work out what on earth the Englishman was talking about.

'So, may I come then?'

'Yes...Yes, of course you may come, but perhaps better on Saturday, if what you have to say will wait that long? On Saturday I will not be working.'

'Yes, well perhaps that would be best then...Thank you.... Right, well, until Saturday then.'

'Okay, see you on Saturday. Michael are you quite alright?'

'What..? Oh, yes, in fact I'm somewhat better than alright, Elin; I've been blind to certain things, you see; very important things, but now I think I begin to see clearly again, and....Well, as you say, best we wait until Saturday.'

'*Very well....Until Saturday then...*'

Michael ended the call, which had not been as he would previously have expected, either, but that had been before today. His life had stood empty and ruinous for too long, and today he had realised that from now on he must not look only at that which had been, beautiful though it once was. History was important, but it must not be allowed to be the only important thing; from now on, he must start to build his future again.

Something else of significance to our story happened during this evening, and of this we should hear before this chapter of our tale closes. After the night of the fire and the destruction of her home, Sharon had found temporary accommodation in the next county. It was just a room, but it had a private bathroom, and it would suffice. She bought new clothes, a computer and a telephone; the stuff with which she could begin to rebuild her life, and in her new home she would sit and contemplate all that had so suddenly happened, and meditate upon the death of Corinne and Fiona. She also contacted various agencies and people whom she knew in the dance business, and let it be known that she was available for work. If nothing happened in this regard soon then she would seek other employment close by, but for now she lived on such money as she had put aside. During these days her thoughts turned often to Megan, the only one of them of whose fate she knew nothing, and during the evening she went on line, and just on the off – chance she entered the name 'Megan Thomas'. There were several women of that name, but one immediately stood out; she had written a brief message, which Sharon read and then read again, as a heat of something like relief rose within her; the message read;

'If any of you survived, contact me.'

There was an email address. Sharon closed her eyes and breathed deeply, the better to bring her emotions to heel, lest they get the better of her. So, Megan was alive; she must have fled her house on the village Green somehow, and she was alive. The horror of the fire still lived within Sharon, but as the days passed she was getting better, and had begun to think of the future, and what must now be done. But from now on, she would not be alone.

Chapter 12

GLEBE HOUSE

Upon a certain day in the late spring, a young tradesman pulled his horse and dray to a halt on the village Green of Middlewapping. He had not been to the village before, and he went from door to door, plying his wares and his skill in the mending of pots and pans, and the sharpening of knives. He was a personable young man, with a ready smile and a quick wit, and he did good business, and so decided to stay overnight, for the weather was mild and dry and he needed no accommodation. He drove to the woods and set his horse to graze on the forest floor, and made a fire from old wood for cooking his repast. By the evening he felt sick, and his head had begun to ache, and within two days he lay dead beside his cart, though his body was not found until some days had passed. Four days thereafter the seamstress fell ill, as did the wheelwright and his family, and within a week there was scarce a household beside and around the village Green where no one therein had succumbed to the sweating sickness, which by now was more commonly known as the Black Death.

The young tinker had come from the city of London, where by now red crosses were everywhere being painted upon the doors of the unfortunates, and the dead were being piled into the plague pits by their tens upon tens of thousands. For this was the spring of the year 1665, and the last great plague had come to London, and none who were there or had been there were safe.

The king, in fear for his life, retired with some of his court and servants to Salisbury, and Parliament to Oxford; anywhere where there was less chance of infection and where some business could still be done, but most of the populous of London had no choice but to stay and take their chances, for most were poor and had no means by which to travel, and in any case they had nowhere else to go; London was their home, and they knew no other. In any case nowhere was truly safe; people travelled from village to village, and town to town, and quite unwittingly brought with them the infection, carried by the parasites which lived in their hair and their clothing, and for the good people of Middlewapping there had been no warning, for there was seldom any warning.

In the cottage down the lane, Thomas Cleves, he who had survived the civil war, was the first to succumb to the sickness, and then his wife, Ethel, and the children buried their parents in the woods, as best they could. Jessica was by now twenty one years of age, and little Tom, who was in fact tall and sturdy of frame, was in his twentieth year, and their sister, May, was eighteen. Nobody could understand why it should be that some became ill, and others did not, but few survived once their skin had blistered and turned black, and the sickness and headaches had begun. And so the children must leave, if they could, and Tom was the first to speak of it to his elder sister, on the day that they had buried their mother.

'But where will we go, brother?'

'We will head south, to the coast. Perhaps there will be places there where the sickness has not yet reached.'

'But we are not supposed to travel, lest we take the infection with us, and how will we make our way?'

'So what would you have us do then, sister; wait here until the sickness take us all, and we are all of us so horribly dead? I say we leave, and take with us such coin and goods as we have and that we can carry. I can work, and you have our mothers' skill in healing, as does May; we will get by well enough, and better that than to stay in this accursed place. Our parents would have had it so; we have said our prayers for them and done as well as we could; they are in God's hands now, but we must away at nightfall.'

But they did not leave that day, for on that day May fell ill, and brother and sister stayed to offer her such comfort as they could during her last days. They buried their sister with her parents, and only then did they depart, taking with them the future of the family Cleves; Thomas carried the name, and he would in time have male offspring, and the name would continue until one day would live Samuel Cleves, who was known to all as Sam, and he would take Vanessa as his wife, and their daughter they would call Emily. And Jessica did indeed take with her her mothers' skill in healing, which she in turn had learned from her own mother, and she also carried the knowledge of the history of the Tillington legacy which Ethel had taught her. The last direct female descendant of the murdered Jane Mary would also survive the plague, and she would have children of her own, and so one day a child would be born who would be called Rebecca.

And so of a certain evening brother and sister walked through the door of the cottage down the lane for the last time, carrying such goods as they could, and neither would return there. It would indeed be many generations hence before anyone bearing the name Cleves would return to the village, and by then any connection between the family and the old cottage had passed beyond all knowledge. Emily would never know that her forebears had once lived and died where her friend Percival now lived.

In time the cottage down the lane would be sold as a part of the Manor House estate, as would all of the houses around the village Green, but for now those who lived there buried and mourned their dead, and some waited for a while to die, or not, and then in time and for a time nobody lived around the village Green, for it had become a place of sickness, and of great sadness.

On the day that the first reports of the sickness reached the Manor House, his Lordship bade that nobody should set foot upon her threshold. The great front door was closed, and the servants were for the most part sent away to their homes, but by then several of those who served the Manor had come and gone, and the closing had come too late. Lady Rosalind, who had been fitted for a new dress some days previously by the seamstress, was the first to complain of the nausea and intense headaches, and she took to her bed, though there was never anything that could be done, and little comfort could be offered to the sick.

Since His Lordship had found such favour with the king, he nowadays attended court regularly, indeed more regularly than had any of his forebears, and he had grown wealthy by means of the importation of tea as well as his incomes from the estate. With a part of this wealth he had had a house built in which his sister, Jane, had but recently taken up residence with her companion. Her companion, who was called Katherine, was daughter to nobility, and was near ten years Jane's junior. Brother and sister had both agreed that though they retained filial loyalty, it would be better if they lived apart, for thus could Jane fulfil her own emotional and sexual needs, and William need think nothing of her circumstance in this regard. The house was some half a days' ride from the Manor, and in a quite isolated location, and Lord William, who was by now fifty years of age, called his son to him. John by now was twenty years old, and his sister Margaret was eleven.

'Father, you called for me?'

'Yes, my dear John, for as you know your mother is sick, and it is not safe for you to stay here. You must take your sister and ride to Glebe House, and stay with your aunt Jane until the danger has passed.'

'But what of you, father? Will you not leave with us?'

'No, my son; I will stay and tend to your mother, for perhaps she will recover, as some do, and I must in any case give her such comfort as I can. I will not risk your falling ill, for it is you who will carry my name and title after I am gone. I have taught you all that I can of my commerce, and should I die then that which you do not know you must learn, and I will leave word that this must be so. If all goes well and I do not succumb then I will send for you in due time, but now you must leave with all haste, and not come back until you hear word from the Manor that it is safe to return.'

And so John took his sister and rode to be with his maiden aunt, taking with him a hastily written letter from his father, which read as follows;

> 'My dear Jane
>
> You will perhaps know by now that the sickness has come to the village, and many have died here. It is with deep regret that I tell you that Rosalind has also become ill, and suffers now greatly, for such is the horror of this malady that there is little comfort that can be given, and no doctor or physician can cure or offer relief. She is in God's hands now, as are we all, and we can but pray for her recovery, and that she does not suffer for long.
>
> I have sent John and Margaret into your care, for they must be kept safe, and I can think of no other way. Do not send riders for news, for after this we

dare not risk any contact between us. I will send
word to you in due time, but for now I urge you
to take all care, and do not go abroad or to public
places, for the sickness it seems is everywhere about.

My prayers are with you, my dear sister, and I ask
that you also pray for us. May God have mercy on
our wretched souls.

Your loving brother,

William.'

And so it was that Lord William, the fifth Lord of that line, became ill himself on the day after he had sent his son and daughter away, and within days his life and so his Lordship had ended. Such servants as remained at the Manor House buried him with his wife as best they could in the grounds of the Manor, and prayers were said over their shallow grave. The servants then departed, to be with their own kin and to get by as best they could, and none of them would catch the infection, which paid no heed to status, wealth or position. To be a Lord, a Peer of the realm, and to have the ear of the king himself proffered great worldly advantage to those few who knew such favour, but gave no advantage in the matter so horrible and painful a malady as plagued the counties of England at this time in her history; a Lord or even a king could die as well as could the most lowly of serfs.

The next time that Keith went to Orchard House he went alone, with notepad and pen. It was on a day when the skies opened and no work was possible on the stone walling, so by mid – morning work was abandoned for the day, Damien, Mike and Will went home, and Keith braved the weather on his motorbike and crossed the county border. His smaller contracts were progressing well enough, and had had decided to give any residual work to Mike. Michael Tillington had assured him that all legal matters pertaining to the property were well in hand, and that there was nothing to prevent work from starting very soon, so in all senses Keith was preparing himself to begin the biggest renovation contract that he had yet undertaken. He pulled his motorbike to a halt by the old front door, removed his helmet and took the notepad and pen from inside his leather bikers' jacket. He unlocked the door with the key which Michael had given him, and walked once again from room to room, taking rough inventory of the materials, pipes, cables and so on that he was likely to need to carry out the work. The old house echoed to his footfall, loud footsteps in bikers' boots on the ancient stone floor, laid at a time long before motorbikes had been so much as dreamed of, and he tried to imagine how life would have been for the first people who had lived here, hundreds of years ago. He knew only that the house had been built in the mid seventeenth century, which with the little that Keith knew of history would place the building somewhere before or just after the restoration of the monarchy. And it had been during the plague years; he thought that the great plague of London had happened about that time, but he was not certain of exactly when it had been. More than during his first visit, however, he was struck by a sense of history which pervaded the house; the house had apparently been standing empty for a long time, and aside from a few rather dated sockets and light – fittings there were none of the accoutrements of modern – day living, and he assumed that the house would not have changed very much in appearance since its' construction, when candles and perhaps oil lamps would have been the only form of lighting. There was not and never had been a central – heating system; the same open fires which had warmed the last people to live here would have warmed the first, whoever either had been. Keith allowed himself a few moments in that which may have been the drawing room, or the music room, to absorb the atmosphere; the rain was falling heavily outside again, but otherwise there was complete silence; if there were such things as ghosts; if the spirits of the dead did indeed walk the earth, then there would be ghosts here for certain.

For Jessica and Thomas Cleves, who had fared better than their parents and sister and had thus far escaped the sickness, these were nevertheless the hardest weeks and months of their lives. They travelled on foot from village to village, often walking many miles each day, but were welcome nowhere, but rather were shunned or turned away, and even townsfolk were wary of strangers amongst them, for strangers may carry the infection. At times the road was blocked, and small communities would allow no one to pass, either for fear of the sickness or because the sickness was already amongst them, and sister and brother were forced to walk a long distance through wood and field to continue their journey in search of a place to stay. And so in the end they lived for a long time like feral creatures, on the outskirts of towns or hamlets, sleeping where they may, and avoiding all whom they saw. In one respect at least were they fortunate, for this was summer, and there were vegetables to be stolen from outlying fields, and traps could be set for wild rabbits and foxes, and thus could they eat on most days, making their fires in secret places, on which they could cook their pottage. They would wash as best they could in streams or brooks, and in fair weather they would sleep in the open, and when the rain came they would seek out a lonely barn or outbuilding and thus find shelter for the night. And so did they live, until by enquiring of passing strangers they would one day learn that the sickness had passed, and that it was safe once more to dwell amongst their own kind; to find employment, and a good place to sleep. But neither would ever forget their days on the road, and never again would they take for granted a warm bed, and good, wholesome food. Brother and sister had survived, and the legacy of their surviving would echo long into the future.

For John and Margaret Tillington, the days after their departure from their home were in certain respects difficult for different reasons. Little Margaret felt with raw, young emotion the separation from her mother and father, though she was too young to realise the implication of all that was happening. John, who was growing now into manhood, began perhaps at first at an unconscious level to realise that their mother may die, and so might their father, and if so then he stood to so soon inherit his fathers' estates and title, neither of which he felt ready to inherit. He understood by now something of his fathers' business, and he had on occasion attended the court of the king, but neither emotionally or intellectually nor indeed in any sense did he feel ready to take the Lordship or business upon himself; affairs of court and commerce were the preserve of older and wiser men than he, who had thus far lived ever in his fathers' shadow.

The siblings were welcomed with open arms by their aunt Jane, who felt great affection for her brothers' children, as did they for her. There was comfort here at least, and none of the material or circumstantial hardship which was by now being endured by Jessica and Thomas Cleves. If in other ways there could be any comparison between their respective circumstances, then Jessica and Thomas had buried their parents and sister, and could mourn their death, an emotional process which would in time find its' own way to restful conclusion. For all of those who now dwelt in Glebe House, however, there could be only doubt and uncertainty. All that the children and their aunt could know was that Lady Rosalind, respectively their mother and sister in law, was sick, and so would probably die, and that his Lordship, respectively their father and brother, lived in mortal danger. Both may die, or neither may do so, for there were some who survived the Black Death, and not everyone became sick. Jane, who had thought hard on such matters, knew that two people could kiss, or drink from the same cup and yet not pass the infection between them, so the sickness was not passed through spittle. People could breathe the same air, and one may succumb and the other not, so either some were lucky and others not, or the infection was not airborne. And yet two people may meet for the briefest time, and one may infect the other, so how was this done? She also was aware that the malady could take some days to manifest, and she watched her nephew and niece with fear and trepidation, and only after a week and more had passed did she feel confident that neither had caught the so horrible sickness, and so in this regard at least could she begin to relax. But still, the uncertainty of the fate of her dear brother and his wife remained, and this could not be found out, for Jane would do as her brother had instructed, and there could be no contact between the Manor and Glebe House. Not even so much as a letter could be passed between them for fear of infection, for not even physicians and learned men at this time knew how the disease was transmitted, and the safety of her nephew and niece must take precedence over all other considerations.

And so, for now, Jane and her beloved Katherine tended to the needs of the two children, and no others were admitted to Glebe House. The two women kept a small kitchen garden, and there was sufficient flour and meat in store to see to their nutritional needs for a short time, so for this time nobody left the confines of the house, and there was no contact with the world outside. The only other person who dwelt there at this time was Holly, who was maidservant and housekeeper to Jane, paid for from the monthly allowance which her brother sent to her, and Holly was under strict instruction not to leave the house under any circumstances, and to admit no one.

And so, for now, all were kept safe, and the days past in a pleasant enough way. Jane indeed took great pleasure in the company of her brothers' children, and perhaps especially in little Margaret, who was pretty and sweet of countenance, though ever did the thoughts of all dwell upon the fate of those who had stayed behind.

Keith pulled himself from his reverie. The visit had been spontaneous, he would not ask for payment for his time, and there was no need for haste; he could spend all day here if he so wished, but he was after all here for practical reasons, and in his capacity as future working contract manager, and to these practical matters did he now turn his thoughts. There was a good deal of preparatory work to be done before any rebuilding could begin; internal plaster must be removed back to the old brickwork, channels fetched out for cables, and holes bored for pipe – work to the bathrooms, and so on. Certain of the floorboards would have to be replaced on the upper floor, although quite how many would only become clear when he had started to lift them. Room by room he familiarised himself with that which would be his working environment for the weeks which would follow; on day one he would need a rubbish container and men with hammers and chisels, and the rest would follow from there. The house would look worse before it began to look better, but in his minds' eye Keith could already begin to see the house restored to its' former glory.

'What will happen, Aunt Jane, if my mother and father are dead?'

This was late one evening, Margaret was abed, Katherine was elsewhere and about her needlecraft, and aunt and nephew were alone in the drawing room; it was a moment of quiet reflection, where quiet words could be spoken.

'We cannot yet know their fate, my dear John. Your father was well when you last saw him.'

'And yet it has been near two weeks now since we left the Manor, and no word has been sent. Surely by now we must begin to fear that the worst has happened.'

'It is true that I have begun to think the same.'

'So then, what will happen?'

'Well, you would inherit your fathers' title and lands; the Manor would become yours.'

'But how will any of that come to be?'

'The king has left London for the west - country; all is presently confusion and uncertainty, but the king will return, and then you would present yourself to him. The lawyers will see that all is done, for there can be no dispute as to your entitlement; you will become the next Lord Tillington.'

'And thus would I have to attend court in my own right, and I have no sense as how to do that, or that which will be expected of me.'

'You need only attend court if wish to do so; there is no law which says that you must.'

'And then there is the matter of my fathers' businesses; I know that my father has invested much in a ship which set sail for China some nine months ago, and that ship will one day return, but I have no idea as to when that will be, or even what to do when it does return. I know that the cargo must be kept in safe store until the merchants and distributers have bought the raw tea, and whatever else the ship may return with, but I am quite unsure as to how any of that will come to be.'

'Your fathers' clerk will help you, John; there are others aside from your father who understand his business, and he has sent such ships away before; you will not be alone, and I will help in any way that I can. If your dear father is indeed passed away, then you and I will study the ledgers and legal documents, and between us we will see what is to be done. Do not forget that my income also depends upon your fathers' profit, which would become yours; I would become dependent upon you, my dear John.'

'In that regard you need have no concern, for you are as dear to me as my own parents; you and my beloved sister will be well provided for, if and when I have control over my fathers' coffers.'

'Then I thank you, my dear John, and for my part I regard you and darling Margaret as I would my own children, but let us not talk ourselves into the worse of news, for your father may yet live, and I thank God that you and Margaret are safe and well.'

'You speak of God, my dear aunt, but nowhere do I see God's hand in this; the good suffer and die with the wicked, it seems. I know that the Catholics would have it that this is God's vengeance upon a sinful world, or so I have heard it said, but as many Catholics are dying as are Protestants, so that makes no sense to me, and yet a loving and benevolent God would surely not allow such suffering.'

'These are mysteries indeed, my dear nephew, and they are not ours to understand; we can but do as we may, and must bide our time until the danger is over.'

'But for how long must we wait? How long must our incarceration here last, and for how long must we prevail upon you? Soon enough the food supplies will be gone, and we must send out or die ourselves from hunger. Should we not send a rider to bring back report from my fathers' house, for I am sorely put to it to wait any longer for news.'

'As am I, my dear John, for your father is dear to me also, and I would know his fate, but let us wait a little longer as your father instructed, for having you here is no hardship, and we have food enough for now; we will know when the time is right.'

And so they waited, but both knew that they could not wait forever.

The rain had eased by the time Keith had completed his tour of the inside of the house, so he next walked once again around the grounds, which would in due course be mostly Damien's domain. He walked the old paths where they still remained, and did his second tour of the boundaries. In one part of the garden were three very old and gnarled apple trees, which he assumed were all that remained of the reason that the house had been called 'Orchard House'. By pushing through some wet and overgrown shrubs quite close to the house, he came upon the head of an old well which would once have provided the household with water. The well had been in - filled, and his thoughts turned for a moment to a certain other well in Daphne's garden, where he and Mike had come upon the remains of Sarah Tillington and her sisters' lover, the young blacksmith who had been called Seth. And from thence did his thoughts turn to his daughter, Tarragon, for she had sung a song about them on her first album; indeed it was that song which had been the beginning of so much for Tara, and now she was somewhere on a world tour with no less a man than Ashley Spears; it was funny how life sometimes worked out; how one ballad written so long ago by some long – forgotten minstrel could have such a profound effect upon those who now lived. By now Keith was hungry, and decided to call in at a transport cafe which he knew of for breakfast, which would actually be his lunch. There was nothing more to be done in any case; he had made his notes and formed his impressions of that which must first be done. He locked the door, put on his helmet and mounted his motorbike; the next time he came he would doubtless be in Damien's Land Rover, and Will would be with them, but he was glad that he had come here once alone. He rode to the gate, or where there would one day be a gate, leaving the ghosts of the old house to their silence.

It was two months to the day after John and Margaret had arrived at Glebe house that any who dwelt there learned news of their father and mother. A rider came in the late morning, and knocked upon the front door. As instructed, Holly informed the rider from behind the still closed door that no callers were to be admitted, but Jane had seen the rider arrive.

'It is quite alright, Holly, please let the gentleman in.'

The gentleman's name was Mark, most trusted manservant to his Lordship, and perhaps the only person whom Jane would have let in; Mark of all people would never have put the children of his Lordship at risk, or go against the spoken word of his master. The door was opened, and Mark requested private audience with Jane, who showed him into the drawing room. This was the first time that Mark had been to Glebe House.

'I thank you for seeing me, my Lady; I regret that I come bearing bad news; the worst news, in fact.'

'I see; so my brother, his Lordship, is dead, then?'

'Yes, he is with God.'

Jane took a moment to compose herself; she had for some uncertain time assumed the worst, and her assumption had grown stronger with each passing day, but there had always remained some small hope.

'And her Ladyship; she is dead also?'

'Ay, it is so, and would that I was not the bearer of such grievous tidings. Her Ladyship was the first, but his Lordship followed soon after, and both have been dead some seven weeks now, and have been given Christian burial as well as may be. His Lordship's last instruction to me was that if he die then you should not be told until the danger had passed, and that I should be the one to tell you, if I was spared the affliction, so I have delayed my coming here until now.'

'Then you did right by him, and by all of us, though long have we waited for news.'

'Many have died in the village, my Lady, and the houses stand now empty, as does the Manor House. Only I remain there, for I sent all others away, and I have acted as watchman, but no new infections have I learned of, so I deem it now safe for his Lordship's son and daughter to return, though there is no one there to attend to them, and I leave the last word to you.'

'Then we will return as soon as may be, for I trust your judgement in this, and will come also to ensure their wellbeing as best I can.'

'Ay my Lady; that would indeed be for the best; if I may make so bold, the house will need a mistress.'

'You may make so bold as you wish, my dear Mark, for now as always have you been a good and faithful servant to my brother.'

'For the most part the tenant farmers have escaped the sickness, though Northfield Farm stands empty. But there will be much to do, and in truth I do not know which of the servants and trades – people will return to their homes, or when they will do so.'

'It will be well, Mark, for so long as I can provide sustenance for the family then all else will follow in time, but I would have you stay with us; we will need you now more than ever.'

'Then I will stay, my Lady, and be glad to do so.'

'Tell me, Mark, how have you yourself got by with no wage these past weeks?'

'My needs are few, my Lady; I have found or begged such food as I have needed.'

'Then you will be rewarded in due time; we also have lived under siege, and I will be glad to once more provide wholesome food for my brothers' children. These are terrible times, and we can but hope that the sickness has truly passed and will not return.'

'Ay, my Lady, that is also in my prayers.'

'We who live must count ourselves blessed, though I have all but given up with prayer, for prayer has taken my dear brother from me, so what of prayer? Anyway, will you stay and take such repast as we can offer you?'

'If I may only slake my thirst then with your consent I will return to the Manor forthwith, my Lady; I do not like to leave the house so abandoned for long; there are desperate people abroad, and those who would take advantage at such times. Do you have the means by which to return?'

'We have horses, dear Mark, and as to your thirst, I can offer you only water. There is no beer, and we have some days since drunk all of the tea which my brother gave me.'

'Then water will suffice. I am glad indeed to have found you all so well, and glad at last to have imparted this news to you, my Lady, though it be the worst of news; this moment has been hanging heavy upon me for the longest time.'

'And you have done your job well, but now if you will forgive me I need a little time alone, for I must prepare myself to tell the children; Holly will see to your water.'

'Of course; then I will take my leave, unless there is any other way that I may be of service before I go?'

'There is not, dear Mark; I will be leaving Glebe House empty for as long as is needed, so there will be some preparation to do; I expect that we will arrive at the Manor on the morrow, before noon.'

'Then I will await your arrival, my Lady, and wish you well until then.'

Mark took his leave, and Jane Tillington sat down heavily upon the settle, and allowed herself a few tears; her beloved brother had been untimely taken from her, which in her heart she had known to be the case, but still, there had always been a little hope. If she was indeed to be Mistress to the Manor House then her life would change from this moment on, for she must also be as a mother to John and dear, sweet Margaret, and she had never until now seen herself in such a role. Their needs would be so different, of course. Margaret would need to be taught such things as a young lady must know, and she was still so young, with all which that implied. John was near to manhood, and would inherit his fathers' title, and in time attend court in his own right. He would become an eligible young man, and must look to marry soon, so there was something else to consider. And first she must tell them, of course, of the death of their father and mother, though John at least will also have guessed that Mark had come with ill news. And she would have to leave her beautiful house, in which she had not long taken up residence, and she wondered when if ever she would return here. She and Katherine would from now on live together at the Manor House. She would perhaps return to her old bedroom, or else sleep with her beloved in the master bedroom in which her brother had slept with his wife. But at least they would be together, and although her love for Katherine and Katherine's love for her had never been discussed with John, he will have guessed their love, for he was a sensitive and intelligent young man. So much would change now; she would have to learn the complexities of her brothers' business, the better to assist his son, for they would need income, and she would be responsible from now on for the running of the Manor House. New staff and trades - people would have to be hired; they would need candles, kitchen staff and people to tend the garden. Rents would have to be collected and new families would live around the village Green, and she would as soon as she could bring some happiness into their lives, for Margaret would not have an unhappy childhood or adolescence; of that Jane was quite determined.

After a few moments she stood up, and prepared herself for the first part of her new life, hoping that the rest of it would be an easier thing. She could not know that only a little more than a year later she would be sitting on the steps of the Manor House, with a sense that all had been achieved. By then John would be established in the court of the king, and would be betrothed to Agatha, a beautiful young woman of good breeding, and little Margaret would be doing well in her studies. By then the ship which had been sent forth by her brother would have returned, and though it would be the last of the ships, a good profit would be made from her cargo of tea, ceramics and textiles, and other exotic goods from China. The Manor House would be fully staffed, and the village Green would once again be a happy place to visit, though for a time she would mourn the loss of her friend Ethel, who had lived in the cottage down the lane.

From her vantage point she would be looking at a distant pall of smoke which had risen two days ago above the city of London. News had reached the Manor House of a great fire which now raged there, for this was the fifth day of September in the year 1666. The fire would do much damage and make tens upon tens of thousands of people homeless, but it would also kill the rats and vermin which had harboured the fleas which carried the plague, and the Black Death would never again bring such suffering to the people who lived in the great conurbation, or to the counties of England. The inferno, which was seen as a curse by all, would also prove a blessing in the longer run of things.

Jane Tillington would never again live at Glebe House, which had been so named because it stood upon that which had once been church land. The house would be in time be sold, for as fate would have it she was mistress of the Manor House by now, the place of her birth, and so would she remain until the end of her days. It would be more than two centuries hence before Glebe House would be renamed, when the new occupants would engage in the business of growing apples, and only thereafter would the house be called Orchard House, which in the next part of our story stands empty and in need of repair.

And then one day will live Michael Tillington, a man with money to invest, and also will live a man whose name is Keith, who will sit one day in a transport cafe with his notepad and pen, and with determination to use his skill as a builder to see to it that this will be put to rights.

But for now Jane Tillington stood up, wiped the tears from her eyes and straightened her dress; she took in and exhaled a deep breath, and went in search of her nephew and niece. She would be their future, now, and they hers, and the future, however that may be, began from this moment on.

Chapter 13

A Very English Ultimatum

'So, welcome, everyone. I think before any of you bring any other matters before us we should discuss the events relating to Rebecca, and particularly Helena. I know that all of you will know something of this, but first of all let me summarise as best I can.'

Charlotte had not after all called an extraordinary meeting of the inner circle, since they were due to meet only a matter of days after Rebecca had been to the white house, and she needed some time by herself in order to think, and having thought, to think again. By now she had spoken to them all by telephone, but this would be their first meeting, and their first chance for discussion, and to air their no doubt diverse views. The ritual had been completed, so the days' agenda could begin.

'As you all know, there has been an attack on the black coven; Helena and Rebecca took it upon themselves to do this, and the coven has I believe been utterly destroyed by fire. As far as I have been told, and thus as far as I know, three of the coven were killed and one only of them remains alive and at liberty. I have only spoken to Rebecca, who came to collect Florence, but I have spoken to her at some length, and according to her it was Helena who instigated the attack, as an act of revenge following the death of her mother and our former leader, Helen. I need hardly say that this was done without my prior knowledge, and if we are to believe Rebecca, she was an unwilling participant. Two things have happened, however, which throw doubt upon the actual events of this terrible night. The first of these is that Rebecca has no memory beyond the burning of Farthing's Well, and it is only her assumption that all three witches were killed prior to the burning. She cannot remember escaping from the scene, her next memory being her arrival at the Manor House in Middlewapping, since when Sophia has told us that she has moved with her infant child into one of the houses by the village Green, which belongs to Michael Tillington, Victoria Tillington's brother. The witch who is called Megan, who lived for a while incognito in this same house, disappeared on the night of the fire and has not been heard of since. That which is perhaps of more concern is that neither has anybody heard word from Helena; she did not return home, and neither has she made any contact with any of us. These are the facts as they are known to me, and the matter is now open for our discussion; I would as ever be grateful for any thoughts that you may have.'

'You say' said Rosalind 'that Rebecca was an unwilling participant, yet knowing Rebecca as we all do, I fail to see how she could have been so coerced. You will all know that I remain ever skeptical as to Rebecca's actions and motivation, but I for one cannot believe that she was so innocent as to be somehow persuaded by Helena into so terrible an act; Helena who has given no indication that she is anything other than a peaceful and conciliatory person.'

The briefest of glances at Sophia, who looked away; she and now Charlotte were the only two of them who knew the truth about the death of Helen. Helena had known, of course, which gave her influence over Rebecca, but now Charlotte would have to lie once more to the inner circle. She had known that it would come to this, there was no avoiding it, but the moment was none the easier for that.

'Nevertheless that is Rebecca's account. Helena I believe kept her intent well hidden from the rest of us; she independently discovered the location of Farthing's Well, and enlisted Rebecca's help. This is as it has been told to me, and unless and until we hear differently from Helena, I will believe Rebecca. In any case it makes no material difference to the outcome; Helena is missing, and well, we must draw our own conclusions from this.'

'Surely' said Sylvia 'we must assume that she is dead, must we not? Nothing else it seems to me would account for her silence.'

'I have reluctantly come to the same conclusion.' Said Charlotte 'I think that Rebecca's account of the night is mistaken; I think that Helena may not have survived the attack, but was assassinated by the black witches. She could otherwise be being held against her will, but I think we would know by now if this was the case.'

'And yet' said Rosalind 'there is another conclusion which can be reached, is there not? Surely it is not such wild imagination to conclude that Rebecca has killed Helena. Perhaps she has conveniently forgotten what happened, or perhaps she has not, but that must also be a possibility, must it not?'

'Yes, it is a possibility,' said Charlotte 'and it is one which I have considered myself, but I don't believe it is so. I am the only one of us who has seen Rebecca, and Rebecca is not as she was, and anyway where would be her motivation in killing Helena?'

'Once again you defend Rebecca,' said Rosalind 'when we all know of what she is capable; she needs little motivation to kill, it seems, and if she assumed that only she and Helena would know of the attack, removing Helena would have made perfect sense to a murderess such as she. '

'Yes, I do defend her, Rosalind, as you always condemn her, because on this occasion I have no reason to disbelieve her. We may question her motivation in helping Helena, but let us not forget the reason that the black coven existed, which was for the ending of the Tillington dynasty, which would involve the killing of children. Let us also not forget that one of the children is Victoria's son, Henry, so that I would suggest would be motivation enough for Rebecca to wish the witches dead. I do not condone her actions, but I do understand them, and you can but take my word when I say that Rebecca felt a great sense of remorse for the killings, and did not kill willingly this time, however she has killed before. Rebecca is I believe as unaware of Helena's fate as are we, and she volunteered her account of the night to me, I did not ask her for it.'

'So,' said Amanda 'if we are to believe that Rebecca has lost a part of the night, how is that to be explained, and how did she get back to the Manor House, since somebody must have taken her there?'

'These are indeed the questions we have to ask, Amanda, and I will tell you my own thoughts, since I have had longer than any of you to contemplate all of this. If we work with the assumption that Helena died during the attack, as I now think we must, then she could not have brought Rebecca back, so somebody else must have done that. We know from news reports that three bodies were recovered from the building, which are apparently burned beyond identification, and Rebecca is certain that there were only three witches there when they attacked. So, if one of the bodies was indeed our dear Helena, then it is possible that another of the witches escaped. It defies logic that it was this witch who took Rebecca away, but when logic fails we must look to the illogical for the answer. Perhaps for her own reasons she wished to keep Rebecca alive, and perhaps she used her craft to remove those hours from Rebecca's memory. After all, Rebecca has never been the target here, but rather a means to their intended end; the death of the Tillington children we assume still remains their first and avowed intent. If they or she decided that Rebecca was still more useful to them alive than dead, then that could perhaps account for such action. That said, there are of course other possibilities; perhaps Rebecca was in league with one of the black witches, or more simply, perhaps she found her own way back somehow and then suffered some sort of partial amnesia, but neither of these scenarios makes any more sense. We know that the witch Megan remains at large, and we know now why she lived beside the Green. Rebecca spoke to her from Farthing's Well, and we can only be thankful that she did not kill the Tillington children when she may have had the opportunity, but now I think we cannot rule out the possibility that two of the coven survived, and only two of them were killed.'

All were silent for a moment whilst they considered the words of the High Priestess, then Rosalind was the first to speak.

'It's a pity that we have not had the opportunity to speak with Rebecca, and that she has not been called before the inner circle to account for herself to us directly.'

'I had no warning of her arrival. She arrived at the café unannounced, so I had no choice but to interview her alone whilst she was here.'

Charlotte could only hope that the tangled web of lies and half – truths which she was now weaving would not entangle her too deeply. She had made her judgment as to how much she would tell the inner circle, and hoped that her reasons justified her untruths, but it was in truth hope rather than certainty. Sophia had had more connection with Rebecca than any of them, and she had been silent so far during the discussion, but she now spoke. She at least understood how it felt to lie to those who should never be lied to.

'I've only seen Rebecca once since she returned to the village, and then only briefly, but my impression and the feeling of other people that I've talked to is that she is different now. I mean she has the baby, of course, and is by all accounts a devoted mother, and apparently she's working very hard these days at her ceramics business.'

'But how, my dear Sophia, does that affect what she may have done? We know that she has killed again, that at least is beyond question, since she doesn't deny it; indeed according to Charlotte she volunteered the information.'

This was Rosalind, whose skepticism remained undimmed.

'Yes, well that may be so, and she may or may not have had good reason to do as she did, but to kill one of us? I don't think so; I think you are wrong in your speculation, Rosalind.'

'All I am doing is suggesting that not everything that Rebecca says can be taken at face value. If indeed one of the inner circle has been murdered then we cannot allow our personal sentiments to cloud our judgment.'

'Which sentiments, Rosalind..?' Said Charlotte

Rosalind let the matter be; she was either unready or unwilling to challenge or engage their leader in direct confrontation, so she said nothing. Sophia, however, had more to say.

'Anyway aren't we talking about the wrong person? I mean Helena may be dead, for goodness sake; isn't that more important?'

'All of the events we discussing are connected,' said Charlotte 'and of course when the time is right and when we are quite sure we will remember Helena and the quite short time that she was with us. In the practical regard we can only wait until the relevant authorities declare her dead; we cannot intervene, for that is the nature of the sisterhood, and has always been so. If she is indeed gone then we will all of us miss her, but she went against the sisterhood, my dear Sophia, and it is because of that that we are in the situation that we find ourselves. The coven at Farthing's Well may be destroyed, but the witches were not all killed, and those who survived may be more dangerous than before. We must not condone the killing of anyone until there is no other way, and no other resort, and if Helena is indeed dead then it appears that she brought her death upon herself, hard though that is to say.'

'Had it not been for her' said Maria, who had so far remained quiet 'we would not have known that Megan was a witch, living in the village and even working for the Manor House. The children were in mortal danger.'

'Indeed,' said Charlotte 'and in that we have been fortunate, but it cannot justify Helena's actions. The children may still be in danger, and perhaps in greater danger now than before.'

'And yet always you seek to justify the actions of Rebecca.' Said Rosalind

'Rebecca was not of the inner circle. Helena knew well enough the responsibilities which come with that, and yet she hid her purpose from us.'

'Her mother had been killed.' Said Maria

'Of course, and had she lived or if by some chance she still lives then this would be mitigation, but it would not be excuse. All matters relating to this should have been discussed among us; that is in large part why we exist as the inner circle, and as the sisterhood. In matters as important as this we should not act alone.'

'So anyway, what can we do about any of this?' Said Sophia 'We could talk all night about the possibilities, but we still only know what we know.'

'Indeed that is so.' Said Charlotte 'Ever it seems do we seek the truth about these matters, and ever does the truth elude us. We cannot yet be sure that there are two of the coven at large, or what their intent may now be. They have lost members of their order; firstly the witch Eve and now whoever the others may be, and they will feel this loss, but it is how they react to that loss which is now the important thing. This is a very ancient order of witches, this much at least we now know for certain, and now Rebecca has quite consciously placed herself in possible danger, so we must consider what if anything we do about that. It will be very difficult now, I think, for the witches to get close to the children. They are safe in the Manor House, and Victoria we may be sure will be more vigilant now, and will not be so trusting of strangers again. Our main concern must be for Rebecca, who is of the sisterhood, and so is deserving of our protection. Sophia is there, of course, and I will give consideration as to what else can be done, but for now at least you all know as much as do I.'

'Yes, well, my being there is no guarantee of anything; there was a bloody witch living in the village for weeks and I completely missed it.'

'You must not berate yourself, dear Sophia; you could not have known.'

'I suppose not, but I'll be watching people more closely in future. The village is behind her; Rebecca, I mean, and Meadow and Keith are there, and they're amazing people.'

'Indeed they are, so perhaps Rebecca is safer than we think, and we can but hope so.'

There were as always other matters to be discussed; this too was an ancient order of healers, and would continue regardless of Rebecca's fate, and the fate of the Tillington Lordship, so little else of consequence was said for now, for nothing was yet certain. For Charlotte in any case this was a difficult subject, and opinions within the inner circle were divided and becoming more so, so for now she would continue to keep her own council. Farthing's Well had been destroyed, and one of their number had probably died in the burning of it, but Charlotte was quite sure that this was not the end of the matter. She had lied to the inner circle, but the lies had been believed, and Rebecca's secrets at least were safe for now, even if she was less certain of Rebecca herself.

'Em, we seem to have a small problem.'

'What kind of a problem?'

William Tucker and Emily Cleves had been enjoying a Saturday night of quite moderate but influential alcoholic indulgence, which had begun quite early. Thus it was that their often passionate feelings for one another found expression first in the downstairs dining room, where they had kissed one another passionately, and by mid evening the situation had quite got the better of them, and they had taken each other to bed. Here their love had found further and deeper expression, and they had had knowledge of one another, but now they had a problem.

'I can't get the knots undone.'

'What do you mean, you can't get the knots undone?'

'You must have been moving around, and tightened the knots up.'

'How can I have been moving around, I've got my hands tied to the bed – head.'

'Yeah, well that's the problem…You must have been moving your hands about; pulling on the ropes, or whatever, and the knots have gone really tight.'

'Christ, well you tied the knots. Couldn't you have used bows or something?'

'Wise after the event, you know…?'

'We've never had this problem before.'

'I was never a boy scout, that's the trouble; knots are not my strong point. Mind you I don't suppose they teach you the best way to tie girl – guides to bed heads; there probably isn't a badge for that.'

'Well never mind about that, just untie the bloody knots. Whose idea was it tie me up in the first place?'

'I think it was yours, actually; heat of the moment, you know?'

'I daresay you agreed to it….'

'Yes, well, always eager to please, you know? Anyway when a beautiful woman says *tie me to the bed – head* most men wouldn't have to think about it too much; weigh up the pros and cons, as it were.'

'Or how to untie the knots afterwards, apparently...'

'Doesn't even enter the arena of their thoughts...Trouble is I'm bit pissed.'

'Well I'm sobering up fast, and I need a pee, so what are you going to do about it?'

'I'm trying, okay? Christ, you must have been really pulling these...'

'Well I've had about fifteen orgasms since you did this, which is definitely your fault.'

'What's that got to do with anything?'

'What it's got to do with anything is that I wasn't thinking very much about what my hands were doing; my thoughts were elsewhere.'

'Yeah, I can see that.'

'Look, if you can't untie me you'll have to cut the rope; get some scissors or something from the kitchen.'

'Yes, well I suppose we can't leave you here all night can we?'

'No we definitely can't....'

'Scissors won't do it though; this is good stout rope; it's the stuff we use for tethering the goats.'

'Thanks for that thought.'

'I'll have to get something from the tool – shed; this is mans' work.'

'Bloody hell, we get some clothes on then and hurry up.'

'Sure...Back in a jiff...'

But then something happened which threatened to make the still relatively simple situation somewhat more complicated. An unmistakable sound came from the kitchen; somebody was knocking on the door.

Michael arrived at Canterbury in the late afternoon. He had only spoken once more to Elin, to arrange a time and place to meet, which in the event was to be at her apartment at eight o'clock in the evening. She after all had to work on this day, having several land disputes and transactions to deal with at present, but she would not be late home, and Michael was pleased in fact that they would meet in the evening; that which he had to say was better said during the hours of darkness, and far preferably accompanied by alcohol. He parked his car in the Municipal car park, and having some time to kill, he visited the ancient and in his eyes very beautiful cathedral, a place which he had not visited for many years. The first and only other time he had been here was with Victoria, and their mother and father, when he would have been about twelve years old, which would have made Victoria nine or ten. Otherwise he walked the equally ancient and beautiful streets of this small city, and stopped for coffee at a street – side café, having bought himself a pack of cigarettes and matches. Michael was not an habitual smoker, and did not always have cigarettes about him, but today was a particular day, and it was definitely a smoking day.

Just prior to the appointed hour he drove the short distance from the city centre to the block of low – rise, high – end apartments in which Elin lived. She opened the door looking in his eyes quite stunning, in a quite short and quite low – cut dress and high heels; dressed apparently for whatever the evening had in store, which was in fact to be a matter of some importance them both.

'Hello Michael….Would you like to come in or shall we proceed immediately to the restaurant; I have booked a table for half past eight.'

'No, well, let's proceed straight there then, shall we?'

'Very well...'

The restaurant was an easy walking distance; a small and intimate just out of own bistro selling international cuisine at in - town prices. They sat at the corner table which had been allocated to them and which Elin had requested, she being a quite regular patron of the establishment. They ordered wine and a first course, and when the wine had arrived and was poured Michael raised his glass, and Elin touched hers against his, although she had no sense yet of what if anything they were celebrating. This was in fact an unusually awkward moment between them, particularly since they knew each other so well, but tonight both knew that there was an agenda, the difference between them being that Michael knew the nature of that agenda. Elin on the other hand had not the least idea what to expect, and in truth was prepared for anything, or so she assumed. Perhaps this was to be a gentlemanly way of telling her that their relationship was over, since she could still make little sense of their last significant conversation. In any case, this had been his instigation, so she would let him speak first.

'Well; here we are, then.'

'Yes…It's…It's good to see you, Michael.'

'You too; so how have you been since last we saw one another?'

The last time they had seen one another was shortly after they had made love in a toilet, somewhere over the north of England, and at an altitude of about twenty five thousand feet above sea level.

'I have been well enough, thank you, but mostly working, actually; there has been little time for recreation.'

'Yes, of course.…'

('What do you mean, 'Yes, of course.'?) The English, she knew, had many ways of saying nothing, and so far nothing was all that Michael had said, until;

'I have some quite significant news, actually.'

'Oh yes..?'

Was this to be it, then; was this the moment when she would understand the reason for this particular meeting?

'Yes; I've come into possession of a very old and very run – down property. It's a big place; several months worth of work, I would think, but it should yield some good returns eventually.'

So, apparently it was not then.

'Well that is very good.'

'Yes, it is; Keith, who lives in the village, is going to do the job for me. He built the extension to the Manor House.'

'I see….'

The first course was delivered to the table; on Elin's recommendation both had ordered vichyssoise.

'Yes, we should be st…'

'Michael….'

'Yes?'

'Whilst this is very interesting, and I would love to hear about your new purchase, can we first please talk about whatever the fucking hell it is that you want to say to me?'

'Oh, right, of course…'

'I'm sorry, but when you eventually returned my call it all sounded rather important, and I have been speculating ever since, so if you would not mind I would like to get to the point of our meeting.'

'Does there have to be a point to our meetings?'

'No, of course not, but….'

'It's okay, I'm also sorry; probably not enough vino yet, you know, but anyway best get to it, I suppose, before the soup gets cold…'

'The soup is already cold; that is the point of vichyssoise.'

'I was joking, actually; sorry, English humour, but anyway…'

Michael took a large mouthful of his wine.

'Anyway, well then the thing is, I've been thinking…'

'Yes…?'

'About us, I mean, and well, if I may be quite honest, I'm not really happy with the way things are between us.'

'Yes, I thought this was the case.'

'And so, well, I think we must find a solution, the point being that I simply don't think we can go on as we are.'

'And so now you wish to tell me that we should be just friends again, is that it? Is this the reason that you are here?'

'Well no, actually, that isn't really it…'

'So, what is it then?'

'Well my solution, which of course is just my idea, is that you and I should probably, as it were, get married.'

Elin had also just taken a mouthful of her wine, upon which she very nearly choked, and it took a moment and some light coughing for her to collect herself.

'Michael, did I hear you correctly?

'Yes, I expect so.'

'And this is not more English humour?'

'No; deadly serious, actually…I mean not now, of course, necessarily, but…Well, marriage isn't really the only thing…I don't think I'm expressing myself very well, am I?'

'You're doing fine, I think, but please carry on.'

'Well the point is, you live and work here, and I live at the Manor House, which is quite a long way apart, isn't it, and well, although seeing you sometimes is very well and good, and I always enjoy our time together, of course, I don't quite see where the future is in it, if you see what I mean.'

'I see…'

'Yes, well there it is, really, so given that, I was hoping that we could, discuss my proposal, so to speak.'

'So you're proposal is that we get married; that I give up my career and my home and live with you in the Manor House, is that correct?'

'I suppose so, yes.'

Elin took another large mouthful of her wine, partly because she needed the wine, but also because of a sudden she needed to think rather quickly, and these few seconds of her life had become important in this regard. Okay so begin at the beginning; take this in stages.

'So why did you contact me, Michael, when you knew already how far away I lived?'

'I contacted you because…Well, I hadn't foreseen how things would turn out between us. I thought we might be friends, but that isn't how things have worked out, is it?'

'No…No, well…But we were already friends, were we not?'

'Well yes, in a way, but only through our parents.'

'Still, even so…Forgive me, Michael, but this is all something of a shock. So in fact you are giving me an ultimation, is that it?'

'Actually the word is *'ultimatum'*, but I wouldn't put it as strongly as that.'

'Would you not? What you are saying to me is that either I marry you and give up my life and my independence more or less immediately, or that our relationship is over, because otherwise you see no future in it, which sounds to me rather like a…what is the word again, please?'

'Ultimatum…'

'Ultimatum; yes, exactly.…'

'It wouldn't have to be immediate; I mean perhaps you could find a similar job nearer the Manor, or something, and London is commutable, of course, and you could take your time in doing that. And then, well, we could scarce live together at the Manor unless we were married, eventually, or at least betrothed, so that would seem to be the thing to do, don't you think?'

Another brief and precious moment of silence followed, whilst Elin tried to calm the storm of surprise which currently raged within her. She was being asked to marry an English Lord; one who had recently lost his wife, and with whom he had a child, and so in time would she become a Lady. She had at times given consideration to their longer – term future together, but the longer term had of a sudden become rather more immediate; her life it seemed had come to meet her, and it was not yet a gentle meeting. She loved Michael, of course, though she knew full well that she was not the most passionate of people, but she loved him, in her own way, and now it seemed clear enough that the Englishman loved her too. But still, for a moment she, the ever calm and sophisticated Elin Tomlinson, was lost for words, and nobody had touched their soup.

'Well, Michael, I must say that you are a man of surprises…'

'Is it really so much of a surprise that I want to spend the rest of my life with you?'

'No…No of course not, but well, actually yes it is, I think.'

'Well, now you know…You don't have to decide now, of course; you can think about everything for a bit if you'd rather.'

'I see, well I thank you for that, at least, and I think I do need a little time, actually. Not because I am uncertain as to how I feel about you, please don't think that, but I am a little confused at present.'

'Yes, of course; I've had time to prepare myself for what I was going to say, after all.'

Elin was lost, and Michael was right, of course; whatever she had prepared herself for it was not this, and the thought which now became foremost in her mind was that she had to get away. If she agreed to his proposal then she might spend the rest of her life with this man, and in principle she had no issue with that, but now he was the only person that she could not be with. If she was indeed to have him, then first she must get away from him; the precious moments of thought had not been enough.

'Look, Michael, I think…I think it better if I leave.'

'Oh, I see.'

'You will not understand, perhaps, but I need time alone now; you have taken me quite aback, to be honest.'

'Right…Right, well then, you'd better go, I suppose; do you want to eat your soup first?'

'No, thank you; suddenly I'm not at all hungry.'

'Me neither, actually…'

'I must think about everything, you see; suddenly there is a lot to think about. Are you really asking me to marry you?'

'Yes; that's the gist of it.'

'And you are quite sure that you want this; that you want me, I mean; is this also in the gist of it?'

'Quite sure; I've had my thinking time; rather too much of it, actually.'

'I see; well then, I suppose it's my turn. What will you do; drive home this evening?'

'I hadn't really thought about it, but yes, I suppose so.'

'I had prepared everything for you to stay the night, of course, but now that would seem strangely inappropriate.'

'Yes, I suppose it would, strangely enough; anyway if you say so…'

'Well then, goodnight, Michael, I will contact you tomorrow, either by telephone or email.'

'So you won't write to me this time then? I thought you didn't like emails'

'A letter would take too long; you will have my answer tomorrow.'

She stood up, walked around the table and kissed him gently. She walked from the restaurant already considering this most unusual of circumstances; the man she had just left would either be her future husband, or she would likely never see him again. Michael watched as she took her dress and her high – heeled shoes through the door and out into the street, and she did not look back.

'Christ, who the hell's this?'

'No idea.'

'What time is it?'

'Just gone nine thirty...And here are you tied to the bed and all; this is awkward, isn't it?'

'Sometimes, William Tucker, you are the master of understatement.'

'You have to see the funny side of it though.'

'If I had my liberation I would hit you right now.'

'It wouldn't be funny if you had your liberation.'

'Well I might hit you anyway.'

'Fair enough...So what should we do, do you think?'

'Well I can't do much can I?'

'I mean do you think we should just ignore whoever it is? Maybe they'll go away.'

The door knocker sounded for a second time, this time more insistently.

'It might be important; I mean who calls 'round at this time on a Saturday night?'

'It's not that late, Em; could be a friend I suppose.'

'Well go and see who it is then, and then get me out of this.'

'That could be tricky.'

'You'll just have to use your initiative, won't you?'

'I'm too pissed to have much initiative.'

'Well sober up then, and cover me up before you disappear.'

'Right, I'm on it...'

Will pulled the duvet over his beloved, to at least afford her some modesty, and to keep her warm during her temporary confinement. He then dressed quickly in trousers and T shirt, and left the bedroom. Whoever was outside would be able to see him walking across the well lit kitchen and dining area; he, however, could not know the identity of the caller until he opened the door, and when he did so he concluded that his particular problem had not become any easier. The caller was Sandra Fox; the vixen had called at the most inopportune moment imaginable, and Will of a sudden was thinking as quickly as he could.

'Oh, hi Sands.'

'Hello Will; not calling at an awkward time am I? I know you farming types go to bed early these days.'

'What...? No, not at all; come in.'

She did so, and sat at the dining table, which is what everybody did. She was wearing a mid – length dress, and heels which as far as Will was concerned were quite inappropriate for the quite long walk from the village, but he had long since decided that unraveling the mysteries of women was quite beyond him.

'Can I offer you a drink?'

'Any wine going?'

'Sure, there's a half – drunk bottle downstairs; just, uuum, just stay there for a minute.'

'Okay; I wasn't going anywhere.'

'Right...'

Will descended the stairs, allowing himself a moment to contemplate this very particular state of affairs. Here was a woman who would be his woman if she had her way, when his actual woman was in the bedroom and tied to the bed; he concluded that he could not have invented or imagined this situation, and that real –life can sometimes catch one unawares. He came back up with the wine bottle, took a glass from the cupboard and put both on the dining table. Sandra watched this process with increasing uncertainty as to that which was going on; something was amiss, and something or rather somebody was missing.

'Will; where's Em?'

'She's…She's not feeling too well, as it happens; she's in bed.'

'Oh dear; what's wrong?'

'Oh, you know…'

'Actually I don't know, which is why I asked.'

'Flu…she's got flu; there's a nasty bug going about, so I hear. She's feeling pretty rotten, to be honest.'

'Poor lamb…I'll go and see her; see if she needs anything.'

'She doesn't need anything.'

'Well I can give her my sympathy at least.'

Sandra stood up.

'No…! I mean, best not; she's asleep.'

'Oh, right…So it's just me and you then. So are you going to help me drink this wine or am I drinking alone?'

Somewhat to Will's relief, Sandra sat down again.

'No…I mean that is to say sure, I'll have a drink in a bit. Thing is, I have to just go out for a minute.'

'Really..?'

'Yeah; got to check on the goats; work never stops for the smallholder you know…'

'I see…'

'So just, like, stay there then; I won't be a minute.'

Will was only too aware that Emily would be able to hear everything which was being said, and had to hope that Sandra would say nothing suggestive or incriminating, as she was wont to do when in his company. Sandra remained unconvinced as to what was going on; Will was acting strangely; she had never seen him like this before, something was up, but by now he had put on his Wellington boots and had gone outside.

Will made it to the tool shed, and now had to make another decision. The best tool for cutting rope would be the long – handled loppers; one lop or rather two lops and the job would be done, the problem being that the loppers were quite large, and as the name suggested had long handles, and would be difficult to smuggle past the unexpected house guest. He could more easily carry the small hacksaw in his back pocket, but then he would have to saw through the ropes, which would take much longer, and the sawing might even be audible from the dining room, which might sound somewhat odd. He had to make a quick decision; he pushed the loppers down the back of his trousers and pulled his T shirt over them. The handles stuck out somewhat, but it was, he concluded, the best that could be made of it, and so long as he kept his back to Sandra all should be well. To his relief, Sandra was where he had left her. He removed his boots and walked in a sort of casual, sideways – fashion toward the bedroom door.

'Will, are you okay?'

'What…? Oh sure; I'll just go and see if Em's awake yet, she would hate to miss you.'

'Okay…Don't wake her up though; I'm sure you and I can f…'

'Right, so see you in a minute then.'

Will walked backwards for the last few paces, trying to make it look as though he always walked that way, and in this fashion he made the bedroom, and not without a certain relief he closed the door behind him; he and Emily would now have to whisper. With some flourish Will pulled the loppers out from their concealment.

'I brought the loppers; it's Sandra.'

'I know. Well come on then, release me from my bondage for goodness sake.'

With two swift movements the chords were cut, and Emily was free.

'Feel the freedom, sister.'

'Will, fuck off.'

'You'd better put some clothes on.'

'Why didn't I think of that…So now I have to have flu, do I?'

'You could say you're feeling better. I'll hold the fort while you get dressed.'

'Christ I need a drink; and a pee, and not necessarily in that order. Remind me never to let you do this again.'

'Okay, only it was your…Never mind, see you in a minute.'

Will reentered the dining room and sat opposite Sandra, who gave him a somewhat suspicious look.

'So, how's the invalid?'

'Feeling much better as it happens; she'll be out in a minute.'

'That was a quick recovery.'

'Well you know Em; not one to be tied down…I mean kept down for long.'

'No indeed.'

'So anyway, it's good to see you Sands.'

Suddenly the change of attitude; Will had visibly relaxed and was back to normal, so what the hell had all that been about, and there was still no Emily. Just then, however, the lady herself appeared, wearing a casual frock and looking fine, actually.

'Hi Sands.'

'Hi Em; how are you feeling, you poor cow?'

'Oh, okay; I think the worst is over; hang on, I just have to visit the loo.'

Emily would now have to fain at least slight illness, when she was feeling anything but ill, and would try to recover slowly throughout the evening.

'She looks okay.'

'Yes, well, trust Em to put on a brave face, eh?'

'Funny, she was always the worst of us when we were at school and she was ill; she was unbearable.'

'Yeah, well, anyway, I'll get a couple more glasses and open another bottle.'

Will went about his self – appointed task; Emily reentered the room.

'There; all better…'

'Are you sure you should be drinking, Em?'

'Oh I'll be okay.'

'Yeah; glass of wine and you'll be right as ninepence, eh Em?'

'So anyway, to what do we owe the pleasure?'

'It's Saturday night, I was on my own and feeling pissed off, that was all.'

Emily sat at table, Will put some music on.

'Oh dear…Well you're not on your own anymore.'

Will joined the two girls; he too was now feeling rather sober after his endeavors to covertly extricate himself and his beloved from their earlier predicament. He thought they'd got away with it, but now he needed a drink to enter into the spirit of this new circumstance. He wondered momentarily whether Sandra Fox had ever been tied naked to anyone's bed – head, and thought perhaps not, but anyway it was not a useful thought or image, being rather distracting in nature, so he quickly abandoned it and instead attempted to join the conversation.

'So how's living back at home, then..?'

'It sucks, to be honest. I mean I'm enjoying the work, but mum and dad are mostly away as always, and Emma spends all her time with Basil, so mostly I'm there on my own, which was okay for a while, but….Apart from the research my life could be summarized in one word, and it wouldn't be a nice word.'

'And I don't suppose you see any of your university friends.' Said Emily

'Such as they are, but no, I haven't seen anyone.'

It took only a little more time and alcohol for Emily to conclude that Sandra was quite seriously depressed; this was more than her having one bad evening. This had happened before, when they had been at school; the doctor had prescribed anti – depressants, and Emily wondered which particular pills she was currently taking, if she was taking any. Sandra had never been the most sociable of people, often seeking her own introspective company, and she did not shine in group situations. She was probably Sandra's best friend, but on the whole Sandra did not make friends easily, and to this day she had not had any significant romantic relationship that Emily knew of. In Emily's view this was ironic, since taking all things into account she had always been the most attractive of their peers, and always seemed to look good. Emily had days when she thought she looked okay, and Will, bless him, never stopped telling her that she was the most beautiful woman in the world, which was a subjective view, of course, and she usually told him not to be so silly, but she hoped he would never stop saying it. And there was more to it than looks, of course. There was a connection which must be made between two people which often defied any rational analysis, and so far Sandra had never made that connection with anyone. Anyone that was apart from Will, but that particular connection only went one way, and it was odd, really, that she should feel the way she so obviously did about him. He was Will, of course, and she loved him, but Sandra was by several degrees more sophisticated and academically gifted than was her beloved man, and she was hard put to it to see any meeting of minds, even if only one of the minds was attempting to meet. Will was tall, and in her view the most handsome of men, but that was also probably because she loved him so much. Nevertheless she could scarce blame any woman for finding him attractive, but with Sandra it went deeper than that. Sandra, she was fairly certain and as far as these things could be defined was in love with her beau, which tended to complicate their friendship somewhat. One did not covet one's best friends' boyfriend, far less become involved with them, unless one's feelings for said boyfriend were strong indeed. Such things were taboo; an unwritten rule existed, but Sandra, Emily was quite sure, would break any such taboos without a second thought should the opportunity present itself, and the feelings be in the least bit reciprocated. Nevertheless Sandra was her friend, and she was depressed, and she trusted her man and his love for her absolutely.

So, what was to be done then? Aside from offering friendship and an open invitation to Jacob's Field, both of which Sandra already had, Emily could see no other or further way of helping, really. She couldn't live Sandra's life for her, and if it was having Will that would make her happy then she would just have to remain unhappy; there was only so much to be done in the name of friendship. In any case the remainder of the evening, which ended sometime after midnight, passed in pleasant enough fashion. Emily knew Sandra well, and she became increasingly convinced that she was otherwise intoxicated aside from the alcohol; she had probably taken something before she had arrived, the effects of which were becoming increasingly apparent as the evening progressed, and which was not mixing well with the wine. This would be uncharacteristic if it were true, but Emily did not otherwise give the matter much thought. Mutual friends were discussed, and Emily briefly considered suggesting a meeting of the girls, but the idea did not get past the consideration. Dawn would be as man – obsessed as ever, and would use the evening to boast of her latest conquests, and Ali would doubtless be her usual highly – strung and neurotic self. Emily loved them both, but currently had no wish to broker such a meeting; she saw no point to it, and Sandra would probably contribute or gain very little to or from the assembly; Will still saw JJ sometimes, although not so often these days, but otherwise and aside from her and Sandra, connections to the old gang had become tenuous.

By the time she left, everybody but especially Sandra it seemed was quite drunk. Whatever Emily assumed she had taken was perhaps more potent than she had thought; she was slurring her words and even having difficulty standing up, or walking in anything like a straight line. Her mood at least had lifted a little during the evening, but there was still a long way up to go, and now she just looked intoxicated. It was Sandra, however, who instigated her own departure, and only then did the conversation become briefly controversial, and the full extent of her frustration with her life become apparent.

'Well I suppose I should be going; no doubt you two will be up early tomorrow, herding the goats or whatever.'

'Shall I walk you home; I'm too pissed to drive.'

This was Will, who thought that Sandra would in fact have difficulty walking the quite short distance alone, aside from any risks to her person in doing so, and even Emily could scarce argue with the sense of it.

'You can't walk home drunk in those ridiculous heels anyway; do you want to borrow some shoes?'

'Thanks Will, that would be nice; and it's okay Em, Will'll hold me up, won't you Will? Don't worry, I'll send him straight back.'

'Yes, well you'd better.'

'He wouldn't stay anyway, would he, Will?'

'Sands, for fucks' sake...'

'Or then again I could stay here and keep you both company. What do you think of that idea, Will?'

Sandra laughed, but nobody else was laughing, and Will thought it politic to intervene.

'Yes, well, when you're ready…'

The two friends kissed goodbye, Sandra aiming straight for the mouth, and she seemed reluctant to let go their lips, or the embrace which followed; she really was having some difficulty standing up now.

'Bye Em, my love; I'll see you soon, okay?'

'Sure; whenever…'

After their departure, Emily cleared away the glasses, and tried to untangle her somewhat mixed feelings about the evening, and particularly the end of the evening. In close retrospect, Sandra's behavior had been beyond acceptable, hadn't it? Sure, she was drunk, or whatever, and sure, what she said had been said in jest, but perhaps only part in jest, and sometimes only when alcohol has seen off inhibition are a person's true feelings exposed. If Emily was reading the situation right, Sandra was desperately lonely, and torn absolutely between her love for Emily and her feelings for Will, which were of a quite different nature.

After that which seemed to Emily to be rather too long a time, Will returned, looking still drunk but quite relaxed, but Emily couldn't quite keep her need to know or her own feelings in check.

'Well, did she make it okay?'

'Yeah, just about, with a little help, you know? Getting there took about twice as long as getting back, but she's home now.'

'And did she try to get off with you?'

Which was said more aggressively than she had intended; none of this was Will's fault, after all.

'What…? No, actually; she hardly said a word all the way, and what she said didn't make much sense, then she slammed the door in my face, which I thought was a bit rum of her under the circumstances. Not that I was trying to get through the door, but….Still, girls will be girls, I suppose, but she was definitely on something, don't you…'

Emily put her hand over Will's mouth, and smiled. So she had slammed the door, which was no doubt further indication of her frustration with her life and her love, but that was not something to think about now; she would think about Sandra again in the morning; Will was here now, and that was the only important thing.

'Sorry, my love…'

'What for..?'

'Nothing, never mind; let's go to bed.'

'Yeah, I'm bushed…'

'Not that bushed, I hope; you can sleep soon, but I want to show you how much I love you first.'

'Fifteen orgasms not being enough, as it were.'

'It was only *about* fifteen, and fifteen orgasms is just getting started, and I don't need to be tied up this time.'

'The ropes have been cut now anyway, but I'll keep the loppers handy in future; just in case, you know?'

Emily laughed, and took her man by the hand, and now it was she who was leading him.

'You think I'm ever going to let you tie me up again? Honestly, Will, the things you make me do…'

He could have mentioned once again that it had been her idea, but that was old ground now, and the look she gave him as they entered the bedroom would stop any mans' normal thought processes in their tracks.

The next time she was in town she would buy red ribbon; that would be prettier, anyway, and much easier to untie, provided that Will was more careful with his knots in future. It would give ribbons and bows a whole new meaning.

'*Megan, this is Sharon, you and I are now the only two. Where are you and when and where shall we meet?*'

This was the email that Sharon had written and sent, and to which she had waited three days for reply. Finally, however, there came the response.

'*Sharon, thank the stars, I thought I was alone. Meet me at the place we sometimes drink coffee, twelve noon on Sunday.*'

Thus was it arranged, and thus would the only two who had survived the burning of Farthing's Well meet, and of this meeting we will hear soon.

Chapter 14

KILLING TIME

All that Isabella had to work with were raw emotion, and such analysis as her young and inexperienced mind could bring to bear, and it seemed to her at times that these two things were working in direct conflict, one against the other. From the emotional perspective, the thought of meeting with Barnabas Overton made her sick to her stomach; to see him again and to talk to him would be horrible, and something which she did not need to do, so why should she do it? On the other hand, perhaps Rachel had been right; perhaps to see him might help to lay the demons of that night, once and for all. He would apologise to her, more perhaps to save his own marriage than for any reason pertaining to her, but any apology was better than none, was it not? She would not accept his apology; there would be no moment of forgiveness to salve his perverted conscience; that she would never do, so where was the point to it, really, aside from her own satisfaction in the refusal? She could leave him to fester in the ruins of his marriage, which may survive this or it may not, and she really didn't care either way. She owed no debt of gratitude or female solidarity to Rachel Overton, his wife, who was for her own reasons so desperate to broker a meeting; he was her husband, and he had raped a helpless and unconscious young woman, so it was up to her to make her own choices.

Isabella was grateful to her in one regard; that she had told her about the others; Neil Finley, Paul Stewart and Ed Fullerton. Two of the marriages it seemed were over; if there was a lesser part to this crime then the lesser offenders would receive the harshest punishment, but of them she need not think further;

they would none of them forget their crime against her, and she would never see them again. No, it was of Barnabas Overton whom she must think, and in the days following her meeting with Rachel she thought about him, or rather the idea of meeting with him, to the point of distraction. She was doing okay; slowly and by degrees the pain of that night was becoming less, so why should she suffer the trauma of seeing him again when in truth she had no idea how she would react? She knew equally well, however, that time was limited. Before long Rachel would have made her decision; either the marriage would end or she would forgive him, and either way a meeting would then be beyond her, because from their perspective at least there would cease to be a point to it. She had to decide quickly, and presently she was torn absolutely between her disgust at the thought of seeing him, and the possibility that she might indeed gain something from the meeting. It might in some perverse way help the pain to go away, and there existed the outside possibility that it might make it go away completely, or then again it might make it worse, and that which kept Isabella Baxter awake at night during these days was whether or not it was worth the risk.

Michael did not see Victoria until Sunday morning. She had retired to her room by the time he had driven home from Canterbury, and he had only briefly said hello to his parents before decanting himself some fine Irish Whiskey, and passing the remainder of the waking night in his own company. He did not sleep well, however, and by five o'clock he was up and smoking a cigarette on the front steps of the Manor House, which was when and where his sister joined him. Habitually he sat next to the place where Victoria sat, whether she was there or not, and here he was sat deep in thought when she sat down quietly beside him, and lit her own cigarette. This was still pre –dawn, and if there was a moon then it was covered by cloud; he had not switched on the light, and nor had she, and the darkness was intense. Neither spoke at first; an owl was calling from somewhere nearby, but otherwise there was no sound, save the occasional early car passing in the distance, and it was she who broke the contemplative silence.

'You can't sleep either, then…'

'I had a few hours…I've not much going on today so I can take a nap later.'

Victoria was in truth not yet fully awake, and it took her a moment before she realized that something was amiss.

'Hang on; I thought you went to Canterbury last night.'

'I did; I drove back.'

'Oh dear; things not going well with Elin then..?'

'I'm not sure, to be honest.'

That which Michael had been deep in thought about was whether after all he had done the right thing. Was Elin right to prevaricate, for both of their sakes; was this still too soon after Rose, for him and for them, and having asked her to marry him, would she accept, or would she simply say no, in which case what would he do then? Perhaps he would lose her altogether; either way it would be difficult if not impossible to go back to where they had been. But still, it was done now, so it was up to her.

'Well I won't ask, unless you want to tell me.'

'I asked her to marry me.'

Okay Victoria; peaceful early morning over; it was time to wake up, and now it happened rather suddenly. She had not expected her brother to be here, and certainly she had not expected this.

'You did what…?'

It had been a whisper, but a rather loud whisper.

'Shhhh; keep it to yourself, will you?'

'So I take it that you've not discussed this with Mater and Pater, then.'

'No...'

'Christ, no wonder you're up and smoking at this God – forsaken hour...So did she accept? I mean I assume not since you're here.'

'No, she didn't.'

'Oh dear, well I'm sorry then, Mike, I think.'

'She didn't say no, either. She said she had to think about it.'

'Well I'm not surprised...I mean I'm sorry Mike but you haven't even long been together, have you, and the last I heard you weren't sure about her, or rather how you felt about her.'

'I wasn't...Well that is to say, I thought I wasn't, but then Keith said something which rather changed my mind.'

'Keith...? What's Keith got to do with anything? I mean what did he say, for heaven's sake?'

'He made me realize that...Well, that there's never a right time you know? That if I wait until I think I'm ready to be with somebody else then it might never happen.'

'Yes, but did you have to ask her to marry you?'

'Yes, I believe I did; otherwise what would have happened, Vics? We would have just gone on like we were, seeing each other every couple of weeks or whatever, and that isn't enough for me. So I thought, well, ask her then.'

'So if she says no, what then?'

'Then I suppose it's over between us.'

'Bloody hell....That's one hell of an ultimatum, isn't it?'

'Funny; that's what she said.'

'Well she has a point...I mean...'

'I know, Vics, but well, I just can't go on like this, that's all; life can be almost unbearably lonely sometimes, you know?'

'You don't have to tell me that, Mike.'

'I know I don't, so perhaps you of all people will understand. There'll never be another Rose, I realize that, but now there's Elin, and well, I have to let myself love her, if you know what I mean. I can't look back anymore.'

She lit another cigarette, offered him the pack and lit another cigarette for her ridiculous brother, whom she loved so much, and whom she understood better than anybody, and she did understand. He was dressed in casual trousers and an Aran jumper; she was in jeans and had wrapped a shawl around her, but neither wore anything underneath, since neither had expected to encounter anyone else at this hour of the day; it was to be a quick cigarette and then back to a warm bed. It was a chilly morning, but there was nowhere else to have this conversation, so here they would stay despite the cold.

'Sure...No of course you can't. And I mean Elin's great, Mike. She's smart, sophisticated and successful.'

'And beautiful...'

'That too, it's just a shock, that's all.'

'Yes; she was surprised.'

'I bet she was; I bet she didn't see that one coming at all...So aside from not committing herself, how did she react?'

'She walked out of the restaurant; we hadn't even started the first course.'

'I see...'

'Do you think that's a good sign or a bad sign?'

Perhaps she had to release some tension, but for whatever reason and despite the serious nature of the discourse, Victoria laughed quietly to herself as she exhaled her smoke.

'Christ, I don't know. I mean the fact that she didn't say 'no' is obviously a positive, or at last it isn't a negative, and I imagine any conversation thereafter would have been rather mundane; you could hardly have gone on to discuss the weather, could you, so her walking out is probably not conclusive either way. So what happens now?'

'She's going to let me know today.'

'How..?'

'She's going to email or telephone; telephone for '*yes*' and email for '*no*' I expect.'

'Is that what she said?'

'No, it's just my supposition.'

'I didn't think she used email.'

'Apparently she's going to make an exception.'

'Well no wonder you can't sleep then. Christ, Mike, I know we've said it before, but when are you and I going to get something right, do you think?'

'In another life, maybe...'

'Yes, probably...'

'I sometimes wonder, you know, how life got this complicated. It should be simpler than this, shouldn't it?'

'I don't think my life's ever been simple.'

'No, well you always were a complex individual, and now I think I'm catching up.'

'I don't suppose life is simple for anyone when it comes down to it; I suppose it depends how you deal with everything, and I've never been very good at that.'

'Other people manage, though. I mean look at Keith and Meadow; they've been together forever and raised three kids on a bus, and neither of them ever seem to be anything but happy.'

'Yes, I know what you mean...Some people are just lucky, I suppose.'

'And here am I, future Lord of the bloody Manor, and I'm taking advice from Keith about the rest of my life; makes you think, doesn't it? So anyway, what's your excuse for being up at this ungodly hour, apart from nicotine?'

'I woke up thinking about Rebecca, and needed a cigarette.'

'Yes, I can see how that could happen. You're not seeing much of her these days, are you?'

'Not recently…I think we both need time out; it happens sometimes, it's how we've always been.'

'So is the business with the witches over, do you suppose?'

Michael, in common with the rest of her family, still knew nothing of the night that Eve had come; there were a great many things that he didn't know.

'I don't know, to be honest; she says everything's going to be okay, but who knows; certainly not me.'

'Well, good luck with that.'

'Are you still okay with her staying in the house?'

'Sure; currently that's about the least of my concerns. Anyway I suppose we should go in, it's freezing out here.'

'I can't feel my feet.'

'Well, come on then, sis; let's get dressed, at least, then see what the brave new day has in store for us, shall we?'

'Especially your brave new day, my idiot brother… You'll let me know, won't you?'

'Of course; I think I'm going to need moral support whichever way it goes.'

She wrapped her shawl more tightly around her, they stood up and entered their ancestral home together, just as the first dim light of morning began to light up the cold eastern sky.

Despite their young age, Basil and Emma lived in certain respects as a couple of more mature years might live. At school they barely saw one another, and scarce ever spoke; this was not their time. Evenings and weekends, however, were a different matter. If Emma's parents were in residence then she would live at number five and she would sleep alone, but the rest of the time, which was most of the time, they would either sleep together in the trailer, or in Emma's bedroom. Such sleeping arrangements were not condoned by Keith and Meadow, neither were they condemned. They were simply accepted, or perhaps better say ignored, once it had been established beyond reasonable doubt that there would be no issue from such an intimate liaison; in other words that nothing would happen which would be of detriment to either of their academic careers. Keith and Meadow could scarce voice strong disapproval in any case, since by the time Meadow was Emma's age, Tara had already been born. Most of the time, Emma would take her meals on the bus with Basil, but perhaps twice a week, Basil and Emma would cook for themselves. They had no earned income, but both had a small allowance from their respective parents, some of which they would use to buy food, and occasionally wine, and on such occasions they would cook their inexpensive but wholesome meal at number five. Sandra's temporary return to this domestic situation had curtailed this activity somewhat, since she could not be seen to be approving of their relationship, and in truth did not approve of it, but she was not always home, and so sometimes they would still have the house to themselves.

Thus did they live, and over course of time they grew to know and love one another in a way that belied their young years, and we join them now late on this Sunday morning as they are entering Emma's parental home, where they would pass the day. Sandra was at home. This was clear because quite loud music emanated from behind her bedroom door; too loud in fact to be appropriate to the time of day, but they thought little of this. Only when a certain compact disc was playing through for the second time did it occur to either of them that something may be amiss. This, Emma knew, was her sister's favorite record, but even so something was unusual, and it was Basil who first voiced mild concern.

'What do you think she's doing in there?'

'I don't know...'

'Entertaining a man, you reckon?'

'What, Sandra...? I doubt that.'

'Well she can hardly be sleeping through those decibels, can she?'

'No; do you suppose she's even there; I mean she might have gone out and left her player on, I suppose.'

'That's even less likely I would have thought.'

'Yeah, I agree; that wouldn't be Sandra at all, so what do you think we should do?'

'I think you should go and check.'

'Sure, okay.'

Emma left the room; Basil heard her knock gently and then less gently on Sandra's bedroom door, which she then opened. The next thing that he heard was Emma's voice, and she was saying something which he heard well enough, and which brought him immediately to attention.

'Oh...my....God..! Basil...Fucking hell...Come here, quickly.'

Basil was beside his beloved in an instant, and that which he saw made his blood run cold. Sandra was lying fully dressed on the floor. She was lying on her stomach, and her head, which was lying sideways, was in a pool of her own vomit.

'Christ...'

'Basil; do something, for Christ's sake.'

He went to the prone form; she was deathly white, and his first thought was that she might indeed be dead, but she had a pulse, and her breathing came in shallow, rasping breaths. He returned to Emma's bedroom where he had left his telephone, and dialed emergency services for an ambulance. He then returned to the scene, where Emma was pulling Sandra's face away from her vomit, and trying to wake her, but there was no response. They looked at one another, but neither knew what else to do.

'Bas; what the hell's wrong with her?'

'I don't know; looks like she might have O – D'd on something.'

'What, Sandra...? She hardly touches drugs, and she's on her own.'

'Yeah, well maybe she's just sick or something. I don't know; the ambulance will be here in a minute, until then I don't think there's anything we can do.'

Emma knelt down and took her sister's hand, which felt too cold.

'Oh God Sands; wake up...What the hell have you done?'

During the next hours of Sunday morning, Michael Tillington was killing time. He had no wish to see his parents for longer than was necessary, given that he was rather distracted by other matters which he could not yet discuss with them, and Victoria and he, whilst not avoiding one another, did not seek out one another's company again after their early morning meeting. Michael would know when he needed his sister, and until then she would wait. Instead he retired to his room, in the corner of which he had set up his desk and filing cabinet, and tried to apply himself to business matters, foremost of which being the beginning of work at Orchard House, which all had agreed would start on Wednesday of that week. This attempt to otherwise channel his thoughts, however, was unsuccessful; he simply could not apply himself. He had intended to stay at home in case a certain lady should contact him, but by the late morning she had not done so, and so he took Prince and Bathsheba for a long walk around the estate lands, which proved to be a better way to clear his head, and to find distraction. He returned some two hours later, and told his parents that he would not be joining them for luncheon; he could not sit at table with them, and in truth had no appetite, so he feigned a slight stomach upset and said that he would eat later. Nobody had telephoned, and it was not until he had returned to his room and checked his electronic mail that his wait was finally over. There in his inbox was an email from Elin's address. So, it was to be an email, then, which according to his assumption would not be good news; she had likely refused him. He opened his bedroom window and lit a cigarette, which was the last in his packet; to hell with it, he couldn't do this without a cigarette. He sat down at his desk and opened the mail, which read as follows;

'Dear Michael

First of all let me say that I am sorry for walking out on you last night. I am sure that this was not the reaction that you were expecting, but to be honest your proposal of marriage was a shock to me, so I hope you understand that I needed time to consider our situation.

Well, now I have done so, (I didn't sleep very much last night) and let me first say that I would marry you tomorrow, and would love to do so. It would in fact be the best thing that I could imagine, and I am most flattered that you have asked me.

I love my home and my city, and am quite content in my job, and cannot imagine working in London. However I think it would be possible to find alternative and similar work nearer to you, and

I am prepared to do so, so that should not be an impediment to our eventually marrying.

Put frankly, the problem for me is the Manor House. I understand, of course, that you cannot leave your beautiful home; yours is an unusual situation, and it cannot be ignored in terms of our future, because the truth is, Michael, that I could not live there.

I have known your dear parents for a long time, and have affection for them both, but I could not live as the 'second woman', ever in your mothers' shadow, as you will be in your fathers' shadow until your time comes to become Lord of the Manor. Then of course we would live at the Manor, and that would be a wonderful thing, but until then, which could be and of course I hope will be a long time, I would want us to have our own home elsewhere.

So, there, as simply as I can express it, is my ultimatum to you. If you are also prepared to leave your home, then I will accept your offer of marriage most gladly. Of course your son could live with us, provided that full time care is a given. As you know I have never wanted children of my own, but am prepared in certain ways to be as a mother to Nathaniel, but not in terms of his daily needs.

I would not expect you to move so far away as Canterbury, and my apartment of course is too small for us, Nathaniel and a nanny, so a house situated conveniently for my future work and your family home would be the only way for us, I think.

So, dear Michael, there is my perspective. If I appear rather 'cold and calculating' then I apologize, but until I know your feelings I cannot allow myself to become emotional. If you want me, those are my terms. I love you, Michael, and I wait to hear from you.

Elin.'

He read the email three times, each time trying to further untangle his feelings. She had accepted, conditionally; she would be his wife, and he could marry again if he could accept her conditions. He should wait, of course, and ponder her words; he should talk to Victoria, and then with his parents; he should make the situation quite clear to them before he responded. That would be the proper and sensible thing to do, but there are moments in peoples' lives when to be proper and sensible is not the thing; when it is better to follow your heart, and at this moment Michael Tillington felt happier than he had felt for the longest time. He moved the curser to 'reply' and wrote;

'Of course I'll move out of the Manor; we can live wherever you want, so will you marry me?'

To which, less than a minute later, came the reply;

'Yes, Michael, I will marry you.'

The ambulance arrived within ten minutes, albeit that they were a long ten minutes. Basil had left Emma with her sister whilst he waited at the front door, and now he showed the two medics upstairs; they were one man and one woman, and they had come with more equipment than Basil would have expected. Once at the scene, the woman gently but firmly pushed Emma aside and looked inside Sandra's mouth, whilst the man put a stethoscope to her chest. It was the woman who spoke first, the question addressed to anyone who would answer.

'Has she been ill lately?'

'No, not as far as I know.'

'Diabetic..? Any long term problems..?'

'No, not at all...'

'Do you know what she's taken, apart from alcohol?'

'No, I haven't seen her for a few days...She's my sister...Is she going to be alright?'

Emma had to ask, although she knew that the question was inane, and it received the answer which she knew it deserved, which was no answer. Some sort of probe was put on Sandra's finger, and a reading taken.

'Eighty five; better give her oxygen.'

The man placed an oxygen mask over Sandra's mouth and switched on the supply, whilst the woman took blood pressure and felt her hands.

'Blood pressure's up...Dilated pupils; it's probably cocaine, and these, I would think.'

She quickly passed Emma a bottle of pills which she had found under the prone body; some kind of anti – depressant, whilst a tube was inserted into Sandra's arm, and some kind of fluid began to flow from a transparent plastic bag.

'Did you know she was on those?'

'No...I had no idea...'

'Well she is now; lots of them I would think.'

The man was now taking her temperature. During the process of examination her dress had partially ridden up to her hips. She was wearing a thong, and stockings; one of her favourite dresses and nice underwear, and she even still had high – heeled shoes on; dressed to go out, and now here was Emma's beloved sister, reduced to so much flesh, muscle and fluid. Even if this had been deliberate; even if she had really tried to kill herself, the organism had taken over and was now fighting for its' own survival; it cared nothing for her state of dress, or her state of mind. The medics went about their impersonal, objective business; she was nothing to them but another person who had overdosed, and another life to save, if they could; they were doing their job, and they saw this sort of thing all the time as they made their daily rounds. Some of them made it, some of them didn't.

'Temperature's up, and her heart rate's all over the place.'

And now the woman was talking to her, looking for a human response.

'Can you hear me; if you can hear me, open your eyes.'

The eyes remained closed; the woman squeezed a muscle by her neck and Sandra moaned at the pain.

'Okay, we're going to have to move her.'

The woman stood up; they would need a stretcher, but now the man spoke.

'The heart's stopped; she's arresting. She's stopped breathing; we're losing her.'

'Okay, let's bag her.'

Emma was in a dream now, and was watching the proceedings as though they weren't really happening, and she wasn't really hearing that which she was hearing; her sister wasn't really dying or already dead, and she would wake up in a moment. In the real world the oxygen mask was removed and now a plastic bag was placed over her mouth, and the bag squeezed, trying to get the lungs working. The man was compressing her chest quite violently.

'Nothing…'

The woman pulled her dress down from the top; Emma noticed the most stupid thing; she wasn't wearing a bra. Two pads were placed on her chest, a small, portable machine gave instructions and finally advised a shock, and now the man spoke.

'Stand clear…Shocking now.'

He pressed a button on the machine, then repeated the process.'

'Nothing...'

'Try again; once more…'

The third and perhaps last time, and this time there was a reaction.

'There's a heartbeat; she's breathing; we've got her back.'

'Okay….adrenalin.'

The woman replaced the bag at the end of the tube; Emma's emotions were taking care of themselves and going where they would, and Basil looked on in hopeless wonderment as to where this would go next.

'I think that's all we can do here; she needs to get to the hospital.'

'So will she be okay now, do you think?'

The woman smiled now for the first time; at least a half - smile.

'Well, we'll see; she's not out of danger yet, but she's young, and I think we got to her in time; maybe only just in time, and we don't yet know what she did to herself, so let's see.'

A stretcher was brought, to which she was strapped with all of the tubes, plastic bags and oxygen mask, and all that was keeping her alive, for now. It took a little persuasion for Emma to be allowed to ride in the ambulance, but she was persistent in her request, and so she kissed Basil goodbye.

'I'll see you at the hospital.'

Basil returned to the bedroom. He cleaned up the vomit and general mess of it, just because he wanted to do something useful, and bring some order back into his thoughts before he left this place, which but an hour ago had been a happy place to be. There was a small mirror lying on the dressing table, which showed traces of white powder residue, which he also wiped clean, placing the mirror in a drawer; and he took the half – empty Tequila bottle to the kitchen. The medics had taken the pill bottle with them. He didn't really know why he did these things; perhaps for Emma's sake, and her parents would have to come home from wherever they were, and better they didn't come back to this. Finally he checked the house over before slamming the front door behind him, as it had been slammed the night before, for a different reason. He walked the short distance home, and within ten minutes Keith had donned his bike – leathers and with his son was following in the ambulances' wake, arriving at the accident and emergency centre only shortly after Sandra's body had been wheeled through double doors to a treatment room. They met Emma there, who hugged Basil and then Keith, and then they all hugged each other.

'So, how is she?'

'She's...Well they won't let me be with her now, but she survived the journey, anyway. She not conscious yet, so all we can do now is hope, I suppose.'

'So what did she do?' Said Keith

'The medic thought it was...Well she thinks it's probably cocaine, and pills, and she'd drunk a lot of alcohol, I think.'

'Christ...And she did all of this alone?'

'I don't know where she was last night, or who she was with.'

'Okay, well we'll stay here for now, of course, and see if we get any news, Basil, 'phone your mother, will you, she'll want to know what's going on.'

'Sure...'

So they stayed, and the last news that they had was that Sandra's condition was stable, and although she had not yet regained consciousness, she was, they hoped, through the worst of it. They would not know the full extent of any damage until she woke up, and were awaiting the results of the blood test, but at least they now seemed more confident that she would wake up, eventually, and at least now she was in the best possible care, rather than lying on her bedroom floor waiting to die. They spent some time in the hospital canteen, and left in the mid - afternoon, having filled in forms and having left their contact details should there be any significant change for better or worse, but there really was no point in their staying any longer. If she was still alive in the morning they could see her then, and if she wasn't, well there was nothing to be done in any case. Keith rode with Emma back to the bus, and Basil took a taxi, and the evening was spent as any family would spend it, when one of their number had tried to kill herself. They all knew well enough that Sandra had never approved of Emma being with Basil, and she had never once been to the bus. Her demeanor had always been somewhat trite when she had seen Meadow at the delicatessen, but at such times such things can be put aside, for Emma's sake at least. Blood, after all, is thicker than attitude.

Victoria's knock sounded on Michael's bedroom door but a few minutes after he had read and replied to the email.

'Come in Vics...'

She entered the room and closed the door behind her. Michael was at his desk, a neutral expression on his face.

'I was passing; I just thought I'd see if you were okay.'

'I've had an email.'

'Oh...Oh dear, that doesn't sound like good news.'

Victoria prepared herself to offer commiseration and the moral support which they had touched upon in the early morning, which seemed to both of them to be a long time ago. Watch the expression, that was the thing; she knew her brother well, and now her brother smiled.

'She said yes, didn't she...'

The smile became broader, and spoke a thousand words, though none were spoken.

'Oh Mike, that's fantastic.'

He stood up and they walked to each other; they were not on the whole tactile with one another, but now they hugged. When they released both were surprised to see that both had tears in their eyes.

'Well, my idiot brother; what the hell have you done now?'

'There's a condition.'

'What condition?'

'Why don't you read the email?'

'Are you sure...I don't suppose she intended that anyone else should read it.'

'You're not anyone else though, are you? Read it; it's not X rated, which is probably the first time.'

Victoria sat at the desk and read the mail; Michael took one of her cigarettes and stood by the window. When she had finished she looked up at him.

'You're smoking in the house.'

'Like you never do...Anyway give me a break; I just got engaged, sort of.'

She stood up and lit a cigarette herself, and both now leaned out of the window; the day was warmer now.

'She has a way with words, doesn't she?'

'Not bad for a Norwegian, is she; you don't get any sense of accent at all when she writes; in a way she writes better than she speaks; she gets her words wrong sometimes.'

'She's only half Norwegian, and most Norwegians I've met speak better English than most English people. You replied to it...'

'Did you read it?'

'And her reply to you; so it's all done then.'

'In writing, which isn't quite what you'd expect from a lawyer, is it?'

'I don't suppose it's legally binding; anyway it sounds as though she means it.'

'Yes, it does rather, doesn't it?'

Both took a moment; thoughts were settling and becoming ordered, and the nicotine was helping.

'So you'll be moving out then.'

'Eventually; it's something that I've been thinking about doing for a long time, and should have done a long time ago. With Rose....With Rose it was always going to be the next house; I'm not going to make that mistake again. Rose never wanted to live here either, and I understand how she feels; Elin I mean.'

'So do I; you need your own place, Mike. I just hope you're more successful than I was, my attempt at escape didn't exactly last very long, did it?'

'I'll have a woman with me.'

'I had a woman with me, too; I suppose it must depend on the woman. So when are you going to tell them, then?'

'Christ knows; not yet, that's for sure; I'll wait until everything's more certain. I haven't even seen her yet.'

'Yes, it wasn't exactly a conventional betrothal, was it? So when are you going to see her, then?'

'Lord knows.'

'Well don't you think you should?'

'Yes, of course; she's working long hours at the moment, so I expect I'll go to her. I'll 'phone her later. Vics; do you think she was being *cold and calculating?*'

'I think she was doing what she had to do; laying down her terms, and good for her. Anyway it would hardly be uncharacteristic, would it? How was it that you once described her;' *cold, beautiful and shallow*', wasn't it?'

'Only by default; I was talking about Norway, I believe. I've found new depths to her since then, anyway, and in certain regards she's not cold at all.'

'I'm glad to hear it.'

'I think we can dispense with '*Shallow*' from now on, anyway.'

'You still get three words; so what's the new word?'

'I'll let you know...So how do you think they're going to react?'

Victoria laughed quietly as she exhaled her cigarette smoke.

'I don't know, Mike; perhaps better than the last one. The difference this time is that they know her; they've watched her grow up, in fact, and since she's daughter to their friends I can't see how they can object, can you?'

'No, I suppose not, when you put it like that.'

'Anyway, well done; congratulations and all; I have to say you've taken us all by surprise with this one. So I suppose you'll have to start looking for houses now; can you afford to buy outright yet?'

'Well no, not now I'm committed to Orchard House; that'll take all my cash and then some, I expect. I'll have to tell Keith to get a move on. Once I sell Orchard House I should be okay;

either that or something will have gone badly wrong, but I'm several months from there yet.'

'She can sell her apartment, I suppose.'

'Yes, although I don't know how much of it actually belongs to her; we haven't exactly got to the finer points yet.'

'And you'll have to get a new nanny; you're not taking Abigail.'

'I wouldn't dream of it. I don't know, Vics; all this has come as a bit of a surprise to me too, to be honest; there's a lot to think about.'

'Well if you will go asking people marry you, you shouldn't really be surprised if they say *'yes'*…So I suppose you'll want me to help you find an engagement ring, will you?'

'Christ I hadn't even thought about the ring…Maybe we could go into town one day soon.'

'Maybe we could…'

'I'll buy you lunch.'

'Then how can I refuse?'

'And you know; keep this to yourself for now, won't you…'

'Don't be silly…God knows I keep enough secrets, so I don't suppose one more will make any difference.'

'What do you mean?'

'Never mind….Anyway I'll leave you in peace, shall I? I expect you'll be wanting to speak to Elin.'

'Could you leave me some fags?'

'Take these; I think I've got another pack somewhere.'

'Right, well thanks, Vics…'

'What for..?'

'Just thanks, you know?'

'You're welcome, and I'm really pleased for you, Mike; Elin's a lovely lady.'

She left. She had not seriously thought that Elin would refuse him, although perhaps that was easy to say in retrospect.

Mike was a gentleman, in the true sense of the word, and a good looking and extremely eligible gentleman at that, and she knew of certain young women who would be bitterly disappointed when the news broke. So what of Elin? Mike had been through something like an emotional maelstrom with Rose; that had never been an easy marriage for him even before she had become ill, so she could see the attraction of somebody like Elin. Mike had never been a leader of men; in his quiet way he would go on to make a success of his business, she was sure, because in the end there was only him, but in general terms he would benefit from having a strong woman beside him, and Rose had had her weaknesses; Percival, for example. It was also the case that Elin was by several degrees of magnitude more sophisticated than Rose had been; she would be an easier person to have around. Mike's love for Rose had gone in deep, she knew that, and it had taken some digging out; little wonder that he was keen to fill the resultant void, and perhaps after all cold, beautiful and shallow was just what he needed. As with all affairs of the heart, however, she supposed that only time would tell.

Rachel Overton was in her kitchen and making herself a bedtime drink when the ring – tone sounded on her mobile telephone. Barnabas was out, probably at his chess club or at the public house; she didn't know any more, and nowadays she asked less often, particularly since he had on her instigation begun sleeping in the spare bedroom. Their relationship was in a strange state of suspension; they went to work, mostly ate their evening meal together, more perhaps by force of habit than any wish to do so, since mealtimes had become awkward these days, and they inhabited the same mid – range semi – detached house. Emotionally, however, they had become estranged from one another, and it seemed to Rachel that the estrangement was becoming more so as the days went by, and every day that the phone - call didn't come they drifted further apart. He had said he was sorry, on more than one occasion, and they had both cried, but she still did not understand. She did not understand how the man whom she thought she knew could have done such a thing, and there was no explanation, since how could there be? In the end therefore there could only be forgiveness, or not. One day they would have to find each other again, and one day if it was ever going to work she would have to sleep with him again, and that she could not presently bring herself to do. She was too young to give up sex altogether, but not with the man she still loved; not yet, and if never then there would be an end to it, sooner or later.

She answered the call; it was a number that she did not recognize.

'Hello..?'

'Hello, this is Isabella Baxter.'

A heat rose inside her, and she took hold of the kitchen work – surface as if it might give her some support. Calm voice, Rachel.

'Hello Isabella...'

'I'll meet him.'

Three syllables which mean so much more than the speaker could realize.

'I see, well, thank you...'

'Don't thank me yet, you don't know what I'm going to say. You have to be there, I'm not meeting him alone.'

'Of course...'

'And it has to be a public place; St Agnes Park, six o'clock tomorrow afternoon.'

'Right; that's fine, we'll be there.'

'See you there then.'

Which was the conversation in it's entirely, which had lasted less than a minute, and which could change Rachel's life, because Rachel knew full well that her life had to change, one way or the other. Her fate and the fate of her marriage now stood with a skinny, teen - aged girl, whom she had liked when she had met her, despite everything. By this time tomorrow she would know then, one way or the other.

Chapter 15

ST AGNES PARK

St Agnes Park was the smallest of the several parks which fell under the care and maintenance of the Borough Council. It was triangular in shape, having wide pedestrian walkways along its' three sides, bordered on their' outer edge by dense, well established shrubberies, in which were also several mature trees, and on their inner edge by a large expanse of grass, which made up the better part of the park, and the entirety of its' centre. The park had three narrow, pedestrian entrances, approximately at the centre of each of its' sides, which led from the three busy shopping thoroughfares which bordered the park. Beside one of these was the building in which tools, lawnmowers and so one were stored, and in which the municipal workers responsible for the parks' upkeep took their lunch and tea breaks, amongst whom as we have learned was Barrington Thomas, on the days when he was working here.

Situated at intervals along each of the pathways were several concrete and timber benches, which during the day and during clement weather were frequented by office workers, shop assistants and so on, for the park was situated at the very heart of the newer part of the town, and here was a pleasant place to bring thermos flasks or take – away drinks, sandwiches and such, and to enjoy the relatively peaceful ambience of the small park for an hour or so at lunchtime. During the evenings, and particularly during the hours of darkness, the park was otherwise used for perhaps somewhat less than saintly activities by courting couples, those paying and being paid for services of a sexual nature, and by purveyors of illegal herbs and other substances, intended for the enjoyment and recreation of the local populous.

It had once been the Council's policy to lock the three small gates at the end of each working day, but the low, stout iron fences which surrounded the park were in a poor state of repair, and proved little deterrent to those wishing to gain entry. It was also the case that the gates were vandalised with such frequency that it was decided at a particular council meeting that they should be remain open, and the first task of the council employees each morning was to carefully clear the park of used syringes and contraceptive devices, and any other detritus which had been left from the previous nights' commercial and other activity.

If the park had a focal point, it was a quite large and mostly enclosed shelter, situated roughly mid – way along another of its' lengths, which provided almost total privacy. It was in this shelter that many of the nights' more nefarious activities took place, and it was to here that Isabella Baxter went at a little before six o'clock on the appointed evening, and it was here that she waited.

A knock on the door of the cottage down the lane; Percival saved the document that he was writing into his word - processor, and from her place on the rug by the fire Lulu omitted a low rumble from her throat which did not become a bark. When she saw who the caller was she ceased her state of semi - alertness and rested her head once more on her paws, only the eyes working. Nothing after all need be done.

'Reginald, this is a pleasant surprise; come in; coffee?'

Reginald was wearing his Sombrero, but was otherwise more conventionally dressed in grey trousers and raincoat, and extremely shiny slip – on shoes.

'Yes, thank you.'

Percival fetched another cup and poured coffee; Reginald removed his hat and coat, which he placed over the back of the chair, and the two men sat opposite one another at the dining table. Percival knew Reginald well enough to know that despite being the caller he would not instigate conversation, nor would he easily reveal the reason for his visit, but he was equally sure that there would be a reason for it.

'So; how's life treating you then?'

'Very well, thank you.'

'Glad to hear it...So, been anywhere interesting lately?'

'I have been to London on three occasions.'

'Oh yes; any particular reason?'

'I believe it was your suggestion that I go there, and I have enjoyed each visit. I have been to the Natural History Museum, the Tate Gallery and the Tower of London, all of which I have been to before, but nevertheless all three were most interesting.'

'Well that's good then. So did you go with what's her name; Gwendolyn isn't it?'

'Yes; she had never been to the Tower of London before.'

'I don't think I've been since I was at school...So things okay between you and her?'

'Yes, we share certain of the same interests, and we enjoy each others' company.'

'Well that's good then; so when's your next trip planned?'

'She wishes to go to Venice.'

'Yeah; Venice is nice, in parts anyway. I enjoyed the one time I was there.'

'So I have read; the problem is that I have never been abroad, and don't currently have a passport.'

'That's easily solved; just visit the website; look up *'Applying for a British Passport'*; it'll tell you what you need to do. When do you intend to go?'

'More or less as soon as I have a passport...'

'Well you can apply by post, which I think is supposed to take no more than three weeks, but that could be for a renewal; I'm not sure about getting a new one. You'll probably need your birth certificate, signed photos and so on, and a word to the wise; get the post office to check your application form before you submit it. Actually it's probably better to go to the Passport Office in London yourself, since you have time; you'll need to make an appointment, but I'm sure all of that can be done on line.'

'I see...So would you be willing to sign the photographs for me?'

'I don't think an unemployed ex – banker would quite cut the mustard; ask your GP or whatever; somebody in a position of responsibility, a lawyer or similar.'

'Yes, I understand. Well thank you for your advice.'

'You're welcome.'

So was this the reason for the visit? Reginald may be a certain and unusual manifestation of humanity, but he was by no means stupid, and Percival was sure that he was quite able to organize the obtaining of a passport without assistance, so perhaps they had yet to hit upon the main subject to be discussed; he would have to dig deeper into his friend's psyche.

'Yes...Well, you'll find Venice interesting, I'm sure.'

'I'm sure it will be, not only architecturally, but also in certain other particular ways...'

So, perhaps the cause of his uncertainty was across the water; perhaps it was Venice where the problem lay; they may be homing - in.

'Of course we'll be staying in a hotel.'

'Well that would be the usual thing...'

Getting closer, perhaps, but Percival still couldn't see it, and then came the realisation, and he had arrived just before Reginald.

'That is, we'll be sharing a hotel room, I would think.'

Reginald would perhaps never have shared a hotel room with anyone, far less a member of the fairer sex, so now they were there.

'Well, that's nothing to be concerned about, is it?'

'Well no, I suppose not; I'm just, as it were, not familiar with the etiquette in such situations. It would be twin beds, of course.'

'Naturally...So, you know, don't hog the bathroom and leave her one side of the washbasin; that kind of thing. Women like to hang clothes up, so let her unpack first and take whatever's left. And take a dressing – gown if the hotel doesn't provide them; you'll be fine. I mean she must know what to expect, and I'm sure she'll be respectful of your modesty, as you will of hers; it'll work out okay. Anyway Venice will provide sufficient distraction; after a couple of nights you'll forget you ever thought there was a problem.'

'Yes, well I'm sure you're right...'

'Sure I am. I'm glad you two are getting along okay, anyway. Next time she's in the village bring her 'round for coffee; I promise to be on my best behaviour.'

'I will be sure to do so; thank you, Percival.'

'Sure...'

'I don't believe she has any friends; at least she's never mentioned anyone in that context.'

'Oh dear, that's a shame. You'll have to share yours then, won't you, a diverse and motley crew though we be.'

'I believe I am very fortunate with my friends.'

'Honoured you should think so.'

'And thank you for the cup of coffee; I apologise that this is to be a short visit, but I have other matters to attend to.'

'Whatever; I'm just doing some writing.'

'What are you writing presently?'

'It's a kind of personal perspective on recent events in the village.'

'I see...An autobiographical work then.'

'I suppose you might call it that, although it's not just about me, in fact it's mostly not about me, and I'm not using real names, not even mine, in fact especially not mine.'

'So will I be characterised?'

'Of course, but not as yourself, so to speak; for example there's one particular scene where an assassination attempt on a young woman is prevented by someone with a tin of anchovies, although in the true spirit of anonymity I suppose I should make them pilchards.'

'So you know about that then.'

'Emily told me; she's always been quite convinced that you saved her life, and she's never forgotten it.'

'I only did what anyone else would have done...'

'Anyone who happened to be carrying a tin of anchovies; you still carry them?'

Reginald reached down into his coat pocket and placed the tin on the table.

'I can't seem to break the habit.'

'Does Gwendolyn know you do that?'

'We have not quite reached that level of intimacy.'

Percival smiled, whilst Reginald reached down into his other coat pocket, from which he produced a canister of powdered ceramic - cleaner and a packet of scouring pads.

'Would these be useful to you?'

'I don't think I've got any of either, so yeah, thanks.'

Reginald placed the tin of anchovies back in his pocket, having read the label.

'They're approaching their sell – by date; I will have to replace them soon. So how much of the book have you written?'

'I don't know, to be honest; the more I write the more there seems to be to write about. Even if I eventually finish it I may never have it published, so unless and until then it's just a kind of personal journal, or whatever one might call it, but some interesting things have happened which I think are deserving of the writing down for posterity.'

'Yes, the village does seem to have more than its' share of unusual people.'

'Yeah, you might say that...Still, not everybody can be normal like us, eh?'

'No indeed. On the other hand I daresay that some people might consider carrying a tin of anchovies in one's pocket to be somewhat eccentric.'

'Do you think so?'

'Quite possibly, this is why I have yet to tell Gwendolyn that I do so. Anyway, I wish you well with your writing.'

Reginald stood up and put on his coat and hat, and Percival could not but ask.

'Why the sombrero; there's hardly a cloud in the sky and the sun's not exactly fierce at this time of year.'

'There is a forty percent chance of rain'

'Well I suppose you can't be too careful. See you soon then, and don't be a stranger. Let me know how you get on with Venice.'

'Yes, I will be certain to do so.'

Reginald left, and having put the cleaning products in the kitchen, Percival sat back at his desk and lit a cigarette. His concentration had been interrupted so he closed down his word – processor, allowing himself a wry smile at his strange friend, combined with the hope that Reginald had indeed found his soul mate, regardless of their future sleeping arrangements.

On the evening of this day, by which time she decided that a decent and respectable length of time had passed, Rosemary made a telephone call. She had kept the scrap of torn – off newspaper in a drawer in her bedroom, and now she entered the number and the name in her contacts list, and made the call. She had no idea what kind of reaction to expect; probably he had forgotten about her completely, in which case nothing would be lost by making the call anyway, and the number could always be deleted. So with this in mind she made the call, which was answered almost at once.

'Hello…'

'Hi; this is Rosemary; we met on a train the other day…?'

'*Oh thank Christ….*'

'What?'

'*Yeah, sorry, I mean of course we did, and I should explain, but first a question; are you by any chance free tomorrow evening?*'

'Ummm, well yes, I think so.'

'*Try to be; you could be my salvation…*'

'I see, or rather I don't see, actually.'

'*No, of course; thing is, you remember my grandmother had just died?*'

'Yes, I remember.'

'*Well my two brothers finally arrived for the funeral; you probably don't recall but I mentioned that I had two brothers?*'

'Tristan and Tarquin, AKA Freddy…'

'*Christ, you've got a memory. Anyway we burned the old dear yesterday, and we managed to get through the funeral without major incident, but now I'm stuck with them for a couple of days; that is*' *they're staying at a local B and B, but one feels duty – bound to entertain them.'*

'Right...'

'So, the thing is we're all going out tomorrow evening; a meal, you know, or something anyway, and I'd be delighted if you would join us.'

'So would this just be the four of us?'

'Yep; just you and the three musketeers, and well, a bit of feminine company's just what we need, I think; might reduce the tension, you know?'

'So I'd be a convenient diversion, so to speak.'

'Well a bit more than that, I hope; I didn't put that very well, did I?'

'Not really...'

'Yeah, sorry, my mouth runs away with me sometimes, but underlying my vocal ineptitude lies the fact that I'm glad you 'phoned, and I would very much like to see you again, with or without the brothers grim.'

'That's better...'

'So, are you up for it, or have you suddenly got a prior engagement? I'd quite understand if you would rather not; that is if you would rather meet up after they're gone.'

'No...No, it's okay, I'd be glad to help out.'

'Brilliant...So shall I send a taxi for you?'

'Nobody can ever find our place; I'll meet you in town; just let me know when and where.'

'I'll call you later, or tomorrow; depends when I can pin them down, and it's all provided they're still talking to each other; it could just be the two of us anyway.'

'Okay, well whatever; I'll speak to you soon then.'

'You will, and you know, I really am glad that you called. I didn't think you would, actually.'

'Sure...'

Rosemary ended the call, which had not been as she had expected, although in truth she had not known what to expect. Anyway, now she had a date with a young man, which was actually the first time, and his two brothers would be there, and that she had certainly not expected, but there it was. Whatever happened tomorrow, it promised to be an interesting evening.

By common agreement among themselves, Keith, Meadow, Basil and Emma would not reveal the true nature of the emergency, or the reason that there had been an ambulance on the village Green. They would merely say if asked, and they would surely be asked, that Sandra Fox had been taken seriously ill, and was now in hospital. Rosie, who had been out or otherwise occupied during the short drama, was the only other person who was told the true nature of the business; that the uncommonly clever and beautiful young woman had almost certainly tried to take her own life. This economy of truth, which was in any case well intentioned, was given credence by the fact that the cause of her physical or mental collapse had not yet been officially or medically confirmed. Basil had told them of the powder residue, which even Emma had not seen, and the pills and Tequila bottle, so the likely truth of it could be deduced only too easily and clearly, but the results of the blood test were not yet known, so nothing was absolutely certain. There also remained the outside possibility that she had simply gone way too far with her self – intoxication, and it had somehow got out of control; nobody knew how many pills had been in the bottle, or how much Tequila had been drunk prior to the night in question. It was also possible that she had wished only and in this most extreme way to reveal the true extent of her unhappiness to the world, but she could not have known that Basil and Emma were going to the house, and that she would therefore be found in time, and the extent of her drug and alcohol abuse left little doubt that this was a serious attempt at suicide.

It was also the case that nobody knew where or with whom if anybody she had spent the hours prior to her near death, except of course Will and Emily, and they knew nothing of any of this until the next morning, and then not until morning tea – break in a suburban garden, when Keith, Damien and Will were making conversation. Damien was the first to raise the matter.

'So what happened to the Fox girl yesterday? We assumed the ambulance must have been for her?'

'Yeah, she got taken poorly; I went to the hospital. We don't know what's wrong with her yet.'

Will, who had been enjoying his goats' cheese and cucumber sandwich, was suddenly attentive to the casual conversation.

'What…? Sandra's ill?'

'Yeah; last I knew she was still unconscious.'

'Unconscious? How did she get unconscious, did she take something or what?'

'Like I say, we don't know, Will…'

'Bloody hell, I mean she was fairly well gone when I dropped her off, but she wasn't that bad.'

'You dropped her off; when?'

'Sometime after midnight on Saturday; she'd been with us all evening, but we were just, you know, drinking wine. Em and I thought she'd done some coke or weed or whatever before she got to us, which we thought was strange, you know? I mean Sandra never does drugs, really, but something was up with her, and she was having trouble staying vertical on the walk home, but it was nothing that out of the ordinary. She was wearing heels, you know, and it's quite a long walk in heels, I would think, but Em has the same trouble sometimes when she's had a few. Maybe she was just sick or something.'

'Yeah…Well no, actually; look, you may as well know since you're going to find out sooner or later anyway, and I would appreciate it if we could keep this between the three of us for now at least, but the general consensus is that she tried to top herself.'

'What…?'

'We think she overdosed on some combination of coke, Tequila and antidepressants; there're no definitive test results yet, and like I say she was still out when we left the hospital yesterday afternoon, so she can't confirm or deny anything, but all the evidence seems to point to it.'

'Christ, that's…I don't know what to make of that.'

'So how was she when she was with you?'

'Well, she was a bit down, you know, but she didn't seem anything like suicidal. If we'd thought there was the least chance that she'd do anything like that we'd never have let her go.'

'No, of course not…'

'And she was the one who said she wanted to go home, so I walked her home, and like I say, she was out to lunch on something, but that's the way it goes, right; I mean we've all done that a few times.'

'More times than I care to remember…' Said Damien

'Well like I say,' said Keith 'let's not jump to absolute conclusions until we hear it from her, or the doctors; she'll tell all when she wakes up, I'm sure, always assuming that she wakes up.'

'You mean there's a chance that she won't? Said Will

'It was pretty serious, Will; Basil and Emma found her and called the ambulance, and they saw the whole thing. Her heart actually stopped beating and she stopped breathing for a minute or so, but the medics brought her back, and she's in good hands now.'

'Good god…I mean for fuck's sake…I'd better tell Em; she'll want to go and see her, and stuff.'

'Do you want to take the rest of the day off?'

'No…No, you're alright; I'll tell Em when I get home; we'll go this evening, assuming she's allowed visitors.'

'Okay well, see how that goes then; Emma's going to report back to us this afternoon. Anyway, let's get to it, shall we; we've got today and tomorrow here, then we start Orchard House.'

'Are you sure Mike'll be okay working alone,' said Damien 'I can stay and give him a hand if you want.'

'No, it's okay; we'll be as good as done here by Wednesday, and Mike's doing a couple of other jobs for me after this anyway, so we're alright; he's quite happy working alone, and one thing about Mike is that you can absolutely trust him to do a good job.'

'Sure,' said Damien 'guy's a legend; he never looks busy but his work output's phenomenal, and his work's always right there; I can see why you work with him, despite the fact that in other respects he's a pain in the butt.'

'I've always thought it was worth putting up with the man for that reason…Anyway we need to get going on Orchard House; Mike Tillington's keen to get started now, and I want to hit the ground running; get the job off to a good start.'

'And once we're there we'll be there for a long time, yes?'

'Months rather than weeks, if you can commit to it…'

'Sure, I'll be there; it'll save me having to look for work; I'll need to be out by spring, I would think, but let's see how we go.'

The three men made ready to return to their respective parts of the stone wall. Will took a few moments to reflect on the news about Sandra as he was mixing the next batch of mortar for the others; he at least would be glad not to have three demanding craftsmen to keep supplied for the whole day. In his mind he replayed Saturday evening, looking for indications that Sandra had been depressed enough to commit the ultimate act of self – destruction, and he couldn't make it fit, but he had been quite drunk himself and perhaps not so sensitive or perceptive as he might otherwise have been. If she really had tried to kill herself, she had kept her intent hidden, or had he and Emily missed something? This was a matter which he and his beloved would discuss at some length over the days which followed, but for now it was enough to establish whether or not her attempt to self – destruct had succeeded, if that was the right word for it, and this they would only know this evening.

The truth of the matter was, that aside from their not wishing anybody to be so out of harmony with their lives that they be left with no choice but to attempt suicide, Keith and Meadow held no particular affection or concern for Sandra Fox. They knew well enough that in common with her parents, she considered Basil to be not worthy of her sister. Their concern was rather for Emma, who was de facto now a part of their family; that which affected Emma affected all of them, and it was to her that they would offer their support during this difficult and uncertain time. It so happened, however, that something else occurred in the quite early morning of the next day which further distracted their thoughts from the young woman who was somewhere fighting for her life in a hospital ward, having apparently tried to end it. Meadow awoke on this day at a little before five o'clock in the morning, to the sound of somebody moving about in the kitchen of the bus, lighting the gas ring and apparently putting a pan of water to boil. Keith became conscious of the disturbance next to him, and also awoke, at least partially.

'What's going on?'

'One of our offspring is up and making tea or something.'

'What time is it?'

'Just before five…'

'Oh well, as long as it's not a burglar, bent on relieving us of our worldly goods.'

'What worldly goods?'

'Exactly my point; unless of course they couldn't find any so decided to make themselves a cup of tea instead…'

'Do you think they're okay, whoever it is; I mean it wouldn't be Basil, and Rosie never makes tea at this hour.'

'Do I take it that you'd like me to investigate?'

'Would you mind…?'

'Sure…'

Keith put jeans on, and yawned as he opened the door which divided their bedroom from the rest of the bus. Someone was indeed boiling water on the hob, and it was indeed one of their children, but otherwise both were quite wrong in their assumption.

'Hi dad…'

'Christ; what are you doing here?'

'That's a nice welcome I must say; here am I travelled half way across the world to see you, and that's all the welcome I get?'

Tarragon smiled, walked to her father and gave him a hug.

'Wake up, sleepy head.'

Meadow was up by now and putting on her dressing gown as Keith spoke to her over his shoulder.

'There's a famous rock musician in the kitchen; I can't quite place her but I'm sure I've seen her before somewhere. You'd better come and see if you know who she is.'

'Tara, what on earth…Is everything okay?'

'Everything's hunky – dory thanks mum.'

Meadow was in the kitchen by now, and mother and daughter embraced.

'But I mean really, what are you doing here?'

'I arrived on a late flight, or rather a very early flight this morning, and got here about three o'clock.'

'Why didn't you wake us?'

'I didn't like to; anyway I'm here for a few days.'

'So have you slept?'

'Not really; I lay on the bed but I'm a bit jet – lagged, you know, and I slept quite a bit on the way over. I'm a bit of a night – owl these days anyway, and then I badly needed tea. What I need most is a shower, actually, but I thought I might wake you up. And as to what I'm doing here, well, we're done in the Far – East now, and next it's America, but we've actually got a break in between, so everybody decided to fly home. We were going to use the time for rehearsal and development, but then decided that we didn't really need either, and everyone's getting a bit home – sick, so it was more or less a last – minute decision, and before you ask why I didn't tell you, well, I thought I'd surprise you.'

'And it's a wonderful surprise; I can't quite believe you're here.'

'Well here I am; who's for tea?'

'All of us, I would think.'

Tara made tea, and they sat at the dining table. There was so much to talk about that for a moment nobody quite knew where to begin, so Keith, who was by now almost fully awake, began with the most general and obvious question.

'So; how's it going then?'

'What can I say, dad, I mean it's amazing; life's just one big adventure at the moment; I wake up in yet another hotel room and kind of forget where I am sometimes.'

'But what about the music..?'

'That's amazing too, of course; I mean there I am standing on stage with all of these fantastic musicians and just surrounded by this sound, it blows me away every time, and there's this huge audience just responding to everything we do, even my songs, you know, and there's no feeling like it, the adrenalin's totally addictive. I leave the stage exhausted and yet on such a high, and within a few hours I'm thinking yeah, I'd like to do that again, please, and you can't sleep for like hours afterwards, so normally I crash at about four in the morning and try and sleep 'til early afternoon. Then it's either on to the next place or we just get together and talk about stuff, and they're all such great people, it's another world, really. Everyone's just so focused on the music, and the performance; we live it, eat it and sleep it, but you can only sustain that for so long, and we needed a break, especially Ash, actually. So we came back, and here I am, and it's good to be home. Mind you it's bloody cold here, I don't miss the English winter weather; I think I've become tropical.'

Meadow still had so many questions, but it was Keith who continued the conversation and she let him do so; she would have Tara to herself later.

'So how many of your songs have you performed?'

'We're stage – ready with about eight or nine now, so we vary it, you know, but I've got a couple of favourites.'

'So which ones do you do from the new album?'

'*Hell can wait*' and '*Under My Skin*' always work really well, and I love singing '*Turn Me Over*'; I mean I'm up there in heels and a skirt up 'round my bum and singing all this sexy stuff; you become something else, like some sort of sex goddess or something, and nobody knows it's just me; it's kind of empowering.'

'So do you get a lot of attention because of that?'

'What; like men chasing me down the street or something? No dad, I'm well looked after, and it's just music, you know? Christ I don't have enough energy for anything else.'

Meadow smiled to herself; Keith would be reassured.

'So anyway, what's been happening around here lately?'

'We're all fine,' said Meadow 'but something tragic has happened; Sandra Fox has tried to commit suicide.'

'Oh dear, what a pity....'

'Tara, at least try to sound sympathetic.'

'Miss Prissy – Knickers finally had enough of being a virgin, has she?'

'Is she...? How do you know that?'

'It's a guess, father, but I mean really, she's always been a stuck – up bitch, so if she's unhappy she's only got herself to blame. She's probably just looking for attention anyway; *look at me everyone, I'm so depressed*; Christ...Ask me, what she needs is a good f...'

'Yes well anyway, Emma's upset, of course.'

This timely introduction was provided by Meadow, who was quite well aware of its' timeliness.

'Sure, but she's going to be okay, is she? What did she do anyway?'

'We're still not really sure yet, but it looks like she took cocaine, Tequila and antidepressants.'

'Well there's ironic then; killing yourself with happy pills. I mean what does she have to be so unhappy about, anyway? She doesn't have a bad life, does she? I mean there're people living shit lives everywhere and getting by, and people who are genuinely ill through no fault of their own, and people like her make themselves sick and cause everyone time and trouble.'

'There are different kinds of illness, my love, and we can't know what kind of a life she has, and it's not all about circumstances. I'm sure unless you've sunk to those levels, well, I don't think we can even begin to understand.'

'So go and see a head doctor then; turning it into this really isn't going to help, is it?'

'I think it gets beyond rational thought, and she's probably tried the '*head doctor*' which is why she had the pills; they must have been prescribed.'

'Yes, I know, I'm probably biased because I don't like her... Thing is, if you really want to kill yourself why not jump off a cliff or something; certain, quick death and it's all over. Anyway, I think we need to talk about something cheerful; anything good happening?'

'I've got a big job starting this week,' said Keith 'I'm renovating an old property for Mike Tillington; it's enough work for a few months, and the money's good.'

'Well done that man...And talking of money, I've sort of got quite a lot of it now; I'm really going to have to put it somewhere sensible when the show's finally over. So, Rosie and Bas okay...?'

'They're fine.'

'Rosie and I are in touch quite a lot anyway, so she keeps me up to speed with things. So have you got the second album?'

'Of course; Basil bought ten copies of it.'

'Did he, bless him...'

Tarragon yawned.

'Sorry, I think I'm about to crash; more news later, I need a shower if I can bear the cold out there, and then some sleep.'

'Of course; anyway we should be thinking about our day, and the others will be up soon.'

'Well if I miss them say hi from me, I'll see them all later; I assume Emma's still sleeping here, unofficially at least?'

'We cannot confirm or deny this rumour.' Said Keith

'Of course; well at least she's not a virgin anyway...'

'And she has my son, and I'm told he's getting more like me all the time, so how could anyone be anything but completely happy?'

'Exactly, pops…I'll come and see you at the deli later, mum, when I'm a bit more myself.'

'Sure, whenever you're ready, sweetheart…'

They all stood up and Tarragon hugged her parents again, then she left the bus. Keith and Meadow exchanged looks between them, and Keith was the next to speak.

'She seems well.'

'Flourishing; she's changed, hasn't she, even since she left for this tour.'

'Seems like it…'

'She's not the shrinking Violet that she once was, that's for sure.'

'I expect singing in front of tens of thousands of people does that to a person, and yet she still comes back here.'

'Of course she does; these are her roots, everyone comes back to their roots, if they have them, and Tara's still about the most grounded person I know. It's what enables her to survive the dizzy heights of stardom, I suppose.'

'I guess so…She was kind of hard on Sandra, don't you think?'

'Perhaps, or perhaps she's just voicing what we all think but aren't saying.'

'Yeah, could be…Anyway, best get to it.'

'It's not six o'clock yet; let's go back to bed for half an hour.'

'That's the best idea I've heard all day.'

Sandra was sitting up in bed in her private room when Will and Emily went to the hospital in the early evening. This was essentially a public hospital, but one part of the building had been set aside for paying clientele, and Brian and Margaret Fox, who were in Holland, had instructed Emma that no expense be spared for their elder daughter. Emma was to use her credit card, which they would reimburse on their return. Sandra still had a tube inserted, and was being kept mildly sedated and on painkillers, and her heart – rate was being monitored. But still, she was awake, and alive, and it seemed that the worst of it was over. Emma was there, as she had been for most of the day, having taken the day off school; their parents were not expected until the next day.

'Oh, hi Emily...Hi Will.'

'Hi Emma....'

Sandra looked at them, and recognition seemed to take a moment, but then it came. She was deathly pale, she looked thin and her voice was weak, as was her smile. But she was speaking, at least, though her words were somewhat slurred.

'Hello you two...I was hoping you'd come.'

'Of course we came,' said Emily 'Will heard the news this morning, and I only heard this afternoon. So, how are you feeling, if that's not too stupid a question.'

'Well, you know...Not too bad considering. My chest's bloody painful but no ribs broken, which happens sometimes, apparently, when, you know...When they try to get your heart going again.'

Emily sat down on the only chair beside the bed, and took her friends' hand, which remained limp, and felt cold.

'Look,' said Emma 'if you three want some time, I could do with getting something to eat, to be honest.'

'Sure,' said Emily 'take as long as you like.'

Emma took her leave, and Will leaned on the end of the bed. It was something of a shock for him to see Sandra Fox in so diminished a state, and she had clearly been worse than this. He had been the last one to see her, and she had said nothing and then slammed the door in his face, and then she had done this. There had been no last – minute cry for help, no last attempt to seduce him as she had done before; the vixen had fled or rather staggered to her lair, put on her favorite record and turned the volume up. The rest he tried not to think about.

'So,' said Emily 'what have you been up to then, you silly girl?'

'I don't know, Em.'

'Well, we can talk about it all later, if you want to, but at least you're going to be okay now.'

Sandra looked away, her somewhat glazed and vacant expression now studying the wall.

'That's what the doctors are saying.'

'And we're sure they're right, aren't we Will? You'll be up and about in no time.'

'I can't remember, you know…How I did this.'

'Do you remember being at our place?'

'Yes, I think so.'

'Do you remember walking home with Will?'

'No; no, I can't remember doing that…What…I mean, what did I do, Will?'

'You just, you know, said goodnight and went in the house; you weren't walking too well by that time.'

'I haven't, ummm…I haven't walked anywhere since either; I can't seem to stand up very well yet.'

'That'll come.' Said Emily 'You've had a nasty shock; it's bound to take a bit of time to get your strength back.'

Sandra said nothing, but tears came to her eyes, and then;

'I'm so sorry…I didn't mean to do this to everyone.'

'Don't be silly, it doesn't matter.'

'And you're still my friends, aren't you?'

'Of course we are, and always will be, won't we Will?'

'Sure, just, you know, go easy on the dope in future.'

Sandra actually laughed; at least it was a kind of a laugh. She then put her head back on the bed – head and stared at the ceiling.

'Christ, what a mess I've made of everything…I'll lose my funding now.'

'Not necessarily.' Said Emily

'Sure I will…They won't want me after…After this. I was always the sensible one, wasn't I? Sandra the fucking sensible…'

'Yeah,' said Will 'well you've beaten us all with this one. Talk about making up for lost time; getting all the nonsense out of the way in one go, got to have respect for that.'

Sandra lifted her head again and focused on Will; every movement seemed to require thought and effort, but she was trying to smile now through the tears. Just then a young nurse entered the room, Will stood up.

'And how are you now, young lady; time for your meds…'

'This,' said Sandra 'is my day – nurse; her name's Sophie Summerfield, isn't that a lovely name? Sophie Summerfield, this is Will and Emily, they're the people that I love most in the whole world, did you know that?'

'No I didn't, and you're not supposed to be getting excited yet, are you?'

'Sorry…' Said Emily

'It's fine; you need to see your friends, don't you, but it's time for your sleep now.'

'Time to sleep…' Said Sandra

'Right' said Emily, 'well we'll be going then…'

'And do you know what…' Said Sandra 'My sister, my lovely sister, doesn't bring her boyfriend here because she thinks I don't like him…Sandra the fucking snob, well that's all going to change now; everything's going to change…'

'Yes, of course it is, you just have to get better first, so drink this and then let's get you laid down, shall we?'

Emily let go of Sandra's hand, which just for a moment held hers. Sophie, who had seen Victoria Tillington through her worst days of intensive care, now helped Sandra Fox to lie down, and made her head comfortable on the pillow. Sandra's last words before she drifted into sleep were addressed to Emily.

'It's all going to change, Em….I'm so sorry.'

Will and Emily went in search of the canteen, where they found Emma, who had just eaten that which would suffice as her evening meal.

'Well, how is she?'

'She's sleeping.' Said Emily

'Good, well I may as well go home then; she'll probably be out 'til the morning now.'

'We can go together in the Land Rover if you like; we can drop you off.'

'That would be nice, thanks. I think she's going to be okay, isn't she?'

'Looks like it…'

'I just don't know what made her do it, the silly cow.'

'I know, and you've had to do this all by yourself, haven't you?'

'Well, Keith and Meadow have been great, and Basil, of course; without them this would have been horrible; I mean even more horrible. You know, I didn't even know she was taking antidepressants.'

'Sure…I don't think any of us knew. So when are your real parents coming, if you know what I mean?'

'Tomorrow, I think…They missed everything, didn't they, which is mostly what they do; makes you wonder who your real parents are.'

'Yes, well, Keith and Meadow are always great…Anyway, shall we go then?'

Emily disliked hospitals intensely, so she was not sorry that their visit had been brief, and now she was keen to leave. How much of that which Sandra had said was influenced by her medication was impossible to know, and perhaps she would be thinking more clearly when next they saw her, but at least she was alive, and was apparently lucky to be so. And who knew, maybe she really was going to change.

'Yes, I'm ready…'

'Come, William, take us all home; I need a stiff drink.'

Isabella had awoken on this morning with a particular and in no way pleasant feeling in the pit of her stomach. She had gone about her daily routine and had gone to school, but she had had no application for it, and academically the day could be said to have been wasted. If her teachers had one criticism of this their most able pupil, it was that she lacked creativity and imagination. She went about her learning with cold, detached logic, and in this way, if one were looking for an example, had she learned to play the violin. For Isabella this was about the precise reproduction of sound, or the exact reading of a given musical score, but she could not compose, any more than she could with any enthusiasm or ease write creative essays or poetry. That which existed in the world was quite enough to occupy Isabella's considerable mental abilities, and in truth she saw no point to creating anything new, even if it were within her natural gift to do so. Thus had she also learned to become a more than competent chess player, by learning from the masters of the game who had come before her, by remembering rather than creating lines of play, the winning of games being a logical end result of this so logical a process.

This, however, was different. Try as she may, she could not apply her cold and detached logic to the matter of her meeting with Barnabas Overton, and it was this which on this day caused her such distraction. Before, when she had been hunting them, when she had been Mirabelle or Alexa, just names hiding behind a computer screen, she had felt safe, because she had been safe; she could have stopped any time she had wanted to, and they would never have known it was her. And then even when she had been Agnes Appleby, and had gone incognito to the chess club and had seen him, he had not seen her, or who she really was. She had been in control then; she had the element of surprise as she removed her dark glasses and mouthed the words; *'Remember me?'*

Then she had had the anger, and the anger had given her courage, but now as she watched from her vantage point as Barnabas and Rachel Overton walked toward her along the path in St Agnes Park, the feeling which had started the day somewhere in the pit of her stomach found its' way elsewhere and everywhere; she flushed red, and noticed that her hands had begun to shake, her legs felt as though they could not move, and of a sudden she needed to urinate. Now she and he were two people meeting who knew that they would meet; there was no anonymity, or surprise; now they would meet as equals. Instinctively her hand gripped more tightly around the cold, steel blade of the kitchen knife which she held in her coat pocket. It was the short – bladed knife which her father used to dress and cut meat on Sundays, and he kept the edge keen. Even now it was not too late; she could stay in the darkest recesses of the shelter, and perhaps they would not find her, or she could still leave, and walk quickly away; perhaps after all that would be best. But she stayed where she was, and in fact she moved to the entrance of the shelter, without knowing how or why she had done so, and now they stood before her, just a few paces away, and time for a moment stood still. Their eyes met; Rachel was no part of it now, this was him and her, male and female, abuser and abused, and for that which seemed the longest time, neither spoke. Later she would try to remember how she had felt during those first few seconds, when their eyes had been speaking volumes to each other, and all that she could recall was feeling numb, and helpless, in a way, and it was Rachel Overton who had to break the deadlock.

'Thank you for coming, Isabella. Barnabas, is there something you wish to say?'

Still the endless silence, until;

'I'm sorry, Isabella; I really am so sorry. What we did…What I did, well, it was unforgivable, but still, I've come here hoping that you will try to forgive me even so, that's all.'

Simple yet no doubt well rehearsed words, and tears now; male tears, and still the numbness wouldn't go away. It was as though all of the bad things that had been done to her, and all of the bad things that she had done; all of the emotions which she had felt; the pain, and the pain that she had caused others had come together in that one moment, and in this one moment of contact with another human being. This was primeval, instinctive and raw; it existed now, but it had existed forever, far back into the mists of long forgotten time, when everything had begun; male and female, rape and seduction, and the ungodly and unending mess of it all, and perhaps in the end all things became equal. There had been so much that she was going to say to him; so many questions, and so many insults; so many words, but they would just be words, and they were beyond words now. Here he stood; her abuser and tormentor, and the man that she had hated so much, and yet a part of her had at last begun to understand why she had come, and that here perhaps also was her savior, and her salvation. If she could perhaps somehow try to forgive him, then perhaps she would be forgiven, and she would be free; free of all that she had done, and all that had been done to her. Here perhaps was her baptism, her confession, and an end to it all, and beyond that end was a new beginning. But still, such things were more easily thought than done; the moment passed, and she felt once again the cold precision of her fathers' knife; just a few paces closer, and she could do the thing which she had imagined herself doing so many times.

'Isabella, you have been brave enough to come here. Is there anything you can say?'

Quite what happened thereafter was unclear to Isabella. He must have walked the last few paces which separated them, his wife by his side, and perhaps she had even walked towards him. Anyway he was close enough now, and he must have offered his hand; so speak then, Isabella; say something, but the words felt like glue in her mouth, and in the end, when the words finally came, she was unsure to which of them she was speaking.

'I can't....I'm sorry, I can't do this.'

The knife was out now, covering the last of the distance between them, and she felt the pressure as she pushed it hard into his stomach, feeling the warm blood on her hand as it poured from him, and seeing the look of abject shock on his face as he realized what had just happened. Isabella must have walked away, although she later had no memory of leaving the park. Her next clear memory was of standing somewhere in the town, alone in the semi – darkness, her face wet, and the numbness had gone.

Isabella walked home in a dream, and it was a long walk. She had met him again, and she had made it through the meeting, and that at least was something, was it not? She walked with her hands in her coat pockets, which were empty as they had been when she had arrived. It was said by some of Isabella that she had no imagination, but the knife and that which she had done with it had felt real enough to her, and perhaps that had helped. She was not yet free, but she had taken another step towards freedom, and perhaps next time that she met him she could say the things that she had so much wanted to say. The next time, if there was to be a next time, and perhaps next time she could leave her fathers' knife where he always kept it, on the hook on the kitchen wall.

Chapter 16

SOMEWHERE TO START

If the beginning of this particular week had been of significance for Michael Tillington, then this significance seemed set fair to continue into its' middle, and certainly if Wednesday was anything to go by. As we have learned, this was the day that work would commence at Orchard House, and in the normal run of things he would have met Keith there in the morning at eight o'clock, to discuss and witness the beginning of the contract. The week, however, was running true to form and thus anything but normally, and as it happened he would have to delay his arrival. This was due to a telephone conversation which he had had on Tuesday afternoon with a certain lady of half – Nordic ancestry, who had but recently accepted his offer of marriage, but whom he had not seen at the time or since.

'Hi Michael...'

'Oh, Hello Elin'

'I have clearance to take tomorrow off work, so we can meet, if this would be convenient?'

'Well yes, of course, but are you sure, about the work I mean?'

'It is quite alright, I have worked some weekends lately and today we completed on two difficult sales and purchases, so my work – load has quickly decreased significantly.'

'Well that's excellent, then; I mean I can come to you, but I can't leave until mid – morning at the earliest.'

'It is quite alright, I would welcome some time away, so I will catch a morning train, and be at Queenswood Station at twenty past ten.'

'Oh, fine then; see you tomorrow morning. So will this just be one day?'

'I think I'll be fine to have Thursday as well; I will return on Thursday evening.'

Later Michael 'phoned Keith, who said that there was no problem, there was quite a lot to be getting on with; Michael could take his time. In truth, Michael was somewhat disappointed that he would miss the very beginning of the project, but any such disappointment was more than compensated for by the fact of his seeing Elin, and under the circumstances he could scarce have not been there to greet her. The last time he had seen her she had been walking out of a restaurant, when their future had still been uncertain, if they had a future at all, and now they were to be married. Both had committed the rest of their respective lives to one another, Elin would now one day be 'Lady Elin', and all of that had happened when they had been in different counties, so it was time indeed for them to meet.

The Kings Head public house was situated close to the centre of the town, and was that which may be called a 'young persons'' pub. Here was music played more loudly than was usual, and the music selected for its' modernity. In former times, when public houses had been gathering places where relatively cheap ales were available, and the smoking of cigarettes was permitted, the Kings Head had been a thriving establishment. Latterly, with the increased taxation levied upon alcohol, the availability of relatively inexpensive wine, and a total ban on smoking indoors, many public houses had become primarily places to dine, some even setting aside areas for those patrons not wishing to eat. The Kings Head, however, had maintained its' emphasis on good ales and basic but inexpensive food, and informal and some might say shabby decor. The building also benefitted from a quite large inner courtyard, where the smoking of cigarettes was permitted, large outdoor heaters having been installed to encourage its' continued use in all but the most inclement weather. The pub had therefore become a favoured haunt for students and a generally younger clientele, and it was in any case the venue for the arranged meeting of a certain young lady whose name was Rosemary Knightman, her new – found acquaintance, Quentin, and Quentin's two brothers.

Rosie arrived somewhat after the appointed time of eight o'clock, not wishing to be first there, and being uncertain of the reliability of her potential companions, but in the event she found the three men seated in the courtyard, the evening being pleasantly mild for the time of year. She saw them before Quentin saw her, and a quick assessment told her that they were all of similar age, that Quentin was probably although not certainly the youngest, and perhaps no more than four or five years separated the youngest of them from the oldest. The reason that they were seated in the courtyard was also apparent, since both of the brothers were smoking cigarettes. Rosie was a person whose attractiveness tended to draw attention to her when she entered any new environment, and despite her being modestly dressed in jeans and overcoat, eyes turned to her as she approached the table, including the eyes of one of the two brothers, who looked somewhat embarrassed when she stood at the head of the small wooden table, and Quentin saw her for the first time.

'Hey; here you are...Everyone this is Rosie; Rosie this is Tris and Freddy, my two elder brothers.'

Quentin had indicated which brother was which; Rosie thought that Tarquin was probably the oldest of them, and it had been Tristan who had been observing her entry with particular interest. She sat down next to Quentin and opposite the others, who quickly assessed and acknowledged her without speaking. Tristan had inherited the same extremely curly hair as had Quentin, Tarquin had straighter and darker hair, but the young lady noted that they were none of them unattractive young men. All were casually dressed, and Quentin was wearing the same Tweed jacket that he had worn at their first meeting, or rather meetings, since they had met twice on the train. Rosie smiled, and addressed the small congregation.

'Not that much older, though.'

'No,' said Quentin 'well our dear departed mother hated being pregnant and didn't like babies much better, and got us all over with as quickly as possible. She actually wanted a girl but gave up after three, so we were all of us as you might say an inherent disappointment to her.'

'I'm sure that isn't true; anyway I'm pleased to meet you both.'

'Likewise I'm sure,' said Tarquin 'so what are you, then, our brothers' girlfriend or what?'

The same cultured if understated home – counties accent, which she would learn that all three shared.

'No, actually...'

'So are you hoping to be our brothers' girlfriend?'

'Freddy for fucks' sake behave,' said Quentin 'forgive my brother, he has a way with words, and it isn't always a good way.'

'It's okay,' said Rosie 'actually I'm nothing in particular; we just met on a train going both ways, and as to what I hope for, that's for me to know, don't you think?'

'Our brother worked his undoubted charms on you, I'm sure.'

'I'm not sure he worked anything on me, actually, but anyway, here I have been invited and here I am, so is anybody going to buy me a drink or what?'

'Tris, your on...' said Quentin

'Yeah; my shout... So, Ms nothing in particular; what's your poison?'

'Vodka and Tonic, thank you.'

Rosie seldom indeed very rarely drank alcohol, but seemed to have walked into a particular situation, and felt that the occasion called for it. She would need to keep her wits about her, but some dulling of the senses and sensibilities might be no bad thing.

'Right; coming up...'

'Anyway,' said Quentin 'I suppose a bit of background is called for; Tris there has a degree in physics and mastered in astronomy, then completely wasted his education and works with charitable organisations abroad, mostly in India; he's a rampant bloody socialist these days, and has kind of become our social conscience. Freddy lectures in Mathematics at a French university, and is also fluent in German, but we've long since forgiven him for being a genius; politically he's pitched himself slightly to the right of Attila the Hun, so we don't talk politics much.'

'And where do you stand, politically speaking?'

'I suffer from the intellectual affliction of being able to see both sides of the argument and not really agreeing with either, so you'd probably have to call me a social democrat.'

Tristan returned with a tray of drinks; Rosie took and actually rather enjoyed the first mouthful of hers, and prepared herself for whatever might follow as Quentin continued his monologue.

'So anyway, we were just getting down to the brass tacks of what to do with the family pile; Freddy thinks we should pull rank on the tenants and give them notice to quit, then sell up and divide the proceeds, I think we should maintain the status quo, at least for now, so Tristan has the casting vote.'

'So this is a democracy then, is it?'

'Sometimes, although that doesn't always work, nobody being particularly willing to accept the view or will of the majority, so mostly we end up fighting, but there've been no fatalities so far, and we've been at each other since we could walk.'

'Couldn't two of you buy the other one out, or whatever?'

'Nobody can afford it, it's a fuck – off big house, and it's in Clandon, if you know what I mean, and none of us are exactly big earners. Anyway apart from the money there's the sentimental aspect, which Tris is hung up on, and I kind of agree with him; it's where we all grew up, and it's not all good memories but it's all we've got.'

'But T...Freddy doesn't agree?'

'Freddy's a mercenary, he sees it as just being a house, and frankly we could all do with the cash, so I can see his point of view; see, that's my problem; I'm the archetypal fence – sitter. I need somebody else to make the decision.'

'So your grandmother didn't live there, then?'

'No, well not for a long time, but she was born and raised there and didn't want us to sell so we respected the old girls' wishes whilst she was alive, and now we find ourselves cast adrift in the ocean of self – determination, and so far we're drifting in different directions, you might say.'

'Oh dear...'

'Yeah,' said Tristan 'and if we're not careful we're going to bore this young lady into an early departure, so let's talk about something else, shall we?'

'The floor's yours,' Said Tarquin 'we're all ears.'

'Okay, well perhaps Rosie would like to tell us something about herself; Quentin tells us you're from Middlewapping; home to the world-famous Middlewapping meteorite; it must be the most photographed village cricket – pitch in history.'

Rosie noted that Quentin had in fact told the others about her, and wondered for a moment what and how much he had told them.

'Yes, we get a lot of visitors...'

'And are said visitors welcome to your quintessentially English rural idyll?'

'Well the village deli does good business because of it, and so does the pub, and since it's my mother who runs the deli, I can hardly complain, I suppose.'

'That's looking at it from a very personal perspective.'

'Yes, well it's the only perspective I've got, actually, so it'll have to do.'

'Fair enough...What's the pub called again?'

'I don't think I've told you the first time, but it's called the Dog and Bottle.'

Quentin sat ready to defend Rosemary should either of his brothers overstep the bounds of decent or polite enquiry, but he was gratified to note that she was doing okay without him, and would thus be earning their respect, which was often hard – won.

'You ever drunk there Quen..?'

'Never have as a matter of fact.'

'So what about the witch...?' Said Tarquin

Just at that moment, which promised to be little uncomfortable for Rosie, the opening track of *All That I Will Ever Be* filled the pub, and the sound of her sister's voice caused her further if better distraction; it felt good to have Tara with her, and they would probably play the whole album.

'What...? I'm sorry?'

'The witch of Middlewapping; how did that particular piece of folklore come to be..?'

'I really don't know.'

Rosie might have been tempted to ask to which of the three witches currently residing in the village he was referring, but she resisted the temptation. If they only knew the power that she could have over them if she was of a mind to use it, but Charlotte had warned her not to so mischievously abuse her particular abilities, so she let the thought go on its' mischievous way.

'So there's no truth in it then;' Said Tristan 'one almost feels disappointed.'

'I reckon there's something in it.' Said Quentin

'Yes, well you always were a sucker for anything like that.' Said Tarquin

'All I'm saying is that there's more going on than we know or understand, and these rumours don't start from nothing.'

'Oh come on for Christ's sake; let's at least keep the conversation in the real world, shall we?'

'Yeah, but I mean, I don't see any reason why there shouldn't be modern – day witches.'

'Jesus, Quen...So what say you, Rosie; any old crones with spinning wheels living near you?'

'Not that I know of...'

'You probably can't get the broomsticks anymore anyway; someone change the subject before our younger brother makes a complete fool of himself. I mean what about the rumour that none other than Ashley Spears lives in a church in Middlewapping; you believe that too, do you Quen? How did that particular piece of fantasy come about, do you suppose?'

'Actually that's true...' Said Rosie 'Well he doesn't live there, not often anyway, and he's on tour at the moment, with Tara Knightman, as coincidence would have it, but he's there sometimes, and it isn't actually a church anymore; it's been deconsecrated.'

There was a moment of silence whilst everybody tried to decide whether the young lady was being serious, and then whether or not they should believe her. Quentin in particular knew that his credibility was on the line; he had brought Rosie here, and he didn't know her well yet, but he decided to risk it and give her the benefit of the doubt.

'So now who's the fool, Freddy? So have you met the great man?'

'Yes; you could say we're quite good friends, actually.'

Which further fanned the flames of doubt and uncertainty, but by now Quentin had decided that his new – found friend was neither delusional nor a liar, at least he had almost decided this, so he pressed on in the sincere hope that he was right, and was not in the end to be made to look a bigger fool than his eldest brother was currently in danger of appearing.

'Well, Freddo; I trust you feel suitably chastened?'

Tarquin fell silent and went about drinking his beer; he was not happy to be have been made to look somewhat foolish, and certainly not by this young girl, and it was Tristan, who in terms of his conviction stood somewhere between his two brothers, who next spoke.

'So what about the album cover?'

'I'm sorry?' Said Rosie

'The first Tara Knightman album shows her sitting on the steps of a bus.'

'Yes, I've seen the album.'

'So there was yet another urban myth going about that she lives on the bus, and that the bus is somewhere down your way, but nobody knows where it is.'

'I believe there may be some truth in that.'

'What makes you say so?'

'I'm just saying; that's all...'

Tarquin saw his chance to regain some credibility, and to undermine that of the speaker, so he re – entered the conversation.

'Quen tells us that you live on a bus, is there also some truth in that?'

So he had told them that as well. In the background Tara had begun the first verse of 'A Song to Nobody', which was a particular favourite of Rosemary's.

'There's quite a lot of truth in that, actually.'

'So does everybody in your village live on buses, or what?'

'No, not everybody; that would be rather unlikely wouldn't it..?'

'This whole conversation is becoming rather unlikely; I suppose you're going to tell us that you know Tara Knightman too...She a good friend of yours as well?'

'No, not really...'

'Maybe you even live on the same bus...Jesus, where did you find her, Quen?'

'Actually we do; live on the same bus that is. Tara's my sister.'

Once again the silence, and now even Quentin had a moment of doubt; was she really telling the truth, or was she actually this good at spinning yarns? Rosie took a mouthful of her drink and looked from one to the other of them, and waited. As she had expected, it was Tarquin who broke the doubtful silence.

'I don't believe you; I think that's all bullshit...'

'Well I don't particularly care whether you believe me or not, but I can prove it if you like.'

'So prove it.'

Rosie looked at Quentin, her expression enquiring, and Quentin understood well enough that which was being asked of him; his was the trust that mattered the most, and this was a test of faith.

'I believe the lady absolutely. How about you, Tris; you in...?'

There was only a moment's hesitation, before;

'Yeah, I'll buy it.'

'So now it's just you, bro; the rest of the nights' beer says it's true; you up for that, or would you care to rethink, in which case I think an apology is in order, don't you?'

'Okay, I'll call it.'

Rosie reached into her inside coat pocket, took out her bankcard and tossed it gently onto the table; had this been a card game it would have been the ace of spades. Tristan picked up the card, read it and smiled; the name Rosemary A Knightman was printed clearly enough upon it. He passed the card to Quentin, who passed it to Tarquin, whose expression remained neutral, but the other two knew that it must have hurt.

'I've got messages on my 'phone if that isn't enough, but those are private.'

'It's enough.' Said Quentin 'So, Fredo, looks like you've been taken to the cleaners by a teenage girl; you want to tell us all how you feel about that, or would you rather just get the beers in?'

Tarquin stood up, gathered up the empty beer glasses and walked away without speaking. Quentin and Tristan exchanged looks and smiled.

'I'm sorry,' said Rosie 'I didn't mean to cause trouble.'

'It's okay,' said Tristan 'if it hadn't been that it would have been something else. And don't take it personally, it's just his way; he's not as bad as he comes across, is he, Quen?'

'No, he's far worse than that. Anyway, so you're Tara Knightman's sister; that must be cool.'

'Must it; why, do you know her then?'

Which Rosie realised was overly defensive; he had believed her, after all, and she had better come out of combat mode.

'Sorry, I mean I love her to bits, of course, so yes, it's cool.'

'No, your okay; I had that coming, but she's got a great voice.'

'Yes, she has.'

'Dreams of Winter' was now playing; one of the more mellow and slow – tempo songs on the album, and one which allowed Tara to use her considerable vocal range.

'And Ash Spears is a legend in his own lifetime, of course, but what's he like, you know?'

'He's the perfect gentleman, actually.'

And so did the evening find its' way to closing time, and having earned her rite of social and intellectual passage into this particular group of brothers, Rosie would in the end conclude that they were in fact at a deeper level a close – knit and cooperative unit, and none of them were as bad as Quentin would have had her believe. Even Tarquin had treated her with something like friendship and at least respect, once he had recovered from his mild humiliation, and everybody in fact bought drinks thereafter. They said goodbye at the door of the public house; from here it was only a short walk to Quentin's rented rooms and Tarquin and Tristan's bed and breakfast accommodation. Rosie had missed the last bus home, Quentin hung back for a brief private moment with her, the others having diplomatically walked on ahead having wished her goodnight, and Quentin insisted on paying her taxi fare.

'Hell, it's the least I can do...Thanks for coming; I hope it wasn't too much of an ordeal?'

'Not at all; I've had a good time.'

'So, will you 'phone me, then; maybe we could get together again soon.'

'Maybe we could, and maybe you could 'phone me next time.'

'Sure; I'll do that, once those two are safely dispatched.'

The taxi pulled up at the kerbside.

'Well, goodnight then, Rosie.'

'Goodnight...'

The taxi pulled away, and Quentin went after his brothers. A chance second meeting on a train, and he truly had not expected her to 'phone, and now there was this. It was a fact that none of the brothers had had any lasting romantic attachment to anybody; their lives thus far having been devoted and channelled to more academic matters. Quentin had had two brief sexual encounters with women whilst at university, nothing having made traction in either case, for either party, but as he walked through the now quite chilly streets of the town, he found himself looking forward very much to his next meeting with Rosemary A Knightman, in a way that he had to admit he had not felt before.

Michael and Elin kissed lightly on the station platform. Michael had noticed that whilst it was the case that Elin went about the business of sex with some enthusiasm, she was in general less inclined to show lesser demonstrations of affection, and rarely did she do so in public, but now she took his arm as they walked to the car. These were unusual circumstances; they had agreed to marry one another, and so their relationship had fundamentally changed since they had last met, but now neither quite knew what to say or indeed do about it. It was done and accepted now, and both had had time to let the matter settle into their lives and their futures, so what was to be said, really? So perhaps this light intimacy was her quiet way of acknowledging their new status, and their newly established importance to one another, and Michael accepted the acknowledgment; enough said, without either having to actually say anything.

'So, how are you, Michael?'

'I'm very well, thank you.'

She looked up at him and they smiled at one another and at their politeness; both knew what was going on, and in a way they were laughing at themselves, which was no bad thing to do.

'I have to go to Orchard House this morning, but I can drop you off at the Manor if you like; Victoria's working today but Mater and Pater are there. I should only be gone for two or three hours.'

'Could I not come to Orchard House with you?'

'Well yes, of course, if you'd like to; it's just work, you know, and I'll have to spend some time with Keith and so on.'

'I would very much like to, actually, and I would rather not be without you.'

'Okay fine, so do you want to call in at the Manor to freshen up, as it were, and to drop off your bag? Orchard House has no working facilities yet.'

'There is no need; we can go straight there if you would like.'

And so they did, and within the hour Michael had driven through the entrance to Orchard House, and had pulled his motor vehicle to a halt on the quite small area of rough gravel which constituted the only parking place within the bounds of the property, and on which Damien's Land Rover was already parked. There was also now a large rubbish container there, and space was limited. In time the area would need to be increased in size, and a double garage would need to be built, but that was still some time in the future, and would he assumed be one of the last jobs to be done.

Michael walked immediately toward the house, Elin did not, but rather she took a moment to view the house from a distance before following him to the front door and across the threshold. Sounds of hammering emanated from the floor above them, but Elin was keen to inspect the ground floor, so Michael gave her the tour, such as it was.

'So these will be the reception rooms, basically a lounge and dining room with an office or whatever off the lounge, and the kitchen will be through here. Eventually there'll be a downstairs toilet and shower – room.'

She followed him to that which had once been the kitchen, where there was still a large old ceramic sink, but little else to indicate the rooms' former use save some rusty iron pipe – work, through which no water had flowed for a long time.

'This is a large kitchen; in fact all of the rooms are very big, aren't they?'

'Yes, it will be a substantial property.'

'And these old beams are beautiful.'

'They may have been old ship – timbers, in which case they would pre – date the house.'

She took in every detail of each room before they ascended the central staircase, and here they entered a somewhat dusty working environment, which smelled of old plaster. The three workmen, who were covered from head to foot in plaster dust, stopped work when they became aware of the newcomers, and introductions were made.

'Elin, this is Keith, who's looking after the contract for me.'

'Pleased to meet you...you'll forgive me if I don't shake hands...'

'Please, it really is no problem.'

So they shook hands, and exchanged pleasant smiles; Mike had not been exaggerating; she really was a most attractive woman, and an unexpected visitor, actually.

'It is unusual to see a man with such long hair these days.'

'Yeah, well some of us never really grow up, you know; one day I'll be big and responsible, but I'm not quite there yet.'

'I'm sure that's not true; Michael has spoken very highly of you, and your hair is very nice.'

'Thanks…My wife likes it, not that she's actually my wife, but anyway she's long since taken over maintenance duties; if I suggest having a go at it myself she hides the scissors.'

Elin laughed, and decided that she liked Keith already.

'And this is Damien, who lives on the village Green.'

'Delighted, I'm sure…'

'Ah, you are a Scotsman.'

'Ay, for my sins.'

'Scotland is a beautiful country; very much like Norway in many ways, and I have always loved the Scottish accent.'

'And this is Will, who lives on a small farm with Emily on what used to be estate land; Emily makes the best goats' cheese in the county, and some way beyond I would think.'

'Hi…'

'Hello Will.'

'And that's the whole team, for now anyway; so how's it going, Keith?'

'Yeah, well you know, four hours in and so far so good…. The plaster's shot and it's coming off okay, so we should be able to leave the brickwork exposed if you want to, at least in places.'

'Will it be difficult to clean up?'

'No more difficult than re – plastering; we'd have to seal the walls, but you'd save on the plaster and labour for plastering. The bricks are great, aren't they; there're hardly two the same size. They used to make each brick by hand in those days; seems a shame to cover them up, but it's up to you of course.'

'Well I'll give that some thought then; I rather like exposed brickwork, but it can be quite dark compared to painted walls.'

'Yeah, well, like I say, it's your call.'

Elin was by now inspecting the various rooms, and Michael caught up with her in that which had once been the bathroom, in which an old bath and washbasin remained, neither of which were fit for reuse.

'This bathroom will serve two of the bedrooms; the other bedroom will be en- suite. That way we don't have to knock any walls down.'

'I see...'

Which was all that she said, busy as she was looking through each window and assessing the views, but Elin was thinking.

'Would you guys like some tea? I think we can rustle up enough cups, and we haven't had a break yet.'

This was Keith, who was addressing Michael, but it was Elin who answered.

'That would be nice, thank you Keith.'

'Right, well let's go downstairs then, into a more conducive environment.'

Once downstairs, Will started a small generator at the front of the house, from which ran a single cable to a set of portable sockets, into which was plugged a kettle. Tea was made, and the day was sufficiently warm for everyone to sit outside on makeshift chairs, the three workman being glad of the fresh air. Whilst Keith and Michael discussed the work in hand and the first delivery of materials, Elin took her tea and walked as best she could around the overgrown garden, looking at the house from all sides and all angles. It seemed to Michael as though she was taking an uncommon interest in the building, but he put that down to feminine curiosity, and thought nothing else of it. Within an hour they were once more in the car and heading for the Manor House.

'Well, what do you think?'

'It is a most beautiful house.'

'Yes, it is, isn't it, or rather it will be when it's finished, I hope.'

'Michael, do your parents know, about us I mean?'

'No, not yet; I thought I would make an official pronouncement in due course.'

'Yes, that would probably be best.'

'I told Victoria, but she won't say anything to anyone.'

'You two are close, aren't you...And what did she say?'

'She was delighted, of course, and I'm sorry, Elin, but I haven't had a chance to buy a ring yet.'

Elin laughed gently.

'It's okay my love, all in good time. None of this has been well planned, has it, and please don't spend a fortune, I will be quite happy with any ring that you buy me. Do you think your parents will be surprised when you tell them?'

'I really don't know; I mean they know we're in a relationship, of course, so it shouldn't come as a huge surprise.'

'Well, it came as a huge surprise to me, not that I'm complaining, it was a very nice surprise.'

She took his hand, and they were silent for most of the rest of the journey; Elin seemed to Michael to be deep in thought, and it was not until they were quite close to home that she appeared to have come to a decision. He drove through the gates of the Manor House and pulled the vehicle to a halt by the steps which led to the front door, but for a moment neither moved. This was to be a significant moment, after all; the first time that she would walk into that which she now knew would one day be her home. It was not this home, however, which had been occupying her thoughts.

'Michael, I have something to say.'

'Yes, I thought so...'

'I would like you to renovate Orchard House for us.'

'What do you mean?'

'What I mean is that I want us to live there.'

Michael was glad she had waited until now to impart her thoughts, and that he had not been driving when she had done so.

'What...? I mean, are you serious?'

'Yes, I am very serious, the house is perfect; it has three bedrooms for us, Nathaniel and his carer, and well, to be honest I fell in love with it as soon as I saw it.'

'Yes, but I mean it's going to take all of my money; I may even have to borrow to finish the job.'

'Well then I will sell my apartment, and I have money of my own; I am prepared to give you all of it to help to finance the renovation, assuming of course that we have joint-ownership.'

Now it was Michael's turn to be deep in thought. Never for a moment had he seen Orchard House as anything other than a quite short – term investment, and as a way to continue and improve the financing of his business. He had also assumed that a part of the money would be used to buy a somewhat more modest house for them, but he had not thought that it would be this house, and he needed a moment.

'Well, now it's my turn to be surprised...'

'Then we are now even, would you not say?'

She smiled at him, and at his reaction, which had been as she had expected. She was right, of course; aside from its' grandeur, in all other respects the house was perfect, and it was a beautiful house, and in truth Michael had always seen it in terms of more than just money, but this was something quite new to consider. And if there was now to be more money available then he supposed the idea was perhaps not so outlandish. In the short time that he had had to consider the matter, he had thought that theirs it would be the next house, but then he smiled inwardly and somewhat wryly at that particular thought; it was a thought which he had had before, too many times.

'We'd have to furnish it.'

'Yes, but that would apply to whichever house we bought, anyway I have some furniture; enough for us to begin with.'

'It's a big house.'

'So we will furnish it slowly and as we can.'

'I see, well, in that case I suppose the idea is worth considering.'

'Well then please consider it.'

'Alright, I'll do that...But now I suppose we should meet your future in – laws.'

'I have met them before, Michael.'

'Yes, but they weren't going to be your in – laws then. So let's get our story straight; we're not betrothed, or engaged to be married or anything.'

'No, nothing like that...'

'And better not mention the house yet; at least I want them to see it first, and preferably in its' completed state, and anyway we haven't made a final decision about that yet, have we....'

'No, not at all, and in any case that will only follow once they know we are to be married.'

'Yes, that's true....Well then, shall we...?'

'We shall, and by the way, there is one more thing I would like to say.'

'What's that?'

'I do very much like exposed brickwork.'

Sandra Fox remained in her hospital bed for two more days, after which her doctor prescribed mild anti – depressants, and declared that she was well enough to go home. She was young, and would quickly regain her strength, and no lasting neurological damage was expected. She was given the contact details of a local psychiatrist, but otherwise the Health Service had done all that they could for her. Brian and Margaret Fox, having arrived home from Holland, spent a good part of these two days at their daughters' bedside, which as far as Sandra was concerned was as good an incentive as she needed to get well and leave as soon as possible; in her current still delicate emotional state, she found their presence anything but curative. Upon their arrival home, her every need and wish was catered for, when in fact all that she wished was to be left alone and to get back to a normal life, and her normal life had little to do with her parents. She had as good as managed to convince them that her intention had not been to kill herself, but that she had lost control of her emotions for a single evening, and that this would not happen again, so they may as well return to Holland. They believed her, perhaps in large part because this is what they so much wanted to believe, and her father did in fact return to work after a further two days had passed, her mother following three days thereafter; they were mid – way through a large and important contract, and their presence was required there. Emma slept at home during these days, and saw little of Basil, so neither daughter was overly sorry at their parents' departure. Sandra had also managed to convince those at her temporary place of work that she had been sick, and she was given leave by her sponsors for a further weeks' absence to convalesce, after which she would return to the laboratory and continue her research. So all then would be well, at least in that important regard, and on the day and in fact the hour that their mother departed the two sisters breathed something like a collective sigh of relief, and sat down to drink tea together.

'Thank Christ for that; she was starting to drive me insane.'

'She means well, Sands; they both do, and they're the only parents we've got, so you know....'

'Yes, I know, we have to learn to live with them, even if most of the time we seem to have lived without them.'

'So maybe we should count our blessings. Anyway if you hadn't gone insane in the first place they wouldn't have had to come back, so try to avoid going insane again, okay?'

'Sure...'

'I mean apart from anything else you've really screwed with my love – life, you know?'

'Yeah, sorry, and talking about that, it's okay if you bring Basil back here; I really don't mind.'

'Well thanks for that at last...I mean sleeping in a trailer's okay, but here's better.'

'And I won't tell them, I promise.'

'Well if you do I'll have to kill you...Oh shit, sorry...'

'As long as I don't manage to kill myself first, right..? In fact....Well, I'd like to get to know him better; Basil, I mean.'

'What's to know...? I mean he's a great guy and he loves me.'

'Yes, well lucky you then...'

'And I know you don't think he's good enough for me, and he'll be the first to admit that he's no academic, but he makes me happy. Anyway I'm not as smart as you either...'

'Don't be silly, of course you are, and probably nobody would ever be good enough for you, so forget what I think, or thought. Anyway I'm so smart I nearly killed myself, so don't use me as an example of smart.'

'So were you trying, Sands, really?'

'I don't know, honestly....I mean it was me taking the pills, so I must have known what might happen, but I think I'd lost control by that time. It's a funny thing; it was me but it wasn't me, so I suppose that's what being mad must feel like, but it's gone now; I really can't remember much about it.'

'But you're okay now?'

'Well yes, I think so; I mean I still feel a bit weird sometimes and I get tired easily, but the doctor said I should expect that. And I mean...Well it wasn't as though I was feeling particularly unhappy, you know? I'd spent the evening with Emily and Will, and that went okay as far as I can remember, and I don't even know why I went 'round there, so the whole mad thing must have started before then, even. The best way...Well, the best way

I can describe it is that I felt numb, like I really didn't care what happened to me, or about anything or anybody else, which isn't true, because I do care about people. I care about you for a start, but I put you through something horrible, and I would never have done that if I'd been myself.'

'Yes, well I'll forgive you this once, but don't do it again. So are you going over to see them; Will and Emily I mean?'

'Yes, I'll have to, but I'll give it a couple of days.'

'Well I'll be here anyway; I can take the week off school.'

'You don't have to do that, really you don't, and I'm not going to do it again, so you don't have to hide the booze or anything.'

'I think mum and dad have already done that.'

'What...?'

'I expect they see it as their contribution to your future wellbeing, not that you couldn't, you know, buy some if you wanted to.'

'Where did they hide it?'

'Don't know, probably under their bed or something.'

'Bloody hell...'

'Did they say anything about the coke?'

'No, not really; it's been kid – gloves all the way, and I promised to be good in future. Anyway the thing is, going back to Basil, I really want to see not only him but Meadow and Keith. I think it would do me good to tell them how sorry I am that I've been such a bitch about the whole thing. So, you know, could you sort that out for me?'

'What do you mean?'

'I don't know, just...Just pave the way somehow, so that...So that when I go to see them it won't be such a shock, or whatever.'

'I can try, I suppose, but the thing is, Sands, Keith and Meadow are great people, I mean they've really sort of looked after me, so you don't have to worry. They won't bear any grudges, you know, and I'm quite sure you'd be welcome anytime.'

'Yes, well maybe, and I dread to think what Tarragon and Rosemary must think of me.'

'Well stop dreading it then, and stop making everything such a big deal; just go over there, be natural and let things take their course; it'll be fine, people are very forgiving, and it's not like you've done anything to harm them, is it?'

Sandra smiled.

'You know, something's happened to you, little sister; you've become wise.'

'Oh that's just bullshit.'

'No...No it isn't, and well, pretty soon I suppose ordinary life will take over again, and if I don't do and say these things now then I may never do or say them. I feel as though I have to make peace with the world again, like tell Emily that I'm sorry that I've been trying to steal her boyfriend since I can remember, and she's my best friend, for Christ's sake, and I really don't deserve her friendship.'

'Sure you do, well apart from the boyfriend thing...Anyway she'll forgive you too, I'm sure, so you know, go and make your peace or whatever it is you have to do to stop yourself going bonkers again. Whatever people may think of you, nobody wants you to die, you know?'

'I know; that was all my idea, but I cocked it up, fortunately, or rather you were there to stop it happening.'

'Yes, well that was just an accident; we didn't expect you to be in, which was the only reason that we came here at all, which is ironic when you think about it, but anyway let's not think about what could have happened; it didn't, you're still here, so try to behave in future. So are you going to see the shrink or what?'

'No...I don't need that; that would just remind me of everything. Right now what I need to do is to rest, get better and then try to engage with the world in a more positive way.'

'That's the spirit....'

Sandra smiled.

'I wish I had your spirit, Emma; I'd drop a few I.Q. points for some of that; how come you got all the happy genes?'

'Well if I did I don't know where they came from; not our dear parents anyway.'

'They must have been recessive then; maybe we had a happy great grandmother or something...'

'Could be...'

They both smiled now. Light and easy conversation with her sister, her first bit of happiness, and her life back, whatever she would make of it. She had been lucky, Sandra Fox knew this; she had been so stupid, but now she had been given a second chance. A few more days to recover and the vixen would be back. She had her research to return to, she had Emily, and she had her beloved sister and her bottle of pills, so that was somewhere to start, wasn't it?

Tarragon stayed at home for three nights and for three days, more or less. During this time she slept a good deal, whilst she adjusted to English time, and in any case sleep was something which she considered that she had not had a sufficiency of since she had last been home. Otherwise she helped her mother at the delicatessen during a part of each day, more by way of their having time together than for any other reason, and Meadow was pleased indeed to have these hours with her eldest daughter. On a few occasions she received quizzical looks from customers; they were to differing degrees certain that they had seen the young woman somewhere before, but could not think where, and neither she or Meadow would enlighten them; this was Tarragon's other life, and here she was anonymous, and wished to be no other way. Evenings were spent in the bosom of her family, and only once did she have significant time alone with her father, when, on his instigation, they rode together on the motorbike which she had bought him, and went wherever the road took them until in the still early evening they stopped at a rural public house, some distance west of the town. In truth Tara had needed no second invitation; more than either of her siblings she loved to ride behind her father. They drank fruit juice, ate bar – snacks and spoke in general terms about Tara's experiences on tour, and only after about an hour had passed did the conversation take a new and for her unexpected turn.

'So anyway, I mean you and I are cool, aren't we?'

'Of course we are, why shouldn't we be?'

'Oh, no reason....'

'Come on dad, what are you talking about?'

'It's just something your mother said, that's all.'

'What did she say?'

'Just about, well, you and I not having much time together and such, I mean in general terms, you know, over the years.'

'Right....I see, I think...'

'I mean you know, in a comparative sense.'

'Comparative to what...?'

'Not so much what as whom.'

It took a moment, and then Tara took a wild guess.

'If you're talking about Rosie...Are you talking about Rosie?'

'Yeah, that would be it. I mean I don't want you thinking that I love her more than you, that's all.'

Tara smiled, and had there not been a table between them she would have hugged her father.

'Don't be silly; God that's so typical of mum, isn't it...'

'What do you mean?'

'She just wants everybody to love each other, and wants everything to be perfect all the time.'

'That isn't a bad thing to want.'

'No, of course it isn't, but don't worry, dad, I know you love Rosie, and well, she needs all the love she can get, and don't think for a moment that I resent that, or ever have done. Everyone's different, aren't they, and everyone relates to everyone else in different ways, you know? I mean take the band for example; underlying everything are an incredibly complex set of relationships between us, and sure I like some of them more than others, but in the end we all love each other, and we can stand up on stage and perform, and that's what matters. We all need different things from each other at different times, and I love Rosie too, you know, and so how could I be anything but happy that you love her?'

'Yeah, you're right, of course, I'm just, you know...'

'I know, but don't worry. I do know that you love me too.'

'Just as much as I love Rosie, right..?'

'Just as much as you love Rosie...'

'Okay, well that's that done then, so we're cool, right?'

'We're cool, papa; very cool indeed, actually.'

'And we're all like, very proud of you, you know?'

'I know; mum keeps telling me that too, and I'm proud of you as well. I mean apart from the fact that you're a cool father to have anyway, it's not everyone whose father has played guitar on a symphony composed by Ash Spears, is it? I mean I'm doing what I do because I can sing, but in a very big way it was you who opened that particular door for me, so I owe you a lifetime of love for that anyway.'

'You don't owe me anything.'

'And why would that be, do you think?'

'What do you mean?'

'What I mean is that it's because you love me, so there's a case in point, so stop even thinking that I think otherwise, okay?'

'Okay, I'm convinced.'

They smiled; enough had been said.

'Anyway, I suppose it's time we went home and joined the rest of the band; your mother won't relax until we're back.'

'Are all mothers like that about their kids and so on do you think?'

'I suppose, to a greater or lesser degree, but your mother probably has a bad case of it. Once you've got children you never really stop being concerned....'

'Even you, eh dad?'

'You'll know if you ever have kids.'

'Yes, well I've got to find someone to have them with first.'

'And right now you life's all about the music, I can dig that, but don't let it be everything, you know?'

'I won't. I just happen to be in the middle of a world tour right now.'

'Of course, and what happens after that, do you think? Tara part three?'

'I expect so...I don't think Ash has run out of songs yet, and the record company will be putting the pressure on if number two sells well, which it seems to be.'

They smiled again; this most unlikely of famous musicians seemed set fair to become more famous yet, and these were things which they both knew.

Otherwise during the roughly three days, Tara spoke once alone with Rosie, who came into her bedroom on the night subsequent to her meeting with Quentin.

'Oh Hi Rosie; are you home this evening?'

'Yes.'

'Good. So, my little witch sister, is everything okay in your world?'

'Yes, actually...'

'Meaning what?'

'Meaning...I had a date last night. Well kind of a date, anyway.'

'What kind of a date, and with whom?'

'It was someone I met on a train.'

'What...? You got picked up on a train?'

'Well not really; I mean I wasn't exactly picked up. We sat opposite each other on the way down to the west – country when I went to see Charlotte, and then by coincidence he was sitting opposite me again on the way back, so we sort of got talking, you know?'

'Yes; mum told me you went down there.'

'It was an interesting meeting.'

'What, with Charlotte or the man on the train?'

'I was talking about Charlotte.'

'Well never mind about that; what about the man on the train...? For a start are you sure it was a coincidence that you sat together twice?'

'Absolutely; he was sitting there first.'

'Okay so what's his name, how old is he, and how did you get talking?'

'His name's Quentin....'

Tara laughed, gently.

'Quentin...?'

'Yes, I know, but the name fits, actually.'

'Anyway, sorry, you were saying...'

'I suppose he's about twenty three or four, he's got a masters' in human evolution from Oxford, and well, he's nice, you know?'

'How nice...?'

'Well, I've only met him once since, but he's...nice, you know? Quite tall, long, curly hair and a posh accent; he lives in town. So anyway we went out....'

'Wait; how did you get to be going out?'

'I 'phoned him.'

'*You* 'phoned *him*?'

'Yes; he left me his number, and so I called him and he invited me out. His grandma died on the day that we met, which is why he was going to the west – country, and so we met in the King's Head with his two brothers, Tristan and Freddy, who's actually called Tarquin, but nobody calls him that.'

'I wonder why...?'

'Yes, well anyway that was it, really. We had a sort of a nice evening together.'

'You and the two brothers...'

'Yes, who are also nice in a weird, intellectual kind of way; they're all about the same age.'

'So are you seeing him again?'

'He's supposed to be 'phoning me when his brothers are both gone. One lives in France and the other lives in India, I think.'

'And do you think he will. 'Phone you, I mean?'

'Yes, I think so.'

'And do you hope he does?'

'Yes, I do...'

'I'll expect updates....'

'Sure...'

Simple days filled with the simple pleasures of being with her family, and Tara was glad of it. On the third day she received a telephone call from Ash; the band were all getting together at his house prior to their departure for Los Angeles. She had been summoned and had to go, and he was right, of course. The absolute intensity of their performing and living together had been lost, for the moment, and must be re-found well before the next performance. It was in a sense like being in a rather heavy and highly – charged relationship with six other people and all at the same time, and their being cast asunder was only a temporary state. There were a lot more performances and a lot more cities to get through yet, and they needed to psyche – up; the love affair was not over yet, not by a long way. Tarragon kissed goodbye to her family, and prepared to take the plunge once more into the deep and dizzy heights of high – performance music on the biggest stages that the world had to offer; the bright lights were calling, and she must answer.

Chapter 17

A MAN FROM LONDON

Sharon and Megan met at the appointed place and at the appointed hour, as they had agreed in their brief exchange of electronic mail. This was a small coffee house on the east coast, in a small coastal hamlet which in the season catered for the more discerning tourists and day – trippers, but now the two witches had the cafe to themselves; a quiet place where quiet words could be spoken, and where they would not be overheard. Light classical music formed the backdrop to good coffee and a sophisticated ambience, and here had the two women been before with Fiona, Corinne and Eve, but now they were only two. Their greeting had been somewhat emotional, as it was bound to have been. They had not seen one another for some time, and neither had known the fate of the other on the night that the coven which had been their home and the spiritual and actual centre of their lives had been burned to ruination. They were the last of their coven; the last refuge of the spirit of Edith, who had walked alone through one lonely night, and on the dawn of a certain morning in the year 1572 had made up her mind that there must be vengeance upon the house of Tillington; that the cruel death of Jane Mary must not be let go. So had she gone against the high witch, her Priestess, and through her daughter Marian her spirit had continued, and then through Marian's daughter, Eleanor, and so on to Eve, the last of her bloodline, who had died on the steps of the Manor House.

They bought coffee and took a corner table, where they took opposing seats, and for a moment let their relief at seeing one another find its' place, and it was Megan, who was by a few years the older of them, who first broke their silence.

'I went to Farthing's Well, after the fire. I thought that you would all be dead.'

'We almost were; I was fortunate to escape; the witch who tried to kill me perished along with Fiona and Corinne; aside from me only Rebecca survived, and she only survived because I allowed it. Otherwise my one mistake was to leave without my telephone, which left me with no way of contacting you.'

'So you have your passport and so on?'

'Yes, I left with that at least, and I had the car keys, and in that I was also fortunate, and so was able to get away.'

'So what happened?'

'I awoke, sometime in the dead of night, and became aware of my would – be assassin just in time, and I overcame her. That is to say I pushed her, that was all, but she must have struck her head.'

'How did she try to kill you?'

'She had a knife, I think, although I never saw the weapon; everything happened so quickly, and in the darkness. All I could think of was escaping, and that I also did just in time, before the fire had really taken hold.'

'So who was she, do you know? Was she a witch?'

'I don't know, but I will find out. The witch Rebecca was setting the fire, and I confronted her by the front door, and I could have let her burn, but I saved her, and drove her to the Manor House.'

'Why? Why did you let her live?'

'I...It was a decision which I had to make quickly, as you will understand, the house was already all but burned when I left with her, and there was no one else alive. I had to know how it had happened, and who had been behind the attack, and thought that if I had killed her then perhaps we would never know. If it was the white coven then she is our only link to them, so I let her live. You may think me foolish, and perhaps I was, but that was my decision.'

'So where is she now?'

'I don't know; at the Manor House, perhaps, but she will not go far; she will not leave Victoria Tillington. I will kill her, Megan, in due time; she will pay for the deaths of Fiona and Corinne, but for now she will have no memory of how she was rescued, or by whom; she will not know me when we next meet.'

'Are you certain of that?'

'Yes, I am certain. Rebecca is powerful, I know, but I am stronger than her, and I had her quite under my spell; she was unconscious for a few moments, then she regained some consciousness, and that is how I left her on the steps of the Manor House, but she will not remember me. Next time we meet it will be I who will have the element of surprise. I did not see Fiona or Corinne alive; I only saw Fiona, but she was already dead, so I left her; I could have done nothing for her.'

'So the one who died, your assailant; they will know that she is dead, surely.'

'I don't know; there were only two of them, which has always struck me as a strange thing, so one assumes that they will know, of course, but perhaps they were acting alone, otherwise why only two? Had there been more of them they could have killed us all, so perhaps this has nothing to do with the white witches. These are all questions which need to be answered, and I intend to find out how such a thing was possible. How in the first place they found out the location of our coven, when we were always so careful.'

'Indeed we were, but you at least survived, my dear Sharon, and for that we must be thankful.'

'So, what happened to you? I went to the village on the night of the fire, but you were already gone.'

'I received a telephone call. Rebecca spoke to me from Farthing's Well, which was her mistake, because otherwise I would not have known. She knew who I was, I think, and perhaps where I was, so I left that night with all that I could take with me, and after that I knew nothing of what had happened, so I went to the coven, and then I left my message. By now they will know who I am, and certainly since Rebecca is still alive they will have guessed, and I cannot now return to the village.'

'I see...So had I killed her then would you have gone back?'

'I don't know, perhaps, but not now.'

'So all of your time there was for nothing, then, and after all I should have killed her.'

'You did as you thought best, and my time was not wasted, actually.'

'I don't see what was gained by it.'

'In a sense nothing was gained by it, but in another sense it was.'

'What do you mean?'

'What I mean is that here is something which I wish to tell you, and it's doubtless something which you will not wish to hear. It's over for me, Sharon.'

'What's over?'

'All of it; I want no further part in it. Our coven is destroyed, and whatever revenge you may take for that is yours to decide, but I will no longer be a part of anything which may happen from now on.'

'Why...?'

'Because...Because I could have killed them... I saw the children, Henry and Nathaniel; they were with their nanny, walking in the grounds of the Manor House, and it would have been so easy. I could have murdered them and made good my escape, but I did not. I told myself at the time

that I had better wait for a better moment, but I have since meditated long on this, and I believe now that I could not have killed them. As long as Eve was alive....But well, she is dead now, and the blood curse died with her, Edith's blood line is broken, and it is now my belief that we should at last leave the memory of Jane Mary to its' rest. Those who live now are innocent of any crime against her, so you, my dear Sharon, must do as you will, but now you will be alone, and this may be our last meeting.'

For a long moment Sharon said nothing. All of the support and guidance which she had expected and had hoped for was gone, vanished in a single moment, and if she really was alone, if Megan would so betray all of those who had come before them, then she must think before she responded, for this was dire news indeed.

'You have devoted your life to this. We all have, as have all of those who have come before us, and now three of us are dead because of our belief that justice must be done for Jane Mary.'

'Yes, I know, but we are neither of us old, Sharon, and I no longer wish my life to be only about this. I was put to the test, and I failed. The hatred has died in me, I think. The hatred was in any case only in a sense academic, felt for a woman so long dead, and for the sisters who have come before us, whose bodies are now dug up and so defiled, and of course I hate them for doing that, but that is another kind of hatred. I cannot so hate any child that I will kill them, I know this now. And aside from that, I have met his Lordship, and believe that he is a good man, regardless of the actions of his forebears. I do not think that I can do that which I must do to give any meaning to our cause, it is no longer in me to do so.'

Sharon was silent again as she processed the words of the woman whom she had for so long loved and respected; words that she never thought she would hear.

'You of all people... You are the strongest of us; you were stronger even than Eve, who had the blood of Edith. Will you really give up, and leave me alone?'

'I cannot now do otherwise, my dear Sharon. For me the burning of the coven was the end of it, and though we may seek our revenge on the living for that, I will no longer seek vengeance upon the dead.'

'So then what of the witch Rebecca, and what of the white coven; will you not avenge the deaths of Fiona and Corinne?'

'I think that Rebecca and the other witch, if witch she was, were alone in this. You are right, nothing else makes any sense, and if so then you do not need me anymore; kill Rebecca if you will, but I have no murder in me. I cannot help you, Sharon, and for that I am sorry. I no longer have a home, and must make my life elsewhere before I grow old and embittered. If nothing else my time in the village has taught me this, and I know myself better now, and I know what I must do.'

'So where will you go?'

'I will go north, I think. I have family there.'

'Family...? It is a long time since any of us thought of our families.'

'Then perhaps it is time, for me anyway. I love you, Sharon, but you and I cannot be all things to each other. I have hidden myself and my life for long enough, and I am tired of hiding, and tired of all the suspicion and the hatred, and tired of those closest to me being killed.'

'So, you admit defeat then.'

'If that is what it is, then yes. Despite everything they found us, so you will do as you must, but I have made my decision, and now you must make yours.'

'So is that your last word?'

'It is.'

'I never thought it would be you who would betray our cause.'

'Our cause is dead, Sharon, and you will not persuade me otherwise. It died with Eve, and you know well enough that our greatest folly was to let her die. She was the way, and the only way, and the woman Meadow was our undoing, and there is nothing now that can be done, it's over, let it be.'

Sharon stood up.

'Well then, if that really is your last word then I think we have nothing more to say to each other.'

'Perhaps not...'

'So, goodbye Megan...'

'Goodbye, Sharon. I wish you well in all that you do, but if you go against Rebecca be careful. Do not underestimate her, or those around her.'

Sharon walked away, and Megan was left now utterly alone. She finished her coffee, and walked out into the dull and breezy afternoon. The free wind was blowing from the south, and she would follow it, wherever it took her.

Sharon walked to the car. She would keep the car, at least. From her vantage point she watched the late winter waves crashing onto the beach below her; the sea was dark grey and angry, which befitted her present state of mind perfectly. Megan had not been there on the night of the fire. She had not known the fear and the horror of that, or how it was to come upon Rebecca in all of the terrible heat and smoke, and to drive away leaving her friends to their death, and their burning. She would keep that fire with her, and within her; it would be her only friend now, and she would not forget it. She turned the key in the ignition and drove away. So, she was alone then, as Edith had been so long ago. She was the last of them, and she would see them avenged, or she would die in the trying.

A low and sustained growl was all that was needed to indicate to Percival that he should be wary of the person who had just knocked at his door. Lulu was on full alert, and so should he be. The time was just after ten o'clock in the evening, and Percival was alone aside from his dog; Sally was working away again, which despite her intentions was most of the time now. He went to the door, and opened it cautiously, keeping the door between himself and whoever was outside; he was not expecting any callers, and his own instincts were telling him that this was nobody that he wanted to see. The figure standing in the half light was male, and someone whom Percival had not seen for quite a long time; not since he had knocked rather nervously on the man's door one night, but he recognised him instantly. Percival said nothing; he would let the caller speak first.

'Good evening.'

The man appeared to be alone, at least, and Lulu now stood up and came to the door and stood beside her master. She had never come close to attacking anybody, but looked as though she could, which was the important thing.

'What business do you have here?'

The man looked first at Percival and then at the German Shepherd dog.

'I don't know, actually; perhaps the same business which brought you to my door, and as I recall I had the courtesy and good manners to trust you, and to let you in. All I'm asking is that you return that trust, and perhaps you would call the dog off?'

'The dog stays; she won't harm you unless I tell her to.'

'So with that understanding....?'

Percival opened the door wider and stood to one side as the man entered. He was dressed in overcoat and jeans, clothes which could easily conceal a weapon, but his manner did not indicate any aggressive intent, and Lulu was following his every move from close range.

'I come as you apparently came to me, which was in a spirit of peace, or so I recall your telling me.'

'Well then, you'd better sit down.'

'Are you sure the dog's okay?'

'Just avoid any sudden movements, those make her nervous, which takes her beyond my control.'

Percival moved papers and general detritus from the dining table as Tony Blackman took a seat.

'Coffee...?'

'Thank you.'

Percival fetched a second cup, Lulu went back to her place by the fireside, although no fire was lit this evening, and she remained alert, watching every move that the man made, whilst occasionally glancing at Percival for reassurance that all was well.

'Tell me, were you expecting to see me? I don't mean tonight, of course, but in a more general sense.'

'Why should I have been expecting to see you?'

Percival took the seat opposite, and lit a cigarette.

'Are you smoking at the moment?'

'Sometimes...'

'And is now such a time?'

He offered the packet and Tony Blackman took a cigarette, which Percival lit for him.

'I would perhaps have come before now, but I've been away for a while.'

'Oh yes, anywhere nice?'

'I've been living in a caravan quite a distance from the town, at the back of a timber – yard. Nice views over the canal and some warehouses.'

'Sounds very pleasant, I'm sure; it's good to get away sometimes, don't you agree?'

'Every day some young kid brings me food and drinking water. Beer if I ask for it, and cigarettes of course. Books, daily newspapers, I even have a television set.'

'Sound luxurious, you must put me in touch with the travel agent.'

'The bathroom facilities leave something to be desired.'

'I'm sorry to hear that.'

'Thing is, it's all been for free, and the other thing is that I have no way of contacting the world outside, and it was made very clear to me from the outset that it would be better for my general wellbeing if I didn't try to leave, or to contact anybody.'

'There's always a catch, isn't there?'

'I was taken there by a man from London. The East End somewhere I would think.'

'Yes, well it's better not to argue with people from there; they can get quite nasty, I'm told.'

'I am being held captive, Percival. I mean there are no bars or chains, and I could have walked away, I suppose, there has been nobody guarding me, as such, but there are people working there during the day, including the young man who brings me the provisions, and the timber yard is locked up at night. High fences, you know, so to all intents and purposes I have been a prisoner.'

'That sounds most inconvenient; I would complain to somebody in the strongest terms if I were you.'

'Yes, it has been rather inconvenient, and furthermore whilst I have been away my house was broken into, and I had to read about that and about my own mysterious disappearance in the local newspaper. Eventually I made the inside pages of the national press.'

'That must have been quite surreal, in a way.'

'I daresay all of my houseplants will have died, and I don't yet know what if anything was stolen, since I have not yet been home. Still, whoever it was didn't get my passport, anyway; that and all of my cash and credit cards were taken from me by the man from London.'

'For safekeeping, no doubt; you can't be too careful these days, as you seem to have discovered.'

'Indeed...So do you have anything to say about any of that?'

'Well, a couple of questions spring immediately to mind. Firstly why have you come all this way to tell me this, and secondly, how did you get away, or rather why did you risk getting away?'

'Well to answer your second question first, I decided that it was time for the holiday to end, so I climbed the fence after hours, and acquired some money by illegal means from a passing stranger, which was enough to get me here, so now I have become a criminal. And as to the first question, I have had quite a long time to meditate upon my situation, as you may imagine, and during my meditations I kept coming back to the possibility that you were responsible for it.'

'Me...? Why would you think that?'

'Well, first let me finish my somewhat unusual story.'

'Please, carry on.'

'A few days ago a series of mysterious deaths began to be reported in Headwater. Three deaths, in fact, which included that of a high ranking local police officer. All of the people, who were all male, by the way, appeared to have died by accident or misadventure, and all died within three days of each other.'

'That does sound unusual, statistically speaking.'

'The coincidence will get more unlikely when I tell you that all of the people belong to a certain organisation to which I also belong.'

'You mean the cult of the chicken – stranglers, I presume.'

'If that is what you choose to call it. They were all high up in the organisation, and included our leader and his second in command.'

'Well, it's tough at the top, they say, and that is indeed most unfortunate, for the organisation as well as the individuals concerned.'

'Yes it is, isn't it; these deaths I have also read about in the local newspaper, and now I would welcome any comments that you would care to make.'

Percival lit another cigarette, and offered one to his guest, who turned down the offer, but now it was he who spoke again.

'You are from London originally, aren't you?'

'Yeah, I haven't always lived in chocolate - box land. My origins and upbringing were what you might call somewhat humble, and rather more urban.'

'And is it true to say, do you think, that you can take the man out of London, but you can't take London out of the man?'

'I don't know. I don't often go to town these days, but one cannot entirely escape ones' roots, I daresay.'

'And the fact that you refer to London as *'town'* rather gives you away.'

'I've never made any secret of my place of birth, and I'm certainly not ashamed of it.'

'No, I'm sure not, but do you see where I'm trying to steer the conversation? Someone like you might know people like the man from London.'

'London's a big city, and I never lived in the East End.'

'No, perhaps not, but you take my point?'

'Your point being that you think that the man from London is in my employ, is that it?'

'Yes, that's it exactly.'

'Well I'm going to say that you're wrong, of course, but I can see how you might have come to that conclusion.'

'How so...?'

'Well, you know, when somebody gets, drugged, tied to a stake and nearly has his throat cut by some hooded maniac, that person might feel somewhat aggrieved, and might even be tempted to get his own back, don't you think?'

'That was a long time ago, and the person who nearly cut your throat is dead, as you well know. It was you who told me how he died, after all.'

'Snakes can grow new heads, metaphorically speaking, and apparently they do, and I still remember the night vividly, as though it were yesterday. I've also heard it said that revenge is a dish best served cold, but of course I speak hypothetically, since as I said before, I'm going to say that nothing which has happened has anything to do with me.'

'Yes, I hear what you say.'

'Good, then I would also say that you, that is the organisation, may perhaps have brought this upon yourselves, and you are in large part responsible for that, as it happens.'

'Is that so, and if so, how?'

'Well, if I may continue my hypothesis?'

'Please do.'

'Well, take you and me for example. The last time we met I offered you peace terms, which you refused, as I recall. You refused to guarantee my safety and the safety of certain others, in return for my eternal silence and my leaving you well alone. You could have strangled every chicken in Christendom and sacrificed them to whatever false idol or philosophy you chose, so long as I had your word that I and said others would be left alone, but you would not give me that word. So, hypothetically speaking, if someone like me were to take it upon themselves to become proactive, then I can imagine a scenario not unlike the one which you describe. If there cannot be peace then there must be war, and in war both sides will use whatever weapons are at their disposal, and someone such as myself might under these circumstances take it upon themselves to crush your small organisation in your small town as though it were a mere inconvenience. One should not fight above ones' weight unless one is prepared to lose, don't you agree?'

'We had no warning, Percival.'

'No more did I when I was abducted, and such is the nature of war, my friend.'

'And there is nobody else like you.'

'Well then I can offer you no explanation.'

They were silent for a moment whilst both drank their coffee and assessed the conversation so far, and its' implication. Once again it was Tony Blackman who spoke first.

'So, in your objective opinion, why do you think it is that I was not killed, but merely got out of the way, so to speak?'

'That's a good question, and off the top of my head I would guess that it's because for now you are more useful alive than dead.'

'Do you suppose that's the only reason?'

'Well, perhaps, but it could also be the case that having met you the man who set this up had some sympathy for you and your position; perhaps even he felt a certain empathy with you, or perhaps again somebody else put in a good word for you, as it were; said that you were not the worst of them, that kind of thing. I don't suppose that whoever is behind this has gone to the trouble and expense to kill gratuitously or indiscriminately, and perhaps they feel that it is not too late to broker a peace deal, in which case it would make perfect sense to keep you alive.'

'And what form would that deal take, do you suppose?'

'The same deal as before, I would imagine. An absolute guarantee that you and your cohorts will keep yourselves to yourselves and to your temple, and that you will never make a move against your perceived enemies, be they male or female.'

'I see...So if I now gave my word that the deal was acceptable, do you think the killing would stop?'

'Almost certainly, I would think.'

'And otherwise it would continue?'

'Again, almost certainly...Your ranks appear to be broken, now, and as we have said before, Headwater is a small town. Once the dam's broken it's hard to keep secrets in such a small place, and if things continue as they are then I would not even rule out another attack on your temple, and baseball bats would be no defence this time. This time it would be the end; this time the chickens would go free, once and for all.'

Tony Blackman took a pack of cigarettes from his coat pocket, offered one to Percival, and they took another moment for mutual consideration.

'I would have to go to my people with the proposition.'

'Of course, although if I were you I would make it an instruction, I think you're past the stage of having any choice in the matter, don't you?'

'Perhaps...'

'Perhaps doesn't do it either; there're no half – measures now. It seems to me that you're alive for as long as you're useful, so if I were you I would make yourself useful, and get this done once and for all. I would hate to hear of someone fishing your mortal remains out of the canal, especially after all we've been through together.'

Tony Blackman smiled a wry smile.

'So what's to stop me just taking off from here and not going back?'

'Nothing, apart from apparently not having the means to do so, but I suppose you could overcome that, but then of course there's the safety of the rest of your organisation. As I see it you are about all that stands between them and a further series of unfortunate accidents.'

'So do you think my safety and their safety is guaranteed, once the instruction is given?'

'So long as it's adhered to; the man behind all of this will have no wish to see anybody else die, I'm sure, but bear in mind that he's got to you once, and he can do it again.'

One final moment of consideration, but Tony Blackman knew well enough that the conversation was as good as over. The meeting had gone more or less as he had anticipated, and if the cult was to continue then there could be no more prevarication, and the survival of the cult was and had always been paramount, and must rise above all other considerations.

'So be it then; the man behind all of this may consider it done.'

'I believe that's a wise decision. It's a pity for all concerned that you did not come to it sooner.'

'So what do you think I should do now; should I go home or back to the caravan?'

'I would extend your holiday for a while longer, just until it's all taken care of. It's a small price to pay for your life, don't you think, regardless of the inconvenience, and I'm sure the man from London would prefer to keep an eye on you for the time being. Look upon it as a safe sanctuary, away from all of the bad business.'

'The man from London...By that would you be referring to yourself, or to the assassin?'

'You mean in our hypothesised scenario?'

'Indeed...'

'Well, as you rightly say, I'm from London, and in the situation which you describe I would be the one as it were calling the shots, would I not?'

'So it would seem, and it would also seem that we would have grossly underestimated you.'

'Well don't beat yourself up, we all make mistakes.'

'So when will I be able to go home and attend to my dead house plants, do you suppose..?'

'When whoever's behind this gives the man from London the all clear, I would think.'

'And when would that be, do you suppose?'

'When you tell whoever's behind this that you've done as you have said you would do, and that there are no dissenting voices in your ranks; nothing but complete and unanimous agreement will do it.'

'Total and absolute surrender.'

'I don't see what else there can be, do you? At least that way you get to keep the nice hooded gowns. You never know, they might even come back into fashion one day.'

'And how would I contact him?'

'Send a letter by courier, it would be quicker that way, and I don't suppose he would want to give you his 'phone number or email address, that would be taking your friendship too far.'

'I could lie to whoever's behind this.'

'Yes, you could, but I don't think you will, under the circumstances. You're on the hit list, I'm sure, so better make certain your name doesn't make it to the top. You seem to be safe for now, but your situation is still vulnerable, and that could very easily change.'

'That sounds like good advice, at least.'

'I do my best...'

'So will I be in trouble for playing truant?'

'If you're back there by tomorrow at closing time I'm sure they will hardly have missed you. The man behind all of this will I'm sure speak to the man from London, and that will give you enough time to speak to the rest of the chicken – stranglers, but I advise you to be back at the holiday camp by tomorrow afternoon.'

Percival poured more coffee for them both.

'I've always had respect for you, Percival.'

'Well thanks for that.'

'We could have had you killed; you know that, don't you?'

'Killing people is easy, but you always knew the risks inherent in that.'

'And yet the risks have come to fruition in any case.'

'Not really; what has happened is really only the beginning, and the end would have meant your death as well. You live because I live; our fates have been drawn closely together since the beginning.'

'So it would seem, and anyway be that as it may I do have respect for you, and always have done. Not many people could have done what you've done; not many people would have had the nerve, or the reach for that matter. Whoever's been working down there is very good at what they do; I mean to kill a police officer...'

'They don't care, these East End guys; no respect for authority. I blame their parents, or perhaps society as a whole is responsible, I'm not certain, really.'

'Nobody knew he was there; we didn't see him coming, and we know most things that happen in our small town.'

'Well, I don't profess to understand everything which has gone on, but I've heard it said that it's not what you know but who you know, and these East End boys can be hard as nails, much harder than you or I. Once their blood's up there's no telling where it could all end.'

'So if I leave now and do as you say, you'll call the dog off, will you?'

'They won't hurt you unless I tell them to.'

Tony Blackman smiled again, and stood up.

'Well then, this could be our final farewell.'

'Don't take it personally, but I hope so.'

'There's just one more thing before I go.'

'What's that?'

'It's a small matter in the bigger scheme of things, but I find myself somewhat financially embarrassed. I don't actually have any money to get back with, and I'll need to stay overnight somewhere.'

Percival searched for his wallet, which was hidden under some paper, on which he had written notes for his book. He took out a bundle of notes and put them on the table, Tony Blackman picked them up.

'Thank you.'

'You're welcome.'

'Do you think I'll get my personal effects back in due course?'

'I'm sure you will.'

'And will there still be money in my bank account, do you think?'

'I would say so, yes. The man from London may be very good at finding people and causing unfortunate accidents, but that doesn't make him a thief.'

'Well that's something, at least. And you were expecting me, weren't you?'

'I thought we might meet one more time.'

'Would that it had been under happier circumstances...'

'The circumstances are of your making. I've always been content to mind my own business.'

'That isn't quite true, is it?'

'I think that if you seek the truth in all of this then you chase after phantoms, my friend; everyone has their own truth, do they not? Only pragmatism can save us both now.'

'Well then, I will try to save us both, and I bid you farewell.'

Tony Blackman looked at Percival for a moment longer; he then turned and walked through the door and out into the night without looking back, and closed the door behind him. Percival followed him and locked the door, and Lulu was by his side, just to be sure.

'It's okay, he's gone.'

Percival poured himself a large scotch and sat where he had sat before. He felt quite calm, all things considered, but he noticed that his hand shook slightly as he held the glass, and thought perhaps that one Scotch would not suffice for the occasion. He had been expecting him of course; it could only have been a matter of time, and Eddie Michel had indeed done his job well. Three deaths, which were in truth more than Percival had been expecting by now, but even he did not have complete control over Eddie; nobody did. Edward Michel had always been a law unto himself, and even in London his name was spoken in hushed and revered terms. 'Eddie the ninja' they called him; that was what he was known as in his home city, although he did not practice that particular martial art.

Victoria Tillington awoke with a start, and to the realisation that she was not quite fully awake, and that she had a dull pain in her head. This was in fact the second time that she had woken up this morning, but this was the first time that she had done so in her own bed, and a glance at the clock told her that the time was a little after ten o'clock. This was not a working day, but she should go and see Henry soon, and this would be on the other side of a shower and some pain – killers; she needed to lose the hangover. Thoughts filtered slowly into her consciousness, chief amongst them being something which she thought best not to think about until her head was clear; perhaps then it wouldn't seem like such a bad thing. In the next instant she understood the reason for her sudden awakening; someone was knocking gently on her bedroom door, and it was Michael, perhaps the last person that at this moment she wanted to see. She could ignore him, he would not be persistent, but where would be the point in that; she had to see him sometime, and perhaps he had something important to say. She leaned up on her elbow, took a deep breath, and tried to gather herself.

'Come in, Mike.'

The previous evening Victoria had walked to the village. She had an idea that she would go and see Percival, for no particular reason, really, but she felt the need for alternative company away from home, and he had asked her for occasional news of Henry, his Godson, and was still reluctant to come unannounced to the Manor. She did not, however, get as far as the cottage down the lane; a light was on in her brother's house, Rebecca might be home, which would be a quite rare thing these days, as she would usually still be at the studio at this time. She detoured across the village Green; it was time that they saw one another, and Rebecca was indeed at home, and was indeed pleased to see her.

'Hello you...'

'Are you busy?'

'I'm just putting Florence to bed, after that I'm all yours.'

Victoria sat on the only chair in the lounge; Rebecca had still not bought furniture. A few moments later Rebecca came down the stairs, carrying something in her hand, which turned out to be a bottle of alcohol; Grappa, in fact, which Victoria knew was her favourite spirit.

'I didn't think you drank these days.'

'I don't, not really, and never on my own, but I've been saving this for a special occasion, and here you are. We can't sit in here though.'

'No, well there's nowhere really to sit, is there?'

'Are you working tomorrow?'

'No, actually...'

'Good; I'll take the day off too then. Let's take this to bed, shall we?'

'If you like...'

'Just to talk, you know? I'll get some olives.'

The next hours were for the most part devoted to their lovemaking, the Grappa quickly seeing off any inhibition or awkwardness of their recent estrangement, indeed the fact of their not having been together saw to it that their passion and desire for one another ran deeper even than was usual. By midnight they were drunk, and intoxicated by their love, and all else was for now forgotten, until finally they fell away from one another. Victoria lit a cigarette, which they shared, Rebecca remaining with her head on her pillow, staring at the ceiling.

'You know, we should do this more often.'

They laughed, and smoked, and felt drunk, and young again. For this moment they had no children, and no responsibilities; they were teenagers again, and they were in love, and there was nothing that they would not tell one another. At least, this was Victoria's hope.

'So; are you going to tell me, then?'

The enquiry was not specific, but even in her drunkenness Rebecca understood the question well enough.

'That depends....'

'On what...?'

'Whether you're going to be angry with me...'

'Why should I be angry with you? I mean I've guessed that I must know him, otherwise you would have told me, and you've told me it isn't Percival.'

'No, it isn't Percival, and yes, you do know him.'

'Well then, who is it?'

'I think I'd better wait, and tell you in the morning.'

'No you won't, and anyway it is the morning.'

'Do you love me, Vics?'

'Of course I love you.'

'Despite all the bad things that I've done..?'

'Yes, despite all of that.'

'I mean you've forgiven me for killing people?'

'Yes, I suppose I must have done, but what's that got to do with the father of your baby?'

'I just want to put it in context, that's all...Just to see what you'll forgive me for. That whoever it is, you'll be okay with it.'

'Bex, why should I need to forgive you?'

'The thing is...I wanted good blood for my child, good genes, you know, and for it to be somebody that I love and admire; you understand that, don't you?'

'What are you talking about?'

'Tell me you understand that...'

'Yes, I understand that.'

'And well, I was different then; I don't think I could do it now, but...Well anyway, it's done now, and you love me, and I love you, and it was the closest that I could get to it being you, wasn't it? Are you beginning to understand?'

'No, I'm not, and you're starting to worry me again...'

One final moment, once spoken the words could never be unspoken. Rebecca sat up in bed, and took a deep breath.

'It's Mike, Vics...'

'Mike who?'

'Michael; Florence is Michael's child.'

Somewhere from somewhere deep within her, through all of the drunkenness, and in this moment of afterglow with the woman that she loved, the dawn of understanding began to make its' way to the clear light of this dark, lamp - lit night. She knew now why she had not told her, and for a moment Victoria held this new understanding in perfect balance, and she had no response.

'Well, say something...'

'You slept with my brother...'

'Yes, well no, not exactly. I mean we had sex, of course, but he doesn't know anything about it; he has no idea that Florence is his daughter. I can do that, you see; I can control people, in a way, and I can make them forget, and I wanted my child to be the best child, so I seduced him in a way that you won't be able to understand. I turned myself into the most beautiful and desirable woman imaginable, which is crap, of course, but I can do that, too, and he had no choice, really; men are so easily controlled. None of this is Michael's fault, and he need never know. Florence will never be Michael's responsibility, but now she is such a beautiful and wonderful child, and that's because of Michael. So come on, get it over with; tell me that I'm a monster, or whatever, but please try to forgive me, like you've forgiven me for everything else, and like you forgave Rose.'

'What do you mean, I forgave Rose?'

'For Nathaniel...I mean it's obvious that he isn't Michael's child, isn't it? Florence has pale skin...You and Mike are both as white as ghosts, and Nathaniel, well, he just looks like Percival, doesn't he? I daresay Mike will never realise it, and of course nobody will ever tell him, but now Michael has a child of his own, and your blood will carry on through me and through Florence, and that can only be a good thing, can't it? I only ever wanted this to be a good thing, Vics, and I would never even have told you, but you kept on asking, so please try not to think too badly of me. I mean....'

'Christ, bex, shut up and let me think, will you?'

'Of course...'

'When did this happen...? I mean of course it was nine months before she was born, but how; I mean where were you?'

'At the Manor House; Mike and I were alone in the house, and he didn't know I was there, and he won't know that I had even been there. I left after, well you know....'

'After you'd hypnotised him, or whatever it is that you do, and after you'd had sex with him against his will?'

'You make it sound sordid, and it wasn't, and it wasn't against his will exactly.'

'You just controlled his will, is that it?'

'That's what seduction is, isn't it? Anyway he didn't see me, or at least of course he saw me, but he isn't aware that he saw me, and he never will be.'

'And you knew that you could get pregnant?'

'Well you never know, do you, but it was about right, you know, and as it happened, well, it was exactly right. It was only once, Vics, and it wasn't for the sex, not for its' own sake; it was for Florence, that was all, and I can't regret it now, I could never do that, no matter what you think of me.'

Somehow this had to be got through. Somehow all of the confused thoughts and emotions which were currently fighting for dominance in Victoria's heart and mind had to be arranged, so that they made sense, or at least began to make sense, and all through an alcoholic stupor, where clear thinking was harder than usual, and was not even supposed to happen. Was she angry that her beloved had slept with her brother? That she had apparently so bewitched him that him he had no knowledge of it after the fact? He didn't know; of course he didn't know, she knew her brother well enough to know that he would not be able to keep that from her, or be so natural about discussing Rebecca and her situation. The fact of his allowing Rebecca and her child, his child, to live here was nothing but coincidence, and a manifestation of his good and kind spirit, so all other thoughts must be banished. But this was wrong; something was wrong, morally, emotionally, genetically, she couldn't yet untangle the wrongness of it, but no matter how she waited for the anger, it didn't come. Rebecca had by now laid her head back on the pillow, waiting for the storm of abuse and accusation, but it didn't come. All that Victoria quite suddenly felt now was tired; deeply and extremely tired. Rebecca, or the absence of her, had been a large part of the reason that she had killed herself, and Rebecca it was who had saved her life, and that which had happened since was almost unbelievable, had she not been there to see it and so believe it. Rebecca had saved little Henry's life, Rebecca had murdered people, and now there was this, and all of the love that she felt for Rebecca and for her own dear brother, who lived every day in the belief that Nathaniel was his son, and his only child, when in fact his actual child was quite elsewhere, and was a girl called Florence, came together in a maelstrom of emotional and intellectual confusion.

'Well; aren't you going to say anything? Can't we even talk about it?"

'Shut up, Rebecca, I think you've said enough, and at the moment I have nothing to say to you.'

'So can we talk about it in the morning?'

'I don't know, stop asking me questions, I need to sleep now...I just need to sleep.'

And so she slept, which was in truth more akin to a drunken stupor, and she awoke with a headache in the early morning. Rebecca was still sleeping, and Victoria dressed quietly and left the house. She walked home in the half light, and went to her own bed, where she slept until she was suddenly awoken by a knock on her door.

'Come in, Mike.'

Michael entered her bedroom, looking awake, freshly laundered and relaxed, and quite unconcerned by the ways of the world, and by the ways of women. She, on the other hand, must have looked quite otherwise in all of these regards.

'Oh, sorry, you sleeping something off? Not ill, are you?'

'No, just hung – over...'

'Oh, right...'

Which was a statement, which was in fact in Michael – speak a question.

'I stayed over at number seven...with Rebecca.'

Rebecca, mother to your daughter; Christ, had last night really happened..? Did she really know everything which she now knew?

'Right, well anyway I'm off to Orchard House. Wondered if you'd like to come with me, that was all. I should only be a couple of hours, that is if you're not busy today, or too hung over, or whatever.'

For no good reason her thoughts turned to little Nathaniel, and to Rebecca's words; was it really so obvious that he was Percival's child?

Victoria had had reason to suspect that he was, and had thus looked for signs of it, but Rebecca had no reason to think that he was anything other than Michael's son. It was another thought to be put away for later consideration.

'What....Sorry Mike, I'm not quite here yet...Actually I think I'll pass, thanks, I feel bloody awful. Anyway, I mean it's only a house, isn't it?'

'Well yes, although actually no, not really...'

'What are you talking about?'

'Look; keep this under your hat, but Elin wants us to live there, you know, when it's finished and we're, you know...'

'When you're married?'

'Yes, exactly...'

'But I thought this was to be your passport to financial independence, or whatever.'

'Well, yes it was, but she seems to have set her heart on it, and you know what women are like once they get an idea into their heads...'

'Yes, I suppose I do...'

If only you knew, my dear Michael.

'Anyway she's going to help to finance the renovation, so it may all work out okay anyway.'

'I see....Well look, in that case can you give me an hour? I need a shower and pain – killers, and strong coffee, and I need to check on little Henry.'

'Sure, okay; I don't have to be there at any particular time.'

'Right, well go away then; I'll come and find you when I'm in the land of the living.'

'Sure; see you in a bit.'

Michael was happy again. Elin was clearly working her Nordic charms on him, and was apparently making serious plans for their future, and Victoria was glad to see her dear brothers' state of being so much improved. Victoria felt awful, but she now and of a sudden rather wanted to see Orchard House, which had now of a sudden taken on a quite new significance, and perhaps some time with Michael would be no bad thing, under the circumstances, and a part of those circumstances were that she did not want to be on her own today, and some distraction from certain thoughts would be no bad thing either.

Somewhat more than an hour later brother and sister were in Michael's car, driving through the gates of the Manor House. Victoria opened the passenger – side window on this quite chilly morning, and lit her first cigarette of the day. She had no idea where Orchard House was located, and therefore where they were going, and this seemed to her to be a fitting metaphor for the way she felt about their respective lives in a more general sense.

'So, are you feeling better now?'

'Ask me in an hour's time, and in the meantime stop being so cheerful, will you?'

'So how's Rebecca, and how's what's her name doing?'

'Do you mean Florence?'

'Yes, that's her.'

'She's bonny, Mike; she's going to be a very pretty child, I think; mother and daughter are both doing well.'

'Good; I'm glad to hear it. So no news of the paternal half of the genetic makeup yet then...?'

'No, she isn't saying.'

'That's queer, don't you think?'

'Yes; I'm quite annoyed with her about the whole thing, actually.'

'Do you think she's embarrassed by whoever he is, or what? I mean I presume we don't know him, so I fail to see where the problem is. I wonder if the poor chap's even aware that he has a child.'

'Yes, I wonder...'

Percival did not sleep well on the night that Tony Blackman had come to the cottage; instead he found himself once again playing back in his mind all that had happened during his still quite recent life. The night that they had gone to rescue Rebecca from the shack in the mountains, the night that he had been abducted and almost killed, set up by Rebecca in order for her to confront the then head of the order, and his subsequent meeting on the Indonesian island with Philippe, who was dead now, murdered by his beautiful assassin. So much had happened, and all of it had lived in the background of his life for so long now that he could scarce remember the time when it had not been there, a time when for a while when there had been peace in his life, and before he had involved others in the situation which was in large part of his making. Keith and Meadow, Will and Emily, and Victoria; all had played their part in the often surreal drama which had played out over the past months of all of their lives. And now, that which kept him awake for a good part of the night was the thought that it may all be over. It had cost him, financially. Eddie Michel did not work for nothing, but if it was truly over then Percival resented not a penny of it. He could, he supposed, have sold Rebecca out to them on condition of his being left alone, but could not have trusted to that, and in any case the night on the bridge had seen to it that he could not have done so, and Rebecca perhaps would also be safe now, at least from the cult whose temple lay in the midst of the Three Brothers. He understood their wish for revenge against her for the massacre at the temple, and had always done so; their blood was on her hands, and one day she still might choke on it, but that was only her problem; he had done as much as he could. Her fate and his had otherwise been intertwined since he had made his choice and decided to take her side, and because of that more people had now been killed on his instigation, and that was something which he must now learn to live with. There were no moral absolutes here, and no angels, that much he understood. Certainly he had never accorded himself angelic status, but there was perhaps the lesser of evils, at least that was how he must try to justify himself to himself. If Rebecca had been murdered then there would not have been Florence, and he tried to convince himself that for her if for nothing else it had all been worth it; a life which would perhaps not have begun had it not been for his intervention. There were still the witches, of course, but of them he knew little, which was enough, and witches were for others to deal with. In this regard Rebecca had Meadow on her side, and it would take a braver man than he to intervene in that particular situation; let the women deal with the witches.

And then of course there had been Rose, who had nothing to do with any of it, but had played her own so significant part in his recent history. He had walked willingly into her seductive arms, and now he had a son, who would one day be a Lord, and that he could not make go away. Victoria knew, of course; she and he had a secret now, and they had both hidden that secret under a veil of necessity and mutual regard, which he would not be the first to uncover, and now he was Godfather to her son, which further bound them together.

Finally during this night he slept, and awoke late the next morning, feeling at least a sense of something like freedom such as he had not felt for a long time, and in this spirit did he begin his day. It was not over yet, but perhaps the final end to it had now begun. It was a little before noon when he heard a car pull up on the lane outside his door, and shortly afterwards his door knocker sounded. This time Lulu was at the door, tail working and in a state of more positive enthusiasm than she had displayed at their last caller; she knew this person, whoever they were. Percival had no idea who the caller might be; perhaps Lulu had it wrong and it was a just a parcel delivery service; most people he knew would be working at this hour of the day. He opened the door, and there before him was somebody whom he would never have expected; a woman this time, and somebody who would change his day completely, and perhaps his life; it would not be the first time, after all. Here was manifestation of a quite other aspect of his recent life, and one for which he thought he had found resolution, of sorts, but apparently he had thought too soon.

'Hello, Percival.'

Their eyes met, and for a moment Percival was lost.

'Well, aren't you even going to let me in?'

'Louise...'

'Well done, you remembered my name, at least.'

She walked past him and sat at the dining table, picked up his half – drunk cup of coffee and drank from it, and lit herself one of his cigarettes; she knew what to do, she had done it so often before. Percival sat opposite her; perhaps it was the lack of sleep, or perhaps last nights' caller had affected him more than he had realised, but he could still not find the words, or perhaps he would not in any case have found the words.

'What are you doing here?'

'Well, you didn't really think I would let you go that easily, did you? One email and it's all over; come on, Percival, my love, you know me better than that, surely.'

'Yeah....I suppose I do.'

'So, Mr Bastard who couldn't even say it to my face, how's your life been since you apparently so easily cast me from it?'

'It wasn't easy, Louise.'

'Don't play the martyr, Percival, it really doesn't suit you. So are you with what's her name, Sally again now then?'

'How did you know that?'

'Call it a woman's instinct; she's been waiting for you to weaken for a long time, poor girl. So her patience has been rewarded, has it, well good for her I suppose. She still work at the bank?'

'She's giving it up, actually.'

'Giving, or given?'

'Giving, she's waiting for the right moment.'

'Why...? I mean why do you think she's giving up on such a glowing career?'

'I'm not sure, to be honest, but anyway that's not your business.'

'Well pardon me, then. So, come on, why did you leave me; it wasn't for her, was it?'

'No, it wasn't for her. I thought I'd explained everything in the email.'

'Oh yes, the fucking email...Well that isn't good enough, I want to hear it from you.'

'I think you know perfectly well; it just wasn't working, was it.'

'You didn't say that when you had your dick between my legs; it seemed to work well enough for you then.'

'I thought there had to be more to it than that.'

'And you don't think there was more to it than that?'

'Yes, of course there was, and that was the part which wasn't working. You need London, and I can't go back there, so how does that work?'

'It doesn't, I know, but that's over now.'

'What do you mean?'

'My great love affair with London is finished; I've done it, Percival; I'm leaving and I'm not going back.'

'Well good for you, then. So where will you go?'

'I don't know yet; the world is my oyster, as they say. So what are you doing today?'

'Nothing that I'd expected to, so far anyway...'

'So shall we go somewhere?'

'What...? I mean, where?'

'I don't know; let's take the dog down to the coast, like we used to. Find some seedy cafe somewhere, drink bad coffee and talk about life; what do you say?'

'I don't think...I don't think that's a good idea.'

'Why not...? Oh yes, of course, you're with Sally now, and it wouldn't do to walk on a beach with somebody else, would it?'

'You're not just somebody else, Louise.'

'So what am I then, Percival? You see that's what I don't understand; you want your quiet life down here and I respect that, and Sally's here, and available, and I'm sure she does good sex, and now she's trying to make herself more like you, make herself into a free spirit or what the fuck ever, but people don't change, Percival, not really, so don't expect that.'

'I'm not expecting anything.'

Louise laughed, she couldn't help herself.

'No, of course you're not, you never did, you just bend with the wind, don't you, and sure, I'll walk away and never darken your door again if that's really what you want, but before I go, ask yourself a question; who do you love, Percival? You write oh such eloquent and meaningful words in an email, but I'm here now, and that's harder, isn't it, and you say you don't love me anymore, but the problem is that I don't believe you.'

'I didn't say that.'

'What didn't you say?'

'I didn't say that I don't love you, but loving you messes with my head, and my head's been messed around enough lately. Things have been happening in my life that you wouldn't understand or believe, probably; I'm having trouble believing it myself.'

'If you say it I'll believe it, Percival, and how can I understand it if you don't tell me?'

'It's too late, Louise.'

'Is it....? So what about the other person; what about me; you ever think about her?'

'Of course...'

'And does being loved by her mess with your head as well..?'

'You could say that.'

'But don't you understand, Percival, my love; that's what love is supposed to do, it's part of the job description. Love sends your soul soaring to dizzy heights of ecstasy, and then drags you to depths of despair that you never even knew existed, or it isn't love. You hurt the fuck out of me, but here I am making a fool of myself and being the angry woman, because I love you, and because I believe that you love me too; have I really got that so wrong?'

'No, you're not wrong....I just couldn't do it anymore.'

'So you went for the safe, predictable option; keep within the tram – lines, was that it?'

'I suppose...'

'The little voice inside your head was telling you to ditch the mad woman and go for mediocrity, as long as you're getting laid what the hell does it matter? Well beware false prophets, Percival, my love; the middle way isn't where love is, and it isn't where you belong, it'll destroy you in the end.'

'Loving you nearly did that.'

'Yeah, but it's a hell of a way to go, isn't it?'

She stood up, preparing to leave.

'I can't do it, Louise....Don't ask me to do it.'

'Oh you poor bastard; you really don't know what you're doing, do you? Or maybe you do, and that's even worse. Look, just give me today, okay? Just one day out of your life. I'm going to leave now, and you can come with me or not, but if you come and if at the end of this day you can look me in the eye and tell me that we're over, then fine, I'll walk away, but you owe me that, at least. Someone else may have your body right now, but I've got your soul, Percival, or I've got everything wrong, and that part of you I intend to keep, so it's up to you now, and I don't think I'm wrong, do you?'

A still, quiet afternoon in a quiet English village, and a car door slamming, and anyone listening would have been hard put to it to tell whether it had been two doors, or only one. Perhaps it had just been an echo, after all.

END OF PART XI

CPSIA information can be obtained
at www.ICGtesting.com
Printed in the USA
BVHW04*0949040518
515323BV00004B/5/P

9 781490 788357